sweet love

Also by Lauren Accardo

Forever Adirondacks Novels
WILD LOVE

sweet love

LAUREN ACCARDO

JOVE
New York

A JOVE BOOK
Published by Berkley
An imprint of Penguin Random House LLC
penguinrandomhouse.com

Copyright © 2021 by Lauren Accardo
Excerpt from *Bold Love* copyright © 2021 by Lauren Accardo
Penguin Random House supports copyright. Copyright fuels creativity, encourages
diverse voices, promotes free speech, and creates a vibrant culture. Thank you for buying
an authorized edition of this book and for complying with copyright laws by not
reproducing, scanning, or distributing any part of it in any form without permission.
You are supporting writers and allowing Penguin Random House to continue to
publish books for every reader.

A JOVE BOOK, BERKLEY, and the BERKLEY & B colophon are registered
trademarks of Penguin Random House LLC.

ISBN: 9780593200315

First Edition: September 2021

Printed in the United States of America
1 3 5 7 9 10 8 6 4 2

Book design by George Towne

*Dedicated to all the girls
who have ever been told
their dreams were too big*

chapter **one**

The shiny, happy couple beamed from Jared's TV screen, hands clutched as they awaited the big reveal.

"Are you ready to see your Forever Home?"

Power: off. He huffed a sarcastic breath as he dumped potato chips into a plastic bowl. Forever Home. The concept turned his stomach—who wanted a *forever* home?—but his all-time favorite show, *Million-Dollar Properties*, was on hiatus. He took notes while he watched that one.

As he emptied a pretzel bag into another bowl atop his kitchen table, the clock ticked to eight. People would arrive any minute. The annual Kirkland St. Patrick's Day party was a tradition his mother started years ago, and since she'd passed away, Jared continued it. While she'd cluck her tongue in disappointment if she knew he didn't drape every surface with green tablecloths or hang paper shamrocks from the doorframes the way she had, he liked having people around, so he took on the legacy. His brother, Sam, could be counted on to show up and otherwise not contribute in the least.

Jared's home phone rang shrilly as he tossed the empty pretzel bag into the trash, and he plucked the receiver from the wall. Pine Ridge, New York. No cell service, barely any Wi-Fi, and every house with a landline. If you squinted, the whole place looked like 1985.

"Hello?"

"Jared, it's Phil. Sorry to bug you so late, but my client would like to take another look at the Balsam Lane property tomorrow. Can you swing that?"

His heart sunk. He showed Phil two properties yesterday, and the difference in price between the two was a cool half mill. Balsam Lane was cute. He'd done cute. He ate cute for breakfast. Cute didn't warrant popped champagne and desperate calls from rival firms.

"Absolutely," Jared said. "Just curious, what did they say about the Silver Lake property?"

"It's just too much house for 'em. They loved it, really loved it. But Balsam Lane is more their speed."

Damn. Another lead tapped out.

"Got it. How's ten a.m.?"

"Perfect. We'll meet you at the office."

With a heavy hand, Jared replaced the receiver. Silver Lake was his white whale. Selling that property would put him in the top tier of Adirondack Park Realtors and propel him into the next phase of his career, not to mention prove to himself and everyone around him he'd outgrown this tiny town.

Until that property sold, he was just another North Country guy hawking vacation homes to midlevel Manhattan jerk-offs. He wanted bigger; he wanted better. He wanted more.

The front door burst open with a satisfying crack, yanking him from his reverie, and he jogged into the foyer of his ranch home. His smile dropped along with his excitement when Sam appeared. When Mila's schedule allowed, she usually arrived early to his parties to help him set up.

"Hey, man, what's up?" Jared's older brother pushed past him into the house, stomping the snow off his boots and onto the all-weather area rug.

"Same shit, different day."

"Is this your spread?" Sam's eyes trailed over the meager snacks, and he ran a hand over his full beard. He shook his head disapprovingly.

"What'd you want, filet mignon? Shrimp cocktail?"

"When you invite people over to get shit-wrecked, you have to at least have sandwiches or something." Sam popped a chip into his mouth. "Mom always had enough food for a football team."

"We both know my version of this party couldn't hold a candle to Mom's, no matter what I do," Jared said. "Mila's bringing dessert. Maybe some other stuff from the diner. That should beef it up."

"Mila to the rescue." A sly smile stretched across Sam's mouth. "Too bad you can't find a girlfriend who saves your ass like Mila does."

Jared's shoulders tightened. *A girlfriend like Mila.*

Who wouldn't want a girlfriend like Mila Bailey? Her drip of an ex-boyfriend, for one. That idiot never really saw her, never understood her weird, wonderful personality. Jared had known all along they were wrong for each other. But what right did a guy have to trash-talk his best friend's dude? The day she'd told Jared she broke up with Marty, his chest lightened as if he'd been wearing a concrete vest for the duration of their relationship.

"Speaking of women who are way better than us," Jared said, "where's Sydney?"

"She had a book club meeting tonight that ended at seven thirty, so she'll be here soon. She's been so busy with the store lately, I feel like I've hardly seen her. It sucks."

Jared grunted a barely audible reply. He'd never been

particularly eager to hear the nitty-gritty details of Sam and Syd's disgustingly perfect relationship.

"What's that look for?" Sam said. "You love Syd."

Jared ran a hand over his face, avoiding Sam's powerful stare. Truth was, Sam and Sydney's relationship made him feel things he wasn't quite ready to confront. After Sam's first girlfriend had broken his heart, Jared looked to Sam as an example of how a woman could ruin a man. The new-and-improved Sam, who stared at Sydney as if she had the answers to all his questions, threw Jared's long-held relationship beliefs into disarray.

"Sure," Jared said. "Syd's great. I just . . . I dunno. You trust her?"

"Of course." Sam leveled his gaze. "I'm gonna ask her to marry me."

"The hell you are."

Sam's eyes popped open, and his chin pulled back in the most overt display of shock Jared had ever seen from his generally subdued brother. Jared surprised even himself with his reaction.

"I mean," Jared said, "so soon? You guys have only been dating a year."

"Does this seriously surprise you? I'm not even sure why we waited this long."

Jared huffed out a breath. Of course Sam would marry Sydney. No one who'd spent more than three minutes with them would object. He was happy for his brother, but Jared's gut hollered at him like a little kid who needed attention.

"Marriage is . . ." *Terrifying. Idiotic. Bad business. A life sentence.* "Forever."

"Yeah." Sam laughed. "Spending forever with Sydney sounds pretty great, actually."

Jared coughed over a sarcastic laugh. "Okay."

Sam raised his eyebrows. "What's the deal, dude?"

"Nothing." A wry smile hung on his lips.

"No, come on," Sam said. "Enlighten me with your extensive knowledge of marriage and how it works."

Jared took a beat. How to phrase this to a guy who had just admitted he wanted to shackle himself to someone for life? "I just don't get it, I guess. Have you ever seen two happily married people?"

"Sure," Sam said. "What about Jorie and Matt?"

"They've been married one year, and he only popped the question because she got pregnant. Try again."

Sam shrugged, returning his gaze to the middling food spread. "I don't care about anybody else. I don't care why other people's marriages have succeeded or failed. I care about her. And I know I can trust her."

Jared's skin prickled with discomfort. "I bet Dad thought he could trust Mom."

The sound of Sam's deep, measured breath filled the quiet space. "You want to get into that conversation right now? You want to dive into how little you actually know about Mom and Dad's marriage?"

Jared knew plenty. He knew they both had their flaws. He knew they both stayed in a tense marriage despite not seeming to enjoy each other's company whatsoever. He knew his mother had a lightness in her step the day after his father died that Jared had never seen before.

Sam's stony face dared his brother to continue. Before Jared could get another word out, the doorbell rang, as if signaling the end of the grudge match.

"Thank God," Jared said.

"This isn't over," Sam called after him. "You're gonna be my best man whether you like it or not."

Jared pressed his lips together, tamping down the threatening grin. *Whether you like it or not.* Groom: professor of love and undying devotion? No thanks. Best man: planner of bachelor parties and composer of killer speeches? Yeah, buddy.

By eight fifteen, Jared's modest home swelled with rowdy

twenty- and thirtysomethings looking to celebrate. Handles of Jameson and buckets of Guinness covered the kitchen countertops, and some heaven-sent partygoer had brought a giant tray of taco dip that disappeared within minutes.

Jared scanned the open space again, but still no Mila. She worked until seven on Saturdays, but maybe she had to stay late. Her boss always suckered her in to refilling one last coffee, stocking one last bakery case, or ringing up one last check. She never said no. Even when she should.

As Jared cracked open his second beer of the night, the front door opened and Mila breezed in, balancing a covered pie dish in one hand. Her wild, dark curly hair danced around her freckled cheeks as the frigid, early-spring wind blew in behind her. She grinned, and her wide-set cat eyes all but disappeared in the brightness emanating from her face. He felt instantly lighter just having her in the room.

Mila squeezed Sydney in a one-armed hug before slipping out of her coat. Syd loved Mila, demanding her friendship after she saw Mila carrying a copy of Beverly Jenkins's *Destiny's Embrace*.

With arms wrapped around her pie plate, Mila caught Jared's eye from across the room. Her lips pressed into a timid smile, and he swallowed down the same twinge of awkwardness he'd experienced every day since their almost-kiss five years ago.

She'd been his best friend for as long as he could remember. Being around her was as easy as being around his brother, but with the added joy of a woman's perspective on everything, from books and movies to relationships and his job. She was fun and smart, and her place in his life was secure.

Until that day at the lake.

Where had those curves come from? How long had she had that electric pink bikini? She'd pulled herself out of the lake and onto the boat—taut, lean muscles glistening in the sunlight, rivulets of water streaming down her flat stomach to collect at her bikini bottom.

His whole world tilted.

In a single, heart-stopping moment, his best friend quietly vacated and some smoking-hot, supercool chick who made his groin tingle had taken her place.

He'd wanted to kiss her. Asked to walk her home, even. But the way she'd looked at him—like he'd asked her to hop in his car and ride shotgun to Pluto—had turned his confidence to dust underfoot. He'd stumbled through some lame excuse about protecting her from a burglar loose in Pine Ridge, and when her face twisted even further into disbelief, he'd jumped in his car and raced home in shame.

For the past five years, that insatiable sense of longing plagued him. Every time she walked into a room, his chest tightened and his ears burned. Five years of wondering why he hadn't gone through with it. Five years of shifted feelings and distracted thoughts.

Five years of freaking exhaustion.

He circled the room, greeting the crowd of guests, before landing in the kitchen in search of another drink. Mila and her best friend, Nicole, listened as Sydney filled them in on that evening's book club event.

"One of these days," Sydney said, "we'll do a midnight book club meeting or something, and you'll be able to come."

"I would love that," Mila said. "Can't believe it's been more than a year since you started and I still haven't been."

With Mila's work schedule, her attendance at social events was as common as an eclipse. At least she'd managed to come tonight. Maybe she'd pulled a special favor.

Would she do that for him?

Jared cleared his throat, snapping himself back into bro mode, and pointed at a ketchup stain splattered across the front of Mila's white T-shirt. "Hey, when I asked you to bring diner leftovers, I didn't mean you should wear them."

"Why do you always have to be such a jerk?" Nicole said, shoving an expertly twisted braid over her shoulder and narrowing her dark brown eyes. Mila's best female friend had never understood their relationship. She treated Mila like a lame duck, a less fortunate friend who always needed her hand held. Mila was no damsel in distress, and she didn't need anyone in her life putting her in that box.

"It's called 'negging,'" Sydney said. "Little boys do it when they shove girls on the playground."

Mila's lips curled into a grin, and one dark eyebrow twitched at him, sending him a tiny signal. *Nobody gets us.*

"Well, it's the twenty-first freaking century," Nicole said. "How about just being kind to the women you like instead of pushing them off the swing set like some kind of Neanderthal?"

"Hey, what kind of pie did you bring?" Jared said, redirecting the conversation. Nicole was the friend you wanted as your darts partner, the one always down for one last drink at the end of the night, and the one everybody went to for advice. But when it came to Mila, she could be as protective as a mother bird over her nest.

"It's a grasshopper pie with chocolate cookie crust," Mila said. "Not very original, but I didn't have tons of time today."

"Even your classics are knockouts," Nicole said. "You should make that one for the bake-off."

Mila's eyes widened at her best friend, her lips tightening as she clutched her beer bottle.

"Bake-off?" Jared asked.

"Oh shit," Nicole muttered. "Sorry, Lee Lee."

"Are you finally entering the Spring Bake-Off?" Jared asked. He'd given up suggesting she enter a long time ago. She hated being in the spotlight, hated any situation where she'd have to put her talents on display. Give the girl a couple of shots and a microphone and she'd bust out all the bad Celine Dion impressions nobody asked for. But when it came to the true genius in her nimble fingers, she didn't want any credit.

"I haven't decided yet," Mila said, sipping her beer and effectively blocking her face from view.

"She's entering," Nicole said. "Go on. Tell them."

Mila rubbed her lips together, her glittery eyes dancing around the small group. She cleared her throat and said, "Before my great-aunt died, she paid the entry fee. She also set up accounts for me at the grocery store and the hardware store so that I can buy everything I need to test recipes. Every penny of the two thousand dollars she'd saved up before she died has been allocated. For this. Apparently she'd always wanted me to enter the contest, too, and she knew I never would on my own."

Warmth touched Jared's chest. He'd always liked Aunt Georgie, even if she was the meanest lady in town. Cashiers at the grocery store saw her coming, and suddenly everybody needed their cigarette break. She had her own pew at church because when Aunt Georgie shared the peace, she left bruises. But she'd always served Jared the best piece of chicken at Bailey family dinners, and her sharp tongue made for some fantastic stories. He saw bits of that fire in Mila when she thought nobody was looking.

"Well, she picked a good year to force you into it," Sydney said.

Sam sidled up next to her and patted her butt, raising the hair on the back of Jared's neck. He should've known his goody-two-shoes brother would end up meeting a cool-ass chick despite the confines of tiny Pine Ridge.

"Why's that?" Mila asked.

"You know," Sydney said. "The hotel thing?"

The group blinked at her, no one having a clue as to what she was talking about.

"You guys haven't heard about this? The new hotel going up outside of town?"

"Great," Sam grumbled. "That's all we need. A hotel."

"Actually, it's great for the area," Sydney said. "It'll lighten the burden on rental properties. Provide jobs. Anyway, they're sponsoring the bake-off this year, since it's the fiftieth anniversary and they want to get on the town's good side. The winner gets a big cash prize, and their recipe will be featured at the hotel's properties all over the country. They're getting a celebrity judge, too. It's supposed to be amazing exposure."

Mila's full lips parted, her eyes locked on Sydney. "Wait . . . seriously?"

"Yeah," Sydney said. "How cool is that?"

"God damn it, Aunt Georgie," Mila muttered. "That's sort of terrifying, right? I bet ten times more people will enter this year. And a celebrity judge?"

"Only you would be turned off by this," Nicole said. "What are you afraid of, anyway? You love to bake. It's as easy as putting a pie in the oven."

Mila swallowed, tucked her chin, and glanced around the circle like the scared little mouse he knew she wasn't.

"Maybe she just likes to bake," Sydney offered. "Not everything in life has to be a competition."

Jared and Nicole both looked at Mila, knowing it wasn't true. Mila had flirted with the idea of selling pies, writing recipes, and taking the next step in some as-yet-undetermined culinary adventure for as long as they'd known her. A combination of cynical family and a lack of funds kept her in her place. But she'd always wanted more.

"I need some air," Mila said. She placed her empty beer bottle on the kitchen counter and slipped past Jared, a faint breeze of diner grease and lilac perfume trailing after her.

"She acts like her pies aren't the best thing since sliced bread," Nicole said. "I should just sneak into her freezer, steal one, and enter it myself. She'd win even with a six-month-old apple tart."

"You know how she gets," Jared said. "You gotta lay off her sometimes, Nic."

Nicole's brow knit as she shrugged, a whisper of regret crossing her face. Jared snagged two more beers from the fridge before following Mila to the back porch. The icy wind stole his breath, and he hunched against the below-freezing temperatures. The thin flannel shirt he wore did little to protect him against the Adirondack spring.

Despite the cold, he breathed deep, giving his lungs a break from the stuffy party air. His eyes slowly adjusted to the inky darkness surrounding the porch, the dense trees just beyond the railing concealing all sorts of bright-eyed creatures. Tonight the air and the woods stood perfectly still.

"Where's your coat, you dope?" She spoke without turning around, knowing it was him and knowing—probably by the chatter of his teeth—he hadn't bothered with outerwear.

"I'm fine." But he knew if he didn't go back for a coat, he'd likely die of hypothermia out here.

In one swift motion, she tugged the scarf from her throat and tossed it at him before zipping her big blue parka up to her nose. He wrapped the soft wool around his neck and shoulders, breathing deeply as her clean, flowery scent filled his head.

"Better guard your fridge," he said. "Nicole's threatening to enter one of your old, frozen pies."

She shot him her warning glare, the tiny diamond stud in her right nostril catching a thin shaft of moonlight. "She doesn't understand how I could not want to enter a competition. You know her. Captain of the soccer team, valedictorian, leader of her Adirondack Mountain Rescue team. She's the queen of Why-do-anything-if-you're-not-gonna-be-the-best? And that's just . . . not me."

He swallowed down the rest of his thoughts on the matter. That's all he'd get out of her. Mila didn't trash-talk her friends. Never had, never would. "I don't think she tries very hard to understand you."

She shrugged, leaning back against the porch railing and tucking her face deeper into the coat. Only her eyes were visible, and they glowed like the lake in moonlight.

"Where's Chloe tonight?" She said Chloe's name the way she always did. Like she had a gnat on her tongue.

"Who knows?"

Her narrowed gaze darted to his face. "You guys broke up again?"

He waited for the delicate pang in his stomach that told him he was bummed that Chloe had finally ended things for good, but it wouldn't come. Hadn't come. Maybe this time he really, truly didn't care. "Yeah. For good, I think."

She nodded slowly. "You seem devastated, J."

"Don't let this stony facade fool you. I've been crying to Adele on my own time."

A short, sarcastic huff escaped her lips. "What happened?"

"The marriage shit again. She's waiting for a ring."

"Five years together and she still doesn't know you at all, does she?"

He shrugged, the frigid temperatures sneaking beneath his shirt and burrowing under his skin like a ghost. "It's for the best. I mostly feel bad I wasted her time."

"She'll get over it."

He cracked a smile. Was Mila happy about this? She'd never been particularly fond of his ex, but he'd always thought it was because they came from different worlds. In high school, Mila drew punk band names on her sneakers with Sharpies during class while Chloe sat in the front row and volunteered for extra credit. Mila was Hot Topic and the Ramones, beer in the parking lot on weekends. Chloe was Britney Spears and Forever 21, pep rallies and pom-poms and yearbook editor.

He'd always thought he was meant to be with a Chloe. He gravitated toward Mila.

"So what do you think about this bake-off?" she said.

"Am I acting like a baby about something that doesn't even really matter?"

Half a laugh escaped his mouth. "First of all, I'm not sure I agree it doesn't matter. I think it's very cool, and it could be huge for you. Second of all, you're totally acting like a baby."

"And Nicole's the bully?"

He licked his lips. "Nicole needs to learn how to tell the truth but be gentle about it."

"Was calling me a baby your attempt at gentle?"

His brain skipped like a stone to something dirty that he'd definitely be gentle about, and he blinked to shake the vision. Why did that keep happening around her? For twenty-five years she'd been an asexual figure in his life, a buddy he'd go to for advice on first dates and girlfriends' birthday gifts.

One stupid pink bikini and he crumbled like a cookie.

"I think," he said, "instead of thinking about the prize money, the celebrity judge, the press coverage—"

"Press coverage?" Her face twisted up, her brow creased.

"Yeah. The hotel will want maximum exposure out of this if they're putting money into it."

An exhale passed her coat, forming a white crystallized cloud in front of her face. "Great."

"My point is, forget the big, scary what-ifs. Focus on the first step. The pies. You've got that down."

She slipped a hand past the neck of her coat to gnaw on her thumbnail. "Not when it matters, I don't."

"What does that mean?"

"Baking for fun is one thing." Her gaze shifted, her mind traveling someplace else. "I just . . . I freeze up when it counts. It might seem like small potatoes to you, ruining a pie, but it's embarrassing to watch someone eat something you made and make a face. Or worse, get sick."

He rolled his eyes. "Dude, stop. That was one time. And it turned out that Cruz kid had a gluten allergy nobody knew about."

"It's more than that." She paused. "I didn't ask for this. I didn't want it. Now I feel like I have to do it. I don't know what made Aunt Georgie think I could succeed at it anyway."

"Maybe because you've got an insane amount of talent? Maybe because you shortchange yourself all the time?"

She dropped her shoulders and glared over the narrow bridge of her nose at him. "Shortchange myself?"

He shrugged. Did he want to bring this up now? She never took criticism very well, no matter how well-intentioned. "It's just that sometimes the things you think you've failed at are just the things you never really gave yourself a shot at."

"Like all the other baking contests I've passed up?"

"You're joking, but . . . yeah. You've lived in Pine Ridge your whole life and never once entered the annual bake-off. You were eighteen before you got your license because you were convinced you'd be a terrible driver."

She rolled her eyes. "I'm still not a great driver."

"You didn't apply to Brown because you somehow knew before you applied that you wouldn't get in."

Her brow pinched, her eyes crinkling at the corners. He'd touched a nerve. "I didn't have the *money* for Brown. I could barely cover the application fees for SUNY Potsdam."

"Sure, Lee. If that's the story you want to stick to." His breath came quicker. He forgot about her inherent ability to drag any conversation from optimistic to cynical in three seconds flat.

"Well," she said with a sarcastic lift of her brows. "This is one opportunity I can't run away from. If I did, I'd basically be flushing Aunt Georgie's life savings down the toilet. Happy now?"

"You know what?" A smile twitched on his lips. "I am. I can't wait to see what you come up with. You're gonna kill it. I know you are."

She licked her lips, her eyelids lowering as she settled her intense stare on him. Despite her propensity for the shadows, once she set her sights on something, her gaze never wavered. When those eyes found him, they stripped away his bravado. The air around them grew thick with tension, and he shifted his weight.

"You need a taste tester? I'm available."

"You're a terrible taste tester," she said. "You like everything."

"Nah, that bacon thing you made last year was disgusting."

With both hands, she shoved him, her tangle of curls brushing the delicate curve of her jaw. He laughed as the dull impact landed.

"All right, fine," she said. "We'll come up with a scoring system from 'bacon thing' to . . ."

"Caramel apple." Just the mention of the decadent creation made him salivate. She'd made the pie for his birthday one year, apologizing because the filling had turned out thicker than she'd hoped. The dessert she'd inadvertently created became his all-time favorite, and he'd polished off the last quarter of it alone on the couch before he went to bed.

"I call that one the happy accident." The bridge of her nose wrinkled.

"Hey, that's what my mom called me." He grinned. "Or was it the *un*happy accident?"

"Oh, stop. She loved you so much."

Angry sparks flared up in his chest, but this pain originated somewhere deeper. Sure, his mother loved him. But she'd never stopped demanding more of him. No grade he brought home was high enough, no article in the school paper had good enough placement. He'd felt like the disappointment since birth, and even after she'd passed, the shame hung over him like a December storm cloud.

The grin melted from his lips. "Not where I want to go right now."

The door opened behind him, party noise spilling out

into the formerly blissful quiet of the porch, and a couple of his brother's drunk friends stumbled toward them.

"Yo, Kirks," Greg said. "You got a lighter out here?"

Mila raised her eyebrows at him and moved toward the door. She unzipped the big blue coat, slipped it off her slight shoulders, and handed it to him. "Here. So you don't catch pneumonia."

He took the coat and watched the door long after she'd disappeared through it.

chapter **two**

Heat accumulated inside Mila's heavy down coat as she darted around her apartment, snagging her purse from her bedroom floor and biting back the curse words threatening to erupt from her lips. No time for bitterness now.

She slipped her feet into trusty black leather boots, reached for her keys, and instead scraped her nails against the dingy white paint of the apartment walls where her keys should've hung.

"Shit." Panic prickled at her throat. Had her mother not dropped in this morning unexpectedly, interrupting her recipe testing and trying her patience all at once, she'd have had an extra moment to look for the keys. Now she had to decide if it was faster to search or jog the mile and a half to the diner so Benny didn't rip her a new one.

She trailed through her bag with fingers tense from kneading pie crust all morning but came up empty. One last check of her bedroom. An empty wineglass and a handful of Ferrero Rocher wrappers littered the nightstand, but still, no keys.

She gritted her teeth, unable to push out her mother's voice. *Don't waste too much time or money on this bake-off thing, hun. You don't want to get your hopes up.*

How many times had she heard it over the years? Basketball tryouts, school musical auditions, the time she alone had prepared a huge Christmas Eve dinner for the whole family and openly told her mom she hoped everyone enjoyed it.

Don't get your hopes up. The Bailey family mantra.

Mila's eyes swept the apartment one more time before she huffed out a frustrated sigh, swapped her leather boots for running shoes, and headed off to work.

She arrived at the diner twenty minutes later, rogue curls clinging to her neck and jaw, and her white T-shirt stuck to her skin underneath her heavy coat. It had been years since she'd sprinted. Her lungs burned, her heart slammed against her ribs. A trip to the gym seemed long overdue.

"There you are!" Amy, her teenaged coworker, rolled her big green eyes and yanked off her apron. "I'm gonna be late for my doctor's appointment. I told you I had to leave at noon today."

Mila tossed her bag and coat under the counter, wishing she had a single moment to catch her breath. But those moments were few and far between these days.

"I'm sorry," Mila said. "I couldn't find my keys—"

"Anyway." Amy cut her off. "I gotta run. Oh, and Ethan called. He's got a cold, so he's not coming in today."

Amy slipped into her jacket and sent Mila a *sorry* shrug. God damn it. Ethan LaMotta had begged for the busser job, told Benny he needed the extra cash for drum lessons his mom couldn't afford. In the three months since the kid had taken the job, he'd called out four times. She'd wanted to rat him out to Benny so they could hire someone dependable. And yet, she held her tongue.

The lunch rush came in a deluge, and Mila zipped around the restaurant, filling and taking orders, checking on regulars, clearing plates, and gritting her teeth against complaints. As soon as she had one table settled, another needed more soda, a clean fork, more napkins.

Freaking Ethan. She'd chew him out next time he was in.

"Excuse me, *miss*, I've been waiting twenty minutes for a coffee refill." Mila spun on her heel, the word *understaffed* hot on her tongue and ready to snap out.

Instead, she grinned. Jared leaned over the counter, a smirk hanging on his lips. He wore his Saturday casual clothes—fitted, faded jeans; a worn blue-and-green plaid shirt; and a navy peacoat—with his fawn-brown hair swept back in one tidy swoop. The lingering spring chill lent a pink tint to his cheeks, and Mila swallowed down the giddiness fluttering in her chest.

"My deepest apologies," she said. "As you can see, we're short-staffed today, and customers who tip most get priority service."

His grin faded, but the sparkle in his eye did not. "Oh yeah? Cash, or do you accept creative tips?"

"I've served you here before," she said. "Your most creative tip was a pile of nickels."

"I was hammered," he said. "I thought you'd think it was funny. I mean, I had to go out of my way to collect nickels from everyone in the restaurant for that gag. No props for effort?"

"Mila! Can I get a side of bacon, hun?"

Mila's gaze flickered to where Annette Bethel waved at her from a corner table, a single egg with toast in front of her. Annette ate at Black Bear Diner every single day. She spent twenty minutes poring over a menu that hadn't changed in twenty years and eventually ordered the exact same thing. As soon as the egg and toast were delivered, she remembered she wanted something else.

Mila leaned toward Jared. "Get your own coffee, yeah?"

He sat up on his counter stool like a puppy that had been offered a treat. "I'm allowed behind the counter?"

"This *one* time," she said. "Don't make it a habit."

With a joyous little-boy glow on his cheeks, he hopped off the stool and scurried around the counter before retrieving the coffeepot and filling a mug.

"Kirkland! Fill me up, will ya?"

Jared shot Mila a *See what you started?* grin and poured dark roast brew into the customer's waiting mug. He shed his coat, tossed it under the counter, and filled another coffee cup. And another. As Mila entered Annette Bethel's side of bacon into the register, she watched her best friend saunter around the diner, the coffeepot held high like some sort of award.

He rolled up his sleeves and continued his rounds, leaning over tables, his shiny white teeth gleaming and drawing smiles from waiting customers. No wonder he'd gone into sales. Even tables with full mugs waved him over to chat.

Mila jotted down orders on her notepad, but her eyes drifted back to Jared. The prickly mood in the diner shifted with his presence. Each table he visited lightened somehow, and as the carafe emptied, he slipped behind the counter and set to work making a fresh pot.

"Hey," she said, sidling up next to him.

Something crackled between them, sparking like drops of water on a hot griddle. He'd been her best friend for as long as she could remember, and yet the air thickened between them lately in ways it never had before.

Well. At least before they'd almost kissed.

No. They hadn't almost kissed. She'd been sun-drunk and happy after their day at the lake, and he'd offered to walk her home, and for the first time in their friendship she'd wondered, *What if?* She'd always pitied other women for falling so shamelessly at his feet, and then when he turned all that deep, soulful attention on her, she'd melted like caramel.

"Get out of my way." His voice teased as he reached around her to grab a coffee filter. The soft skin of his forearm brushed her elbow, and she inhaled sharply. Was she imagining things? Or did he go out of his way to touch her? She couldn't remember what life had been like with him before that day at the lake.

"Do you even know how to do that?" she asked. "Mr. Nespresso."

He raised a single eyebrow as he fit the filter into the machine and filled it with grounds. "You forget I worked that summer at McDonagh's Bakery."

Laughter shot past her lips. "That's right. The summer they had to shut down over an *E. coli* scare?"

"That was totally unrelated."

She bit her lip as he flipped the Brew switch on the machine and wiped his hands on a dishrag.

"Thank you for helping me," she said. "You don't have to hang around. I think the worst of the lunch rush is over."

"What are you talking about?" His beautiful face twisted. "I'm having a blast, and I've got nowhere else to be today. I'll stick around. LaMotta called out again, didn't he?"

Her throat dried up. She tried—unsuccessfully—to stop seeing everything he did through the lens of the almost-kiss. Did he stay because he wanted to be around her? Or was it simpler than that? Nicole was always telling her that men rarely had some secret hidden agenda. Most meant what they said. And if that were true, Jared had nowhere else to be today and he actually enjoyed serving coffee to the grateful people of Pine Ridge.

The lunch rush tapered off just as the early-dinner crowd amped up, and Jared remained. He wiped down tables, cleared plates, filled coffee mugs, and enhanced the mood in the diner threefold. Customers tipped more, complained less, and by the time Mila's shift ended, she barely even noticed the dull ache in her heels and shins. She liked having him around. His presence made even the most grueling aspects of the job somehow manageable.

Edith O'Hare's daughter arrived to relieve Mila, and Mila grabbed her purse and coat from under the counter. Recipe testing awaited her, but the thought of imagining an inventive, delicious pie for the bake-off seemed nearly impossible. Her brain could barely calculate how she'd navigate herself back home, let alone dream up something cool enough to win a contest.

"That was fun," Jared said as he grabbed his own coat. They walked together to the door and into the dark, icy evening. Mila tugged the zipper of her coat past her chin and snuggled down into the depths of its warm down layers.

"You want the job?" Mila said. "I'll get Benny to fire Ethan in a heartbeat."

Jared laughed, an airy, noncommittal chuckle that let her know he'd sooner give himself a root canal. Working at the diner had never been Mila's dream, but she didn't mind the work. Jared had always been destined for greater things.

"Where's your car?" he asked, glancing around the parking lot.

She exhaled a long audible breath that sailed out past puffed-up cheeks. "I couldn't find my keys this morning, so I jogged here."

A grin spread across his lips as he shoved his hands into the pockets of his coat. "Why don't you use that remote key finder I got you for Christmas?"

Ah yes. The remote key finder. A plane flying over Pine Ridge with a *Platonic* banner would've been far subtler.

"I lost the remote," she said.

He shook his head and combed his fingers through his hair. "Come on, I'll walk you home."

"Or you could drive me," she said.

"My car's at Sam's shop," he said. "Some muffler thing. I can't pick it up till tomorrow."

They stood opposite each other in the parking lot, the

purple glow of evening lighting his face and forcing her jaw to clench.

He wanted to walk her home.

Or did he? Her apartment was on the way to his house. Maybe it was a stroll of convenience?

"All right," she said. "Let's go."

They fell into step beside each other, the crunch of shoes on gravel the only sound. Mila breathed deep, filling her lungs with fresh, sweet mountain air.

"You feeling any better about the bake-off?" he said.

"No." She winced as the cynicism snaked out of her mouth on a single syllable.

He huffed a laugh. "You're a trip."

"I did some testing this morning," she said. "It . . . didn't go that well."

"That's why you test, though, right? Get the mediocre shit out of the way to make room for the pure genius?"

A smile curled onto her lips, and she stole a glance at his happy, open face. "If I have pure genius somewhere in me, I don't know where it's been hiding all these years."

"Hiding?" They rounded a bend in the road and diverted from the paved sidewalk, both deciding but neither voicing the decision to cut through the expansive lawn behind the community center.

"Listen," she said. "My pies are good. I'm just nervous I'll be competing against professionals and get laughed out of the competition."

Crisp, frosty grass crunched under their feet as they trudged across the field, and the violet sky blurred into indigo. Mila's breath formed crystallized clouds in front of her face. Early spring in Pine Ridge all but erased her memory of warm weather.

"Hey." He hooked a hand around her elbow and gently yanked her toward him. The glowing moon illuminated his long eyelashes.

"What?" she said, fidgeting inside her coat. "It's freezing."

"Listen to me."

Kiss me kiss me kiss me. She couldn't fight the plea running through her mind. She loved him as a friend, as someone who knew her better than anyone, as someone who'd had her back from day one. But being alone with him dredged up something else these days. Something she couldn't ignore.

"You're really freaking talented," he said. "I don't know what makes one pie better than another or why McDonagh's pecan pie is good but yours finds its way into my dreams."

She bit back a laugh.

"I'm not kidding," he said. "I told you about that time I dreamed I was in math class—"

"And I was your teacher, and the problem was about percentages and I was using a pecan pie to demonstrate?"

"Exactly!" He flashed a half smile. His hand lingered on her elbow, the physical connection breathing new life into her tired limbs. "Your stuff is so good. Just give it a shot, all right? An honest shot. What do you have to lose?"

She tucked her thumbnail between her teeth. She had plenty to lose. *Don't get your hopes up.* What would her parents say when she didn't get past the first round? How many years would they bring up her failure at the dinner table, laughing about the time she thought her humble little pies could compete against professional-quality baked goods?

Jared's breath whispered past his lips in an icy cloud. The faint bitter scent of diner coffee and grill grease emanated from his otherwise pristine coat, blending her worlds together. He'd eased the chaos of her day with his easy optimism. Maybe she could borrow a bit for the competition ahead of her.

"My mom came to my apartment this morning," she said. "I was just finishing this chocolate-bacon-orange thing, and she gave me a big ole dose of her patented Bailey family cynicism."

His brow pinched as he retracted his hand, slipping it

into his coat pocket. The air around her grew somehow colder the second he broke contact. "That explains it."

"She's not wrong, you know?" She heard the words come out of her mouth and immediately wanted to take them back. She didn't want to be another negative voice in the Bailey family chorus, and yet the mentality haunted her all the same. "There's a fair chance I'll fall flat on my face."

"Well, you should definitely not do it, then," he said. "In fact, you should never try anything new. It's the only guaranteed way to make sure you never fail."

She pursed her lips and glared at him. "Don't be a jerk."

"I'm not." He shrugged. "It's the truth. There's no guarantee of success. Ever. But man, it feels good when it works out."

A chill skittered across her skin, and her shoulders tensed in response. How did he really feel about her? What if they tried? What if they failed?

She swallowed down the attraction tickling her periphery and looked up. Stars sprinkled across the blue velvet sky, the tiny, innumerable pricks of light like glittering grains of sand.

"I feel sorry for people who can't see the stars," she said. "Can you imagine looking up and the night sky is just one big blur because of city lights or smog?"

A long, defeated breath whistled past his lips. When she looked back at him, a shadow cast over his features. "I dunno," he said. "There are other upsides to living in a city."

Her pulse sped up. He'd threatened to move away from Pine Ridge since the day he got his driver's license. His imminent departure loomed over her like a black cloud.

"Sure," she said. "There are upsides to everything. But there's something really special about being able to see the sky like this."

She looked up again, sensing his gaze on her. She imagined confessing her feelings, opening her mouth and letting all her complicated emotions pour out over him. And then she imagined the horror. The sympathetic grimace. He'd think her a fool.

"Jesus, it's cold out here," she said. "We should go."

She turned toward her apartment building and headed home.

The white-walled community center roared with a hundred voices, all clamoring to be heard over one another as the residents of Pine Ridge and beyond found empty folding chairs. People had come from as far as Albany and Rochester to enter the Pine Ridge Spring Bake-Off and to receive additional information from Indigo Hotels directly on what to expect.

Mila shrugged off her coat as she settled into a second-row seat next to a couple of eager young women wearing University of Albany sweatshirts. She breathed deep, nerves twisting in her belly, and wondered about the level of expertise in the room. Would most of the entrants be college kids hoping for prize money? Experienced pastry chefs with professional training? Amateur bakers like Mila?

"Yo." She looked up to find a pink-cheeked, breathless Jared squeezed in between the college girls and the row of folding chairs in front of them. The girls went suddenly quiet, staring up at him with glassy eyes and timid smiles.

Who could blame them?

"What are you doing here?" Mila asked.

"I had a showing this morning over on Grange, and I saw this mess while I was driving by. Came to see if you needed moral support." He turned his attention on the college girls and flashed his million-dollar smile. One of them actually gasped. "Do you mind moving down a chair so I can sit next to my buddy here?"

Mila's side pinched as if someone had jabbed her with a tiny knife. *Buddy.*

"Of course," one of the girls said. They moved down a chair but never took their eyes off him.

"Good grief." Mila groaned as he settled into the chair. "You should try asking for a foot rub. I bet they'd do it."

"Maybe later. These shoes are a bitch to take off." He winked, his hazel-green eyes sparkling in the fluorescent lights, and opened the informational pamphlet Indigo Hotels had handed out at the door.

"Anything good in there?" she asked as he pored over the pamphlet.

He wore his work clothes, a fitted black blazer over a crisp white shirt. Even in more casual outfits, he stood out among the casual Pine Ridge crowd, but dressed to sell property, he belonged on the cover of a Brooks Brothers catalog.

"You talking about this pamphlet or my suit?"

Heat rose to her cheeks, and he grinned, watching her squirm.

"Ooh, damn, Mila. You really were checking me out, huh?"

"Keep it up and your big head won't fit through the door." She turned over her shoulder as if searching for someone, but he could surely see right through her. No amount of salty retorts would cover up her burning face.

He was her friend.

Her friend who had filled out in the last few years, turning from a gangly teenager into a full-grown man right before her eyes.

Nope. Not full-grown. Nothing grown about him. Just a friend.

Just. A. Friend.

"It says here," Jared said, "the hotel will employ three hundred locals. From front office to housekeeping and everything in between. Pretty good, right?"

He raised a hand to his ear and scratched the sharp angle of his jaw, revealing a fancy silver watch and the thick, powerful tendons in his wrist. Could a man's wrist be sexy? The pressure between her legs screamed *YES*.

She swallowed, trying and failing to moisten her throat. "Yeah. That's great, actually."

"I wonder if, uh . . ." His eyes darkened, and his face turned serious. "Nah."

"Wonder if what?"

"Nothing." He lifted his gaze to the front of the room, and the moment passed. He didn't do serious very often. She'd have liked to poke around in that intense thought and explore. "They're gonna start."

"Hello!" A booming voice crackled through the loud-speakers, and the crowd slowly quieted, the squeak of chairs as bodies settled in echoing through the room. "Hello, everyone, and welcome."

At the front of the room, atop a rickety platform and behind a microphone, stood a man about Mila's age clad in a crisp red-and-blue plaid shirt, dark jeans cuffed at the ankle, and expertly worn-in brown leather boots. With his hands on his hips, he grinned out at the sea of people in front of him.

"Guy looks like an Instagram influencer," Jared grumbled.

She shifted her gaze to look at him. "What does that mean?"

"Thank you so much for coming," the man onstage continued, drowning out Jared's reply. "I'm Vin Ortiz, head of marketing for Indigo Hotels, and I'm beyond thrilled to join you today and introduce you to the world of Indigo."

"Who names their kid *Vin*?" Jared said. "Like Vinny or Vincent but they got lazy and dropped the second syllable?"

"Maybe his name *is* Vincent," Mila said. "And Vin is a nickname."

"Even worse. He *prefers* to be called Vin."

Mila squinted at him. "What's your deal with this guy?"

Jared's face fell, and he licked his lips. "What? Nothing. I'm just skeptical of this whole hotel thing."

She stared at him, waiting for the rest of it. A few days ago he'd been excited about the hotel coming into town, and just a few minutes ago he'd praised them for hiring locals. Suddenly the rep started talking and *poof*—he turned anti-Indigo?

Vin Ortiz continued, laying out the hotel chain's mission statement, along with details on the Adirondack property, which sat just twenty miles from Pine Ridge. After a quick rundown of employment opportunities within the company, Vin turned the conversation to the bake-off.

"We couldn't be more excited to get our feet wet in this incredible area of the country by sponsoring the Pine Ridge Spring Bake-Off. We hear there are a ton of incredible pastry chefs nearby, and we can't wait to taste what you've come up with."

Mila's gut twisted. *Incredible pastry chefs.* Experienced bakers with degrees and finely tuned skills from working in professional kitchens and studying the greats. All she had were old cookbooks with splattered pages and a knack for knowing how to perfect crust.

"Tomorrow," Vin said, "official registration closes, and our monthlong competition timeline begins."

He went on to lay down the parameters and guidelines for the first round of the contest, including the stipulation that each contestant use New York–sourced ingredients for at least half the recipe.

"Those lucky ten bakers who make it past round one," Vin said, "will be invited to a private dinner at the brand-new Indigo Hotel Adirondack Park property, and then participate in the final bake-off during an all-weekend festival right here in Pine Ridge."

The room erupted in applause, and Vin raised his hands skyward, grinning wildly at the crowd like a preacher on a pulpit. "It's amazing to hear that you're all as excited about this as we are. And we appreciate your patience while we put the finishing touches on the property. We'd have loved to host both rounds of the competition at our spectacular new site in Adirondack Park, but we're also grateful to share the hosting duties with the incomparable town of Pine Ridge."

Mila ran her suddenly damp palms down the legs of her jeans. Thank God both rounds weren't at the massive new hotel. A little bit of familiarity by way of the Pine Ridge community center would go a long way in soothing her ever-increasing nerves.

"Details of the final event will be announced in a few weeks," Vin said. "But rest assured, Indigo Hotels puts on a spectacular party. The bake-off grand prize includes the winning recipe featured at every Indigo Hotel property across the country, fifty thousand dollars in prize money, and the title of Pine Ridge Baker of the Year."

Fifty thousand dollars covered her parents' mortgage. A new car. Deposits into savings accounts for her sisters' kids. A voice inside she'd tried to shut down a thousand times whispered, *Culinary school.*

"Wow," Mila whispered. "Fifty thousand?"

"May I suggest investing in real estate with your winnings?" The corner of Jared's lips curved skyward. Her seat offered a prime view of the suggestion of stubble peppered across his strong chin. He shaved every single day. Always so pulled together, so . . . *on purpose.*

She glanced down at her own ensemble. A greasy dribble of ranch dressing decorated the curve of her left breast. She cringed. Sexy.

Maybe if she won this contest she'd invest in a larger apron.

"Now," Vin said, "we know you've paid good money to enter this contest, and we know you're the best this community has to offer. So impress us. Blow us away. Knock our socks off. We want your weird, your wonderful, your incredible creations. Does anybody have any questions?"

Hands shot up around the room, and Mila leaned back in her chair, allowing her imagination to drift. Would her chocolate-bacon-orange creation be enough to get her to the final round? Her mother's sour expression when she entered her apartment as she baked said otherwise. Sourcing local ingredients threw another wrench into her plan, and doubts crept in like ghosts.

Aunt Georgie's voice sounded in her ear. *You're as good as them, Lee Lee. Better, even.*

Mila crossed her legs and tucked her hands between her thighs. What did Aunt Georgie know about baking, anyway? Cooking, sure. She had her five-dish repertoire. But baking? Not a chance. The woman treated Entenmann's like the Second Coming.

As the information session wrapped up and people began tucking themselves into outerwear and drifting out of the room, Mila stood from her folding chair and stretched her legs.

"So?" Jared said, standing to meet her and tugging on his coat. "You feel any better? Empowered? Or you feel worse?"

She raised her eyebrows. "Same?"

He laughed. "Hey, maybe whipping up a caramel apple will boost your confidence?"

"Wow, J, thank you so much for the suggestion. You're a peach." She zipped up her coat and slung her purse across her chest as they made their way through the throngs of people to the front exit. "I have to add my name to the registration list and make sure they have Aunt Georgie's check on file."

"Okay, cool. I'll catch you later, then."

"Hey." She touched his wool coat sleeve as he turned away, catching his attention before he bolted. "Thanks for sitting through this with me."

His smooth cheeks flushed blotchy red, and he blinked at her. "Yeah. Sure. No sweat."

For a moment, they stood staring at each other. Something unspoken flowed between them, but she couldn't be sure what it was from his side. Did he ever think about that night after the lake? She remembered it all the time.

He'd stared at her so curiously, so heavily, that she couldn't ignore the shift. When he followed her to her car and offered to walk her home, she thought maybe he'd bridge the chasm of friendship and tell her he wanted more. But as they stood outside next to her car, both shifting awkwardly in the summer air, he blathered something about a burglar on the loose in Pine Ridge and then bailed. A few weeks later he told her he'd hooked up with Chloe, and Mila took it as a sign. A big fat sign. *Never gonna happen.*

Jared coughed into a fist and broke the spell. "Well, all right. See ya later."

She turned to make her way to the registration sign-up sheet when she rammed shoulder-first into another body.

"Oof, Jesus," she grunted. "Sorry."

She looked up to find Vin Ortiz grinning down at her. His heavy cologne assaulted her sinuses, forcing tears to her eyes and reminding her of middle school, when boys began discovering drugstore body spray.

"My fault." He grinned. "I wasn't looking where I was going."

She offered him a tight smile and took a step toward the registration table.

"Are you entering the bake-off?" he said before she could fully move past him.

"Yeah," she said. "I am."

Cool, Mila. Very cool. What if he had something to do with judging?

"That's great," he said. His attention lasered in on her, and he took a step closer, crossing his arms over his chest. "Are you from Pine Ridge?"

She nodded. "I've lived here my whole life."

"Wow, really? Must be a very special place."

He had a kind face, an easy smile. The cologne was a total turnoff, but not the worst she'd ever dealt with. Nicole would tell her to flirt a little, put herself out there. It wasn't every day a single man arrived in Pine Ridge and paid her attention. She should capitalize on the opportunity, even if Vin didn't quite do it for her.

She smirked. "It has its perks."

"Well, I'm here until the contest ends. Maybe you could show me around?"

A single laugh escaped her throat. "Yeah, we'll start at the gas station and end at the diner. If we have time, I can show you the stoplight. You'll be blown away by the booming metropolis that is Pine Ridge."

His smile widened, revealing impossibly straight, white teeth.

"Whatever you love about it," he said, "that's what I want to see."

She wanted to laugh. It had been years since anyone had so shamelessly flirted with her, and even then, it was only Marty, and he'd turned out to be the most boring boyfriend in history. He loved football on Sundays and tan pants, and when she'd asked him to sample her persimmon pie, he'd grimaced and said he didn't eat seafood.

Her whole life she'd decided how she felt about new people within moments of meeting them. Marty was a basset hound, reliable and boring but ultimately safe. The handful of guys she'd dated before Marty fell somewhere within the same safe-but-boring spectrum. And where had that gotten her? Lusting over a friend.

Nothing could ever happen with Jared. The churning feelings would pass, Jared would move on to bigger and better things, and she'd move on, too. She'd take the next step without him, date and possibly marry a man she hadn't even met yet. It had to be that way. Maybe now was the time to step out onto the ledge and take a chance on someone different.

"Sure," she said. "I'm Mila, by the way."

"Vin," he said, extending his hand.

She dragged her own sweaty palm against the fabric of her coat as she pulled it from her pocket. His warm hand enveloped hers, and he lingered for a moment after she'd already let go.

"Very nice to meet you, Mila."

"Nice to meet you, too."

He tugged his phone from the back pocket of his fitted jeans, unlocked it, and handed it to her. "You want to put your number in there? I'll shoot you a text and we can set something up."

With cautious fingers, she took his phone. "This isn't against bake-off bylaws, is it?" she said. "Am I gonna find out later you're a judge and I broke the rules?"

"Nah," he said. "I'm an employee of Indigo, but I don't have anything to do with judging."

She forced down the warning bells in her gut, typed in her number, and handed the phone back. "I should go. I still have to sign up."

He nodded, one side of his mouth turning up in a grin. Smooth. The guy was very smooth. "See you soon, Mila."

chapter **three**

The icy air barely grazed Jared's cheeks before he remembered he'd left his scarf inside. He turned on his heel and hurried back into the community center just in time to see that Instagram-influencer wannabe hand his phone to Mila.

Jared stopped short, and the woman behind him tumbled right into his ass.

"Oh!" she yelped. "Excuse me, son."

He stepped to the side, tucking himself against the wall to keep out of traffic's way. Why was Vin smiling at Mila like that? She gnawed at her thumbnail the way she did when she got nervous, and a single toxic curl of jealousy wound through Jared's gut.

He'd never been jealous before. Never had a reason to be. Mila hovered under the radar of most men in town, and there wasn't anyone to date in Pine Ridge anyway. Her last boyfriend, Marty, barely counted as a romantic partner, and she'd confessed once after a couple of tequila shots that the guy refused any sexual position but missionary. Jared would've been more threatened by a golden retriever.

But this was something new. Mila tapped something into Vin's phone and handed it back, the flickering, awkward smile never leaving her glowing face. When she walked away, Vin stared, checking out her ass.

Before he knew what he was doing, Jared strode across the room to stand directly in front of Vin.

"Hey, man, how's it going?" Jared reached for Vin's hand without waiting for his handshake to be accepted. He tightened his grip, and Vin winced.

"Fine, thanks." Vin shook his hand out before crossing his arms over his chest.

"Pretty cool about the bake-off," Jared said.

"Yeah, man, it's a great program. Indigo is big into community outreach and supporting the areas they build in."

"I'm in real estate myself, so I can definitely see the risks in coming into a small-town area like this."

What the hell was he doing? He never got into pissing contests, and he never boasted about his career. Something about this guy got under his skin, and he hadn't even done anything wrong.

"Ah, cool," Vin said. "What do you do exactly?"

"I'm an agent. Are you looking to move to the area? I could definitely hook you up." He bunched his mouth, immediately regretting the offer. His brain was on autopilot. Sell, sell, sell.

"Nah, man, I'm here short term. Thanks, though."

"You need a rental?"

Vin's dark eyebrows rose past his glasses and into his forehead. "The company's putting me up at a hotel just outside Utica."

"Wow, really? That's like, an hour from here. Without traffic."

Vin ran a hand over his mouth, and his gaze drifted to the registration table where Mila scribbled on a clipboard.

She flipped her hair to one side, chatted amiably with the woman at the table, rocked back and forth on long legs. Why hadn't Jared noticed when he'd walked in how beautiful she looked today? Why hadn't he told her? The curl of jealousy tightened around his lungs.

"Huh," Vin said. He looked back at Jared, his brow furrowed in thought. "Maybe I should be closer. Plus I've got a buddy coming into town, and it'd be easier to have him stay with me."

Shit. What had he done now?

Jared sniffed, forcing himself to chill. Mila was his friend. Did he want her to end up single and alone for the rest of her life? Why shouldn't she go on a date? Even if he let himself admit there may have once been the possibility of something more between them, he'd never get married.

Ever.

To anyone.

And if Jared wasn't going to marry her, then somebody should.

"Here's my info." Jared handed Vin a business card. "Cell service in Pine Ridge is almost nonexistent, so if you call and I don't answer, just leave a message."

"Jesus," Vin said. "No cell service, no Wi-Fi. How does anybody get anything done around here?"

Jared bristled. He'd said the same thing himself a thousand times, but he'd be damned if he'd let anybody talk shit about his town.

"We find a way."

Vin raised his eyebrows and held up the business card. "Thanks for the offer, man. I'll be in touch."

Jared rolled the rough plastic casing between his fingers, set his feet, narrowed his gaze, and propelled the dart toward the bull's-eye.

"Damn it." Eighteen. Again.

"You're distracted," Sam said, retrieving the darts. "Get your head right, brother."

Jared balanced his weight on the barstool and sipped his beer, the hoppy liquid cascading across his tongue. The alcohol soothed his anxious mind.

"I'm not distracted."

Lies. He hadn't been able to think straight all day. Slept like shit last night. This morning he'd poured orange juice in his coffee.

Sam yanked on the brim of his baseball cap before tossing a dart at the board. The stupid thing landed right in the bull's-eye.

"That's game," Sam said.

"Good," Jared said. "I'm done anyway. Those darts are all messed up."

Sam slowly shook his head as they took seats at the bar. The bartender set a water in front of Sam and another IPA in front of Jared.

"How many is that?" Sam nodded toward Jared's beer.

"Two." As much as he wanted to argue, he knew where it would get him. Sam could be cool about his friends drinking, but when it came to his little brother, he monitored alcohol intake like a mama hawk.

"Just be careful," Sam said.

"What do you mean? Be careful of what?"

Sam's face tightened until he turned and caught Jared's shit-eating grin. "Very funny."

Sam ran a hand over his beard and stared into the row of taps behind the bar. Utz's was quiet tonight, with only a smattering of people perched along the bar, watching the basketball game on TV and sipping their respective drinks. This was their place. His and Sam's. The place they always talked.

"Sorry, dude," Jared said. "You make it too easy."

"Syd always tells me I should lay off," he said.

"You give her a hard time about drinking, too?"

"No," Sam said. "Lay off of *you*."

Jared sipped his IPA. Sam had never been shy about reminding him of their father's alcoholism or what a slippery slope awaited if Jared didn't watch himself.

"I knew I liked her," Jared said.

"Then why are you such a hater about us getting married?" Sam lifted the water bottle to his lips, took a long drink, and returned his patient gaze to Jared.

Shame creeped across Jared's skin. He rotated the pint glass between his clammy hands, watching the foam head pop and dissolve. "I'm not hating. Seriously."

Sam scoffed. "Right."

"You and Sydney are perfect for each other," Jared said. "If anybody in the world should get married, it's you two. I guess I just have a hard time . . . seeing the appeal. Personally."

"I don't know, man." Sam folded his hands on the bar top. "Imagine getting to spend every day with your best friend."

Jared's throat dried up like the Sahara in the summer.

"And then imagine," Sam continued, "your best friend is incredibly sexy and she listens to you when you're down and sometimes she bakes chocolate chip cookies."

Or caramel apple pie.

"Syd bakes?"

Sam laughed. "Break and bake. But I'm not complaining."

Jared nodded. The Indigo Hotels weasel featured prominently in his thoughts lately. What if he and Mila hit it off? What if they got married? Would the weasel see her the way Sam saw Syd? Would he savor every bite of each incredible baked good she came up with? No guy who wore ironic flannel would ever truly appreciate Mila's dry wit or impossibly bad taste in grunge rock.

All of a sudden, imagining Mila married to some other guy made his stomach hurt.

"Syd's one of the good ones." His voice betrayed him, and he felt the weight of Sam's stare on his face.

"Damn right she is." Sam paused. "You know, there are other good ones out there. I hope you don't think you've met every woman on the planet. Maybe somebody's out there who could change your mind."

Jared huffed a bitter laugh. "It's not a matter of meeting the right person."

"Just don't want to see you end up alone."

"Why not? Doing what I want, when I want? Yes, please."

The mantra he'd used his entire adult life suddenly sounded hollow.

Sam shook his head and smiled. "Okay."

Jared swallowed the last of his beer. "All this marriage talk is giving me heartburn. I gotta get out of here. I'm showing a house off Tucker Road tomorrow at eight o'clock."

"The Fullers' old house?"

"Yeah."

Sam whistled. "Damn, J. That'll be a nice commission for you. That place is huge."

At four thousand square feet and sitting on a stunning, heavily wooded three-acre plot bordering Fourth Lake, the Fuller house was definitely too much for one person. But Vin Ortiz screamed *poser*, and if the guy didn't want to educate himself about the area, Jared would let the jerk pay way too much. No skin off his nose.

Jared tossed a twenty down on the bar and bunched his lips. "Eh, it's not huge. Just a rental."

"Who's renting that big old place this time of year?"

Jared couldn't bring himself to say it. His voice would probably give him away. *Some dude who's hard up on Mila, and I'm pissed off because I don't think she should date anybody, but I'm not even sure why I feel that way.*

"Some tourist," Jared said. He buttoned his peacoat and clapped his brother on the shoulder. "Hey, when are you proposing, by the way? Want to make sure I've got a bottle of sparkling cider in the fridge for you."

Sam glared. "So thoughtful."

"Kidding, of course." The heavy mood required an easy dig. He admired Sam for always being the sober one in the room, for turning down whiskey shots when everyone taking them knew they were a bad idea. The guy had a level of discipline Jared couldn't fathom.

"It's happening soon," Sam said. "I've had the ring for a while."

"It's . . . good. For you guys, I mean." Jared cleared his throat and closed his hand around the keys in his pocket. The sharp metal house key dug into his palm as he fought against every natural urge to crack another joke about marriage or drinking or Pine Ridge or any of the other deep topics creeping under his skin like a rash. "Sorry I'm such an asshole."

"When it comes to relationships, I expect nothing less." Sam grinned. He'd seen his younger brother through every stupid one-night stand, every Chloe breakup, every crush. Jared's reputation as a commitment-phobic lothario was no secret to anybody in town.

Except lately something had shifted inside him, and he didn't know why. The code he'd always lived by, the single-till-I-die persona everyone knew him for, had begun to wear thin, like bad jokes in a seventies sitcom.

With one last gentle punch on the shoulder, Jared said goodbye to his brother and walked out. He made it as far as the sidewalk outside Utz's before he stopped short. He'd know that curly mop anywhere, and with the grocery store light illuminating her from above, his eyes were drawn to her like the brightest star in the sky.

Mila tilted under the weight of what looked like a thousand grocery bags, teetering and struggling as she exited the grocery store. He hurried across the street toward her.

"I think it's illegal within city limits to carry more than your own weight in groceries," he said as he hooked a hand under the straps digging into her shoulder.

A relieved but disapproving grin spread across her lips

as she looked up at him. She hated his corny jokes, but her response only encouraged him.

"I'm sick of stopping here every day," she said. "I thought I'd try to kill a bunch of birds with one stone."

He snagged another bag from her hand as they headed toward the parking lot together. "You stocking up on recipe-testing supplies?"

"Yeah," she said. "This one's totally wonky. I don't even want to tell you what I'm thinking."

He raised an eyebrow, waiting for her to continue, but she simply smiled, her lips curling slowly upward as her gaze narrowed. She was baiting him.

"Don't make me beg," he said.

They reached her car, and she slid the key into the trunk lock. He wanted to rib her for the umpteenth time about her lack of automatic locks, but he sensed her weariness tonight. She had every right to be. The girl never stopped.

"Coffee praline," she said as she lifted the trunk. "I smell nothing but coffee every day of my life, so I've always veered away from it, but today it hit me. Something sweet and crunchy and spicy . . ."

He bit his lip, tried to focus on what she said, but all he could do was stare down. Her trunk overflowed with crap—a dozen half-empty water bottles, an old grease-stained towel, three ice scrapers, crumpled fast-food bags, and a variety of discarded sneakers—but on top of all the chaos sat a pair of jeans, a balled-up white T-shirt, and the tiniest scrap of purple panties Jared had ever seen.

His tongue turned to cement. He'd seen hundreds of pairs of women's underwear in his life, everything from G-strings to granny panties, but he'd never been turned to ash like he was at the sight of Mila Bailey's thong.

"Yikes," she said, following his gaze and snatching up the undergarment. She shoved it behind the greasy towel as her cheeks flushed. "I'm practically living out of my car these days."

"Damn," he muttered. "You're that busy?"

She arranged the grocery bags around the clutter in her trunk and then shoved a hand into her curls, flipping them to one side and giving Jared a moment to collect his scattered brain cells. If he gave himself enough space and time, he'd start envisioning what she looked like in that little scrap of lace.

A deep exhale passed her lips as she looked up at him. Her eyelids were heavy. "I'm just tired. On top of working and recipe testing, I'm helping my mom with this food and clothing drive she's organizing at the church."

"Your mom asked you for help even though she knows you committed to the bake-off?"

His skin prickled. He often viewed Mila's life as a tug-of-war, with Nicole and himself on one side and the Bailey family on the other. One team wanted Mila to own her life and follow her heart, while the other team wanted her feet and dreams planted firmly on the ground. He couldn't imagine monopolizing Mila's free time when she needed every moment of it to win the contest.

"It's not a huge commitment," Mila said. She slammed the trunk closed. "And it's for a good cause. How could I say no?"

He gritted his teeth. Surely her mother knew that when she asked.

"Hey," he said. "Why don't you let me help your mom with the charity thing? I have lots of time."

She tipped her head back and laughter burst from her lips. "You're sweet, but I got it."

"Seriously, I'd be happy to jump in—"

She placed a gentle hand on his chest, the pressure of her touch searing straight through to his thumping heart and stopping the words on his tongue. "Thank you. I appreciate it. But you don't have to swoop in and save me every time my life gets a little chaotic, okay?"

Didn't he? He wanted to. He also didn't want to push her.

"You sure?" he said.

"You and Nicole," she muttered. "I'm a big girl, all right? I can handle myself."

He rubbed his lips together, wanting to argue but knowing he shouldn't. She was right. She could handle herself. The people in her life needed to recognize that about her. Himself included. "Okay."

She patted his coat, and as she headed toward the driver's-side door, she called over her shoulder. "I'll see you later."

With his heart in his throat, he watched her drive away.

Jared's Camry hugged the winding curves of Route 9, and Vin stared out the passenger window as the scenery sped by in a blur of green and brown. The hipster wannabe wore a pair of Dickies, his boots, and a gray beanie that probably didn't even keep his head warm.

Amateur.

"So, where do you live full-time?" Jared asked. He'd already decided the guy was from New York or LA.

"Denver."

Prick.

"Ah, that's cool. You ski?"

"Yeah," Vin said. He pulled out his phone, checked the home screen, grunted, and replaced it. "This house you're showing me has Wi-Fi, right? I'm losing my mind up here without service."

"Yeah, of course."

The car sped around a tight turn, and Vin gripped the door. Good. Silly fuck in his silly fucking hat.

"Hey, thanks for this, man," Vin said, his gaze returning to the window. "You're right, Utica is really far. And Indigo really wants me close to the property, spending time in town."

Jared took a deep breath and focused on the task at hand. *Rent this guy a house, make the commission.* It wouldn't be a lot, but every little bit helped. Maybe Vin would fall in love with the area and want a vacation home come summer.

"It's no problem," Jared said. "If you want some info on stuff to do in Pine Ridge, too, I'd be happy to fill you in. I know it looks like a nothing little town, but there are some great bars."

"Yeah, that'd be cool." He paused. "Hey, uh, that girl you were with at the bake-off meeting. Mila. You're not with her, right?"

Jared's throat turned to sandpaper, and he gripped the steering wheel. "Mila? Uh, no. We're just friends."

Vin looked at him, steady gaze staring from behind his thick-rimmed glasses. "Did you ever hook up with her?"

The commission. One wrong word about Mila from this dick, and he'd have to forgo the two thousand bucks. "Nope."

Vin nodded. "She's hot."

Jared steadied himself, waiting for the rest of it. But Vin simply returned his gaze to the pine trees blazing past his window and checked his phone once more.

They pulled into the driveway of the old Fuller house, and it took Vin only a few minutes to walk the spacious home before deciding to take it. After a total gut renovation, the Fullers listed the house at a ridiculously low price despite Jared's advice, and now one lucky renter was making out like a bandit.

"Cool place," Vin said, eyes glued to his phone. "Too bad there's no dock. It'd be cool to take a Jet Ski out or something when the weather gets warmer."

Jared choked back the words threatening the gates of his mouth. Everybody knew only selfish pricks disrupted the serenity of the lake with Jet Skis. "Yeah, too bad."

Vin walked to the window and looked out over the snowy expanse of lawn to the mountains beyond. "It's weird looking at mountains like this when I'm used to the Rockies."

Jared clenched his teeth. He'd heard it so many times from out-of-towners. *But the mountains are so small!*

"If you're into outdoor stuff, though," Jared said, "you'll love it here. Tons of great hikes, kayaking, fishing."

"Hey," Vin said, "just throwing it out there, but Indigo has a whole real estate team. They scout out new property locations, work the deals. Most of the people who work in that department have backgrounds in real estate. Not sure how married you are to this area, but if you ever wanted to move on, I could introduce you to the right people."

Jared froze, temporarily caught off guard. For all his job searching, hunting across websites and referral services, drooling over TV shows featuring slick agents earning six-figure commissions, he never expected an offer like Vin's to pop up during a rental showing.

He shoved down the adrenaline suddenly coursing through his veins and forced his face into a neutral gaze. He didn't want Vin thinking he cared too much.

"Wow," he said. "Really?"

"Yeah," Vin said, checking his phone again. The dude was a Wi-Fi addict. "Indigo is based in North Carolina, but it's a pretty big outfit. Listen, I have to jump on this conference call. You mind if I take it here? It'll take ten minutes."

Jared blinked, trying to keep up with the shifting conversation. "Uh, yeah. Sure."

"Thanks. And let me know about Indigo. I can make some calls."

Before Jared could answer, Vin said hello and disappeared into the kitchen.

Jared made his way outside and into his car, cranking the heat and rubbing his hands together against the frigid temperatures. Winter in this town seemed endless, with snow beginning to fall in October and steadily increasing, finally tapering off in April or May.

For a moment, as he gazed out over the matted grass,

studded with patches of melting gray snow and framed by spindly trees, he envisioned what his life might look like in a new city. No snow. Cell service whenever he wanted it. New faces, new bars, new restaurants.

New women.

No stars.

His phone buzzed, still connected to the Wi-Fi in the house.

PIE! Requires immediate tasting.

Mila attached a photo of a chocolate pie with a twist of orange in one corner, and a smile curved onto his lips.

He'd spent hours upon hours examining his feelings for her. Before that day at the lake, he'd never even imagined kissing her. And after, he couldn't imagine anything but. The thing that killed him was that the old feelings of friendship didn't disappear with the feelings of lust, they just combined to create one giant fireball of overwhelming emotions. It confused the shit out of him.

Chloe had arrived in his life like a Happy Meal when what he really needed was a green salad. But food was food, and a man had to eat. He'd hooked up with her for the distraction. She'd been pissed off when he'd called it quits for good, but ultimately, they both knew it was best. She wanted to get married. He didn't. End of story.

"Hey, thanks, man." Vin climbed into the car and shivered against the cold. "Jesus, the weather up here is no joke."

Jared threw the car in reverse and pushed all thoughts of his love life aside. Maybe he should just go back to hooking up with whoever looked good to him in the moment. That had always worked before.

"While I was in there, I texted that Mila chick," Vin said. "We're gonna have dinner this week. Looks like Pine Ridge has more to offer than just bars, you know what I mean?"

Jared's stomach turned as cold as the temperatures outside. He shot Vin a look, but the guy was staring out the window with a dopey grin on his face, totally unaware of Jared seething beside him.

"Yeah," he said through his teeth. "I know what you mean."

chapter **four**

The heavenly scent of browned crust, caramelized pears, and toasty cinnamon filled Mila's apartment, and she breathed in like the air itself was a gift from the heavens. Ginger? Maybe the crust needed fresh minced ginger.

As the gently thrumming sounds of Jimmy Eat World cascaded out of her Bluetooth speaker, she jotted a note in her flour-splotched notebook and wiped her hands on her apron. Benny told her he could source pears from a friend with a greenhouse, and he promised to look into a few other options for fruit, but so far everything she'd tasted was lackluster. Grainy pears; chewy citrus; bland, mealy apples. Baking in the winter with only locally sourced ingredients provided a special kind of challenge.

Mila trailed her powdery hands over the notebook, remembering when Aunt Georgie gave it to her. Georgie remained a mediocre cook, at best, but she loved cooking all the same. The rules, the measuring, the experimentation. Like Mila, she loved its solitary nature, the ability to create something from scratch all by herself, without assistance or interference. Something that was all hers.

Mila could still hear Georgie scolding her grandnieces to "get the hell out of the kitchen!" The old woman didn't have a sentimental bone in her body—at least not that she'd ever revealed to Mila—but her sharpness held truths. Truths a girl could trust.

Mila's doorbell rang, and she checked her wall clock as her heart leaped into her throat. Vin couldn't be picking her up yet, could he? Only five forty-five, and she still had to shower.

Uneasiness stirred inside her. She'd given Vin excuses for the first two dates he'd suggested earlier in the week, and by the third option, she realized she had to say yes or put an end to the whole thing. Her rational mind couldn't find a reason why she shouldn't go on a date with a perfectly pleasant guy who seemed interested in her, and so she gave in. Dinner. In town. An excuse to put on makeup and wear heels and get to know someone who might eventually save her from her post-Marty drought.

"One meal," Nicole had urged. "He seems like a per- fectly nice guy."

Perfectly nice. So why did Mila's stomach bubble and pop like sauce boiling over?

She hit the buzzer and a minute later opened the door to find a grinning Jared.

Relief flooded her veins.

"Hey." She smiled. "What are you doing here?"

"You sent me that photo. The pie? Don't tease me with baked goods, dude."

"The photo I sent you almost a week ago?" Mila said. Typical Jared. On his own schedule. Always. "I gave that pie to my mom, and my parents have probably long since polished it off."

"Shit. Sorry I didn't text you back." He ran a hand over

his expertly coiffed hair before sniffing at the air. "Something else smells pretty good in there."

She pursed her lips and allowed herself a moment to take him all in. The sweetness in his gaze that turned steely when he closed deals. The sharp jaw formerly hidden by pubescent pudge. The scar over his left eyebrow from the time they'd ridden their bikes down a dangerous trail and he'd flown over his handlebars, sailing forehead-first into a gnarled oak tree.

Her friend Jared. The face she'd always known. The face she'd relied on over the years to put her worried mind at ease. The face that, more recently, made her stomach fizz in a very different way.

"All right," she said. "Come on in."

He beamed and brushed past her on a wave of spicy cologne. It took all of thirty seconds for him to strip off his coat, kick off his shoes, and settle down at the kitchen counter with an eye on her cinnamon pear pie.

"It just came out of the oven," she said. "So you have to give it a few minutes. And I have to take a shower. When I'm done, we'll cut it, all right?"

"Perfect. I'll just wait here and will it to cool down with mental telepathy. That is, if this ridiculous music doesn't distract me."

Her playlist had skipped to "Sugar We're Going Down," an emo song featured prominently at every Pine Ridge High School dance for years on end, and she rolled her eyes. "Don't you dare touch my music. The pie needs to be surrounded by good vibes as it cools. I'll know in the first bite if you messed with it."

Wanting to spend a few minutes with Jared before Vin arrived, she sped through her normal shower routine and avoided shaving her legs, a silent promise to herself that no matter how charming Vin might turn out to be, she'd made the decision ahead of time that sex was off the table.

She dried off in the bathroom, tucked the towel around herself, and scurried into her bedroom. As she rounded the corner, a looming male figure appeared, and she yelped.

"Dude!" She clutched the top of her towel to keep it from slipping as Jared turned over his shoulder. His eyes blazed as if she'd shocked *him* and not the other way around.

"Sorry!" he said. "I was just looking at your paint job. You should let Sam come in and redo this. Is this lead paint? Did you ever get that checked out before you moved in here?"

"Holy hell." Her heart hammered against her ribs as she struggled to catch her breath. "You scared the shit out of me. You're checking out the paint job? Get the hell out of here so I can get dressed."

For one quiet moment, he stared at her. His eyes and smile softened, and he slipped his hands into the pockets of his jeans. The simple gaze lit her skin on fire, and she twisted the towel between her fingers to make sure it was still there and she wasn't standing stark naked in front of him. That's what it felt like. Like he could see right through her.

"Go on." Her voice whispered, barely audible. "I have to get dressed."

He breathed in, his chest rising and then falling under his simple gray sweatshirt, before brushing past her and closing the bedroom door behind him.

When she emerged from the bedroom fully clothed and supremely confused, he sat at the kitchen island holding a fork and staring at the pie like an oracle.

"It's probably still not cool enough to cut," she said. She tucked a loose curl into the bun she'd quickly twisted on top of her head, but it fell back down almost immediately. She hoped Vin was into unruly hairdos.

Or did she? Was it normal to hope a guy didn't like you enough to want a second date before you'd even gone on the first one?

After retrieving a knife from the drawer, she turned

back to the island to find Jared staring at her like he'd been staring at the pie. Openmouthed, wide-eyed.

"What?"

"You look hot." He pressed his lips together like he was sorry he'd said it. "I mean, I can't remember the last time I saw you dressed up."

"The funeral."

He snorted a laugh, and all at once she remembered why they were such good friends. She didn't need to explain to him that it was a joke, or that he didn't have to be delicate with her. They could be themselves.

"Seriously," he said. "You, uh . . . you look good."

She tugged at the sleeve of her fluttery red blouse. The neck dipped low, exposing a stretch of cleavage typically hidden under stained T-shirts and heavy winter garb, but she figured date night called for something outside her everyday look. She'd even slicked on a deep berry-colored lipstick. The way Jared gawked at her, she guessed it worked.

"Thanks," she said.

"Where are you going?"

She pressed her lips together and tried to swallow the discomfort tickling her throat. "To dinner."

His eyes narrowed. "With that Indigo weasel?"

She shook her head and sunk the knife into the pie, averting her eyes. "He's not a weasel. He even asked to take me to dinner instead of meeting up with him and his buddies at Taylor's the way most guys in this town do."

"So the bar was already at an all-time low. Well played, weasel."

"Stop." Her voice lacked conviction. "He's nice."

Jared scoffed. "Nice? I showed the guy a rental property. He's a total douche."

"A rental property? In Pine Ridge?" She stopped cutting mid-slice and looked at her friend, whose cheeks had turned blotchy.

"The company put him up in Utica, so I told him he'd be

better off renting a place nearby to cut down on the commute. He's renting the old Fuller house."

She waited for the rest of the story, but Jared sat stone still, simply watching her like he'd done during the staring contests they used to have as kids. "Well, that was nice of you."

He pursed his lips and turned back to the pie. "Just trying to make that money. Are you gonna cut that or what?"

"Why is he a douche?"

Vitriol colored Jared's tone. She needed to know why.

"I dunno." His eyes remained trained on the pie.

"I'm going on a date with this guy, so if there's something I should be aware of, can you just spit it out?"

His jaw worked back and forth, and he crossed his arms tightly across his chest. The color remained in his smooth cheeks. He still wouldn't look at her.

"*Jared.*"

He looked up. The golden kitchen lights bathed his face in a warm glow, and his green eyes burned right through her. Tension tugged at his mouth.

She swallowed, but the parched feeling in her throat remained. What if all Jared needed was an opening? Would he admit something was different between them? She had to ask. She simply had to. "Is there any reason I shouldn't go on a date with this guy?"

He unfolded his arms and ran a hand through his hair, sending it sticking up in uncharacteristic chaos.

Sex hair.

She tightened her thighs as if somehow just the thought of him in bed might send her off an orgasmic cliff.

"No," he said. "I'm just . . . protective over you. That's all."

Her heart sank into her stomach. Protective. Right. Definitely not wild with jealousy at the thought of her with another man. She tiptoed backward from the edge of the cliff.

"Fine." She slid the knife through the pie and then used a serving utensil to lift the dripping slice out of the pan. "See. I told you it was too hot."

*   *   *

Seven o'clock came and went. Jared lingered at her place, sneaking forkfuls of the pear pie she'd already deemed subpar based on fruit quality. As much as she didn't want him in her apartment when Vin arrived, she also didn't necessarily force him out.

At six forty-eight he'd asked, "Lemon or lime?" and thirty minutes later, they collapsed into hysterical laughter as the game devolved into gems like, "One ply or two?" and "Would you rather smell like tuna for the rest of your life, or every time you burped, a tiny word cloud appeared over your head with the exact thought you were thinking at the moment of the burp?"

"Oh shit," Mila said, rising from the couch and noticing the time. "Did I get stood up?"

"Maybe he heard your shitty music from the hallway and thought twice about dating you." Jared grinned, settling back into his regular spot in the corner of the couch.

"Twenty bucks says you have a Randy Travis album in your car right now." She trailed her tongue across her lip and reached for her cell phone. "You have absolutely no room to weigh in on what good music is."

The phone in her hand *dinged* with a text notification from Vin, and she checked the screen.

Call me?

She picked up her home phone and dialed his number, avoiding Jared's stare as best she could. He didn't even pretend not to listen in.

"Mila, I'm so sorry," Vin said as soon as he picked up. "I was on my way to pick you up and I got a call from the hotel that a pipe burst, and they need me on-site. I hate to do this, but can we rain-check dinner?"

A weight lifted off her shoulders. Did normal girls expe-

rience unfiltered relief when their dates canceled on them?
She crossed her arms over her chest and turned further away
from Jared. He'd have a field day if he saw any trace of joy
on her lips.

She promised Vin it was no problem, hesitantly agreed
to a drink on another night, and hung up after he apolo-
gized once more. After she replaced the phone in the cradle, she turned back to Jared, who quickly erased the hint
of a smile from his face.

Forced disapproval knit his brow. "Dick move," he said.
"Canceling after you're already late?"

She shrugged. "There was an emergency at the hotel.
We're gonna grab a drink next Monday night."

Jared nodded slowly and ran a hand across his chin, the
sound of skin on stubble like nutmeg on the grater and eliciting the same warm, tingling sensation in her chest.

"Bummer." Sarcasm hung heavy on the word. "So, you're
free tonight?"

"I guess."

"All dressed up and no place to go."

She narrowed her gaze and placed her hands on her hips.
"I was canceled on. What's your excuse?"

"You're right." His lips curled into a grin. "I should see
if I can scrounge up a date."

Even joking, the thought of him with another girl summoned tension to her shoulders. Jared's past was common
Pine Ridge knowledge, and more than once they'd had to
switch tables at a restaurant or hurry into another aisle at
the grocery store to avoid an awkward run-in with someone
he'd slept with and never went out with again. He told Mila
he was always honest with the women he hooked up with,
but she wondered.

"You should," she countered. "I'm sure there are at least
two or three lonely women at Utz's or Taylor's right now,
just waiting for your smarmy ass to walk in the door and
shake up their evening."

The grin faded from his lips, and the taut column of his throat constricted as he swallowed. As the urge to lick him from clavicle to chin washed over her, she took a step backward, brushing up against the refrigerator. When would these lusty feelings pass? What would it take for her to stop seeing him this way?

A mind eraser.

"I'm not like that anymore," he said.

"Oh, you're not? Forgive me. I must be misremembering the last time you and Chloe were on the outs and you took home that semiprofessional rower who was in town on vacation."

His cheeks flushed, and he lifted his gaze, his forest green eyes blazing. "That was a year ago."

"And now you're reformed?"

"Forget it." He pressed on his knees and stood up from the couch. "I'm gonna go."

He grabbed his coat and brushed past her, moving steadily toward the door.

"Oh, come on," she said. "Now you're gonna pout?"

He turned sharply, a delicate wave of warm, spicy cologne washing over her. He stood close enough that she could see the heavy lashes overlapping at the corners of his eyes. The closeness paralyzed her.

"I'm not like that anymore." The gravel in his voice shivered down her spine. "Seriously, Lee."

"Okay."

"You don't believe me." His jaw tensed.

"I'm sorry," she said. "But you just broke up with your long-term girlfriend because she wanted to get married. You physically flinch at engagement ring commercials. And up until . . . apparently . . . a year ago, you were king of the one-night stand. I'm just drawing logical conclusions here."

He shook his head. "I can be anti-marriage and also not want to treat women like shit."

She drew in a deep breath. *Anti-marriage.* So not everything about him had changed. "No one ever said you treated women like shit."

"Well, I did. I don't need anybody to say it out loud to know it's true."

She tucked her arms across her chest and ran her tongue across her teeth. He used to carry the reputation like a badge of honor, grinning and laughing and slapping hands when one of his guy friends joked about the Kirkland swagger or how Jared hadn't experienced a sex drought since he lost his virginity at the ripe old age of sixteen.

"Maybe you're growing up," she said.

He pinched the bridge of his nose and dragged tense fingers across his eyebrow. "Or maybe I'm just tired of doing the same old shit."

Something in her chest deflated. Did he include her in that statement? Was being around her the *same old shit*? She ran a hand over her arm, suddenly chilled.

"Speaking of the same old shit," he said. "You wanna go get a drink?"

"Actually," she said, "if I have a whole night free, I should test out some more recipes. I don't have all that much time to dedicate to testing with my work schedule, so this is sort of a gift."

His face clouded over. "Ah, okay. I'll head out, then. Leave you to it."

"No!"

The second the word shot out of her mouth, his eyebrows rose into his forehead. "It's not goodbye forever, weirdo."

She nestled her thumbnail between her teeth, properly shielding half her face. What was her problem lately? Spending platonic time with him felt like having an itch in the middle of her back she couldn't quite reach.

"I just meant you don't *have* to go. You know, if you don't have any other plans tonight."

"No offense, but I've been in the room when you're testing. You're not the most . . . social."

Okay, he had her there. With the pressure of the contest and the money at stake, she'd be even more focused than usual. And the truth was, she didn't know where to go from here. The cinnamon pear pie was good, but it wasn't anything to write home about. She could practically hear her mother's voice.

No, it's good. Really, Mila. Very tasty. Hey, you know who makes a good pie? Safeway.

"That's fair," she said quietly.

He studied her, his eyes darkening with seriousness that made her stomach tighten. These moments happened more frequently lately. The young, goofy Jared mask slipped, and they connected over something deeper. Like he was trying to show her another side of himself. Another possibility.

"How's all this going?" he asked. "You feel like you found the recipe yet?"

"Mm." She stared at the pie plate, one giant wedge and several additional forkfuls missing. "No. This was okay."

"Are you kidding?" he stammered. "This was legendary. You better add this to the rotation no matter what."

"You're sweet. It's just the fruit . . . It's March, you know? The worst season for fruit. And we're in North Country, where I have even less access to quality produce." Mediocrity threatened her fingertips. Pine Ridge's famous pie baker couldn't get past simple fruit combinations and chocolate tarts. "I feel a little stuck."

"Of course you feel stuck. You've done nothing but work and bake and work and bake for the past, I dunno, twenty years of your life? When's the last time you let your hair down?"

"Let my hair down?" She grinned. "Golly gee, I'm not sure, Aunt Georgie."

"Ha. Ha." His lips downturned into a sarcastic smirk. "I mean it. You need some fun in your life."

"I had fun at your party."

He dropped his chin. "You had two beers and left at ten o'clock."

"Okay." She raised her arms and let them slap down against her thighs. "So take me out, Kirkland. Let's have some fun."

"Don't tease me."

She laughed. "I'm not."

"We're gonna have fun?"

"Yes."

"Fun that lasts past ten?"

"Yes."

"Fun that includes calling Sam at two in the morning to ask him to come pick us up and then having him yell at us not to puke in his back seat during the ride home?"

Her cheeks burned at the memory. Pine Ridge had one cab company, and Herb knew Jared far too well to risk picking him up after midnight.

"Yes, J." She brushed crust crumbs from her hands. "Let me just go change."

"Nuh-uh." He grabbed her wrist, sparks shooting up her arm. "If Vin was gonna get this version of you, then I want this version of you, too."

From the waist down, her body turned to jelly. He bit his lower lip and blinked, as if realizing what he'd said. His hand slid away from her wrist, and he stepped backward.

"You think I'm arm candy, huh?" Did he hear the tremor in her voice?

He cleared his throat. "Obviously. You know me. If I'm not making the other guys in the bar jealous, I don't want to be there."

With one last mind-clearing breath, she grabbed her purse. "Okay, Fabio. Let's go."

chapter **five**

know where we're going."

Jared's secretive gaze slid over to the passenger seat in his car, but he remained silent. He said he wanted to surprise her, but there was no such option for a Pine Ridge local who knew every cool spot within a hundred-mile radius.

"That coffee shop that serves local beer at night, right? Jam's or something?"

His eyebrows jumped into his forehead as if to say, *Maybe*, and he turned his attention back to the road. Twilight settled into the dense forest surrounding them, coaxing the melodies of nightfall out of the wildlife within. Crickets chirped, furry animals scuttled along the forest floor, and bats flapped overhead. Anyone who came to the Adirondacks for peaceful, quiet evenings had never been in the woods at night.

Mila leaned against the cool glass and soaked in the blurred view. She loved Pine Ridge. The inky nights, the sparkling lakes, the air so pure and clean it melted on your tongue like ice cream. Her life hadn't always reflected the postcard-perfect scenes sold at tourist shops in town, but nothing in life was perfect. The town suited her best that way.

Jared's silver Camry rounded a tight corner before slowing abruptly and turning into a parking lot filled nearly to capacity. At the far end of the lot stood a dark wood structure with a pink, neon sign blazing on the roof. **EAT AT JAM'S**.

"Wait," Mila said slowly. "Is this the same place?"

"How about when I tell you something's a surprise, you let the unknown of it just wash over you?" He closed his eyes, fluttering his fingers dramatically across his cheeks. "Letting it all just *waaaash* over you."

She slapped his hand, and he smacked himself in the face, his eyes flying open in mock outrage.

"How dare you?" he said through laughter. "You know, you try to do something nice . . ."

"Hey, have we met? I don't like surprises."

He huffed out one long, dramatic sigh. "It's just a cool spot with good food and live music that happens to be owned by a guy who bought a house from me a few years back who *also* happens to own a pretty serious vineyard in the Finger Lakes."

Her gaze narrowed. "Okay?"

"A vineyard with grape crops. Concord grapes."

The words rang in her head like a bell. *New York–grown fruit.* She wet her lips in anticipation.

"Grapes he'd be willing to part with?"

Jared shrugged. "Won't know until we ask. Right?"

Visions of tarts, cakes, and pies danced in Mila's head. The mouthwatering Concord grape cookies Edith O'Hare baked up for last year's Harvest Festival. The tangy grape quick bread Karen Walsh gifted the Bailey family the day Aunt Georgie passed. The classic grape pie Mila whipped up at the diner after closing last year. The possibilities seemed endless. Unique. And New York grown.

Mila and Jared crossed the parking lot, and the second he yanked open the door for her, music spilled out into the night. The thrumming, guitar-laden sounds of "Little Miss Honky Tonk" pulsed through the wide-open space and, despite her aversion to country music, drew Mila in like a spell.

Giant well-loved beer signs and an endless array of stickers covered the towering walls, while long communal tables lent the only bit of organization to the otherwise chaotic space. A buzzing hive surrounded the bar, and all manner of people shouted in jovial tones into one another's ears to be heard over the live band. Mila's cheeks warmed in the humid air as Jared sidled up next to her.

"Good surprise?" He leaned in, maybe to be heard over the music. She let her mind roam free.

"Good surprise."

He tilted his head toward the hostess stand and held up two fingers at a bubbly young woman with a clipboard. They followed her to two empty seats on the same side of a table far from the main stage, where a six-person band sawed and swayed and jammed out to Brooks and Dunn covers. Despite their distance from the stage, the music still rattled Mila's bones and forced a wide smile to her face.

"Drinks?" the hostess shouted.

Jared stood to give their drink order, gesturing wildly and trying to get his point across to the confused young woman. Finally, she nodded emphatically and gave Jared a thumbs-up.

"Got you an IPA," he said. Again, he leaned in close, his warm breath whispering across her neck and raising goose bumps despite the tropical atmosphere.

"Thanks."

The band announced a short break, ushering in slightly softer hard-rock tunes over the sound system, and their waitress reappeared to set down two overfilled pint glasses and sticky menus.

"What are you in the mood for?" Jared asked. "Or better yet, what would you have ordered if the Indigo weasel himself were here? Cute-girl side salad? Dainty-lady hummus and carrots? Ooh, look, they have a 'diet' section on the menu! My favorite. Cottage cheese and half a grapefruit."

He leaned on his elbows, hunched over the menu, and tilted his torso toward her to deliver his corny jokes. She rolled her eyes, but her brain rattled with his close proximity as the scent of his subtle cologne and vaguely vanilla-scented hair product wafted toward her.

He licked his lips and turned back to the menu. She physically shook her head. The stomach flutters, the leg fuzzies, the light-headedness. No time for all that. No time for adolescent foolishness. No time for inconvenient crushes on lifelong friends.

"Did you guys decide what you want?" the waitress asked abruptly, roughly three minutes after she'd set down menus.

"I'll have the fried chicken sandwich with fries, please," Mila said.

Jared ordered a burger before lifting his gaze and pursing his lips. "Fried chicken and fries, huh? Not a very date-friendly meal."

She resisted the urge to smack him. He'd known her too long to assume she'd alter her eating habits for a guy. "Oh, if I'd been with Vin, I'd have ordered that cottage cheese deal you mentioned."

"I knew it." He sipped his beer and glanced around the room. "I want to know what you're like on a date, Lee."

"First of all, no one I've ever dated has called me Lee Lee."

"No one outside your family calls you Lee Lee."

"Nicole does."

He grinned. "I said 'family.'"

Mila's chest warmed. Her older sisters had always had each other, even going so far as to move to Buffalo together after college, and Mila had Nicole. When Mila lost Jared to crushes and school sports for a couple of years in middle and high school, she'd bonded with Nicole in ways she'd never known were so valuable. She considered Nicole and Jared as close as family. Closer, maybe. For better or worse.

"All right," he said, leaning back to survey her. "So we know what you'd wear. We know what you'd prefer to be called. We know what you'd eat. What would you say?"

Her stomach fizzed. What *would* she have talked about with Vin? In their minimal interactions, she deduced that he'd probably carry the conversation. She'd sit pleasantly across the table and smile when appropriate and, if she felt secure enough, add her own anecdotes about a controlling mother and a docile father and overbearing sisters. She'd tell him she went to a state university nearby, but she'd leave out the part about her family not being able to afford student housing.

"For you!" the waitress said, breaking into their intimate cocoon of conversation. She set down two shot glasses filled with clear liquid and a tiny dish of lemon slices. "On me."

Before the waitress turned away, Mila caught her wink. Jared's lips curled into a smile—*that* smile—and the waitress squeezed his shoulder and sashayed away to the next table.

"I bet you wouldn't do *that* on a date," Mila said. She snatched one of the shot glasses and downed it, not caring what the liquor was, only that it stung her sinuses and relaxed the knots in her shoulders. *Holy shit, cheap vodka.* She tightened every muscle in her face and tucked the tart lemon slice between her teeth, sucking on the citrus like a baby on a bottle.

His smile deepened, his eyes sparkling in the neon lights. "Nah, I try not to flirt in front of dates. But sometimes I just can't help it, you know?"

She raised one eyebrow. "Gosh, J, I thought you weren't like that anymore."

An icy wall crackled between them, and he sat straighter in his chair, his eyes darting around the room. He reached a strong hand out and nudged the second shot glass toward her.

"Go ahead."

He never drank vodka.

"You sure?" she asked.

"Yes. Just the smell of it makes me want to puke."

She narrowed her gaze. "Why is that? I know you don't prefer it, but I never realized it was a visceral hatred."

A dark cloud settled over his face, drawing his sharp, beautiful features down into something grave and somber. "Just makes me think of my dad. The bad times."

As if propelled by the memory, she tossed the shot back, sucked the lemon, and followed it quickly with a long drink of beer. Would she smell of it now? If they kissed, would she taste of it?

Her stomach turned sour. Why would they kiss?

"What's with that look?" His eyebrows lowered as he studied her face.

"Oh, nothing." *Just fantasizing about your mouth on mine. No bigs.* "I didn't know that. About your dad."

He took a long drink of his beer and licked the froth from his cupid's bow. "He mostly stewed in silence when he was home, but a couple of times he got belligerent, and I started to recognize the smell of vodka on those particularly fun evenings."

The word "fun" fell off his tongue like a bad penny.

"I thought he never got violent?"

"He didn't." A wry smile settled on his lips. "Never violent. But Jesus, could he yell. I'm not even convinced he knew how loud he was. Just pissed off at everything. The batteries in the remote were dead; the commercial breaks on TV took too long; one of us left the front door open too long when we walked in. The guy lived like he had rocks in his shoes all the time."

Mila had never spent time around Mr. Kirkland, only truly befriending Jared after he'd passed away. The stories Jared told about his father always made light of his frequently inebriated state. In the moments when Jared turned morose, the truth seeped out like poison.

"Must've been hard on you guys," Mila said. "Walking on eggshells all the time."

"Oh my God," he groaned, his face slipping into a smile. "Was that a *baking* joke, you goofball?"

She tilted her head and gave him her best *Are you kidding me?* glare. "No."

He scratched his chin, turning his attention back to the room as the band took the stage again. "They're good, huh? I'm not the biggest Brooks and Dunn fan, but they're killing it."

"So we're done talking about real things?"

"I thought you wanted to know what I was like on a date. I wouldn't bring up my dad until at least three months into a relationship."

He offered her his cheesy smile again—the one that reduced most women to puddles at his spotless shoes—and raised his eyebrows.

"I never asked to know what you're like on a date." She drank the hoppy IPA to settle her suddenly frayed nerves. Maybe she hadn't melted, but part of her did liquefy. *"You* asked *me."*

"Oh, right. Okay, so far, we've got the smokin' hot outfit, the desire to be called by your full legal name, Mila Beauregard Bailey, the fried chicken, and the . . . two shots? Is that right? Damn, Vin has no idea what he missed out on. It's like having dinner with a bangin' truck driver."

Laughter exploded from her lips. "Mila," she choked out, "Beauregard Bailey. I forgot about that." She clutched her middle as tears pooled in her eyes.

He joined in, the two of them attracting curious stares from the strangers at their communal table. She finally caught her breath in time to watch Jared dab at his own ruddy cheeks, the traces of laughter still skipping off his tongue.

"It was tough sneaking that long-ass middle name onto Ms. Mac's attendance sheet," he said, "but oh man, was it worth it."

Mila's smile hurt her cheeks, but she couldn't stop. "I was so pissed at you until somehow that middle name made it to my school record, and my mom's head nearly exploded when she saw it on my report card. That was priceless."

He trailed his teeth over his bottom lip, the joy glittering in his eyes as he looked at her. "You never ratted me out to her."

"It was easier to blame it on the school."

Tingling warmth cascaded across her shoulders as he continued to stare. *It's so easy with him*, she'd tell Nicole before her friend rolled her eyes and raised one accusatory eyebrow. Nicole hated that excuse. She'd tell Mila that of course it was easy. No sex involved. The minute sex entered the equation, everything went haywire.

"You have to stop looking at him like the gold standard," Nicole always said. "He's not perfect. And no guy will ever measure up to him if you keep seeing him that way."

But Nicole didn't get it. She'd met her husband, Calvin, in their first year of nursing school and hadn't looked back. They bonded over their Jamaican heritage, their career interests, their love of baseball, and their shared goal of having lots of babies and a house on the lake before they turned forty. Nicole considered sparks and chemistry and soul mates as reliable as astrology.

Mila read her own sun and rising sign horoscopes every day.

As the band settled in to begin the next part of their set, someone clapped a weathered hand on Jared's shoulder. Jared leaped out of his chair, his energy shifting dramatically.

"Patrick!"

"So good to see you, Jared." The wiry man extended a hand, and Jared shook it vigorously. "Sorry it took me a minute to get over here. We're slammed tonight."

"I can see that." Jared scanned the room before turning back to Patrick. "I haven't been here since it reopened. You've got 'em packed to the rafters."

Patrick lifted narrow shoulders and ran a hand over his shockingly black hair. Judging by the leathery texture of his skin, Mila guessed boxed hair dye was to thank for the coif.

"Patrick, this is my friend Mila."

Friend. Oof. What had she expected? *Patrick, this is the woman in my life I stare too long at and give wobbly knees to but can't really say anything more about.*

"Very nice to meet you," Mila said, standing to shake the man's hand. His grip made her wince.

"Pleasure, Mila. Have you dined with us before?"

"Never," she said. Nerves snapped like rubber bands in her stomach as she suddenly became the focal point of the conversation. What if this guy didn't want to part with his grapes? Concords were harvested in the fall and hard to come by in the off season, and if Patrick made wine, he'd surely need every grape possible to make his profits.

"Well, I do hope you enjoy. Try the banana pudding. It's my wife's recipe, and it's kept me in Weight Watchers since I met her."

Patrick patted his concave stomach, and Mila shot a side-eyed glance to Jared. He raised his brows as if to urge her forward.

"Uh, Patrick," Jared said. "I actually brought Mila here to meet you."

"Is that right?" Patrick's toothy smile appeared behind wrinkled lips. "Well, what can I do for you, Mila?"

Her throat tightened, the words lost somewhere on the back of her tongue, stuck there like autumn leaves in wet cement.

"Ah," she said. "I'm in this pie-baking contest. Well, not necessarily pie baking. The contest is for baked goods in general, I just happen to be making a pie. Or . . . I hope I'm making a pie. And you have grapes. Or, um, Jared told me you grow grapes."

She grimaced as Patrick looked to Jared for further explanation. Damn those vodka shots. Instead of giving her courage, they'd shot her insecurities into overdrive. Patrick would surely think she was some sort of idiot, unable to string words together like a toddler trying out her voice for the first time.

"Mila is an incredibly talented baker," Jared said, smoothing over her gaffe. "She finally entered the annual Pine Ridge Spring Bake-Off, but she's such a perfectionist, none of the available produce is up to her standards. I told her I knew an amazingly generous guy who had Concord grape reserves frozen, and he might be willing to part with some of it."

How did Jared do that? The sales pitch floated effortlessly from his mouth, melodic and easy.

Patrick tucked his arms across his chest, his lips pinching suspiciously. "Hm. Well, I do have grapes."

The tightness in Mila's gut loosened momentarily. "You do?"

"Yes, but unfortunately, they're slotted for ice wine. Have you had it? It's a dessert wine, and we sell it in spades over at the winery. You should come out and try it sometime. Are you familiar with Skaneateles Lake?"

Mila forced her face into a neutral smile despite the disappointment dragging her down like gravity on steroids. "Uh, yeah. Sure. Skaneateles Lake."

"It's really a treat," Patrick said. "I'm sorry I couldn't help you out, Lola."

"It's Mila."

Patrick's lips pinched again. "Forgive me. Mila. Enjoy your dinner. I'll send out some of that banana pudding when you're done."

Patrick shook Jared's hand again and turned away as quickly as he'd arrived. Shame bloomed in Mila's cheeks as she slid back into her chair and tried to avoid Jared's pointed stare.

When he didn't sit down, she looked up. His lips parted in confusion.

"You've gotta be kidding me," he said.

"I know, right? The guy can't part with a couple cartons of grapes? How much ice wine could he possibly produce?"

"Not him," he snapped. "You. You're just gonna take that answer? One no and you're out?"

The embarrassment on her face deepened to something bordering on painful. "What am I supposed to do? Follow the guy home and steal them?"

"Get your butt up and convince him." Jared stepped back and lifted an arm as if to guide her toward further humiliation. "I know you, Lee. You're already thinking about Concord grape recipes, aren't you?"

She gnawed on her thumbnail. A leftover fiber from the lemon stung a raw patch of skin on her lip, and she winced. "No, not really."

His jaw tightened. "Ask him again, Mila. And don't take no for an answer."

"It's not the end of the world. Nicole said her uncle can hook me up with apples. . . ."

"Mila." He bent at the waist, his nose nearly brushing hers. His steely eyes forced her hand to her lap. "I put myself out there for you. Now *you* have to put yourself out there for you."

Maybe it was the vodka. Maybe it was his smooth, creamy skin so dangerously close to hers. Maybe it was the fear of disappointing him. Whatever forced her up and out of her chair, the relieved tug of his lips as she stood made it completely worth it.

"Go get 'em." He squeezed her upper arms before gently turning her around and nudging her toward the bar.

Patrick stood tucked between two patrons, chatting conspiratorially with a server waving her hand around. For a moment, Mila faltered. Their heads bent toward each other, deep in conversation. She shouldn't interrupt.

I put myself out there for you. She refused to appear weak in front of Jared. She'd been his easygoing best friend her whole life. Tonight she wanted to be more. More than just his hometown friend. More than just herself.

"Excuse me, Patrick?" She touched his elbow, and he turned abruptly, holding a finger up before turning back to the server.

Mila firmed her shoulders and stood her ground. The band started up again, the blaring guitar filling any quiet space that formerly existed in the raucous restaurant.

Patrick finally turned to face Mila, his face twisted in discomfort. "Yes?"

She gritted her teeth, realizing she'd have to lean in and shout if she wanted to be heard. Meek Mila took a step back as she reached down deep for her boldest self.

"I know you said you didn't have any grapes to spare," she said, nearly shouting six inches from the man's ear. "But I had to give it one more shot. I have this idea for a savory sweet pie, and I've already dreamed up the recipe, and I'd only need two pints. Max. I'd gladly pay you for them, and I'm told there will be media coverage for the finalists, so if I make it that far, I'd plug your winery every chance I got."

Patrick blinked as if she'd startled him with the idea. She blinked back. She'd startled herself.

"I'm really committed to winning," she shouted. "Finding quality produce has been so challenging. I know if your grapes are as good as Jared says, it'll make all the difference in my pie."

Patrick ran a veiny hand across his mouth, and she expected the "Sorry" to hit her any moment. Another three seconds passed, the twangy chords of "Boot Scootin' Boogie" covering any awkward silence. Mila prepared to make one last-ditch effort when Patrick said, "Okay."

A rush of serotonin flooded her brain. "Okay?"

He shrugged his bony shoulders. "Sure. What's two pints? In fact, you can have four if you like. We usually end up throwing a few of them away by the time the whole process is said and done."

Her sinuses pricked. She hadn't cried in front of anyone when Aunt Georgie passed, and she wouldn't cry now. But God, she wanted to. "Thank you. Thank you so much, Patrick."

"I've got 'em in the freezer here, actually. Before you head out, let me know and I'll grab 'em."

"Will do." Before her rational brain could stop her, she fell forward and squeezed his skeletal frame in a hug. His arms remained pinned at his sides as she stood upright. "Seriously, thank you. It means so much to me."

"I'm holding you to that promotion," he said, raising a stern finger to her face. "Seems like you've got a lot of confidence in yourself and your skills, so maybe you just might get there."

Mila muttered one more thank-you before shaking Patrick's hand and making her way back to the table. Jared turned his face toward her, matching her elated smile the second he saw it.

"Shit yeah you did!" he said.

"I haven't even told you what happened yet," she said with a laugh. But he'd already bounded to his feet, crushing her in a hug. His warm, clean scent flooded her nostrils, and she sank into his tight embrace as if they were the only two people in the room.

He pulled back, guiding her back to her seat. She sat, not trusting her rubbery legs to hold her upright. When was the last time she'd stood up for herself? When was the last time she'd heard no and refused it? As a small child she fought back all the time, but the older she got, the more her parents drilled into her that submission was typically the easiest route through life. Until recently, she'd believed them.

The food Mila and Jared had ordered appeared shortly thereafter, and they happily indulged, letting the music provide the conversation. Mila filled her belly with as much fried chicken and fries as she could handle. By the time the banana pudding arrived, bliss radiated through her like she'd been dipped in radioactive jelly.

As the waitress cleared their dishes, the band slid from driving rock country into a slower number, and Jared stood up from the table. He extended a hand, a mischievous smile finding its way to his lips.

"Care to dance, m'lady?"

"My my," she said. "How could I turn down such a gentlemanly offer?"

A breath of hesitation passed between them, and Mila watched other couples take to the open space in front of the stage. They wouldn't be alone or on display. Still, uneasiness stirred in her gut.

She met his gaze as his face lifted in a hopeful grin. The same grin he employed at Bailey family dinners when Caryl asked who wanted the drumstick. His little boy grin. The grin that cracked her heart.

She tucked her hand into his and let him lead her to the dance floor.

As the band slipped into a sweet acoustic version of "Neon Moon," Jared tucked his strong arm around her waist, drawing her into the warm cocoon of his chest. One hand cupped his shoulder while the other clutched his outstretched fingers. They found a steady, rocking rhythm, neither of them particularly adept at dancing but graceful all the same.

His eyes bore into hers, the dim bar lights shimmering off his long lashes. *Magical.* Her breath caught in her throat, and she tugged him toward her, desperate to shield her face.

What would he see there? A dopey girl developing an incredibly unhealthy crush on the guy she used to joke with about *Family Guy* and inconvenient boners. His small-town friend, the one who wanted to stay in Pine Ridge and have kids someday while he left this place in his rearview. Someone who wanted to hold him back.

"You smell nice," he murmured into her hair.

Shit. If she didn't want him to see every pie-eyed thought in her head, he'd have to stop saying stuff like that.

"Thanks."

"Like vanilla."

God, Jared, shut up already. "Probably the pudding."

He laughed, the rumbling sound deep in his chest, forcing her ribs to constrict. The most beautiful sound and so much better up close.

"Maybe." His long, powerful fingers closed around her hand, and suddenly he drew her closer, tucking her arm in like a swaddled baby and pressing their intertwined hands against his heart.

She wanted to look at him, every muscle in her body screaming, *This is a sign, you idiot!* But she stayed frozen, paralyzed with uncertainty, her eyes squeezed shut and her face turned over his shoulder.

It wasn't a sign. It was the way Jared operated. He'd surely danced this way with a hundred women, leading them all to the same conclusion.

She wouldn't be just another girl. Let him pull out every first-date move, make her feel special in ways he hadn't even intended, but he wouldn't force her to go there. Jared wasn't the fall-in-love-and-stay-there kind of guy. And so he'd never be the guy for her.

The last chord of the song echoed through the room, and the couples on the dance floor awoke from their dreamy haze. Some clapped. Some kissed. Some hooted and hollered as the next upbeat jam rattled pint glasses on the tables.

Mila stepped backward and let her hands fall from Jared's. She wanted to look up. She could feel his eyes on her. Instead, she tucked her desires away, turned over her shoulder, and walked back to the table. Asking for grapes was one thing. Asking her best friend to love her was another.

chapter **six**

Jared leaned back in his ergonomic office chair and placed his hands behind his head with a sigh. He loved real estate because it connected him with people, got him outside, challenged him to use his voice and make the sale. On the days he had to catch up on emails and paper pushing, he nearly crawled out of his skin.

This week, his blazer had been gripping him like a straitjacket.

He'd spent a thousand nights with Mila, drinking and talking and even, on a handful of occasions, dancing. He'd stolen her for a song at their senior prom, spun her around the dance floor at Jorie and Matt's wedding, bounced around to pop hits on late-night radio in her parents' house.

But a few nights ago at Eat at Jam's, the tiny kernel deep in his chest that he'd been trying to ignore for five years had popped open with aplomb. The way her soft, curvy body nestled against his chest, the vanilla-lilac scent rising up at him as if she'd baked it into her skin. He wanted more.

And then she'd refused to look at him.

To make matters even more confusing, she'd gone out last night to meet Vin for a drink. Their first official date. His gut felt like the bottom of a dredged-up lake. Disturbed.

"Hey, Kirkland." His boss, Steven, called out from behind his glass-walled office. "Come in here, will ya?"

A slow, deliberate shiver crept up his spine. Steven didn't usually hassle him. Jared loved that quality in a boss but also wondered if the lack of needling left him complacent. Unmotivated. Uninspired.

But that day, Steven summoned him. Had he seen Jared's Web browser open to job postings in LA? He'd only been casually perusing. Nothing serious.

Yet.

He shoved back from his desk, swallowed down all thoughts of Mila, and entered Steven's office, lowering himself into the chair opposite the sleek, minimalist desk his boss preferred. The office lived somewhere between Manhattan chic and Adirondack rustic, appealing to anyone who might wander in from out of town, as well as locals who preferred the homey vibe.

"How's it going with the Silver Lake property?" Steven asked. His bald head reflected the lamplight, and he ran a hand over the few wisps of hair he had left.

Steven knew North Country as well as anyone Jared had ever met. He could recite market trends as far back as the 1940s and accurately predict which towns were due for a boom, where to mine potential clients, and which listings were doomed to fail.

When he'd given Jared the Silver Lake listing, his eyes glinted with knowledge. "This is a big one, son," he'd said with a crooked smile. "A real challenge. This house has already been listed three times with not a single nibble. Good luck."

"Eh." Jared ran a hand over his jaw, trying to summon

up an optimistic response. "It's all right. There are only so many interested buyers for a property like that."

Steven nodded. "That's the bitch of this job, though, son."

Jared grimaced. *Son* sounded as positive coming out of Steven's mouth as it had coming out of his mother's.

"It's your job to find the buyer," Steven said. "You've exhausted every network?"

"Three times over," Jared said. His chest burned. Impotence reigned over every facet of his life lately. And what was this newfound pressure on selling Silver Lake? When Steven had assigned it to him, Jared thought they'd shared an understanding. *Sell it if you can, but nobody will blame you if you can't.* A fun challenge, not a yoke around his neck.

Steven worked his thin lips and crossed his arms over his blue flannel shirt. Jared had long since refused to succumb to the company "dress code" of jeans and flannel. He wanted to sell million-dollar property, not rent out tents in the backyard.

"We need this one," Steven said. "*You* need this one."

"I'll do another round and then try some unconventional avenues. I've got a few friends who might have leads. I'll see what I can do."

"We have to unload this property, Kirkland. We're coming up on the end of the contract."

"If you don't mind my asking," Jared said, "what's with the pressure all of a sudden? I thought we both knew there was a good chance the contract would run out and that would be that. I've made some good commissions in the meantime."

"The truth is," Steven said, "I'm not sure I've got the overhead to keep everybody on."

All feeling vacated Jared's body from the waist down. "Sorry?"

"I've already reduced Gabby's hours, and we're doing

without an intern this year. But I'm not sure how much more fat I can trim without a boost in sales."

North Country Realty boasted only four full-time employees, Steven excluded. How could the company survive without Jared's revenue? Or had he not generated enough of it to make himself indispensable?

"Now, don't panic," Steven said. Though the deep lines in his face told Jared to do something like it. "Nothing's been decided yet. We've just eh . . . We've been having a tough year. I know I told you there was a good shot this property might not sell, but I really thought you'd do it. When I hired you, I hired the flashy, town pretty boy. The kid who could sell sand in a desert. I thought Silver Lake would be easy as pie."

Easy as pie. Mila hated that saying. *Pie is* not *easy.*

"I still believe in you," Steven said. "And I'm not saying if you don't make it happen, I'll let you go. But it'd make it a hell of a lot easier to keep you on if you did."

Jared liked the guy well enough, but in moments like these, he wanted to stand up, flip his chair, and scream out *I quit!* His legs ached to carry him across the country, where million-dollar properties sat like low-hanging fruit, instead of the volatile boom-or-bust area he grew up in.

His mother never wasted a moment reminding Jared that Pine Ridge was a small town, oppressive as summer heat, and if he wanted more for himself, to stretch out and grow and change, he'd have to leave town. Pine Ridge suited her eldest son just fine, but her youngest required more. Jared had spent most of his life torn between the idea of a hometown he loved and a big world he knew very little about.

"Listen," Steven said. "I know Pine Ridge isn't Aspen or Vail or, hell, even Lake George. I know full well you may move on from here if the deals aren't challenging or lucrative enough for you. I know it's not your dream to make $30,000 a year selling one-bedroom cabins to retirees. But I'll tell you right now, there's money to be made here. This won't be the last challenging million-dollar property that lands on your plate if you stay in Pine Ridge. You've got to get creative. It's the only way to close this type of deal."

Frustration tickled Jared's fingertips. Steven knew better than most how difficult a property like Silver Lake could be. North Country had good years and bad, feasts and famines. Even the most talented real estate agent couldn't make leads materialize out of nowhere.

"I know, sir." Jared's voice tightened. "I want to sell this property more than anything, and I want to get more just like it."

"I hope you do." Steven shot him a weak smile. "Let me know if you need help on this, son. I can loop in somebody else if you're not up to it on your own."

The frustration turned to simmering anger, and Jared's cheeks flushed. *Help? No way.* He'd sell this place on his own or not at all. "No way, Steven. I don't need help on this. I'll get it done."

Steven nodded once. "Good. Very good, Kirkland. And keep that bit about belt-tightening around here to yourself, okay? The threat of downsizing is never good for morale."

Jared shuffled back to his desk and clicked into his contacts. He'd made Steven a guarantee he didn't know if he could pull through on. But he knew he had to try.

The crowd at Utz's swelled around Jared, and he took another sip of bourbon. Either the alcohol or the people would drown out the thoughts in his head. Something had to.

"Hey."

He breathed in. Lilac perfume. Traces of sweet vanilla. Mila invaded his space. She sat on the barstool next to him, grinning with those perfect lips, her lashes curled and lengthened to frame the deep dark depths of her glowing amber eyes.

"Are you sitting here drinking alone?" she asked.

His gaze trailed down and back up her body, taking in the ripped-up jeans, biker boots, and loose white T-shirt that made up her uniform. The thin gold chain at her throat sparkled against her soft skin, while a tiny aqua gemstone dangled over the chasm of her breasts.

"Okay," she said slowly. "And now you're staring at my tits?"

Laughter burbled up from the depths of his soul, a long-awaited release of tension he'd been carrying all day. "Sorry."

"And you're drunk." She waved at the bartender. "Can I get a water for this drunk asshole here, and a Mueller Homebrew Kölsch for me, please?"

Jared licked his dry lips and raised the smooth, syrupy bourbon to his mouth. "I'm not drunk."

He was drunk.

"Here, Kirkland, drink this." The bartender slid a pint glass full of water toward him, but Jared sneered.

"I'm not drunk, man."

Mila exhaled, a single breath of disdain. "What's wrong?"

"Nothing. Everything is great." Only because of the damned bourbon it came out like *Effer-sing great*.

Her lip curled in disgust. "What was that?"

"How was your *date*?" That one came out clear as day.

Her eyebrows bounced as if to say, *Eh*.

"Wow, that good, huh? Who could've seen that coming?"

"If you're gonna sit here and be a jerk and not tell me what's wrong, then I'm gonna go back to Nicole and Calvin and leave you to wallow in your toddler tantrum. Okay?"

"So go."

He really was being a jerk, and she didn't deserve it. Spending time with her last week had confused the shit out of him, tugging at his emotions in a way he didn't much care for. Add to it the showdown at work, and the lack of control weighing him down had to release somehow.

Cue the booze. And the snark.

Mila pressed her lips together and grabbed her beer before turning away toward the back of the bar.

Damn it. He didn't deserve her anyway. She was talent and sparkle, and he was an afterthought, fighting for any scrap of attention or success anyone wanted to give him. Things that came so easily to her were held at arm's length from him.

"Does she know you're in love with her?"

Jared looked to his left where the voice originated. Next to him, straddling the barstool like doll furniture, sat a tall, lanky dude with floppy black hair and a lopsided grin. The beer he sipped looked like a child's cup in his big paw.

"What'd you say?" Jared asked.

The guy grinned wider and swallowed half the pint glass in one go. "I asked if that girl knows you're in love with her. Kinda seems like maybe she doesn't."

Honesty threatened his lips and the bourbon gave it a nudge. "No. She doesn't know."

The guy smiled triumphantly. "What's the problem?"

Jared laughed, a slow, steady stream of ironic laughter whistling through his teeth. "Where do I begin, dude?"

The story flowed out of Jared like lava. His parents' tense marriage, his father's alcoholism, Mila's steadfast place in his life, the newly discovered lust he harbored for his best friend, and the sudden arrival of a new guy who wanted to take her out. The floppy-haired dude nodded along, adding in an appreciative laugh or a sympathetic sigh where necessary. By the end of the diatribe, the guy had downed two more pints of Coors Light.

"Hey, bro," Jared said. "You better slow down."

The guy laughed, a deep, booming sound that caught the attention of a few women in the bar. Jared sized him up. Handsome-ish. If you were into big, hunky dudes who took up a lot of space and drank shitty beer.

"I'm all right," the guy said. "I've got a pretty high tolerance."

"Me, too, dude. Me, too."

The guy's face pinched as he studied Jared. "Listen. I get growing up without a positive example of happy, loving parents, and trust me, I *totally* understand not wanting to get married. But you've gotta figure out how you feel about this girl. Otherwise you'll lose her as a friend, too. And you don't want that, right?"

Jared breathed deep, fighting and losing the urge to look across the bar at Mila. She and Nicole leaned toward each other, deep in conversation, while Nicole's eyes darted toward Jared every few minutes. Mila, no doubt, grumbled about what a colossal jerk he'd been to her. He wanted to be over there with them, not marooned at the bar like some sad, lonely drunk.

"Nah," Jared said, turning back to his new friend. "I don't want that."

"Maybe give it a shot, you know? Give her some hints that you might be interested in being more than friends, and she'll give *you* a hint one way or the other."

Jared rolled the cocktail glass between his hands, studying the melting ice cubes. He dropped the last of the remaining liquid into his mouth before shoving the glass away from him.

"What about this Vin guy?"

The big guy laughed. "I know Vin. Trust me. You've got nothing to worry about there. He's a short-term relationship kind of guy."

Jared looked up as if seeing the guy for the first time. "Hey, who are you, anyway?"

"Denny Torres." He stuck out his giant hand and nearly crushed Jared's fingers by way of introduction. "I'm a spokesperson for Indigo Hotels, so I'm here to judge this bake-off thing. Vin's a friend, and I didn't have anything else to do, so I came out early."

Jared's gaze narrowed. "Dude."

"Yeah?"

"Stay away from Mila."

Denny's face split into a wild grin, and his booming laughter bounced off the ceiling. When he looked back at Jared, he wiped the corner of his eye as if the warning was the funniest thing he'd ever heard.

"First of all, I'm not looking for a hookup. Second of all, you just told me you're in love with her. What kind of asshole would I be if I went after her now?"

Jared's eyes trailed slowly back to Mila. She sipped her beer, touched a delicate finger to the diamond stud in her nose, scratched her arm. She shifted to allow him full view of the long oval burn scar running along her forearm. A memento from late-night baking after one too many Jäger shots. But damn, they'd laughed a lot. And the cake tasted all right, too.

Mila. His Mila. Mila Beauregard Bailey.

He smiled.

"So." Jared turned back to his new friend. "What do I do?"

"To get her?" Denny said. He swiped a hand across his mouth. "I dunno, man. What's she like?"

"She's, like . . . perfect." Jared sighed. "She's seriously perfect, dude."

"Damn, brother, you got it bad. I mean, what *does* she like? Is she a flowers girl? Special dinner? One of those chicks who breaks in half over stupid shit like mowing her lawn before she gets home from work?"

Jared attempted to focus his bourbon-addled brain. Flowers? Maybe. Special dinner? He'd have to drive her an hour outside Pine Ridge for that, and she didn't have time. And she lived in an apartment, so the lawn thing was out, if he even knew what that meant.

"I dunno," Jared said. "Flowers, maybe?"

"Great," Denny said. "Send her a bunch of flowers. Tell her yellow means friendship, but then put some red ones in there, too, and let her figure out what that means."

Denny raised his thick black eyebrows and nodded as if he'd discovered the cure for cancer.

"All right, man. Flowers it is." Something about Jared's decision didn't sit right. Flowers meant funerals and apologies, and hadn't he heard Mila groan over a bouquet from Marty once? But in the hazy bar with this big, weird dude encouraging him and the memories of last week's closeness weighing on his mind, he went for it. "I'll call the flower place when I get home."

"How late are they open? It's already eight o'clock. Try 'em now. From the bar phone."

Before Jared could think twice, he was bent over the bar, the landline's cord stretching across the taps, and instructing April's Flowers to send Mila a beautiful yellow bouquet—"With some red ones thrown in there for love."

He slurred his credit card number over the line, and when he handed the dismayed bartender the receiver and settled back onto his stool, Denny clapped him on the back.

"You're golden, bruh. Well done. She's gonna love 'em."

Damn, he hoped so. He'd never sent Mila flowers before, had never even given her a Christmas gift aside from that remote key finder that had gone over about as well as a pair of socks. Was it too bold? Should he call April's back and cancel?

He studied Denny for a moment before his brain sloshed into a different train of thought entirely. "Hey, man. You wanna buy a house?"

Denny laughed and swallowed the last of his pint. "No, thanks, man. Not really in the market. But I'll drive you home if you want."

"Dude, you're hammered."

Denny laughed again, stood up, and walked the straight line of the floorboard. "Totally fine. Told you I had a high tolerance. Come on, lovebird. Let's hit it."

chapter **seven**

Mila tried to argue with the kid, tried to tell him there was no way the flowers were for her. Edith O'Hare's grandson raised his shoulders, shook his head, and refused to take the bouquet back. He raced out of the diner as if Mila might toss them at his head instead of enjoy them.

"Whoa." Nicole returned to the counter after taking a phone call outside. "Who sent you flowers?"

Of course Nicole happened to be at the diner when the delivery arrived. No way to hide it now.

Mila couldn't begin to guess who'd sent her flowers. Her dad, maybe? Once in a while he did sweet things like that out of the blue. Definitely not Vin. The frustration in his jaw when she'd left him at the front door of her building after their very quick drinks date two days prior rendered little to interpretation, and he hadn't texted her since. Flowers, at this point, wouldn't make any sense.

Nicole reached for the card, but Mila snatched it instead.

"Don't you dare."

"If I find out you've been dating someone and you didn't say anything about it," Nicole said, "I'm gonna need you to return the *-st -ends* half of our friendship necklace."

Mila flipped open the little white card, smearing mayonnaise on the edge.

Mila—For friendship. Red for love. Jared

Mila's brow pinched. She read it again. And again. Nicole finally caught her off guard and plucked the card from Mila's fingers.

"Huh?" Nicole said, matching the confused stare on Mila's face. "What does that mean? Did you bake him something recently?"

Mila scratched her nose and tried to ignore the nagging in her gut. *Red for love.* If Jared really did have feelings for her, the last thing he'd do is send a bouquet of yellow daisies and red roses. Flowers reminded him of funerals.

It was decidedly not Jared. It was decidedly not her.

"He's such a weirdo," Nicole said. She tucked the card back into the bouquet. "Not the prettiest flowers, either, right? I'm surprised April didn't talk him into something a little more . . . sophisticated."

"I dunno." Mila trailed her fingers along the soft rose petals. "I can't remember the last time I got flowers that weren't from my dad. Even if they're kinda ugly, it's thoughtful. Right?"

Nicole rolled her eyes and took a slug of coffee. "Sure, Lee Lee. Whatever you need to tell yourself."

The order bell dinged, and Mila retrieved the plates, deftly delivering a tuna melt—hold the pickle—with fries on the side to Karen Walsh at her usual table up front.

"Thank you, doll," Karen said. A wide grin pressed into her face, warming Mila as if she'd stepped into a patch of sunshine.

"Can't believe you skip the pickle," Mila teased. "That's the best part."

"I trust you on most things culinary," Karen said, "but that's not one of 'em. Can you bring me a bottle of steak sauce?"

Mila dipped her chin. "Steak sauce? On tuna?"

"For my fries." Karen's bushy gray eyebrows wiggled in her forehead, and Mila grinned as she snagged a bottle of steak sauce from the counter and deposited it on Karen's table.

"Hey," Nicole said as Mila returned to the counter. "Does the grape hookup mean you don't need my uncle's apples? Or are you gonna work out some New York State fruit medley pie? That could be fire, Lee."

"Hm." Mila's brain ticked through flavor combinations as she nibbled on her thumbnail. Apples and grapes would be okay, but nothing like the next-level concoctions she'd been dreaming up lately. "I don't think I'm going to use apples this round. But thank Uncle Paul for me."

"He'll be heartbroken," Nicole said, her dark brown eyes twinkling. "He knows how good you are. He thought your fortune and fame might make Williams Farm a household name."

Nicole's great-grandfather had traveled to North Country from Ocho Rios, Jamaica, as a teenager, working as a seasonal apple farmer before eventually securing visa sponsorship from the farm owner. Teddy Williams developed such a close relationship with the owner and his family, they sold the property to Teddy once they couldn't run it anymore. Generations later, Williams Farm employed dozens of locals, hosted the Pine Ridge Spring Festival every year, and made the best apple butter Mila had ever tasted.

"Uncle Paul is going to make that farm a household name anyway," Mila said. "He's a marketing genius. Didn't one of those daytime cooking shows call to interview him once?"

"Yeah, but nothing came of it." Nicole licked her lips as if weighing her next words carefully. "Maybe you can do something with apples for the next round."

Mila's chest tightened. "Don't jinx me. There's no guarantee I'll make it to the next round."

"Good Lord." Nicole slipped her black wool coat over her puppy-patterned scrub top and tugged on a ski cap. "Cynic of the Year goes to Mila Bailey."

"It's not cynicism," Mila said. "It's called being realistic. There are hundreds of people entering . . ."

"Yeah, yeah, I know." Nicole snagged a plastic-wrapped muffin from the bakery tray near the register. "The odds are against you; it's a long shot; you've got a snowball's chance in hell. I've heard it all."

Mila gritted her teeth and looked back to the flowers. The ground swayed under her feet, and she gripped the counter to steady herself. Even the earth's axis seemed off today. Or maybe she'd just forgotten to eat.

"I have to get back to work," Nicole said. "If you do end up wanting those apples, just let me know. Even if it's only to bake your best friend and her lifesaving coworkers a loaf of cinnamon apple bread."

Nicole flashed a bright smile, and as she pushed open the front door, she waved the muffin in the air and called over her shoulder. "Put it on my tab!"

Mila rolled her shoulders, refilled the coffee at table four, and returned to the counter where the flowers mocked her. She didn't know why he'd sent them, but it certainly wasn't to declare his feelings. If anything, they said, *Here's some flowers that were about to be thrown out. You look like you could use a pick-me-up.*

"Hey, Mila?" Mr. Nimitz called from across the diner. "You got any more of that lemon pie?"

"Mr. Nimitz, are you serious? This will be your third slice. If your wife comes in here and asks who gave you extra dessert, my name had better not come out of your mouth, do you hear me?"

Mr. Nimitz's face collapsed into a smile, wrinkling like an old paper bag, and she delivered the slice with glee. She'd offered a couple of her regulars pie in return for their honest opinion. She didn't dare waste the bulk of her Concords on testing, but the sweet-and-sour lemon-and-grape combination proved surprisingly tasty.

The positive response to her first attempt with the grapes trickled into her sense of confidence, buoying her spirits as she returned to the counter. With her heart beating in her throat, she grabbed the diner phone from behind the register and dialed Jared's number before she could think twice.

"'Sup, girl?"

Warmth bloomed in her chest, and she clutched the phone tightly. "Yo."

"How's it going?" he said. "Are you in need of a taste tester for that ridiculously incredible lemon thing you're hawking over at the diner?"

"How could you possibly know that?"

"Word travels fast in this town." He cleared his throat. "I was at the gas station and heard somebody talking about how you were giving away pie. You shouldn't give that away for free, you know."

"I shouldn't give my pie away?" A smile played on her lips.

"Mila. When you're a pie baker, you sort of forgo the luxury of pie-related euphemisms. It's just too easy."

The return to casual banter distracted her, brought her back to a time when their friendship was easy and not always laced with fraught sexual tension. He sounded happy. Light.

Then she saw the flowers.

"Hey." Her voice careened shrilly. She coughed. "Why'd you send me flowers?"

Silence. She gnawed on her thumbnail as the pause stretched on.

"I mean," she said, "thank you. Very much. I just . . . You never do shit like that."

"That's right."

Again, she waited. A rosy-cheeked couple with a baby strapped to the mother's chest walked into the diner. Mila's phone time ran short.

"Sorry. I, uh . . ." He laughed, a dry, brittle sound. "I forgot I did that."

Her stomach twisted in on itself. "What?"

"I was on a good one," he said. "I'd had a few drinks, and I thought it would be funny. You know, 'cause we both think flowers are kind of lame."

A wave of nausea rolled through her. Funny? Humiliating was more like it.

"Mila!" Benny yelled from the kitchen. "Table eight! Hello?"

The family with the baby glanced around, sending Mila worried stares. Perhaps if they didn't get their coffee within thirty seconds of sitting, they'd combust.

Didn't they realize she was in the middle of complete and total embarrassment? She tamped down the annoyance and remembered she was at work. Getting fired wouldn't lessen the instability weaving through her life.

"I have to go," she said.

"Wait, no . . ."

"For the record," she said. "This isn't funny."

He groaned. "I didn't mean *funny.*"

Her skin crawled, anger itching at her fingertips. The gate in her mind that typically prevented controversial thoughts from slipping past her lips remained firmly open, unwilling to close.

"You think it's a joke that I could receive flowers?" she said.

A long pause. "What?"

"You think this is funny," she said. "Someone sending me flowers is funny."

She heard him swallow.

"Of course not."

She waited, the family with the baby fidgeting as they searched for someone to serve them.

"I . . ." His voice scratched over the line. "Okay, it wasn't a joke. I wanted to send you flowers. I just thought maybe you'd think it was lame."

Heat burned her cheeks. "What?"

"I felt bad for being a jerk to you at Utz's last night, so the flowers were a goodwill gesture," he said. "But you're always so cynical about that kind of stuff, so I . . . lied. About the reason. I don't know, it sounds dumb when I say it out loud."

Her brow pinched further, her grip on the counter tightened. "You decided to send me flowers, then you lied about it, now you're blaming the lie on my cynicism? Do I have that right?"

More silence. She waited. Jared seamlessly navigated relationships with every other woman in his life, from casual one-night stands to long-term girlfriends, and yet he fumbled so badly when it came to his best friend. Didn't he know Mila at all?

"Freaking Denny," he grumbled.

"What?"

"Never mind. I'm sorry, Mila. I wanted to do something nice, and it came out . . . like that."

"Excuse me!" The woman with the baby called out, her voice shrill and desperate. "Could we get some coffee?"

Mila bit her thumbnail. Hard. "I have to go."

"Wait," Jared said. "Are you around tonight? Let's get a drink—"

She punched the power button on the cordless phone and replaced it in the cradle. Fuck him for making her feel stupid. For pretending like he'd made an effort at doing something nice, only to turn it around and blame her for the awkwardness.

Queasiness churned in her gut, and as she grabbed the coffeepot and two mugs, she bit the inside of her lip. Maybe whatever had simmered between her and Jared really was over. Maybe it had never even begun.

Mila entered her apartment later that night, her lower back aching after her long day at the diner. Benny had asked her to wait around for the last table to finish their ice cream sundaes before she closed up, and the table had lingered like they never wanted to go home.

The wall clock's hands slid to eleven and six, and she massaged her pulsing temples in an effort to quiet her blood. Every bone in her body told her to wash her face and get in bed, but the kitchen beckoned, coaxed her into its loving arms with promises of clean measurements, exact weights, and pies fit to be photographed for the cover of *Gourmet* magazine.

She poured a glass of water and took a long, cold drink. A few taps on her phone, and Stone Temple Pilots' acoustic version of "Plush" flowed out of her wireless speaker. She breathed deep, surveyed her waiting kitchen, and got started.

Hours later, as the moon glowed brightly through her tiny kitchen window and the stretches of icy white snow dampened even the subtlest sound outside, Mila's phone buzzed with a text from Nicole, momentarily pausing Eddie Vedder's warbling voice on "Can't Keep."

You up?

A smile crept across Mila's lips as she wiped the Concord grape juice off her hands and onto a dish towel. Neither she nor Nicole had ever been great sleepers. When they were teenagers, Nicole would text *You up?* and they'd talk in hushed voices over the phone to each other until dawn. Conversations consisted mostly of Nicole droning on about her latest crush or the injustices of middle school, but the company comforted Mila. She liked knowing she wasn't alone.

Mila texted back.

Of course I'm up. Can't win the Pine Ridge Spring Bake-Off if you require luxuries like sleep.

Mila's home phone rang seconds later.

"Hi, Nic."

"Hi, Lee. Whatcha baking?"

The creamy purple mousse shimmered in the moonlight, the crimped golden crust still emitting a warm, toasty scent. That was the one. She didn't need anyone else to taste it. She didn't need to test it again.

"I finally did it," Mila said, her voice hushed and reverent. "I think I found the recipe I'm going to use next week for round one."

"Yeah, you did! What is it?"

"It's sort of a sweet and savory . . ."

"Ugh, really? Savory? I was sort of hoping you'd do something super decadent, like chocolate on chocolate on chocolate."

Mila shook her head. Nicole's tastes were simple. For her birthday, Mila usually whipped up a classic apple pie. One year she'd played around with ginger graham cracker crust, and Nicole ate only the filling, innocently inquiring if the crust had gone bad.

"I have to be really inventive if I want to win," Mila said.

"Did you ever get to the bottom of those flowers?" Nicole asked.

Mila's skin prickled. The heat from the kitchen had dissipated quickly after she'd turned off the oven, and now she needed a sweater.

"You saw the card," Mila said. "Jared sent them."

"Yeah, but why?"

Mila swallowed, swiping at a thin trail of flour on her Formica countertop. She hadn't told Nicole the details of the trip to Eat at Jam's, the slow dance, the way her body curled toward Jared's. How could she explain her feelings without Nicole laughing in her face, reminding her that a union between Hometown Mila and Anywhere-but-Here Jared could only end in heartache?

Mila cleared her throat. "He, uh . . . he said he forgot he sent them."

She figured a half-truth was better than a complete and total lie.

"Are you kidding me?" Nicole said.

"It's not a big deal." Mila's voice jumped a register. "We all know Jared can be an idiot."

"Sure," Nicole said, "but he's not allowed to be an idiot to *you*. He's not allowed to hurt you or treat you with blatant disregard."

"He's not my boyfriend, Nic. He doesn't owe me shit."

Nicole released a deep, guttural groan. "Demand more from him, Lee Lee. You have such low expectations for the people in your life."

Mila gritted her teeth. Did Nicole realize she fell into that group, too? Of course her friend loved her. She showed up to birthday dinners and called regularly, but she shoved Mila in directions she wasn't quite ready to go. The weird pineapple pie she made should've been apple, she should've worn hoops instead of studs to better suit her face, the dishrags Marty gave her for Christmas should've been called out instead of accepted with a fake smile. Nicole never let her friend slide. She never gave her a pass. Sometimes Nicole's quest for greatness bled into Mila's life and exhausted her.

Mila glanced out the window at the moon. Her chest tightened, as did her grip on the phone. When would she finally say "Enough"?

"You're right." Mila's voice hummed low and even. "I do. I have very low expectations for the people in my life. Nobody really understands me. Nobody gives me as much as I give them."

"Exactly."

Nicole still didn't get it.

"So maybe I'll start making some changes."

"Yes!" Nicole yelped. "Good for you."

"Starting with you."

"What? Me? Oh, please, I was not including myself in that statement."

"Yeah, I know you weren't," Mila said. "But you should've."

"Okay, so my advice is a little harsh sometimes. Occasionally, though, you need a push. I have only ever wanted the best for you."

"I'm not disputing that," Mila said. "I just wish sometimes you would recognize that I don't need a push. I need support. You think you always know what's best for me, but we're not the same person. What you need is not the same as what I need. You know what I mean?"

Mila's heart thumped wildly inside her chest, reminding her that a confrontation like this could have maximum consequences. What would she do without Nicole in her life? How could she get by without her closest girlfriend?

In a tiny voice Mila had never heard before, Nicole said, "No. I don't know what you mean."

Mila licked her lips, lowered herself onto a kitchen stool, and tried again. "You've created a really specific life for yourself. You're good at everything because you put a hundred percent of yourself into everything you do. And that's fine, I'm not asking you to change. I love that about you. But I need you to see me. I'm not a super competitive person, and I think that's okay. I just wish sometimes you would be . . . gentler with me."

For as long as Mila could remember, Nicole had something to say. And now, silence.

"Nic?"

Nicole sniffed. "I didn't realize."

"Jesus, are you crying?"

"Lee, I love you so much. I didn't know you felt this way. I thought I was being helpful."

Mila inhaled a shaky breath. "You are. I know you want me to be the best version of myself. But I need to do all that in my own time. I've felt this way for a while. I never said anything because I didn't want to hurt your feelings."

"Well, you did." Nicole laughed, her voice thick with emotion. "But it's good. I'm glad you said something. God, that's how I've always felt about my mom. Nothing's ever good enough for Deb."

"You are *nothing* like your mother."

"Oh, please. I'm exactly like my mom. Except for my marriage. I tried really hard there."

Mila pressed her lips together. She didn't want to say that Nicole had chosen a man *exactly* like her father, from the way he took his coffee to the town in Jamaica their families hailed from. But Calvin and Nicole were equals. That she made sure of.

"You and Calvin are perfect," Mila said. "You don't treat him like your mother treats your father in any way."

Nicole sniffed again. "Thanks for saying that."

Mila's heart slowed, the weight of the conversation releasing something inside her. Nicole hadn't freaked out or walked away from her. She'd listened. She'd really heard her.

"Thanks for being so receptive," Mila said. "That was . . . really fucking hard for me."

Nicole laughed. "I've literally never seen you confront anyone in my entire life, so yeah. I'd imagine."

"I love you."

"Love you." Nicole cleared her throat. "Get some sleep. See you at Sunday dinner? Your mom called to remind me, so I'm assuming that means attendance is mandatory."

"Can't wait."

"How's it going?" he asked.

"Fine," she said. "Busy." She turned away from the counter and made a slow rotation of the restaurant, offering coffee to those with both full and empty mugs.

"So, what's up with you two?" Jared asked.

"Nothing." Vin spat the word out. "I took her out for some drinks last week, we had a good time, and then she practically raced home. Didn't even invite me inside. She been dicked over or something?"

Jared's adrenaline soared. They all had their skeletons, but Mila had taken on burdens no kid should have to deal with. As soon as Aunt Georgie moved into her parents' house, Mila's older sisters started spending less time at home, and Mila took on the role of Georgie's nursemaid. She cooked to Georgie's specifications, did her laundry, cleaned the dishes. Her parents worked all hours of the day and night, leaving Mila to run the house. She did it without being asked. She did it without complaint. And she'd turned into one tough chick because of it, not so easily swayed by some city punk in a tight hoodie.

"Yeah," Jared said. "I mean, she's been through some stuff."

"Eh. Not the first frosty chick I've worked miracles on." Vin turned his attention back to the menu. "God, the food here sucks."

"Then why are you here?"

Vin turned again and looked at Jared quizzically. "Trying to make inroads, dude. I'll eat a bad burger if it softens her up, you know?"

This guy begged for a punch in the jaw. But Jared had only ever punched one man, and that man was blood. His brother had deserved it, too.

"Why bother?" Jared said. "You're only in town temporarily, right?"

"Probably." Vin continued to scan the menu, shoving his hipster glasses farther up the bridge of his nose. "But now that Indigo's gonna have a property here, I'll be back and forth a bit. I like to have options when I'm out on the road. It's not like I can hop on Tinder in this town."

Color rose in Jared's cheeks, setting his face on fire. His hands clasped atop the counter, trembling and shaking as if begging to sock this guy in the mouth.

"Dude," he said, forcing a simmering calm into his voice. "She's not somebody to fuck around with. She's not somebody you sleep with and then disappear on. If you promise her things you can't deliver on and then hurt her, I will personally—"

"What's going on?" Mila returned, her forehead creased with concern. "Why are you all red, J?"

A tiny, amused smirk played on Vin's lips as he watched Jared twist and squirm. He closed his menu and turned his attention on Mila. "Can I get a grilled cheese, babe? With fries?"

Babe. Did Mila grimace? She hated pet names. Marty had tried to call her *honey* once, and she mimicked throwing up until Marty got pissed off and left the bar.

"Sure," she said. "You want a little mayo on your grilled cheese? It's way better that way."

"That sounds amazing," Vin said. "Good call."

Vin turned to Jared, the same smug grin on his face. "Sorry you were interrupted. What were you gonna say?"

Every nerve in Jared's body blazed, anger coursing under his skin like hot lava. Vin didn't deserve to be within three feet of Mila let alone date her. Jared's only solace lay in the fact that she hadn't slept with him yet.

Jared raked a hand through his hair. He'd forgotten to bring product with him to the gym, and his usually tamed style fell over his forehead. He tried to push it back again. Even his hair wouldn't do what he wanted.

"I gotta go," he said. He pushed away from the counter, eliciting a confused stare from Mila.

"Didn't you want to eat?" she asked.

He shook his head. "Honestly, I wanted to talk to you. But it doesn't feel like the right time."

She swallowed, the hollow in her throat shifting and causing her tiny, sparkly necklace to glint in the diner lights. Was she still mad at him? She should be. After their incredible night at Eat at Jam's, he'd snapped at her and tried to cover his tracks with the most clichéd gesture imaginable. He'd really messed up. And now she had somebody after her calling her *babe*.

Her eyes flickered to Vin before returning to Jared.

"I can take a quick break." She cleared her throat. "If you want."

He didn't trust his voice to respond, instead nodding awkwardly as she removed her apron and headed toward the rear exit. He followed her through the kitchen and out the back door. The chilly spring air cooled his cheeks.

She crossed her arms tightly over her chest and looked up, making it obvious he'd be the one to speak first. The clear day lent a glassiness to her copper eyes and revealed golden streaks like rays of sunshine in her irises.

"He's visiting you at work now, huh?"

A bitter laugh huffed past her lips. "A week of avoiding me and this is what you wanted to talk to me about?"

He scolded himself internally. Why couldn't he summon his trademark charm in moments like this? Was it so hard to treat Mila as someone more than a friend? He wanted to. Bad.

"No," he said. He shoved his hands in his coat pockets. "I wanted to talk about the flowers. Again. About how I'm an idiot."

The corner of her lips quirked into the first hints of a smile. "You've piqued my interest."

A whisper of relief wove through his chest. "I know you hate flowers. I wanted to do something nice for you, and I should've thought a little bit harder about what you might actually like."

She blinked and readjusted her arms across her chest. "I don't hate flowers."

"You don't?"

"No, *you* hate flowers. Which is why that bouquet was so confusing."

He'd always associated flowers with funerals and apologies. When his father messed up, his mother received a standard delivery from April's Flowers the next day. She always smiled and thanked him, but disappointment would line her eyes.

He swallowed down the sick feeling in his throat. One misstep with Mila and he reverted back to bad behavior instilled in him at birth. He'd pulled a move his father had pulled a hundred times.

"I don't hate flowers, either," Jared said. "I hate what they represent."

Mila quirked an eyebrow. "Love? Joy? Celebration?"

He bit his lip. "I was thinking sympathy and regret."

"Ah, I get it. Aside from funerals, you think men only send flowers when they're apologizing. Is that it? A flimsy attempt at making things right after a dick move?"

He shrugged. She'd nailed it.

"I remember in kindergarten," she said, "my teacher got flowers delivered to her in the middle of the day. She said her husband had sent them *just because.* She spent the rest of the day on cloud nine."

"You sure he wasn't apologizing for something?"

Mila shook her head and dropped her gaze to the cracked pavement at their feet. "Didn't look like it."

She looked back up at him, the sparkle absent from her eyes.

"Okay," he said. "Now I know."

"Now you know what?"

"You like flowers."

Her gaze narrowed. "You planning to do something with that information?"

Panic crept up his neck. Was he? Would he send her flowers again? He thought of Vin—that smarmy weasel—sitting at the counter, hoping for another chance to get in Mila's pants. She didn't deserve that. She deserved beautiful flowers just because. And why couldn't Jared be the one to send them?

"Maybe," he said. Could she see through him? In the past few years, he'd tried diligently to hide his true self in front of her. It grew harder every day.

"Okay," she said. "I'm . . . intrigued?"

He ran his tongue over his lower lip. God, he wanted to kiss her. Would she pull away? Would she slap him? Was that heavy rise and fall in her chest because of anger or impatience?

"Mila!" Benny's voice called through the screen door. "LaMotta's sucking wind in here without you. You about done?"

She lifted her gaze to Jared again as if giving him one more shot. But now wasn't the moment. He couldn't leap across that giant chasm while Benny barked at her to get back to work and the scent of burnt fry grease filled the air and Vin waited at the counter for his grilled cheese with mayo.

No. It wasn't now. But it was coming. That much Jared knew.

The first round of judging for the Pine Ridge Spring Bake-Off began with much less fanfare than the finale promised, but Jared entered the community center with a knot in his stomach the size of a golf ball and just as dense.

He scratched his nose, bit his lip, jiggled his hands inside his coat pockets. Sam elbowed him in the ribs.

"What's your problem?" Sam asked. "You'd think you were baking today."

"He's just nervous for Mila," Sydney said. "Leave the kid alone."

The three of them huddled near the back of the room where bite-size pieces of every baked good would eventually be placed after the judges received their tastes. Long white folding tables lined the room, with tiny cards marking the name of each contestant and the name of their creation.

Jared's eyes returned over and over to the little card on the end that read, MILA BAILEY. SWEET AND SAVORY ROSE-MARY CONCORD GRAPE PIE.

He couldn't believe he hadn't tasted it before she decided it was the one. She'd typically be more than willing to share her creations, but she'd held the bake-off pie close to the vest.

"Sounds kinda gross, right?" Nicole's voice broke through his thoughts.

"Yeah, kinda. Knowing her, though, it's probably insanely delicious."

"She does have the knack." Nicole crossed her arms across her chest and examined Jared with narrowed eyes. "You talked to her lately?"

"Sure." He'd always assumed Mila and Nicole shared everything with each other, but he didn't know how much Mila had said about Eat at Jam's, the flowers, the moment at the diner. And if she hadn't shared it with Nicole, maybe none of it had mattered to her as much as it had to him.

Nicole nodded slowly, more subdued than he'd ever seen her.

"Jared," Nicole said.

He waited for the rest, waited for Nicole to push and prod until the truth fell out of him. "Yes?"

"What's going on with you? Are you dying or something? You've been off your game lately."

Mayor Sweeney entered the community center, and the room erupted in applause. "Thank you all for coming!" he said, raising his hands in the air. "We'll begin in about fifteen minutes."

Jared cleared his throat and shifted again.

"So?" Nicole pressed.

He should've known better than to think she'd drop it.

He opened his mouth, and before a single syllable passed his lips, she gasped.

"What?" he said.

Her mouth hung open in an odd smile, and her dark brown eyes glittered. "You're in love with her. You are totally in love with her, aren't you?"

A blush crept into his cheeks, revealing every bit of fear decorating his insides and refusing to allow him the secret. He was truly screwed now. Girlfriend telepathy had probably already kicked in and Mila was mimicking throwing up somewhere behind the scenes.

"I didn't say that."

"You didn't have to," Nicole said. "I'm not sure why I never noticed it before. You are totally in love with her."

"Stop saying it." The last thing he needed was someone to overhear and shout it from the rooftops. Sam and Sydney chatted, sickeningly smitten with each other and blissfully unaware of the conversation going on three feet to their left.

"Is that what the flowers were for?" Nicole asked, her face twisting in confusion. Mila and Nicole were polar opposites, Nicole's emotions always shining clear through her face, while Mila had practiced her neutral stare to perfection.

"I got some bad advice," Jared said.

"Aw, Jare." Nicole placed a kind hand on his arm. "This is new for you, huh? Normally you'd take a girl for drinks, send her some mediocre bouquet, and seal the deal the same night. But with Mila . . ."

Jared exhaled. The more he talked about it, the easier it got. "Don't say anything to her, all right?"

A sympathetic smile crossed her face. "Sure. But what are you gonna do about it?"

"I haven't figured that out yet. I just want some time to decide."

"Whatever you do," Nicole said, "make sure it's really her. You know what I mean? You're not gonna find advice on wooing Mila Bailey on Google. And I recently promised her I'd stop pushing her into stuff she didn't want to do, but I will absolutely be your girl on the inside should you need me."

He grinned. Nicole's face practically glowed with optimism.

"Thanks," he said. "If it does get to that point, I'm really hoping she won't need too much convincing."

Nicole shrugged. "Either way, dude. I'm in full support of this."

The mayor took the stage again. "Okay, everybody, listen up! The annual Pine Ridge Spring Bake-Off will begin in five minutes! Contestants will wait in the adjacent room until the judges narrow it down to the top twenty desserts, after which time the selected contestants will approach the judges and explain their creations. You'll then have a chance to sample the desserts as the judges deliberate on the final ten. We hope you're just as excited as we are!"

More of their friends joined, and Jared and Nicole's conversation filled the space between them. The secret sparkled in her eyes, and she looked at him every couple of minutes with a timid smile. The promise in Nicole's face gave him a nudge of hope. Surely if her best friend was on board, Mila would be, too.

Or at least, he hoped.

chapter **nine**

The low-ceilinged room buzzed with voices and the electricity of competition. A steady drone of anxious conversation surrounded Mila as she sat alone at the end of a long folding table and tried to distract herself with Scrabble on her phone.

She checked her watch. It was 1:44 p.m.

Judges had been at it for an hour and forty-four minutes. God only knew how much longer it would take them to taste and take notes on the 134 entries. The contestants had been served sandwiches and beverages from the diner, but Mila's stomach churned. She'd grabbed half a turkey club, but now it sat limply on the paper plate in front of her with a single bite missing.

She didn't want to be nervous, had tried willing it out of her system. The bake-off hadn't even been something she'd wanted. Damn Aunt Georgie for putting the idea in her head. Damn her for shoving Mila into a competition she actually believed she had a shot at winning.

Now she wanted it. She wanted it badly. As she fell asleep the previous night, visions of quitting the diner danced in her head. When she'd taken the job her first summer out of college, she never imagined it would become her long-term career. Four years in, the quicksand of steady work and easy money held tight to her feet, slipped past her ankles, and threatened to swallow her for eternity.

The prize money promised a way out. A ticket to culinary school. A safety net. A few months to breathe and stretch and try something new. Possibility tickled her brain, refused to be ignored. How could she ever go back to her mundane life after this?

"Ladies and gentlemen!" Vin's assistant's shrill voice sounded from the doorway of the cramped community center annex that most often served as a meeting place for Girl Scouts and recovering alcoholics.

"Finally," the woman next to Mila said with a sigh. She ran a comb through her bright red curls. "I was about to lose my damn mind in this room."

"The least they could've done is served booze, right?" Mila joked. She'd been sitting next to the woman for nearly two hours without a single word exchanged. Her nerves occupied all her brain space, demanding she explore every possible outcome of the next few hours. The good, the bad, and the ugly.

"Exactly!" The woman laughed, a hearty sound that came straight from her chest. "What I wouldn't give for a sidecar right about now. Gosh, I've been so nervous I didn't even introduce myself. Sorry about that."

Mila smoothed down her sweater. She'd chosen a soft purple wool pullover with slightly puffed sleeves today. The color and silhouette of royalty. Nicole had approved.

"Don't apologize," she said. "I felt exactly the same way. I'm Mila."

The woman extended a hand. "Kim. Good luck to you, Mila."

"Thanks. You, too."

Heat rose to Mila's cheeks. *Here we go.*

"I'm going to announce the names of the twenty finalists," Vin's assistant said. "After you answer a few questions from the judges, they'll cut the group down to ten. Please listen for your name and line up in front of me in the order I call you."

Mila drew a shaky breath into her lungs and took a sip of Coke from the nearly empty can in front of her. The last thing she needed after taste-testing pie all week was more sugar, but her throat threatened to dry up completely if she didn't wet it.

Vin's assistant began reading names, in no discernible order, and Mila gnawed on her thumbnail. Three names. Four. The older gentleman in the purple windbreaker. The cute blonde in the trendy jeans. Her new friend Sidecar Kim. Another name. And another.

"Mila Bailey."

Her nerves shot into overdrive as she pushed away from the wall and grinned at the smiling faces around her. A few called out, "Congratulations!" She yelled back thanks despite having no idea who'd said it.

Her skin tingled from her head downward, and she crossed her arms over her chest to stop the shaking.

Step one.

She'd have to speak in front of the panel of judges, which included Vin's friend and hunky former football player Denny Torres; Mayor Sweeney; Constance Hathaway, head chef at Indigo Hotels Adirondack Park; and Harry Sepinski of local cable access fame.

Despite the usual fears churning in her gut, another emotion tapped at Mila's insides. Excitement. She'd made it past round one. The first hurdle cleared, with a little lift from Aunt Georgie.

The rest of the top twenty lined up behind Mila, and Vin's assistant led them into the hallway. "They'll announce you individually, and you'll stand on your mark in front of the panel. Each judge will be seated with your baked goods in front of them, and they'll ask you a couple of questions. Please answer honestly, and when they dismiss you, go through the far door into the opposite hallway, where Vin will be waiting for you."

Mila traced her teeth over her bottom lip and focused on her breathing. *In and out. In and out.* It was just the townspeople and their families, for the most part. She'd seen these people every day for as long as she'd been alive. How scary could they be?

Her mental pep talk only took her so far, and when her name crackled out over the community center sound system, her stomach flip-flopped into her chest.

"Go!" Vin's assistant hissed.

Mila walked carefully into the room, cursing her high-heeled boots. She should've worn sneakers. Nobody ever tripped over themselves in sneakers.

She made it to the center of the room and forced a smile at the judges. Four pairs of eyes, all fixed on her like spotlights. While she waited for them to greet her, her gaze lifted over the crowd, and there, at the back of the room with fists pumping in the air, was Jared.

A blinding grin dominated his face, and when they locked eyes, he thrust his arms into the air. He mouthed "Yeah!" at her and fist-pumped again. A rush of joy flooded her chest. Despite the awkward ending to their dinner and dancing, and his lame attempt at some sort of gift, he showed up for her when it mattered. She returned her gaze to the judges with renewed confidence.

"Hi, Mila," Mayor Sweeney said. "We're so happy to see one of Pine Ridge's own up here."

"Thank you," she said. "I'm so glad you liked the pie."

"This is a very unusual flavor combination," Denny Torres said. "How did you come up with it?"

Mila cleared her throat. "I was very lucky to be introduced to a local vineyard owner who had frozen Concord grapes to spare." Her gaze flickered to Jared at the back of the room, the wild grin still gracing his lips. "As soon as I heard 'Concord grapes,' my brain just sort of took off. And I've always loved the idea of a savory take on a dessert, so this is what came of all that."

Each judge scribbled a note.

"That's all, Mila." Chef Constance grinned. "Thank you very much."

Mila's smile faded as she waited one more beat. Had they only meant to ask her one question? Was her answer so boring, so mundane, that they'd unanimously and silently agreed they were done with her? Someone in the room coughed, breaking through the moment, and she turned to exit.

Vin waited in the hallway, where the first eight contestants milled around chatting with one another. His eyes lit up behind the hipster glasses, and he pulled her into a bear hug. Her whole body stiffened as he squeezed, and when he finally let go, she took a step backward.

What was her problem with this guy? He smelled good; he had interesting things to say. He'd been attentive but respectful, and he'd paid for every drink when they went out. But she couldn't get over the hump of hesitation. He was like the vanilla pudding in the buffet. Perfectly fine, tasty even, but nobody's first choice.

They hadn't discussed the fact that he lived far away, and anything that might happen between them would be temporary. All the same, what was wrong with getting some? She should want to have fun, and yet every time he tried to get close to her, she pulled back.

"You're amazing," he said from behind straight, shiny teeth. "Congrats on making it this far."

This far. Huh. Did he question her ability to go further? She had too many people in her life already doubting her skill and competence. She certainly didn't need another.

"Thanks." She swallowed down her discomfort and

crossed her arms over her chest. "They only asked me one question. Is that weird?"

"I don't think so. Maybe they already know everything they need to know. Hey, you wanna grab dinner after this?"

"Oh, um." His brain must've flickered like a bad light bulb. "My friends are here, so I think we might all go out."

He nodded slowly, his face falling in disappointment. "Okay, cool."

Be polite, you asshole. "You could come with us, if you want?"

His eyes lit up. "Sounds great."

The rest of the contestants filtered through the community center and into Vin's hallway, and before she knew it, nineteen other people surrounded Mila, all fidgeting nervously as they awaited the final results.

Within minutes, the results were in.

"Okay, everybody," Vin said. "We're going to bring you all in at once. Go ahead and stand in one line across the front of the room, and when the judges call your name, please step forward."

With renewed anxiety, Mila followed the group into the main room. Her chest fluttered and her stomach gurgled. Too much Coke, not enough food.

Oh well. There'd be plenty of time for consolation eating after her name wasn't called.

"Ladies and gentlemen," the mayor said after they'd all stopped in their designated place. "Thank you again for joining us. We know the Spring Festival is going to be a weekend to remember here in Pine Ridge, and the Indigo Hotels–sponsored bake-off will be the ultimate cherry on the sundae! Pun intended."

The room let out a polite laugh, and Mila saw Nicole's eyes roll from all the way in the back of the room.

"Now," Mayor Sweeney said. "I'll announce the ten finalists who will compete in the final bake-off in three weeks' time. Good luck to all of you."

Mila clasped her hands behind her in an effort to remain calm and appear poised, while she felt anything but. Her teeth clenched, and her knees buckled. Every ounce of energy went into standing upright and presenting a collected front.

"Our first finalist is . . . Mila Bailey!"

The room tilted in front of her, and she stepped forward on wobbly legs. She inhaled sharply as the space boomed with applause, and the loudest voice, shouting over everyone, was Jared's.

He bounced up and down in the back of the room, and she wondered, for one hazy moment, if the idiot had brought a trampoline. She bit her lip to contain her laughter, and when Sam shoved Jared, momentarily pausing his elation, a single chuckle escaped her lips.

The other nine finalists—Sidecar Kim included—stepped forward and accepted the adulation of the crowd. The mayor asked everyone to wait for a moment to receive additional information on the dinner that weekend at Indigo Hotels Adirondack Park, and by the time he handed out thick black folders filled with paperwork and pamphlets, the room around Mila spun like she'd just stepped off the Tilt-A-Whirl.

She grabbed her coat and purse from the waiting room and made her way to the back of the community center, where scraps of pies, cakes, cookies, and breads sat discarded on empty platters, and her friends congregated in one big, buzzy group.

"Lee Lee!" Nicole shrieked, lunging and squeezing her in a swinging hug. "You talented bitch! I knew you could do it!"

Mila's face heated, her skin on fire from her chest to her hairline, and the sensation cascaded through her limbs and out through her feet. Surrounding townspeople migrated toward the group, and some turned to her with expectant smiles. The attention, the praise, the eyes on her. She wished for an invisibility cloak or Alex Mack's turn-into-a-silver-puddle thing.

Get me the hell out of here.

"Hey, let's clear out. They probably want to start cleaning all this shit up." Jared tucked his warm, strong hand into hers, and just like that, they slipped through the crowd like eels.

The cold air slapped her face as they stepped outside, and just as quickly, Jared draped her coat around her shoulders. She looked up, lips parted, momentarily stunned.

"Thank you," she said.

He grinned. "You had a solid twenty minutes of gushing ahead of you. Figured you'd rather be dead."

Every inch of her prickled, the goose bumps coating her skin like armor. God, Chloe was lucky. Lucky to have been cared for by Jared, to have been seen by him. To have been chosen.

And yet, she remembered them together. Biting remarks and sarcastic comments that often devolved into petty arguments and dramatic exits. She'd heard his guy friends grunting and joking about their wild sex life, but Jared had never mentioned it in front of Mila. Thank God.

Jared treated her with a kindness she'd never seen him employ with anyone else, save for a rare moment with his mother before she passed. Mila wondered if she was special.

Yeah, special like a sister.

"You still want to go eat?" Jared asked. His gaze had softened while she mulled over her best friend's ex, and now he looked at her with pinched brows.

"Yeah," she said. "Seems like it might be okay to celebrate just a little bit. Right?"

His lips parted, his teeth gleaming in the early-afternoon sunlight. "Yes, Mila. It's okay to celebrate."

Nicole, Sam, Sydney, and the rest of their group swarmed around her, and the whole team descended on Utz's, demanding trays of nachos and something Nicole called "Lee Lee lemon drops."

"Trust me," Nicole said, peeling away her coat and settling into a chair at Utz's biggest table. "Two Lee Lee lemon drops, and you'll be dancing on the tables."

"Nobody's dancing on the tables without me." The booming voice, the heavy footfall, the wide grins from those facing the door. Even without turning, Mila knew her father had walked in.

"Dad!" She bounded up from her chair, and his arms pulled her into a tight hug before she even caught a glimpse of his face. Cold air clung to his New York State Electric and Gas standard-issue nylon coat, the scent of pine and spring enveloping her as she buried herself in his chest.

"I am so sorry I missed the announcement." He released her to remove his coat, and the face that looked down beamed with happiness. "I'm so freaking proud of you."

"Thank you." Her cheeks hurt from the effort of keeping them neutral, the smile she wanted to give him straining at her mouth. But she had to be cool. *Don't jump the gun. Nothing to properly celebrate yet.*

"Hey, Mr. Bailey!" Jared reached across the table to clap Lloyd's hand between his own. "So glad you made it. Nicole said you might have to work."

Mila's father held tightly to Jared's hands as if in solemn prayer. When Lloyd Bailey looked at you, he really looked at you. The warm eyes, the kind smile, the unwavering eye contact. She'd once heard Edith O'Hare call him a "Paul Newman type."

"I didn't think I'd be able to get my shift covered," Lloyd said, "but at zero hour, a friend of mine called and said he could take it. I'm just sorry I didn't get to taste the . . . what was it? Rosemary maple syrup Concord grape monstrosity?"

Mila bit her lip, suppressing a smile. "It was not a monstrosity, thank you very much."

"It was insanely delicious, in fact. The judges went completely nuts." Vin appeared at her side, and Mila rolled her eyes at the overindulgent compliment.

Sweeter than a Little Debbie oatmeal pie, and just as fake.

She wished Vin hadn't tagged along. He didn't fit into the warm, supportive circle around her.

"You want a beer?" Vin asked.

"This girl needs champagne!" Nicole bellowed.

From across the bar, Hank the bartender chuckled. "I don't have champagne, girl. I got the champagne of beers. Will that do it for ya?"

"Ugh, this town," Nicole said. "Fine, Hank. Just bring us a round of lemon drops, will you? We're calling them Lee Lee lemon drops today. In honor of my best friend."

Mila laughed, raising an eyebrow at Nicole. Since their phone call she'd been laying it on thicker than buttercream. But at least she was trying.

"I'm not drinking a lemon drop," Sam grumbled.

Sydney pinched his earlobe. "You will if it's to celebrate Mila."

Sam shook his head, the matching grins spreading across their faces as they stared at each other with googly eyes. Mila softened, the tension in her shoulders melting away. She wanted what they had. Simple love, pure love. Love that flourished without fanfare. Love that just seemed to *happen*.

Her attention drifted to where Vin chatted with Calvin. Love was certainly not in the cards for them, much less an all-consuming, world-changing love. She couldn't force herself into spending time with Vin, no matter how logical it seemed that she should go out on a date with the new, single guy in town. She'd have to tell him soon. Having him around—especially with Jared in the room—felt like wearing an itchy wool sweater two sizes too small.

"Hey." As Jared's hand brushed hers, she nearly leaped out of her skin.

An audible yelp escaped her throat, and his lips screwed up. "Ya all right, weirdo?" he asked.

"You scared me." Her heart beat against her rib cage, reminding her that *that* was a reaction. That was worth getting out of bed for.

Or into *bed for.*

She cleared her throat, wishing she'd had that lemon drop already.

"Listen, are you into this guy?" Jared thumbed subtly over his shoulder to where Vin still talked to Calvin, whose brow pinched in what seemed to be agitation. "You don't look super comfortable around him."

"I don't know," she said. "I'm not *un*comfortable around him."

Lies lies lies.

His forehead wrinkled. "Why would you go out with somebody you're not into?"

"I'm not." She licked her lips. "Going out with him, I mean. Our one date was lackluster, so I'm not gonna do it again."

His gaze deepened, the intensity of his eyes seeping into her skin like hot, melted butter. She had so much more to say to him: that she'd rather spend time with him than anybody else; that she itched to cross the friendship line; that all he had to do was say the word and they could find out together what else was out there for them. What greatness they were meant for.

"I support that," Jared said.

She tucked her arms across the chest of her purple power sweater. Except she didn't feel so powerful right now. She licked her lips. "Glad you approve."

He paused, staring her down for another moment, something much more than his lukewarm sentiment playing across his face. But the moment passed as quickly as it began. He shoved his hands into his jeans pockets and forced a tight grin.

"I'm really proud of you," he said.

"Don't start." She rolled her eyes, despite the warmth spreading across her chest. She didn't want gushing praise from her family, but the tiniest bit of it from Jared made her year.

"All right," he said, holding his hands up in front of him. "I won't say how incredible you are or how delicious that weird pie was or how you basically blew every other dish out of the water. I'll just be cool and say, 'Good job.'"

Would he go on? She loved the praise, and all at once, her mother's cynical voice sounded in her head, telling her she was jinxing the whole thing.

"Thanks for holding back," she joked.

"Get a little hammered today, all right?" he said. "You deserve it."

Hank delivered the shots, and after everyone—including Sam—had downed theirs, another round appeared, and the group moved past the bright wishes of congratulations and into easy conversation.

Mila glanced around the big round table at the faces she'd known most of her life and the new additions who fit right in. When her gaze landed on Vin, something sour stirred in her gut. He didn't fit. Not here, not in Pine Ridge, and not in her life.

"That kid's a clown," Lloyd said.

Mila nearly choked on a sip of hard cider as her father slid into the chair next to her.

"Jared? I know, he always has been."

"No," Lloyd said. He leaned back in the chair, testing the integrity of the wood with his generous frame. He draped a long arm over the back of her chair and sipped his beer. "*That* kid."

Mila followed the line of his raised eyebrows until she landed on Vin, who leaned much too close to Nicole and gestured with angry hands. Nicole's disinterested stare and closed-off body language would steer most people toward giving up on the conversation, but Vin rambled on.

"You went out with him?" Lloyd asked.

Mila's skin prickled, and she ran a hand over her arm as if to chase away the goose bumps. "Yeah. Once. Not many young, single guys pass through here, you know? I figured I should at least give him a shot. He's not terrible. He just doesn't do it for me."

Lloyd's eyes glittered, his trademark smile spreading across his face. Mila could see clear back to his molars when he smiled like that. He always seemed a little lighter when her mother wasn't around. More himself.

"What?" she said. "Don't give me that look."

"I'm not looking any way." He laughed. "I could've told you from ten feet away that's not your kind of guy."

"Oh yeah? Who's my kind of guy?"

"Eh, you don't want to hear about that from me."

She shook her head. Just like him. Tease an opinion and then pull it back. A mouse in lion's clothing. "Dad, sometimes I think you still look at me like a little girl."

"*Lee Lee*, sometimes you act like a little girl."

She turned to face him straight on. He took a long drink from his pint and faked an innocent expression.

"You want to man up and explain that one to me?" she said.

"Oh really now?" The smile still tugged at his lips. "*Man up?* Are you getting tough with me?"

She'd confronted Nicole. Could she confront her father, too? All the nerves in her body buzzed, telling her to cut the conversation short.

"Maybe you're the one who needs to *man up*." He tugged on a strand of her curly hair, and with the release, sent it bouncing against her cheek. "Don't shuffle meekly through life like I did, all right?"

Her gaze narrowed. "Shuffle meekly through life?"

"You heard what I said."

Maybe they were finally getting to the meat of it. She inched her chair closer. "Is that how you see yourself?"

He shrugged, the smile all but fading as he gazed around the table. Confidence and ease oozed from his limbs. "You're the quiet one, Lee. Like me. Your sisters were always so independent. It's how eldest kids usually are. But you were the baby, and you got saddled with a lot. Especially when it came to Georgie."

Tension wound through her scalp, tightening around her temples and threatening a mind-numbing headache. "I didn't get saddled with anything," she said. "I helped out."

"That was more than helping out." He ran a hand over his mouth, his weathered, handsome face growing somber. "You've been the rock for a lot of people. Still are. But we don't need you the way we used to."

"Oh, you don't, do you?" She nudged his solid arm with her elbow and coaxed half a grin from his lips.

"Listen," her father said. "Maybe you don't want my advice. What do I know anyway? I haven't done everything right."

"Dad." Mila's voice filled with warmth. She recognized her father's flaws, but his virtues stood out just as clearly. His humility, his kindness, his generosity. Every resident of Pine Ridge would describe him exactly the same way.

"I'm not looking for pity," he said. "I just want you to know that I let things pass me by. I had a lot of responsibilities when I was a kid, too, and I never stopped feeling responsible. For my parents, then for your mother and you and your sisters, and then for Aunt Georgie. I don't want you to let your sense of responsibility give you an excuse to back away from the things that *you* want. You hear me?"

A trickle of fear descended in her chest. "Are you talking about something specific? Because Aunt Georgie already forced me into this bake-off. I'm not letting that pass me by, no matter how much I'd like to."

"Georgie always got her way, didn't she? One way or the other." Lloyd laughed and pinched the bridge of his nose. "No, I'm not talking about the bake-off. Although that's a step in the right direction."

"Well, what, then? Quit speaking in code."

A shrill, prolonged squeak created by wood on wood punctuated the room as Jared stood up from the table and walked over to Mila and Lloyd, a quiet smile on his lips and an empty pint glass in his hand. He clapped his free hand on Lloyd's shoulder.

"You owe me eighteen holes, old man. As soon as the snow melts, it's on."

"You cheat," Lloyd said. "I'm not playing with you."

"Cheat?" Jared's voice jumped an octave. "Nice try. First your shoes don't fit properly, now I'm cheating? Every excuse in the book."

Lloyd clapped a hand to his chest, the full smile lighting his face up again. "All right, all right. I'll give you another shot. And this time I'm breaking in my shoes *before* we play."

Jared grinned and squeezed Lloyd's shoulder before resting his eyes on Mila. His face shifted, his shoulders lowered. Every inch of air space in the room filled with tension.

"You guys need anything?" he asked.

Mila's throat suddenly closed up. She shook her head.

"I've gotta head out after this one," Lloyd said. "But thank you, Jared."

She watched him walk to the bar, and by the time she turned back to her father, the old man had resumed his glittery-eyed stare.

"What now, Dad?"

"You know what, Lee Lee." Lloyd swallowed the last of his pint and stood up, looming over his daughter. "Don't let the good stuff pass you by."

chapter **ten**

Mila tucked the cordless phone between her jaw and her shoulder and continued stirring the batter. Like she had time to make banana bread on top of everything else. But Dad requested it, and so she baked.

"Everybody else has turned me down." Mila groaned, hoping her desperate tone would convince Nicole to accompany her to dinner.

"Well, darling Mila, people work. What do you want?"

"This is going to be so cool, though! I'm actually excited about it. Don't you want to see me be genuinely excited and optimistic about this?"

Nicole laughed. "I'm actually happy just to hear your voice like this. You *do* seem excited."

Mila poured the speckled batter into the buttered loaf pan and scraped down the sides of the bowl with a rubber spatula. A light fuzziness sparkled in her stomach. Is this what eager anticipation felt like?

"I guess maybe I'll just go alone," Mila said.

"You cannot go to a fancy dinner at Indigo Hotels Adirondack Park by yourself. That's so lame." She paused. "What about Jared?"

Mila slowly slid the pan into the hot oven and closed the door, leaning her hip against the counter as her friend's suggestion settled in her brain. Jared? He'd been the first person she'd wanted to invite. But things between them were tenser than ever, and she couldn't yet summon the confidence to invite him to an official dinner date.

"I don't know," Mila said. "He probably has to work, too."

"He would totally leave early with you if you asked him. You know that."

Mila gnawed at her thumbnail. In a perfect world, Jared would accompany her to the upscale dinner at Indigo Hotels Adirondack Park, smelling like deliciously subtle cologne and cracking jokes to ease her nerves. He'd hold her hand, tell her if she had something in her teeth, and let her eat off his plate when she inevitably wanted a taste of whatever he'd ordered.

But they weren't living in a perfect world. They were in an awkward limbo somewhere between the familiar and the fantasy.

"I don't know."

"Will you quit saying that?" Nicole snapped. "I know I promised to be gentler with you, but right now I think you need a little tough love. Do not go to this thing alone. Put on your big girl panties and call him."

Mila gazed down into the mixing bowl and scooped up a trace of leftover banana bread batter. She licked her finger. Sweet brown sugar, tangy banana, silky butter. Damn, that recipe was delicious. "Remind me why you can't come."

"I told you," Nicole said. "Calvin already bought us tickets to some concert."

"That sounds made up."

"Girl, bye."

The *click* sounded in Mila's ear, and she hit the power

button but held on to the phone. She studied the raised white buttons, the numbers telling her Jared was a mere seven digits away. What if he said no?

She heard Nicole's biting voice in her head. *He won't say no!*

She gritted her teeth, all but closed her eyes, and punched in the numbers. With her teeth clamped around her thumbnail, she prayed he didn't answer.

"Yo."

Despite her brain telling her to chill, her heart bloomed like a flower in spring.

"Hi."

He sniffed. "What's up?"

"Not much."

Silence stretched over the line. "Are you being held hostage and forbidden from giving explicit information over the phone? Do you need me to ask you a series of questions where you answer 'pineapple' for 'yes' and 'Yo-Yo Ma' for 'no'?"

Laughter bubbled up and out of her, and she leaned on the counter to brace her jittery bones. "You're so weird."

"What's up, Bailey?"

"Um, so hey. I was thinking. I have this dinner tomorrow night at Indigo Hotels. The new one?"

He released a single chuckle. "Yeah. I'm aware."

"So, um." She cleared her throat. Why was this so hard? "Do you wanna, like . . . go with me?"

"Do I wanna, like, go with you?"

"Yeah. To the dinner."

"Sure."

"Oh," she said. Just like that. No big deal. *Sure.* "Okay?"

"Did you want me to say no?"

She ran her tongue over her teeth. Did she? "No. Of course not. I just . . ."

He waited for her to continue, but words escaped her. She wanted him to go more than anything, but the easier path would have had him politely declining. Now she had to face the music.

"Was this a courtesy ask?" he said. "You didn't want me to be home alone on a Friday night, so you thought, 'I'll throw my old buddy Jared a bone.'"

She shoved a hand into her hair, massaging her scalp. This boy gave her a headache.

"I asked you because I thought you might want to go with me. And because I thought having you as my date might be fun. Is that good enough?"

"Totally. I'm always in for a free meal." He paused. "Hey, uh. Is Vin gonna be there?"

"Probably." She hadn't spoken to Vin about it, but she'd also avoided him like a bill collector in the last week.

"Vin sucks."

She laughed. "So you've mentioned."

"All right," he said. "So, tomorrow night. Dinner."

"It's cocktail attire, although I'm sure I don't have to remind you to look nice. And the dinner is at seven, but before that there's a tour of the property, a kitchen demonstration, and a cocktail hour, so we have to be there at five. Can you leave work early?"

"For you, sweet Lee Lee, I'll take the whole day."

Her stomach caved, and her skin lit on fire. Jesus, was she in for it now.

Mila's four-inch heels clicked on the fresh black pavement, and she clutched Jared's forearm while carefully avoiding black ice. The parking lot had been cleared and salted, but she didn't need a broken ankle. Not tonight.

"This place is insane," Jared said.

Mila tore her eyes from the pavement and looked up. "Wow."

The massive log cabin–style hotel sat nestled in the surrounding forest like the crown jewel of the landscape, red

pine, balsam fir, and white spruce trees guarding the property like swaying, stoic guards. A sweeping front porch
welcomed guests, inviting them to perch in cozy Adirondack chairs draped with vibrant Hudson's Bay blankets.
Vin stood atop the wide plank staircase. He grinned wildly
as Mila and Jared approached.

A cool breeze blew in across the lake, and Mila admired
the glistening water as she clutched her black wool coat
tighter around her. Jared slipped a warm hand over hers,
drawing her into his body for added stability.

As they drew closer to the property, Vin's gaze narrowed, and the smile fell from his face.

"Hey," he said. "Jared. I didn't know you'd be here."

Jared closed his hand around Mila's until his grip
pinched her fingers. "Ouch, dude."

"Sorry," he muttered.

"Jared's my date," Mila said. "I was allowed to bring
somebody, right?"

They ascended the staircase to meet Vin at the top, and
he licked his lips as he stared Jared down. Mila's chest
swirled with bubbling nerves. Now or never. The awkwardness couldn't continue.

"Hey," she said, turning to Jared. "Can you give me a
minute? I'll meet you inside."

Jared's brow pinched, the biting-cold temperatures turning his cheeks and the tip of his nose bright pink. He ran
his tongue over his bottom lip and squeezed her hand.

"Sure."

"Hey, man," Vin said, "Just don't go too far. The place
isn't finished yet, and there are a bunch of things you need
to know before you go in, all right?"

"Jesus," Jared grumbled. "No problem."

He trailed a hand over Mila's lower back as he brushed
past her and into the hotel. The warmth that spread across
her skin defied the weather.

"How are you?" Vin asked. He stepped closer, invading

her space and drawing tension to her shoulders. She stepped backward, and his face darkened.

"I'm great," she said. "Really excited to be here."

"Good," he said. "I'm really glad you're here, too. Kinda sucks you brought your friend, but maybe I can steal you for a minute later. There are some spectacular views of the mountains from the Spruce Suite I'd love to show you."

Nerves tightened her jaw, but she pried her mouth open and forced the words out. "Hey, listen. Vin. I think you're a really great guy, and I had a really nice time on our date . . ."

"Oh God." He rolled his eyes and stepped away from her, crossing his arms over his chest. "All right, Mila, I get it."

Her lips parted. "You get what?"

"You're here with him, he looks at you like you're freaking Beyoncé, and now you're giving me the 'You're a nice guy' speech. I get it, okay? I wasn't all that into you anyway."

Her limbs turned to lead as the vitriol poured out of his mouth. What a colossal asshole. "Oh, no?"

"No." He sneered. Literally sneered. Had she ever seen anyone *literally sneer* before? "You're cute, but you're probably dying to pop out babies soon, right? I am so not that guy. I just wanted to have some fun."

He pulled out his phone, and she stood still. She didn't have a ton of experience with breakups, but this was one for the books.

"Okay." Her voice hovered above a whisper. Was he texting the judges right in front of her, telling them she shouldn't be considered for the bake-off finals after all? Had she sealed her own fate? The consequences of rejecting him hadn't occurred to her until this very moment. And now they threatened to drown her.

"Not sure that dude's Indigo Hotel material, either," Vin said.

"What?"

He looked up, his lips curled in disgust. "He was interested in a job with us. I thought he might be a good fit for the Raleigh-based development team at Indigo, but maybe he's just a small-town guy. Not that there's anything wrong with that, it's just not really what Indigo corporate is all about."

Mila's hands tightened into fists inside her coat pockets, fighting the urge to smack this guy in the mouth. Let Vin do his worst to her, but no way would she let him insult her best friend. Contest be damned.

"Wow," she said. "Small-town guy, huh? How repulsive. I bet you find kindness and dependability and upstanding morals really off-putting, too."

His eyes snapped back to his phone while a single, sarcastic huff escaped his lips. "Hey, go on in. I'm texting my assistant to give you all the info."

Mila willed her feet to leave the ground and move her inside, but her face remained frozen in surprise. Jared greeted her in the vestibule just inside the front door, and within moments of seeing her face, he touched her elbow.

"What happened?" he asked.

"I told him I didn't think we should see each other again, and he sort of . . . turned into a jerk."

Jared straightened another two inches as his jaw tightened, his usually bright eyes turning cold. "What did he say to you?"

Bits of her conversation with Vin trickled back into her mind, but what really stood out was his claim that at one point, there had been a job on the table for Jared. And Jared hadn't mentioned it to her.

"It doesn't matter," she said. "He seems like a guy used to getting his way, and this time he didn't. I just hope he doesn't have a say in the bake-off outcome. Something tells me if that's the case, I'll finish dead last."

She wanted to ask about the Indigo Hotels job, about Jared's plan to leave Pine Ridge. But something held her back. If his departure was imminent, she wasn't sure she wanted to hear it out loud.

His jaw ticked, a scowl on his lips.

"Was he rude to you?" Anger simmered in his voice.

Before she could reassure him that she could hold her own with guys like Vin, the assistant from the bake-off popped her head into the vestibule, grinning at them warmly and clutching a clipboard in her hands.

"Are you two ready? I'll take your coats and lead you in."

With wide eyes and held breath, Mila followed Vin's assistant past the front door and through the arched doorways and vaulted ceilings of richly decorated rooms, under glittering chandeliers and vintage taxidermy. Fireplaces crackled and roared, the scent of pine and cinnamon wafted through hallways, and twangy folk music cascaded through each warm and woodsy space. The entire place radiated Adirondack warmth with accents of high-priced luxury.

The assistant left them just outside the kitchen doors, where the rest of the bake-off contestants and their partners would meet them. Jared placed a gentle hand on Mila's lower back, sending chills skittering across her skin.

"I didn't even get a chance to tell you how beautiful you look." His words whispered across the delicate skin on her neck, traveled down her collarbone, and landed somewhere in her chest, sending sparks through her body.

Nicole had lent her a formfitting long-sleeved blue velvet dress that dipped low in the back and reached to her knees. She typically strayed from any clothing that highlighted her figure, but after Jared's response to her date-night blouse, she found the courage to step outside her comfort zone. Nicole practically leaped with excitement when Mila came out of her bedroom to model the look.

Mila looked up into Jared's eyes, a warm pine-tree green highlighted with flecks of gold. His long, dark eyelashes blinked once, drying her throat and lips all at once. Seemed the dress had done its job.

"Thank you," she said.

His mouth quirked up. His hand remained on her lower back, and she leaned into it, forgetting to care that he was her friend and that closeness wasn't allowed.

"Ladies and gentlemen!" A booming voice commanded the attention of the huddle of twenty people who had congregated without Mila even noticing. She looked to the front of the group, where Chef Constance, one of the judges from round one, stood clad in blindingly austere chef's whites.

"Welcome!" she said brightly. "My name is Constance Hathaway, and I'm the head chef here at Indigo Hotels Adirondack Park. You may remember me from round one of the contest. It's my great pleasure to welcome you to the hotel and to be your guide on this tour of the kitchen. If you have any questions, please don't hesitate to ask. We're delighted to share this space with you."

Chef Constance pushed the kitchen doors open and waved as the group filed into the kitchen, a sequence of "ooh!" and "aah!" rushing from the contestants' mouths. Mila grinned at Chef Constance as she passed by, and the moment she entered the kitchen, the rest of the world faded away.

All around her, shining, silver commercial appliances gleamed in the fluorescent overhead lights. To her left, a massive grill station sat positioned to receive only the most exceptional cuts of meat. Heat radiated off the surface as a white-jacketed chef coated thick slabs of rib-eye steaks with salt, readying them for the searing metal of the grill.

Massive ovens, imposing cooktops, and giant hoods surrounded the group on all sides, and Mila glanced around with an open mouth as the kitchen team scuttled by like ants with covered bowls, prep containers, and a rainbow of ingredients. The symphony of the kitchen whirled around them—blenders whirring, frying pans sizzling, all occasionally punctuated with a "Hot behind!"

"God, isn't this *cool*?" Mila gushed.

Jared shrugged. "I dunno. It's kinda like the diner, right?"

"Are you freaking joking?" Mila scoffed. "This is nothing like the diner. Look at the pastry station!"

A large square surface covered in tiny ramekins of creamy pots de crème sat at attention while the pastry chef topped each creation with a flourish of lime rind. What Mila wouldn't give to work in this space instead of on the two-foot-by-two-foot countertop in her kitchen in Pine Ridge.

The group wandered the kitchen, murmuring over the meticulousness, the efficiency of it all. Chef Constance explained each station, each chef's role, and how the kitchen staff functioned like a finely tuned machine. It only worked if each person completed their job down to the last crumb.

While the rest of the contestants filtered out of the kitchen, eager for cocktail hour, Mila lingered. She watched the pastry chef pipe perfectly uniformed domes of whipped cream onto the pots de crème, her fingers plying the pastry bag with gentle fingers.

"It's beautiful, isn't it?" Chef Constance sidled up to Mila, looking on as her pastry chef created art out of sugar and butter and cream.

"It really is," Mila said. "It sounds silly, but I think people who've never really tried to work with pastry don't understand how difficult it can be to make it look that good."

"You know," Chef Constance said, "Indigo offers apprenticeships. It's not great money, but the experience is invaluable."

Mila's heart lit up. "Really?"

"Sure," Chef Constance said. "Our team here is second to none. You may have learned the basics in culinary school, but the real-world experience you'll gain here is invaluable."

"Oh," Mila said. She swallowed down her disappointment. "I've never been to culinary school."

Chef Constance's round face softened. "Ah. Well, you're young. There's still time."

As Chef Constance brushed past her, Mila deflated like a balloon. She may have won the first round of a small-town bake-off, but she was still light-years away from owning a place in the culinary world. She watched the pastry chef finish the flourishes on the pots de crème and, with a heavy heart, pushed through the kitchen doors.

Jared stood in the hall outside the kitchen, idly gazing at a wall display of black-and-white photos featuring log cabins and stone-faced families posing for the camera. Mila paused, taking him all in.

Tonight he'd chosen a gray wool suit, the fabric hugging the powerful curve of his shoulders as if its sole purpose in life was to make him look good. As he slipped his hands into the pockets of his well-fitted trousers, the vent at the bottom of the jacket split and the rounded curve of his ass came into view.

She scolded herself, but only for a moment. So what if he was her friend? She couldn't admire God's handiwork? Jared used to be skinny, with chicken legs sticking out of his cargo shorts, but in the past couple of years, his body had transformed. Those formerly skinny legs now curved and dipped into the athletic form of a man. No trace of boy left, save for his smile.

He turned and caught her staring, his curvy lips quirking up on one side. His jaw ticked as he watched her, as if waiting for her to approach. They stood for a quiet moment, staring at each other while sparks traversed the width of the hallway between them.

Maybe she was past the point of getting over a crush. Maybe she'd moved on to full-blown, all-consuming lust.

Without a word, he extended his hand, and she slipped hers easily into his waiting palm. Hand in hand, they entered the dining room.

Mila gasped.

Massive chandeliers made of deer antlers and lined with electric candles hung from the impossibly high vaulted ceilings, filling the spacious room with a glow like the inside of a fireplace. Round mahogany tables stretched before them to the far side of the gymnasium-size space, and each table featured place settings straight out of *Adirondack Decor* magazine. Creamy white china plates sat atop buffalo-plaid tablecloths, and a single sprig of rosemary wrapped around name cards adorned the natural linen napkins at each place.

Brass candelabras with dripping red candles perched in the center of each table, the candlelight flickering in the windows and multiplying as if even the forest itself had been festively adorned. The room had been decorated top to bottom, but their group would be its only occupants tonight.

"I think we're here," Jared said. He placed a hand on the small of her back and motioned to the cluster of people surrounding the imposing wood bar at the far end of the room.

If he didn't stop touching her there, she'd melt into him and ask him to forget their friendship altogether. Her head swam every time his thumb passed the border of velvet fabric and brushed her skin.

After ordering a glass of pinot noir for herself and a Knob Creek on the rocks for Jared, Mila found an empty space amid the chattering contestants to size up the competition.

"You're definitely the youngest." Jared leaned in, whispering and sending warm breath across her neck. The air crackled around them, enveloping them in intoxicating magic. Did he feel it, too? He'd touched her more in the last hour than in the entire history of their friendship, but she didn't trust her gut to lead her in the right direction.

She'd been wrong about him before. That night after the lake. When he sent the flowers. She'd misread every sign, jumped every gun. She'd need more than subtle gestures to bridge the chasm of their friendship.

"That doesn't mean anything," Mila said. "We need to find out if anybody here is a trained pastry chef or some sort of under-the-radar food TV star."

Jared sipped his bourbon and shoved his free hand into his pocket, lowering his gaze in exaggerated skepticism. Mila's chest burned. He'd always been good-looking in a generic way, like a JCPenney catalog model or the kid at camp everybody had a crush on. In the last few years, his features had sharpened, his jaw broadening and his cheeks slimming to turn his face from baby pudge to certified dreamboat.

He licked his lips and nudged her elbow. "That guy. If anybody in this room is anybody, it's that guy."

Mila tore her gaze away from Jared's perfect face to a couple across the room dressed in obviously expensive garments. An eggplant-toned bandage dress hugged the woman's curves and highlighted the shock of expertly dyed blond waves cascading down her back, while the man's charcoal suit coat stretched across broad shoulders, unbuttoned to accommodate a round belly. A salt-and-pepper goatee framed his protruding lips. He ran a hand over the curve of his date's butt as they surveyed the room just like Mila and Jared.

"I remember him from the first round of the competition," Mila said. "He looked familiar then, too. Maybe he is a professional."

"Come on." Jared hooked her elbow and took a step toward the couple. When she resisted, his eyes narrowed in confusion. "We're just gonna stand here and speculate?"

"I don't know," she said. "What would we talk about?"

"Lee." His voice dropped to a gentler tone as he wet his lower lip. "You talk to people at the diner every day. This is the same thing. I love you, but I don't want to stand here like the socially awkward townies all night."

Her face froze in a half smile while the lower half of her body turned to jelly. *Love?*

She blinked.

He blinked.

"Sure," she said, her voice catching. "Yeah, let's go. Talk to some people. No sweat."

She brushed past Jared, her snug velvet dress restricting her breathing and the long strides her legs ached for. With a forced smile, she pushed the l-word into the back of her brain.

Love.

Of course he loved her. They used to say it flippantly all the time. Recently, however, the word had all but disappeared from their vernacular as if overnight it had morphed into some all-powerful entity with the ability to decimate anyone in its path. Tonight it ravaged her brain and tore up her heart.

"Hi there." Mila grinned widely at the paunchy man and his svelte date. "I love your dress."

"Oh, thank you," the woman said, sliding a hand down the front of her toned body. "I had no idea how to dress for this thing. I'm glad to see you're dressed up, too. Those earrings are gorgeous."

Mila touched the dangling gold earrings she'd snagged from Nicole's jewelry box. Her friend would be thrilled to know how well the look had gone over tonight.

"Thanks."

"I'm Rachel Santangelo," the woman said, extending her hand. "And this is my mute husband, Bob."

Mila shook the woman's fragile hand as Bob rolled his eyes.

"Pardon me," he groaned. He shook Mila's outstretched hand. "Not my kind of thing, you know what I mean?"

"Totally," Jared said, sidling up to Mila and flashing his smile at Rachel and Bob. "Free food, free booze, cool place, exciting competition. What a snooze."

Rachel giggled at Jared and adjusted her shoulders until her ample breasts strained against the bodice of her dress. Mila waited for the woman to wipe the drool from her chin.

"I keep telling him to enjoy it." Rachel took a step closer to Jared as if Mila didn't exist. "He entered the competition on a whim, and wouldn't you know it, he finals? Just like that."

Mila tightened her grip on the wineglass and took a calming sip of the smoky pinot noir. Of course this pompous man entered a competition Mila had worked her ass off for and then skated through to the finals. She remembered Bob from the first round. He had rolled in fifteen minutes late and spent the duration of the judging process on an obnoxiously loud phone call with his financial adviser.

"Well," Jared offered, "I'm sure it wasn't *just like that*. So many people entered. The level of competition was really up there."

"Come on." Bob laughed. He downed the last inch of brown liquid in his rocks glass. "It's not *Top Chef*. It's the freaking Podunk Potluck. Rachel's right, I entered on a whim, and now we're using these next couple of weeks as a break from real life. The town's kinda cute. Probably some all right fishing."

A devastating retort clawed at Mila's throat, but she held back. It wouldn't do anyone any good for her to start a petty argument with this arrogant asshole, and it wouldn't make Pine Ridge look any more distinguished if the only resident in the room turned angry.

Jared swallowed, a placid smile settling on his lips. "*Great* fishing," he said. "And you're right, the town is cute. So cute, in fact, the region experienced thirty percent growth in tourist revenue last year alone, and with Indigo Hotels moving in, an even greater uptick is expected. Local businesses are thriving, and the Pine Ridge bookstore was just featured on *Good Morning America*. You'd be hard-pressed to find lakefront property under half a million these days."

Mila bit down on her lower lip, pride in her hometown swelling inside her belly. So many people drove through

Pine Ridge on their way to somewhere else, giving the town a passing glance. Those who stopped found something worth exploring. Those who called it home experienced its magic every single day.

A condescending smirk curled onto Bob's trout mouth. "Forgot I was talking to the competition's only local finalist. How embarrassing for me."

"Oh, shut up, Bob," Rachel said. She slapped his arm and huffed out a breath, her eyes darting back and forth from Mila to Jared. "He's just joking. We really do love it up here."

Mila stood a little taller. "It doesn't really matter to us if you love it here. But since you're part of the competition helping to support our economy, it would be nice if you looked a little deeper into why so many other people love it."

Jared grinned at her, his cheeks filling with a mottled blush. Under any other circumstances she'd high-five him. In her velvet dress and heels, surrounded by opulent fixtures and creamy linens, she settled for a squeeze of his hand.

"I need another drink," Jared said. "Can I get anybody anything? No? Okay, then, we'll see you at dinner. Great meeting you."

A smile exploded on Mila's face as they turned toward the bar, leaving Bob and Rachel openmouthed and speechless.

"God, that felt really good," he said as he motioned to the bartender for another round. "Maybe we don't have to mingle after all?"

"You should work for the Pine Ridge tourism board," she said. "Is that true? What you said? Thirty percent growth?"

"Absolutely," Jared said. "This place is about to boom."

Doubt coiled around her gut and tightened. *So why do you want to leave?* Vin's words echoed in her brain. Jared wanted a job with their *Raleigh-based team*.

Sure, Pine Ridge couldn't compete with a big city. A girl

could barely get a bite to eat after nine o'clock, and in the winter, darkness swallowed the town whole. The snow and quiet and short days could be debilitating.

But it was home. Her home. Quirky and kind and pine scented. And if Jared believed his own sales pitch, there was money to be made here. A lot of money. Leaving didn't make any sense. At least not now.

Maybe not ever.

chapter eleven

guess we oughta introduce ourselves." The silver-haired gentleman dressed in a baggy brown tweed suit clinked a fork against his water glass and grinned around the table with graveyard teeth. "I'll go ahead and assume I'm the grandpa of the group, but that's okay by me. I'm grandpa to ten grandchildren, so I'm used to it."

The group chortled politely, but Jared could scarcely remember the joke. How could he focus on anything with Mila sitting four inches to his right and looking like *that*?

Had she dipped herself in honey and rolled around in magic glitter before she got in his car tonight? Her skin practically glowed in the candlelight. With every movement, a new, gentle wave of amber-scented perfume wafted toward him, making a mess of his head. The stretches of her visible skin shimmered, the rest of her covered in a clingy, midnight-blue dress that showed off a backside he wanted to trail a hand over more than he'd ever wanted anything in his life.

Her outfit distracted him, but the way she'd torn into Bob Better-Than-You stirred something inside he hadn't yet figured out how to squash. He liked her fiery.

He liked it a lot.

But it was Mila. *Mila*. His friend Mila. No tight dress or snappy retort would turn her into anything but that.

"I'm Mila." Her voice cut through his thoughts, and he took a sip of water to steady himself. "I was born and raised in Pine Ridge and still live here now. I'm a home cook, never had any proper training, and the recipe that got me here was a sweet-and-savory rosemary-Concord-grape pie. And this is my friend Jared."

Jared raised a hand while nineteen sets of expectant eyes lighted on him.

"Hi."

Mila lowered her chin, encouraging him to say something, but he hadn't heard a word the others had said. For maybe the first time in his life, words escaped him.

The tiny, red-haired woman to his left cleared her throat before taking her turn. "Hiya! I'm Kim. Originally from Potsdam, but now I live in Buffalo. . . ."

Jared swallowed the last of his water and trailed trembling fingers across the gleaming cutlery on the table in front of him. He couldn't remember the last time he'd been nervous around a girl. But nobody looked like Mila; nobody knew him like she did.

As if reading his mind, she placed a hand on his wrist. Her eyes narrowed in concern.

"What's wrong? Are you sick or something?"

"No." *Shit*. He didn't want the focus to be on him in any way. Tonight was her night. And in a dress like that, who else could it belong to? Nobody in the room stood a chance. Not even Rachel in her *Look at me, look at me, have you looked at me yet* dress.

"Hey," Mila said. She raised her hand to her mouth, paused, and placed it in her lap. Probably dying to chew her thumbnail. How many times had he teased her for the bad habit? She only did it when she was nervous or uncomfortable. His stomach clenched at the thought of what might come out of her mouth next.

"When I talked to Vin earlier, he said something about you being Indigo Hotels material. What does that mean?"

Jared huffed out a ragged breath. "Eh, nothing. He's a dick."

Mila tilted her head, a loose curl trailing along her shoulder. Lucky curl.

"J."

Jared ran his tongue across his teeth and leaned back in his chair as the rest of the group continued their introductions. "He mentioned their team hires people with real estate backgrounds to scout out new locations for Indigo properties. Development type stuff. He said he'd put in a word if I wanted."

Mila swallowed, the concern on her face melting away. "Oh, wow. Really? From here? Or . . ."

"Ah, no. He said they have locations all over the country, but they're based in North Carolina."

Her gaze narrowed. His blood suddenly ran cold. What would it mean to her if he moved away?

"Wow." She cleared her throat. "That's an amazing opportunity for you."

"I guess." His brow pinched. Since when had he downplayed career opportunities? In another life, his best friend, Mila, would be jumping up and down in excitement for him. Lately, something heavier lined their conversations. Maybe their lives were more closely entwined than he thought.

"What do you mean, you guess?" She crossed her arms over her chest, her breasts shifting in response under the velvet of her dress. He forced his eyes upward.

"I mean . . . what about Silver Lake?" he said. "I've been working on that property for a year now. I can't just give it up to go work for some soulless corporation."

"No offense, but you've wanted to work for soulless corporations since you got into real estate. Pine Ridge has always been a jumping-off point for you."

"That is not true," he said.

She raised one eyebrow in her signature stare.

"All right, fine, it's sort of true. But maybe I've been wrong. Or maybe I will move on from here someday, but who knows if it's with Indigo."

"Why wouldn't you at least give it a shot?" she said. "You've got nothing to lose."

The air around them stilled, framing the moment like a photograph. Her oval face glowed in the candlelight, the flames flickering against her glossy dark hair and sparking her tiny jeweled nose stud like someone had conjured her from a vision. She trailed her front teeth over her full bottom lip and tightened her arms across her chest.

Nothing to lose.

Didn't he?

"I don't know about that." His voice barely lifted over the low din of the group, and she leaned forward. He heard his mother in the back of his mind. *If someone had handed me a ticket out of Pine Ridge twenty years ago, I'd have snatched it in an instant and never looked back.*

The problem was, if Jared left, he wouldn't need to look back to know what he'd left behind.

"What'd you say?"

He cleared his throat. "Nothing."

Mila's lips parted, ready to challenge him into continuing, when Vin approached.

"Good evening, folks!" He raised his hands, his phony smile beaming. That guy was lucky it was Mila's night, otherwise he'd have to knock out one or more of those blindingly white teeth.

Conversation at the table quieted as the group greeted Vin.

"We're so glad to have you here at the brand-new Indigo Hotels Adirondack Park," Vin said. "You're in for a treat tonight. Chef Constance and her team have created a very special menu with all of you in mind, so get ready for something truly spectacular."

A stream of waiters clad in crisp red plaid shirts appeared, balancing plates in the air and followed by the bright, clean scent of citrus and ginger.

Each dish that appeared before Jared tasted better than the last, with a steady stream of crisp vegetables, delicate sauces, and slow-roasted meats delighting the table. Jared enjoyed every single bite, but better than the food was Mila's reaction to everything.

"It's duck à l'orange, but this *sauce*!"

"Parsley? This is parsley! J, this is parsley!"

"Did they put this on *toast*? Genius!"

With every plate, her eyes rolled back in her head, she pressed a hand to her chest, she moaned in pure delight. By the time dessert arrived, he didn't know if his pants were tight because he was full or aroused.

The waitstaff brought coffee and tea, and as they departed, Vin reappeared.

"Hello again, everyone." His smile didn't reach his eyes. "Listen, I have some good news, and I have some bad news."

Mila's gaze, formerly trained on the tiny cookies served alongside her coffee, lifted to Vin's face. "Oh no. What?"

Vin released a deep exhale. "We just got word that a storm is moving in. Fast. From the south. Radar tells us it'll hit us in about thirty minutes. The good news is that you'll have the good fortune of seeing some incredible views from the dining room. The bad news is that the one road leading in and out of the hotel has been closed."

A collective groan rose up from the table, and Mila's posture collapsed. "You have *got* to be kidding me," she said.

"It's April!" someone exclaimed. "How is it still snowing this hard up here?"

Mila met Jared's eyes, and they shared a smirk. Snow in April? It wouldn't even make the papers.

"I know," Vin said. "It's crazy, right? But this storm is pretty bad, and the state is taking every precaution to ensure safety. We'll keep an eye on the radar and the roads, but another piece of good news is that you happen to be stranded at what will soon be Adirondack Park's most preeminent hotel."

Jared rolled his eyes. *Preeminent.* Thank God Mila had put an end to their fling. The thought of the two of them together made him want to claw his own eyes out.

"So," Vin continued, "while not all of our rooms are completed enough for occupancy, we should be able to ensure everyone is comfortably accommodated for the night. We'll have toiletry kits available, and if anyone has any special needs, just let me or my assistant know."

"Shit." The expletive slipped out of Mila's downturned lips as she scraped a fork across the last remnants of maple panna cotta on her plate. "I'm supposed to work tomorrow morning at seven."

Jared's gut churned with uneasiness. A tiny part of him hoped she might be happy to spend more time together. She was always running home early to go to bed or disappearing from social functions to go to work. Tonight he had her all to himself.

"Benny will understand," he said. "I mean, what are you gonna do, right? We're stuck."

She lifted her gaze, her eyes the color of golden autumn leaves. A shiver skittered across his skin, and he tried to swallow down the sensation but couldn't. It remained, like the first frost in winter.

Vin instructed everyone to see him once they were finished with the meal, and he'd hand out room keys and toiletry kits. Jared told Mila she could stay seated and finish her coffee while he retrieved the keys. He'd happily intercept any Vin interactions for the rest of the evening if it meant saving Mila from this jerk.

"Hey, man," Jared said when it was his turn in line. "I guess we'll need two rooms."

"Ah, sorry, dude." Vin's eyes remained trained on his iPad and he tapped twice. "We're down to one room. We can set up some blankets for you in one of the ballrooms, but you'll have to use the lobby bathroom."

All the color drained from Jared's face. This guy really *was* dying to be hit.

"Come on, man," Jared said. "Seriously?"

"Look," Vin snapped. "We didn't plan on having guests tonight, all right? And we've got to put up the hotel and kitchen staff since they can't get home, either. We've got ten available rooms for the contestants. Everybody else brought a spouse, so you're the odd man out. Take it or leave it."

With a deep inhale to steady him, Jared said, "What's your problem? So she doesn't want to go out with you. Are you really that thin-skinned?"

Vin's lips tightened, and he thrust a single key card forward. "Here's Mila's key. We'll get those blankets for you in the Black Bear conference room. It's just down the hall to the left. Next to the kitchen."

Jared snatched the key and the two denim Indigo Hotels–branded toiletry bags from Vin and stalked back to the table where Mila chatted with red-haired Kim from Buffalo by way of Potsdam. As he approached, she looked up, gifting him with a gentle smile on her lips.

"Did you get the keys?" she asked.

An annoyed exhale sailed through his lips. "Key. Singular. Apparently they only have ten rooms available, so I'm sleeping on some freaking blankets in the conference room."

Her lips pursed in disapproval. "No way. You can just share with me."

Jared swallowed. A thin sheen of sweat appeared on his forehead and he prayed his blush didn't give him away. *Share. With me.*

"Oh," he said. *Be. Cool.* "Okay. Thanks. You're sure that's okay?"

"Of course. We're adults. We can share a hotel room."

She patted her mouth with her napkin before tossing it down on the table and standing up. Practical, reliable Mila. Always making the sound decision. And apparently, tonight, the sound decision involved being adult about sharing a hotel bed because of course they were capable of being alone in a room with a bed with absolutely nothing sexual happening between them.

Her matter-of-fact attitude sobered him as they wished the other contestants good night. If she was committed to keeping it platonic, so be it. He had his answer. When she'd invited him tonight, he thought maybe, just maybe, she'd had something more on her mind. *A date*, she'd called it.

Interpreting her signals confused the shit out of him. One minute she stared at him with those sparkling copper eyes, sending his body into overdrive, and then another minute she reminded him they were just friends. It was like hopping from an icy pond into a hot tub and back again.

"Hey," Mila said, as they reached the front of the room. "Wait here?"

She sauntered to the bar where Vin's assistant tapped away at her phone, and Mila grinned as she asked the young woman something. The assistant grinned back and within minutes, handed over a bottle of wine and two glasses.

Mila returned to where Jared waited and winked, her grin spreading. His stomach tightened. Were they seriously adding wine to their hotel room situation? Was *that* a signal? They'd been drunk together a hundred times before, and many of those nights they'd been alone.

But this was new. Something sparkled between them that had never existed before.

When she reached him, her brow furrowed. "What's wrong? You're looking at me weird. Did you want bourbon instead?"

"No," he said quickly. "This is perfect. Sorry, I was just . . . thinking."

As they made their way out of the ballroom and followed the signs toward their room, Jared tried to channel Denny Torres. *Be bold, bruh.* His feelings toward Mila confused him, but for years, the attraction had grown. That much he knew for certain.

So, he didn't want to get married. Was that the worst thing in the world? Mila had talked about getting married and having kids someday, but it didn't seem like her top priority. He knew how she'd grown up—with parents who treated each other like roommates and sisters who dominated everyone around them, including their spouses. He couldn't imagine Mila was dying to replicate any of that.

Maybe she wanted a friendship with benefits. Maybe she felt the way he did and, just like him, had been afraid to express it.

When they reached their room, she dipped the key card into the slot and pushed the door open. Two warm floor lamps glowed from beneath buffalo-plaid lamp shades, illuminating the room in soft, golden tones.

"Wow," Mila said on a breath. "Gorgeous, right?"

A large leather armchair sat in the corner with a nubby camel throw draped over one arm, and creamy, textured wallpaper and sleek, dark wood furniture completed the room. The bed loomed large in the center of the far wall, piled high with champagne-colored Sherpa blankets and big, puffy pillows.

One bed. He inhaled deeply.

"It is gorgeous," he said.

She kicked off her heels and wandered over to the window, peering through heavy green wool curtains. She gasped.

"J. Come here and look at this."

With nerves churning in his stomach, he joined her at the window. He craned his neck to see over her shoulder, inhaling the sweet amber scent of her skin before turning his attention outside.

Snow swirled through the air, blocking everything a foot beyond the glass with a wall of white. When they'd arrived a few hours ago, the air had been cold but clear. In an instant, everything had changed.

"Wow," he said. "Guess they had reason to close the road. What a mess."

"It's so beautiful, though." Her voice filled with wonder, breathy and curious. Her ability to find fresh adoration for Pine Ridge, the mountains, even the shitty weather, forced him into a new perspective. If she loved it that much, maybe there was more for him to uncover, too.

She let the curtains fall from her fingers. He didn't move. He wanted to be close to her, wanted to see if her skin felt as smooth and soft as it looked. Being next to her drew him in and held his attention, with no room for thoughts of anything else.

Slowly, carefully, she turned to face him. Mere inches separated them as she lifted her long, dark lashes and gazed up into his eyes. His breath left him entirely.

"Jared." His own name floated from her throat across his lips and landed on his tongue.

With his heart firmly lodged in his throat, he croaked out, "We should drink that wine."

The hopeful look on her face softened, and she pressed her lips into half a smile. "Oh yeah? That's what you're thinking about right now? The wine?"

His throat tensed. Would she be the one to push them past the boundary they'd been dancing toward for five years? He'd slid easily into every single one of his past sexual encounters, charming women with slick conversation and focused body language. It only took a smile, a lean, a touch of her arm. Most girls were the same. They wanted attention.

Mila was different. He knew her too well, cared about

her too much. She'd be immune to his charms. In fact, she'd probably roll her eyes. So, what then? How did he do this? He remembered Nicole's advice. *Whatever you do, make sure it's really her.* He'd have to think well past flowers on this one.

"I don't know," he croaked. *Smooth.*

"Come on, J." Her voice remained breathy and light, pleading and teasing and making a mess of his head. "You've been here before. A dark hotel room, a bottle of wine. Don't pretend like you don't know what to do."

She was wrong. He'd sure as hell never been *here* before, standing inches away from someone who meant everything to him just as she was and had the power to change his whole world if they took it one step further.

"Are we doing this?" he said. "Are we having this conversation?"

"Are we?" She lowered her shoulders as if readying for battle. "Or are you scared?"

His lips parted in a wry grin. "Scared?"

"Yeah," she said. "Scared of something that might not be as easy as what you're used to."

He nodded slowly, refusing to put space between them. He breathed in. That had to be new perfume. He'd never smelled it on her before. The heady scent messed with his mind in the best way.

"You think everything is so easy for me?" he said.

"I think sometimes things in your life have been easy. And you're cool with that. You've happily accepted the things that are easy. But the things you really want are things you might have to work for."

Was she serious right now? Every single thing coming out of her mouth could be spit right back at her with accuracy. But she wanted something out of this conversation. He knew what he wanted. That dress in a puddle at her feet. The taste of her velvety skin on his tongue. He wanted them to push past the friendship line as if it had never existed.

"I'll put the work in," he said. "Whatever is worth working for, trust me, I'll do it. I think you know that about me."

Her eyes blazed. All the years of subtle flirtations, and they stood across from each other, daring the other to leap.

"What about you?" he said.

She licked her lips, her pout glistening as she looked up at him. Her copper eyes shone with questions. Did he have it in him to keep going? His gut told him to slow down, but the heart racing in his chest said, *Keep going.*

"I think you're up for it, too," he said. "You've changed, Lee Lee. It's like you finally believe in yourself or something."

She shrugged. "Maybe it's getting easier."

"It looks good on you."

Waves of sparkling chemistry flowed between them as they stood perfectly still, gazes firmly locked. This was it. His moment. All he had to do was lean in and see if she met him halfway.

The old familiar doubt crept along his spine, crawled up his neck, and teased his brain. *You can't do this. She wants more than you can give her.*

"What's going on in your head?" She tilted her face, her eyes crinkling at the corners.

If she only knew.

"I'm not sure I could vocalize that at the moment," he said. "Maybe we should um . . . relax. You know? Sit down?"

Relieve the tension in this pressure cooker?

His adrenaline pumped as if he'd been at the open door of an airplane, gripping his parachute, readying to take the leap. She adjusted the tight velvet fabric at her waist and winced.

"This dress," she said. "It's not exactly the best lounging outfit. I'm definitely not gonna be able to sleep in it."

His nerves prickled again, and he flexed his hands to shake them. So *that's* how she'd do it. He should've known she wouldn't say it out loud. Subtly. The Mila Bailey way.

He cleared his throat. "I could sleep in my underwear if you want to wear my shirt?"

Did his eyesight short-circuit or did her cheeks flush? She shifted as if settling into the idea, narrowing her eyes as silence hung between them.

She rubbed her lips together. "Okay. Thanks."

He hadn't felt this fidgety and awkward around a woman since his junior year of high school, when Natalie Adams said she'd show him hers if he showed her his. Turned out Natalie had seen a lot of them, and she told him his stacked up quite nicely.

He summoned the courage he'd had with Natalie Adams, the boldness he'd utilized with every woman since. "I'll be right back," he said.

Would leaving their warm cocoon next to the window break the spell? If he gave her a moment alone, would she rethink the scenario altogether? As he grabbed his toiletry kit and closed himself in the bathroom, he realized he didn't care. The fragile moment required a pause. For both of them.

He gazed at his tortured reflection in the mirror. Whatever happened next, he'd focus on Mila. His best friend. The woman in his life who was sometimes frozen with insecurity but always the warmest presence in the room. The one who'd never gone back on a big decision. The one he could trust.

He brushed his teeth with the little plastic toothbrush and rinsed his face with water before peeling off his suit. When he'd stripped down to his black boxer briefs, he took one last look at himself in the mirror. He'd let her lead. The night was hers to dictate.

With one last deep breath, he emerged from the bathroom. As he took a few steps into the room, a slow smile curled onto her lips. She'd seen him shirtless before, but everything was different now.

He bit his lip, quelling the urge to scoop her into his

arms and sink into the plush bedding. This was Mila. He had to take his time. "The shirt's in the bathroom."

Her gaze dropped to the carpet as she breezed past him and disappeared behind the closed bathroom door.

His eyes trailed across the expanse of king-size bed next to him. He knew what he wanted to happen, but he needed her to vocalize her feelings. No room for interpretation. If they simply slept next to each other tonight, that was fine.

He laughed. *Slept*. No way would he get a single wink of sleep tonight if she lay a foot away from him, half-dressed in his shirt and smelling like springtime.

The bathroom door creaked open, and suddenly, any doubt he'd had upon entering the hotel room vanished. Without so much as a kiss, they'd crossed into the land of no return.

The crisp button-down shirt reached just below her butt, shockingly white against her smooth, olive skin. Thin white fabric hugged her hips, and she trailed one hand modestly across the buttons. But that's where all rationale ceased.

The buttons. She'd left them open all the way to her chest, the lush line of her cleavage displayed beyond the split. The subtly protruding mounds of her nipples brushed against the front of the white shirt, and a strangled huff unconsciously slipped past his lips.

Jared squeezed his eyes shut and blinked as if suddenly blinded. His heart thumped inside his chest, threatening to break free of his ribs.

"Do you have any idea what you're doing to me?" The words escaped his lips before he could stop them.

He ran a hand over his mouth, trying to gather his thoughts while her silhouette teased him, backlit by the bathroom light. She chewed on her thumbnail, as his old friend Mila made an appearance alongside underwear-catalog-model Mila squirming inside his shirt.

He couldn't say it. Once it was out there, their friendship was toast.

But he had to. The way he felt right now had singed any level of platonic he could ever hope to regain.

He walked slowly toward her. By the time their toes brushed, he'd made his decision. He couldn't keep doing this. His heart couldn't take it.

"You're so fucking sexy."

Her lips parted, but her face remained neutral. If he'd affected her at all, she didn't show it.

He only stood a few inches taller than her, but from this vantage point, hovering over her, her breasts were on full display. He'd give his right eye to be that glittering jewel dangling from the chain at her throat and nestled against her skin.

"J." The single syllable floated across his bare chest.

"You're right," he said. "I'm scared of difficult shit. I sure as hell don't know how to do *this*. But I can't shake this feeling. We're friends, and I still want you to be my friend. I mean, if I lost you as my friend I'd be totally screwed."

Her lips flattened, and her cheek quirked. The stupid words fell off his tongue like rocks. He really *didn't* know how to do this.

"What I mean," he said, "is that for a few years now, I've just felt different. About you. Did you get hotter since you turned twenty-one?"

She broke into a laugh, loud and barking and typically reserved for bad comedy movies. She placed a cool hand on his chest while tamping it down, and for a moment he thought that was it. He'd opened himself up to her, and she'd never heard anything funnier. Friendship: dead.

With one last gasping inhale, she looked up at him, tears shining in the corner of her eyes. Her hand slowly slid upward from his chest to his neck, and her fingers burrowed into the hair at the nape of his neck. Nerves prickled underneath his skin. Every hair on his body stood at attention.

Her gaze deepened. She took a step closer. All the breath seeped out of his lungs.

"I'd always wondered what kind of moves you used to get girls in bed," she said. "The magic words that made them fall for you. This isn't what I envisioned."

Had the tips of her fingers not traced tiny circles against his scalp, effectively turning his rational mind to soup, he'd have been insulted.

"When it's just some girl, I'm Leonardo DiCaprio. When it's you . . ." He released a deep breath.

She tilted her head, studying him with a warm glow in her deep copper eyes. Freckles decorated the skin across her nose and cheeks, her tiny nose stud sparkling like a diamond in the dust. He swallowed down the urge to kiss those freckles. Maybe she wasn't there yet.

Something about the way she touched his neck gave him the tiniest glimmer of hope.

He tried again. "I have feelings for you, Mila. Feelings I've been trying to ignore for a long time now that just won't go away."

She pursed her lips subtly, like she was reading a menu or working out a math problem. The gentle movement of her fingers stopped.

In that one moment, everything hung in the balance. His friendship, his faith in her, her belief in him. If she decided he'd stepped too far, his whole world would shift again, and this time she wouldn't be in it. He'd have lost her. With one stupid comment about how hot she was.

"Say something." His voice choked out barely above a whisper. "I fucked it up, huh?"

chapter **twelve**

Jared breathed so heavily she could see his ribs expanding and contracting under the firm planes of his bare chest. She hadn't seen him shirtless since last summer at the lake, and since then, his muscles had taken on a life of their own.

The soft, thick hair at the nape of his neck felt like home, and she dragged her hand upward to bury her fingers in more of it. She'd never touched him like this before. It felt easy. Natural.

How would the rest of it feel?

"No," Mila said. "You didn't fuck anything up."

His sweet face slipped into a relieved grin. "Really?"

Her jaw trembled like she'd been outside in the snow for too long. Her old friend Jared stood in front of her, but a different possibility blossomed between them. She just had to take one step forward.

"I have feelings for you, too." She forced strength into

her voice. "There was this day a few years ago. We were at the lake, and you asked if you could walk me home."

A sharp exhale sailed past his lips, and his stomach contracted, tightening the flat muscles and drawing her gaze downward. He certainly wasn't her gangly teenage friend anymore.

"Yeah," he said. "That was the day."

Her brow pinched. "What day?"

"Literally the day everything changed. I don't know why. It was like somebody knocked on my brain and said, *Um, hello. Look at her.* Like I'd never really seen you before."

She nodded slowly. Her hand trailed down, past his ear, to settle on the smooth curve of his neck. The first traces of stubble at his jaw prickled against her thumb, and her legs went numb imagining how it would feel against her more sensitive spots.

"You offered to walk me home," she said, "but it was so random. You'd never done that before, and then you got all fidgety and weird and you said that thing about there being a burglar on the loose in Pine Ridge or something. I had no idea what you wanted."

"I didn't, either." A timid grin settled on his lips. "I knew I wanted to kiss you."

Her tongue turned to sawdust. So he *had* wanted to kiss her. All her suspicions of the last five years were confirmed. The lingering glances, the innuendos turned awkward. That day at the lake had changed things for both of them.

"But you didn't." She needed him to acknowledge the reasons why he hadn't kissed her that night. The reasons neither of them had crossed that line since.

"You're so important to me," he said. While her thumb still caressed his cheek, his arms remained firmly at his sides. "I've bulldozed enough casual friendships with sex. I didn't want to risk what we have."

She bit down on her lip. Hard. Was it worth risking now?

"But," he continued, "I've tried ignoring these feelings. It's not really working. So it sort of seems like maybe we should just . . . see how it goes."

Oh, Jared. Always the little boy. Unabashed bravado on the surface, timid like a mouse when it came to the tough stuff. Apparently she'd have to be the brave one tonight.

"See how what goes?"

His eyebrows lowered, and he tilted his face toward hers. Every nerve in her body screamed at her, warned her that with one touch of his lips, everything would change.

She didn't care. If the buildup was that good, what would the rest of it be like?

"See how this goes."

Jared raised both hands to her face, cupping her jaw before gently pressing his warm lips against hers.

Every inch of her softened. Thank God he held firmly to her face or she'd have melted right into the plush carpet beneath her feet. He inhaled as his mouth opened and his tongue slid past her lips, the moment as sweet and tender as she could've hoped for.

With the initial shock still radiating through her core, she returned the kiss, tasting smoky bourbon on his tongue. He cradled her jaw, the tips of his fingers skimming her neck, and she sunk into him, feeling whole and cared for and on fire all at once.

Just before they broke apart, she reached forward and brushed the smooth skin at his waist. He flinched, pulling back and staring at her wide-eyed.

"What?" she whispered.

"I want more."

His boldness brought a smile to her lips. "Oh yeah?"

She glanced down, the erection visible through the thin cotton of his briefs. It should've been weird, experiencing her friend in this vulnerable state. Instead, it felt right. Like she'd been wandering all her life and finally made it home.

"I'd apologize," he said, "but I'm not even sorry. I've known how you smell, I've known how you feel, and now that I know how you taste . . ."

Her stomach caved like someone had scooped out her insides. Since when did her goofy best friend know all the right things to say? The kiss had rattled something in her head and then her heart and, now, something farther south.

"Just . . ." He paused, his hands still holding her jaw. "Before we do anything we can't come back from, we're on the same page. Right? You want this, too? I feel like my gut's been telling me for a long time now that something was different between us, but maybe I'm just hoping."

Sparks flickered inside her body. "I want this, too. I've wanted it for a long time. I just didn't know how to do it."

His golden-green irises warmed, shifting his expression from worried to hopeful.

He leaned down again, pressing his mouth against hers. His featherlight touch did nothing to quell the electricity coursing through her veins. Her hand snaked around his neck, and she pressed up onto her toes, dragging her body along his.

With every caress, she returned the kiss with something deeper and more urgent. She breathed him in, slid her hands through his thick, dark hair, and moaned as their tongues tangled.

"God, you smell good." He dropped his face to her neck and trailed his teeth along the flesh that pebbled at his touch. "Different. Like flowers and honey."

She laughed, the moment lightened with a reminder that he really knew her. She'd purchased the perfume from a gift shop in town because new adventures required new scents. Little did she know what type of adventure she'd embark on.

He ran his tongue along her collarbone and planted kisses across her chest, as his hands slid down the crisp fabric of his white shirt and lighted on the buttons. He paused, gazing up at her with heavy-lidded eyes and swollen lips.

His beauty stole her breath. All that focus, all that delicious attention, all for her.

He paused, standing upright, with his fingers still idly toying with the buttons. Did he know his knuckles brushed briefly over her nipples every time he moved? Her body screamed with impatience.

"I know so much about you," he said, "but I uh . . . I don't know anything about this part of you."

She took his chin between her thumb and forefinger and touched the tip of his tongue with hers, their mouths melding together in a slow kiss.

"That's the fun part," she said.

Without moving his lips, he popped one button, then the next, and then the next. The cool air breezed against her exposed stomach, and he finally pulled back. His eyes started at her neck and moved slowly down. He'd stared at her chest before but typically averted his eyes the second she caught him. Tonight she let him linger.

His warm knuckles brushed against her nipples as he ran his fingers down the placket, slowly pulling back the fabric like the last present on Christmas morning. With a gleam in his eye, he pushed the shirt over her shoulders.

"You are . . ." He shook his head, his hands skimming the outer curves of her breasts before lighting on her hips and coaxing her forward. She tipped her chin toward his, desperate to taste him again, and he gifted her with another slow kiss.

Desire pooled between her legs as his erection pressed against her lower abdomen. "I'm what?"

"You are so beautiful, Mila."

Her chest tightened, and for a moment, sadness washed over her. She prayed this worked. If it didn't, they'd never recover.

As he sat down on the edge of the bed, she ran her hands

through his hair, delighting in the soft, full strands between her fingers. His head dropped back, and his eyes closed as she gently scraped her nails through the tresses. Finally, after years of holding back, she could touch every part of him.

"Lie back," she said.

His eyelids opened, and he paused, studying her.

"Come on," she said. "Please?"

Her pulse thrummed with need, wanting to please him as much as she ached to be pleasured herself.

He shoved himself back on the bed, and she slid her fingers under the elastic waistband of his briefs. Slowly, savoring each exposed bit of his skin, she slid the shorts down his toned legs and tossed them onto the floor.

She stared, taking him all in, bracing herself for the generous erection that awaited her. Her core throbbed, telling her to skip all this and take care of the ache she'd tended for years now. Instead, she crawled over his legs, gripped his cock, and slid the head past her lips.

A tiny yelp escaped his mouth as she slid the head back on her tongue, dipping and enjoying everything he had to offer. The velvety soft skin shifted against her hand and in her mouth, tightening with his arousal.

When she lifted her gaze to look into his face, he greeted her with a pinched, openmouthed stare. "Jesus," he huffed. "That feels incredible."

Was he surprised? Had he ever imagined her this way? God, she hoped so.

She closed her eyes, delighting in all the ways she could make him squirm, and finally, his hands closed around her arms, urging her upward. She slithered along his body, his skin on hers like cool water to a burn.

"It's not fair," he said, his breath coming in ragged gasps. "I can't have all the fun."

"Oh, trust me," she said. "I'm having more fun than you are."

A devilish smile curled onto his lips. "Not yet, you're not."

He sat up, and she rolled onto her back. His eyes roamed her body as if just seeing her naked was enough for him. He dragged the delicate lace of her thong down her legs, and positioned himself over her hips.

She trembled with anticipation, ready for whatever he wanted to give. When his fingers slid between her legs and coaxed her thighs apart, she felt certain she'd explode right then.

"Are you gonna tell me if you don't like this?" he said, his breath warm on her skin and sending her body into overdrive.

"I couldn't lie to you if I tried. Especially not now."

He exhaled a laugh and bit his lower lip. With his green-eyed gaze still locked on hers, he planted a soft kiss just inside her hip bone. As if following a treasure trail, he kissed along the dip in her abdomen until he reached her aching core, desperate to be touched and feeling wholly neglected.

The tip of his tongue edged along her clit, and she clamped her eyes shut, the overwhelming pleasure pulsing through her arms and legs. Her toes tightened, her breath quickened. His mouth pressed and licked against her, each moment better than the last.

He pressed up onto his hands, his mouth firmly covering the most sensitive flesh on her body, and just like that, she crashed. Her hips bucked, her stomach caved, and behind her closed eyelids, the most insanely vibrant display of fireworks popped off like the Fourth of July.

"Wow." She clutched a closed fist to her chest as he lay back down on the bed next to her, running a hand across his mouth but not erasing the smile.

"I didn't think it would get better than seeing you in my shirt, but watching you come is the hottest thing I have ever witnessed."

Slow laughter bubbled up out of her mouth, and she turned her head to face him. "You wanna see it again?"

He matched her grin before pressing his hungry mouth against hers. "Yes, please."

She stretched out on the bed as he rolled on top of her, the full weight of his muscular frame covering her and pressing her down into the whisper-soft Sherpa blanket. Jared, her childhood friend, had left the building. The man covering her, playing her body like an instrument, was someone entirely new.

Their arms extended overhead, fingers linked and chests melding into one. Her breasts crushed against his ribs, and she rolled her hips against him, desperate for pressure he hadn't yet given her. Despite the all-consuming oral sex he'd just delivered, something inside her still felt empty.

"You don't, by chance, have a condom, do you?" she asked in the spare moment between kisses.

A sheepish grin tugged at his lips. "Yeah. I do."

He slid off the bed in one swift movement. When he returned from the bathroom, he held a gold condom packet between his fingers.

Of course the man had a condom. He probably had one tucked in every corner of his house, his car, his office, the heel of his shoe. A splinter of doubt dug its way into her brain.

"You always have one, don't you?" she said.

If he hadn't been gazing at her with those dreamy forest-green eyes, she'd have laid it on even thicker. She knew he'd been with a lot of women—most of whom she knew from high school—but she refused to linger on that now. Reality had no place in this hotel room.

He crawled back onto the bed, draping himself across her and nuzzling into her neck. With one arm massaging her breast, and the other hooked over her head, gently touching the hair at her temple, he said, "I don't always have one. Call it wishful thinking, but something told me I'd need it to-night."

She closed her eyes, sinking deeper into the mattress. She wished it could swallow her whole. Not only would their friendship never recover, she wasn't sure she would, either.

"You're saying all the right things," she whispered. She turned her face, and their noses brushed against each other.

"I'm just being honest. It's easy with you."

She traversed the centimeter between them and closed her teeth around his bottom lip, tugging gently until a groan escaped his throat. With one hand around his package, she slipped her tongue past his lips and pressed her mouth against his.

He exhaled sharply. "Shit, Lee. You're dirtier than I thought you'd be."

She held back her laughter, settling instead for a grin. "This is nothing."

His cock twitched in her hand, and she snatched the condom from his fingers. She tore it open and slid the latex onto him, rolling and stroking until she achieved a perfect fit.

"I'm clean, by the way." His eyelids drooped and his voice grew ragged. "In case you were wondering."

Because you've slept with a lot of women, you knew I'd be wondering? She pushed the thought out of her head. She didn't want to talk about their pasts. In fact, she didn't want to talk anymore at all. She lifted her knees and let her legs fall open, and the dopey look on his face told her he'd already forgotten the conversation.

He trailed a hand gently across her slick seam, already wet and ready for round two, and positioned himself between her legs. Her hips shifted and twitched, anxiously awaiting what came next.

He gripped himself in one hand and balanced his weight

on the other, staring deep into her eyes. His full lips pursed and parted, and she craned her neck upward to kiss him again as he pressed into her entrance.

With both hands framing his face, she let her head fall back, taking in every bit of sensation from his firm cock sliding inside her. She hadn't been with anyone in so long, and she stretched and tightened around him as he breathed into her neck.

"Oh God," he breathed. "Jesus, Mila, you're so tight."

"You feel so good," she said, muttering the words directly into his ear. "*Deeper.*"

She wrapped her ankles around his legs, gently rocking her hips as he thrust deeper and deeper still. The pleasure mixed with pressure, and she squeezed her eyes shut tighter. Pure, unadulterated bliss infiltrated her bloodstream, and she clung to every moment.

As he rocked harder, their bodies slick with sweat, he dragged his arms down to hold tightly to her shoulders. She pressed her face into the sweet curve of his neck and sucked on the skin there. One part of him inside her was not enough. She needed him like air.

"J," she breathed. "Oh God. J . . ."

Waves of adrenaline shot through her, and she came again, tightening around him as she shattered, her nails dug firmly into his back.

An expletive exploded from his lips as he thrust one last time, shuddering against her and touching his open mouth to her cheek as he shivered. His chest heaved. Their bodies moved in sync, his labored breaths matching hers.

She trailed a hand up his neck and into his thick nest of mussed hair, her nails tracing patterns against his scalp. The breath on her tongue tasted of him, the air in the room filled with their scent. She wanted to live here forever and bask in the warm glow they'd created.

He lifted his head, his eyelids dark and his cheeks pink, a stark contrast against the loose strands of dark hair falling over his eyes. He had the face of eighteenth-century nobility, worthy of being immortalized in a painting.

"Wonder if Vin knew what he was doing when he threatened me with blankets in the Black Bear conference room," Jared said.

The laughter trickled out of her, adrenaline and dopamine mixing in her blood to create the perfect high. "We'll have to thank him later."

Jared rolled onto his back and settled his hands behind his head. She stole a glance at his satisfied smile and tugged the covers up under her chin.

She wanted to ask what happened now. Were they dating? Sleeping together? Friends with benefits? Her body flooded with desire just thinking about having him again, but how did that mesh with the close friendship they'd developed in the last twenty-five years?

"Room service is probably too much to ask, huh?" he said.

She laughed. "Seeing as they barely had rooms for us, I'm gonna guess there's no on-demand dining."

He turned his face toward her, his eyes darkening as he studied her face. The quiet of the room roared in her ears, her body still buzzing and high.

"I enjoyed that," he said.

Her smile stretched. "Always nice to hear."

"No," he said. "I mean . . . that could've been a disaster, right? And it wasn't."

Uncertainty tickled her chest. "Right."

He sighed, grinning as if he'd said all he needed to say. Did he wonder about the state of their relationship now? Did the same doubts course through his mind like they did hers?

"Come on," he said. "Roll over. Unless you want to be big spoon?"

For the moment, she quieted the questions plaguing her brain. His smile was too sweet, his hair too perfectly disheveled. She'd never been the type of person to risk ruining the constants in her life, to throw caution to the wind when it came to people and relationships that formed the bedrock of her world. But as Jared slipped an arm around her waist and pressed his smooth cheek against her neck, she didn't have space in her heart for caution.

chapter **thirteen**

Jared shoved the metal cart over the threshold to their hotel room, grimacing as the covered dishes rattled and stirred Mila's formerly sleeping form under the downy blankets.

"Sorry," he said. "Guess I'm not as stealthy as I thought."

Mila's cloud of curls appeared, followed by her heavy-lidded gaze and timid fingers gripping the edge of the quilt. "Why hello, bellman," she said, her voice thick with sleep. "I hope you plan on feeding me whatever you've got under those domes. I heard it was a service of the hotel, and I won't accept anything less."

Jared bit back a grin. God, he loved her like this. Sexy and tousled and flirty. He wanted to forget the food and get down to it.

"Your wish is my command, Ms. Bailey." He lifted the dome off a plate of thick-cut French toast, releasing the rich aroma of maple syrup and cinnamon.

"Wow," Mila said. "Whatever that is, give it to me. Give it to me now."

"God, I wish you weren't talking about the food."

Her nose crinkled in a laugh, and she tucked the covers up under her arms, ready and waiting for her meal. "Come on. Before it gets cold."

Jared arranged trays and plates in her lap and across the bedspread, ripping off his pants before scurrying back into bed with her. She hadn't waited for him. He hadn't expected her to.

"Oh my God," she groaned. "This bacon has a sweetness to it. Maybe brown sugar?"

"Yeah," he said. "That's what the sign said. I tried to get a little bit of everything from the spread. Can't believe they pulled all this together last minute. Chef Constance said they hadn't planned breakfast, but they made it work."

"Damn," Mila said. "This is them *making it work*. What an insanely talented group of people."

He sipped his coffee and snagged a piece of bacon. The crispy strip shattered on his tongue in a blend of sugar, salt, and fat. He couldn't stop his eyelids from lowering in pure, unadulterated pleasure.

"That's really freaking good," he said.

"Everything is really good." She lifted a forkful of fluffy scrambled eggs to her lips and hummed.

"It's gonna be pretty cool when you get to work alongside them," he said.

She paused mid-bite as the joy melted from her face. "Maybe."

"It's not gonna be cool?"

"I might not get to work with them."

He trailed his teeth over his bottom lip and massaged his eyes with the heels of his hands. Blinding morning sun seared his brain. They'd never closed the curtains last night. Much more important things to tend to.

"There's that Bailey optimism," he said.

She swallowed, her gaze dropping to the plate in her lap. She set the fork down before raising her thumb to her lips. "Can we just enjoy our breakfast?"

The mood chilled as if they'd opened the window. He wanted to press on, remind her that she had all the talent necessary to settle in among the staff of Indigo Hotels Adirondack Park. But after last night, he wasn't sure of his place with her. Could he still badger her into positivity like he'd done when they were just friends? Did he have more license now?

And yet, what were they? The thought of defining their relationship unnerved him, his stomach tightening around the food he'd swallowed.

She ate quickly, her attention focused on the meal, and before he'd finished half his plate, she was up and back in her velvet dress and checking her phone. Was she pissed at him? Had he pushed too far? Or had she finally had time to think about what had happened between them and begun to regret it?

"Are you ready to go already?" he said.

"I have to get to work," she said, eyes trained on her phone. "The roads are clear, and Amy can only cover for me until eleven."

He cleared his throat. "Is something wrong?"

"J," she said gently. "Honestly, I just have to get to work. I can't afford to miss out on hours right now, much less piss Benny off and risk losing my job altogether."

"Lee . . ."

She hovered near the door, giving him a smile he'd seen her use on customers at the diner when she listed the specials for the seventieth time that day. "Just get dressed, okay? I'll wait for you in the lobby."

She didn't wait for a reply. Before he could speak another word, the door closed behind her.

He dressed quickly despite the nagging queasiness in his stomach. He thought they'd climbed a mountain last night and come out the other side unscathed. Exploring her body had been the greatest gift, and he'd hoped he'd get to do it at least once more this morning.

Was she annoyed because he had only one condom? He scratched his head as he slipped on his shoes. That would be a weird thing to be upset over. Plenty of fun, dirty stuff could be accomplished without condoms.

He looked at himself in the bathroom mirror. Hair stuck out in every direction, a result of her incredible blow job, a distractingly good orgasm, and a very deep sleep. He tried to finger-comb it, but nothing helped.

Was it possible she regretted it? Had he come on too strong? He thought he'd read all the signs. When she came out of the bathroom with that shirt half-unbuttoned, he couldn't stuff his feelings back in. She had to know that.

But last night she'd slowly migrated to the far edge of the bed, and this morning she'd treated him like a one-night stand she wanted to disappear. Anxiety swirled in his chest, tempting him into believing something he didn't want to believe.

Maybe Mila was just like every other woman, changing her mind whenever it suited her.

He stared at his own face, dragged his hands down his cheeks.

No. Not Mila. He knew her inside and out. And now he *really* knew her inside and out. Something else was wrong. He'd just have to figure out what it was.

Denny aimed the dart, his hulking frame a solid foot closer to the board than anybody else's. Who could blame him? The guy was big. He'd have to stand across the street from Utz's to even the playing field.

"But," Denny said. He paused mid-toss and turned to Jared. "You said the sex was good?"

Jared shoved his chair backward to avoid getting a dart

in the eye. "Better than good, dude. Maybe the best ever. We were laughing . . ."

"Laughing?" Denny's face screwed up, and he turned back to the dartboard. He launched the dart at the wall and it bounced off, landing at the feet of two female tourists who'd been eyeing him like prime rib.

"Yeah," Jared said. "It was great. It was comfortable. I mean, I thought it was comfortable."

"Laughing, comfortable sex sounds like my nightmare, dude." Denny took a slug from his pint of Coors Light and winked at the tourists. "Are they cute, or am I hammered?"

"Can we focus?" Jared gathered up the darts and tossed them onto the bar. He wasn't in the mood for games. The drive home from the hotel had been as quiet as the deep woods in winter, and when he dropped Mila at her apartment, she'd given him a pleasant wave and a "see ya later."

"Sorry, bruh." Denny slammed the last of his pint and motioned to Hank for another.

"Hey. Sorry I'm late." Sam hurried into the bar, sniffing against the cold that still lingered in Pine Ridge. The winter season stretched far beyond the calendar around here. Jared prayed they wouldn't have snow for the bake-off weekend.

He tried to catch Denny's eye to let him know the Mila sex talk was not a conversation for his brother's ears, but the big dude shrugged, his face creasing in confusion.

"What's your deal?" Sam asked, catching his brother's frantic hand motions. "Are you having some kind of fit, J?"

Jared ran a hand over the back of his neck. He didn't want or need his brother's advice on the situation. He'd chime in with some bullshit about not sleeping with your friends, and how Mila deserved more than he could offer.

"Nah, he's looking for sex advice," Denny said. "I dunno, man. I don't really know what to tell you, except for maybe she's just not into it, you know? Maybe she doesn't like you. Maybe it was a pity bang."

"Oh God," Sam groaned. "Who is it now? Chloe again?"

For a moment, Jared saw an out. "Yeah, Chloe."

"Thought you said her name was Mila?" Denny said.

A long, groaning exhale escaped Jared's mouth as Sam's wide-eyed stare fell on him. "Wait . . . what?"

"Nothing," Jared said. His cheeks burned with the shame of having messed up a decades-long friendship. His brother would never let him live it down.

"You slept with *Mila*?"

Jared glanced nervously around the bar, but no one seemed to be listening in. "Keep it down, all right? Until I know how she feels about it, I don't know if I should be telling people. I thought this idiot could keep a secret, but maybe he took one too many hits in the league, you know what I mean?"

Denny pursed his lips. "Hey, not cool, bruh. I didn't know it was a secret."

"So," Sam said. He leaned over the table, his interest fully piqued. "What happened?"

Jared gave him the PG version of their night at the hotel, beginning with their almost-kiss five years ago and culminating with Mila's nonplussed attitude that morning.

"Wow, brother," Sam said. He ran a hand over his hair. "Can't believe you went there. Were you guys drunk?"

"No," Jared said. "I mean, we'd had a few glasses of wine, but we were both totally fine. We talked about it beforehand. I said I'd been into her for a while, and she said she felt the same. I don't know what changed between last night and this morning."

The front door to Utz's creaked open, and as if summoned by the mere mention of her name, Mila entered. Her boot caught the floor, and she stumbled when her gaze landed on Jared.

"Hey, Grace is here!" Jared said.

She huffed out a short, nervous laugh, but her cheeks turned bright red as she hurried toward the bar.

"What the hell are you thinking?" Denny's hushed warning forced the grin from Jared's face. "Go talk to her. And try not to treat her like your little sister."

Jared tucked his pride down deep and approached Mila as she asked Hank the bartender for her takeout order.

Hank scuttled into the kitchen, and Mila tucked her elbows into her body and huddled over the bar, sinking into her coat like a turtle hiding from a racoon.

Jared leaned in next to her and studied her face.

"Hey," he said.

"Hey." Her lips turned upward, just short of a smile.

"Sorry for uh . . ." He waved in the general direction of where she'd tripped. "Old habits die hard."

"Nobody asked you to stop joking around with me," she said. Her eyes remained trained straight forward on the rows of dusty liquor bottles.

"How was work?"

She shrugged. "Scintillating as ever."

He opened his mouth, but before he could get a word out, Hank appeared with a large paper bag. "Here ya go, darlin'. Two chili cheeseburgers, three fries, one onion rings, and a hot dog."

"Thanks, Hank." She grabbed the bag and sent her *Can I get you anything else?* smile to Jared before backing away from the bar. "See you later?"

"Well . . ."

"I have to get to my parents," she said. "Before the food gets cold."

With a wave to Sam and Denny, Mila exited the bar. A flare of defiance rose up in Jared's chest.

Nuh-uh. No way would they continue on like that.

He shoved the door open and jogged into the parking lot, blocking her car door before she grabbed the handle.

Subtle anxiety tightened the corners of her eyes as she looked up at him. The wind blew through her hair, the curls twisting slightly in the chilly spring air. The bright, late-afternoon light did her smooth skin every favor. She glowed, the tip of her narrow nose shining in the cold.

"What's up?" she said.

He snatched the takeout bag and her keys from her hand, opened the car door, and started the ignition. With the bag of food securely settled in the driver's seat, he closed the door and turned back to her, crossing his arms over his chest. He dared her to slither out of this one.

"*What's up?*" he said. "You've been acting weird since this morning. I want to be cool and pretend to be aloof, too, but I'm not. I am not cool about this. I want to know why you're acting like we went bowling last night instead of . . ."

She sucked her bottom lip into her mouth and shoved her hands into the pockets of her big blue parka. "I'm not."

"Lee." He stepped closer, demanding her attention. When she finally lifted her gaze, her eyes glassy in the wind, his breath caught in his throat. She'd always been beautiful, but now that beauty belonged to him. Like each of them had given up parts of themselves they'd never get back.

He couldn't abandon it now.

"What?" she said.

"Last night was . . ."

"What?" The word escaped her lips on a breath as if she feared the answer. "What was it?"

His brow furrowed. "Last night was incredible. I haven't stopped thinking about it. I hoped we could do it again this morning, but you were so weird when you woke up. I don't know what I did."

The crease in her forehead softened. "You didn't do anything."

He waited. A big, beat-up Buick cruised past them in the parking lot and caught Mila's attention before she looked back at Jared. Still nothing.

"Is this all in my head?" he said. "You're being the same Mila and I'm the one who's different?"

"I'm sorry," she said. "No, you're not making it up. I had

this moment of panic last night that we'd done something we can't undo. And that maybe you regretted it."

His chin dropped. He couldn't hide his surprise. "Regretted it? *Hell. No.* What did I do to make you think that?"

"Nothing."

He searched his memory for any boneheaded remarks he may have made in bed. Had he cracked a joke? Had he teased her about something? He'd been waiting for sex to change everything about their relationship, but all it had done was make him care for her even more.

She exhaled. "You didn't have to do anything specific. We're friends. *Best* friends. And after we slept together, we didn't even really discuss it. In the deep, dark depths of my cynical mind, I sort of thought, *Well, that's it. One and done.*"

His jaw ticked. "Is that what you want?"

"No!" Her eyes widened until he could see the whites all the way around her sparkling amber irises. "That's not what I want at all."

"Well, good." He dipped his chin and caught her lips with his, her body relaxing under his hands. When he pulled away, he let his lips linger over hers. "That's not what I want, either. And that's not how I felt last night. I'm sorry if you wanted to talk and I missed the cue."

"I'm sorry I'm asking you to pick up on cues."

"Uh-uh," he said. "Don't be sorry. It's something I should've been doing as your friend all along. And this whole *more than friends* thing is new. And kinda weird."

She nodded, and her tiny jeweled nose stud caught the sun. "Very weird."

"Just talk to me, okay? Don't let me wonder." He traced his thumb along her jaw. "If I wonder, then I start talking to those guys, and I get the worst advice ever."

"Don't forget Denny is a friend of Vin's, so I'd take everything he says with a giant grain of salt."

"Oh man, that's right. But Denny's a good guy. Vin is . . ."

She shook her head, a smile playing on her lips. "A dick."

"You have every right to kick him in the nuts."

"As long as he's got anything to do with the bake-off," she said, "I will show restraint."

Had Jared been in earshot of their conversation, he'd have had trouble defining the word *restraint*. "All right, Saint Mila."

She ran her hands down the front of his sweater, pausing as she reached his belt. When she looked back up, something sinister glittered in her eyes. "Gosh. What can I do to get you to stop thinking of me like that?"

His limbs went suddenly numb. "I'm sorry it took me twenty-five years to see this side of you."

As her hands left his body, he shivered.

"You should get back inside," she said. "You're always running outside without a coat on."

"You're always making me chase you."

She raised an eyebrow. "Well. Maybe not anymore."

His chest swelled. Maybe this *could* work.

"Hey," she said. "Why don't you come to my parents' for dinner tomorrow night? They haven't seen you in a while, and my mom's been on my ass about it."

"Yeah, of course. What's for dessert, though?"

He'd meant it as a joke about her always showing up to places with pie. The smile that curled onto her lips shoved his mind and his groin in a very different direction.

She licked her bottom lip and then reached for the car door handle. "Guess you'll find out."

chapter **fourteen**

Mila slammed the car door shut behind her and curled her shoulders against the chilly evening air. She sent a silent prayer into the sky, begging the weather gods to be on her side for the Spring Festival. While the bake-off would be held in the newly finished ballroom at Indigo Hotels Adirondack Park, the rest of the festival featured events outdoors at Nicole's family farm. It wouldn't be a Spring Festival in Pine Ridge without the mingled scents of freshly popped kettle corn and cut grass, the sounds of delighted children as they won carnival games, and the vibrant yellows, reds, and purples of Williams Farm's famous tulip beds.

If the weather didn't cooperate, they'd be forced to shrink everything into the barn and nix the outdoor components that made the weekend so special. No amount of crepe paper or silk flowers could match the colorful, apple-blossom-scented splendor of Williams Farm in the warm sunshine.

She hurried up her parents' front walk, refusing to take this

April cold as a sign, and pushed through the front door. The rich, spicy scent of baked sweet potatoes blended with the heady aroma of garlic and sizzling meat, wrapping around her like an old blanket.

"Lee Lee?" her father called from the kitchen.

"Are you joking me?" Mila peered over her father's shoulder, her eyes widening as she caught sight of the perfectly marbled rib-eye steaks waiting to be seared on Dad's prized grill pan. "What's the occasion?"

"You said Jared was coming," Caryl said, scurrying in from the living room.

Mila wrapped an arm around her mother's shoulder as she sprinkled salt onto the raw meat, kissing Caryl's warm, powdery cheek. With three grown adults huddled into the postage-stamp-size kitchen, there was barely room for the food. But the kitchen drew people in, and Mila felt most at home in that particular room of the house.

When Caryl moved to Pine Ridge with Lloyd in the early eighties, she didn't know cumin from paprika. Along with a few tips from Aunt Georgie, Mila had essentially taught herself to cook and, over the years, shared a few tips and tricks with her mother. Caryl absorbed them despite her best efforts.

"Jared's been here for dinner a hundred times," Mila said. "I recall rib eyes being served maybe twice. And one of those was the night we celebrated Nicole's engagement."

Caryl replaced the box of salt in the cupboard and wiped her hands on a dishrag. Her eyes flitted over Mila and then rested on the pie plate in her hands. "What's today's kooky flavor?"

"Brown-butter vanilla custard with graham cracker crust. I don't know if it's any good." Mila slid the pie plate onto the cluttered counter and shrugged off her coat. The tinfoil-covered pie mocked her. She'd spent all day testing fillings. Nothing tasted right. Spicy cherry was lethal cough syrup. Chocolate ganache with homemade crisped rice cereal was twice the effort for half the quality of what came in the box at the supermarket. Pecan coconut was a bad protein bar.

The contest date loomed large on her calendar, and with every passing day, the pressure on her chest grew. Why had she entered this stupid contest in the first place? She knew her pies were good. She didn't need a public humiliation to prove otherwise.

"Well, we'll find out, won't we?" Caryl said. "What time is Jared coming? I can't let the steaks sit out too much longer or they'll spoil."

Mila released a tight breath. Even her mother's anxiety over the food set her on edge. When Aunt Georgie was alive, she'd stand hunched over the stove, calmly stirring and peppering and salting, waiting patiently for one of the few dishes in her arsenal to reach perfection. Everyone knew not to rush her, and everyone knew the cold leftovers in the fridge later that night would taste even better than the original.

Her mother's cooking, on the other hand, seemed to inherit the tension she infused into it as she cooked. Tasty but tough. Nothing like Aunt Georgie's practiced, methodical dishes.

"You keep the heat in this house at sixty degrees," Mila said. "They won't spoil. Plus the longer they sit with the salt, the better."

"I know you're not trying to tell me how to cook in my own kitchen," Caryl snapped. Her mouth bunched; her hands firmly planted on her full hips.

"No, ma'am." A few years ago, the words would've sounded like an apology. Tonight they bordered on sarcasm.

"Lee Lee," her father said, handing her a full glass of cherry-red wine. "Why don't we go into the other room and let your mother finish up here?"

The hair on the back of Mila's neck stood on end, and she followed her father the short distance into the living room. Despite being only a few feet away from the stove, she released a deep breath in the partial privacy.

"I think I could own a Michelin-starred restaurant and she still wouldn't believe I can cook."

Lloyd's smile widened as he shook his head and leaned back in his recliner. His legs stretched far beyond the footrest. When Mila was a kid, she'd hide under that footrest and pretend she lived in a cave guarded by a giant.

"I can't wait until you have kids," he said. "And you have a headstrong daughter who comes into your kitchen and tells you she knows better. I sincerely hope I'm alive to see the day."

"Oh, please." Mila rolled her eyes and sipped her wine. The bright, fruity flavor swished across her tongue and coated her throat, relaxing her frazzled nerves. "I'll encourage my daughter to know more than I do. I'll welcome it."

Lloyd laughed, his affectionate gaze landing on his younger daughter. "All right, Lee."

"I'm serious. Why wouldn't I want my daughter to be smarter than me? To be more ambitious, to have bigger goals in life?"

The smile faded from her father's face. "You think your mother doesn't want that for you?"

"I *know* she doesn't. I just can't figure out why."

The front door burst open, bringing a fresh blast of cold air along with Nicole and Calvin and their heated conversation about the pros and cons of fixing up their old SUV. Mila's conversation with her father halted abruptly.

It was just as well. They'd had that discussion more than once, and Mila had yet to have her mind changed. As far as she could tell, Lloyd would defend his wife to the death. No matter what.

"Happy Sunday," Nicole said, wrapping an arm around Mila's shoulders and kissing her cheek. When she pulled back, her eyes narrowed. "Are you wearing makeup?"

Mila's heart leaped into overdrive. "What? No?"

Nicole's full eyebrows pinched in the middle, and she

nearly poked Mila's nose with her own. "You are, too. What are you wearing makeup for? You have a hot date after this?"

"Nic!" Calvin called from the kitchen. "Mrs. Bailey is making steaks!"

Mila would've thought it a physical impossibility, but Nicole's brow tightened even further. "Is someone coming for dinner? A guy? Are you bringing a *date* to dinner?"

"Are you warped?" Mila tugged out of Nicole's death grip and settled back into the couch, snatching her glass of wine from the side table and sipping gratefully. "It's just Jared."

"Jared, huh?" Nicole's gaze met Lloyd's, and she crossed her arms over her chest. "Steaks and makeup for Jared?"

"I didn't *ask* her to make steaks."

The people in her life could sniff out a hint of drama like a shark sniffed out blood in the water.

"You smell different, too." Nicole stared at Mila as if trying to solve the world's greatest mystery. "Are you wearing new perfume?"

"Cut the girl a break," Lloyd interjected. "There's wine in the kitchen, Nicole. Go ahead and pour yourself a big glass."

Nicole's face softened, and she squeezed Mila's hand. "*Sorry*. Sorry. I'm leaving you alone now."

Mila's heart thumped in her chest like the world's tiniest bass drum. Earlier, she'd debated putting on makeup for this very reason. She knew Nicole would call her out. But the thought of sitting next to Jared at the dinner table looking like plain old Mila, the Mila she'd been before their night at Indigo, made her eyeball twitch. She needed to be new Mila. Cute Mila. Mila 2.0.

She took another sip of wine. And another. She held the glass in her vibrating fingertips. *Not enough wine in the world.*

When she'd invited Jared to her parents' house it had seemed mundane. He'd been here a hundred times. But as the hour approached, she realized in one night everything had changed. And she'd have to be around her friends and family pretending it hadn't.

As Mila stood up from the couch for a refill and to see what snacks she could pick on in the kitchen, a loud rap on the front door startled her to attention.

"Hello!" Jared had been inside a thousand times over the years, only knocking when he was a little boy and his mother told him it was rude to just barge into people's homes. At some point in the past ten years, he'd stopped believing the Bailey house wasn't his home.

Mila peered down the front hallway in time to see him run a hand over his hair, sniffing against the cold. He tugged the scarf from around his throat, revealing the square jawline and taut, strong lines of his neck. With one deft hand he tossed his coat onto the coatrack and stole a glance at himself in the entryway mirror.

As he pressed his lips together and wrinkled his nose, Mila grinned. He was nervous. Usually he'd bound into the house with abandon, Caryl calling after him to leave his shoes at the door. He'd hug Lloyd like he'd been born a Bailey, not a Kirkland, and he'd poke fun at Mila before the scent of cold outside air had left his skin.

Tonight, he paused. He ran a hand across his mouth, straightened his crisp button-down shirt. Preparing.

"You gonna come in, or you want us to serve your dinner in the front hall?" Mila called out.

His head snapped to the left, a smile creeping slowly across his curvy lips. She wanted to kiss him. Bad. Anticipation seeped into her veins as she realized she couldn't so much as touch him tonight without tipping off everyone in the room.

"I don't want your mom to yell at me for getting her floor wet," he said. With great care, he unlaced and tugged off his boots, holding her gaze as he went. Her cheeks burned with the same fiery passion simmering in her gut, the sensation threatening to set her whole world ablaze.

Check yourself. She swallowed down the emotion churning inside. There was a time and a place. Sunday night at her parents' house was neither.

"That's right," Caryl called out from the kitchen. "Don't you dare get snow and salt on my floors."

Mila stood at the end of the hallway, blocking his entry into the living room. He made his way slowly toward her, his green eyes saying all the things his mouth wasn't allowed to. She hadn't meant to tease him, but the way he cocked his head, the way his jaw ticked, she knew she'd done something like it.

Just before their bodies met, he raised a single eyebrow and, much too loudly, said, "'Sup, girl?"

He squeezed between her body and the wall to slink into the living room and crush Nicole in a hug. Had her two best friends discussed what happened? Was Mila so transparent that Nicole smelled the dalliance from a mile away? She hated lying, hated keeping things from anyone who mattered to her. She'd have to tell Nicole.

Eventually.

As Jared settled into the house like a long-lost cousin, Mila stood in the doorway trembling. In just a few short days, he'd gone from her bro-y best friend to a man who could decimate her with a single smirk.

Jared lowered himself onto the couch, chatting amiably with her father, and Mila retreated to the kitchen to refill her empty wineglass. She snagged the open bottle of cabernet from the counter and within seconds, Nicole pressed up next to her. Even the confines of the tiny kitchen wouldn't force her that close.

"Gosh, Nic," Mila said. "Thirsty?"

"I'm not interested in the wine."

Mila paused mid-pour. She knew when she turned to

look at Nicole, there would be a devious gleam in those all-knowing eyes, a smirk on her lips. She didn't want to have to face yet what Nicole seemed to already know.

"Okay, well, you know where the beer is." Mila set down the wine bottle and avoided Nicole's stare, hoping to avoid the awkward conversation for at least another hour.

"Lee," Nicole said, her voice lowering as she leaned closer to Mila, "please don't forget that I am the one and only person in the world who knows that half your parents' liquor bottles are filled with water, and who knows how loose my lips might get after a couple of glasses of wine."

Mila tried her best to summon a threatening stare, but a smile was the best she could do. She and Nicole had slowly but surely dipped into her parents' liquor cabinet the summer after their senior year of high school, and Caryl and Lloyd didn't drink enough to notice.

"You wouldn't dare." Mila pinched Nicole's wrist, and Nicole grabbed Mila's hand in return.

"Don't test me. Come on." She dragged Mila out of the kitchen and into Mila's old bedroom.

Mila's eyes slowly adjusted to the darkness, the chilly air settling over her. The room was never properly heated, an addition added somewhere over the years when the previous owner realized they had too many babies and not enough bedrooms.

"It's like she's always waiting for you to move back in," Nicole said.

The room lived firmly in the early aughts, partially redecorated after Mila's older sisters had moved out, and complete with powder-pink comforters on the twin and bunk beds, Panic! At The Disco posters on the walls, and a butterfly lamp on the sticker-covered desk. Mila and her sisters had been scolded for the first few heart-shaped Valentine's Day stickers they'd affixed to the drawers, but Caryl soon gave up, and Mila added her own punk-rock touch once the room became hers. Now it was a living testament to the years the Bailey sisters occupied the room.

"Maybe you and I will have daughters and they'll want to have sleepovers here," Nicole said.

Something in Mila's chest stirred, warming like chocolate in a pan. She saw two little girls, separated by a few years based on Nicole and Calvin's family aspirations, giggling to each other across the nubby blue carpet while Caryl warned them from the kitchen that they better be quiet and get some sleep or there'd be hell to pay. One of the little girls had Nicole's sharp tongue and Calvin's dimples, the other had Jared's mischievous streak and Mila's eyes.

Mila used to think her mother's jokes about future generations occupying her old bedroom were foolish. But maybe they weren't so silly after all.

"*Soooo.*" Nicole's eyes sparkled in the moonlight streaming in through the single pink-curtained window. Her mouth pressed and twitched, a smile threatening beyond. "Tell me! Tell me. Right now."

"What am I telling you?" Mila's stomach turned to ice. She wasn't ready to say anything. She wanted to keep what had happened at the hotel her own little secret. She wanted clandestine smiles across the room and fiery, featherlight touches that no one else saw.

"Fine, you want to pretend? Then I won't ask you *if* you slept with Jared. I'll ask, How many times? How was it? And when did you two finally admit that you have feelings for each other?"

Mila's cheeks burned, and she was suddenly grateful Nicole had never flipped on the light. Was she smiling? Her cheeks hurt from holding it in. She wanted desperately to share the news with Nicole, but how quickly would that news spread through Pine Ridge? How quickly would the pressure of an entire town's expectations land squarely on Jared's shoulders and push him away?

"Nic . . ." She had nothing else to say. How many times? Not enough. How was it? Mind-bending, soul-crushing, world-shifting. When had they admitted their feelings? Not soon enough.

Nicole grinned. "He told me, you know."

A half croak escaped Mila's throat. "Wh—what?"

"He told me he was into you." Nicole's eyebrows jumped, and she crossed her arms in satisfaction. "At the bake-off."

Mila's skin tingled like a kid in summertime standing under the sprinkler. "He did?"

Nicole shifted her weight, a smug smile on her lips. "I think this is great, Lee. I think it's amazing. I've always wondered why you two never got together."

All at once, Mila deflated. *Why you two never got together.* They'd never gotten together because their futures looked as different as could be. Jared wore Pine Ridge like a too-tight suit, busting at the seams and begging to be shed. He talked more about leaving than anybody they grew up with, and he practically salivated over any TV show featuring house hunting and exotic locations.

He didn't want to live a small-town life. Mila *was* small-town life.

"We're not together," Mila said, directing her statement toward a faded poster of Brendon Urie. Her mother really needed to give this room a face-lift, future generations sleeping here or not.

"What does that mean?" Nicole asked. "You're just hooking up? No way."

"Listen." Mila licked her lips and took Nicole's hand in hers. "I'm not trying to keep this from you. I promise. But can we have this conversation when my parents aren't in the next room?"

Nicole gave her a sympathetic head tilt. "Don't you dare try to dodge me."

Mila exhaled. In a perfect world, she and Jared could go

on doing as they pleased without an explanation to any-body. Including themselves.

"I'm not dodging you," Mila said. "We'll talk. We'll get a giant bottle of wine and sit on my couch, and I'll share every detail. Just . . . not tonight."

Without waiting for an answer, Mila slipped out the bed-room door and joined her mother in the kitchen. The two women worked side by side, Mila leaving anything skill-based to Caryl but effectively avoiding the men in the other room. If Nicole could tell within minutes that something had happened between her and Jared, how long would it take her parents?

Caryl announced dinner was ready, and everyone settled down at the table. Over the years, as Caryl and Lloyd's blood children had vacated the home and their surrogate children had filtered in, they'd each claimed a regular spot at the table. Jared always chose the seat next to Mila.

That night, with Jared's soft, peppery cologne compet-ing against the heady smell of hot, sizzling rib eyes, Mila wished for TV trays in the living room. How could she fo-cus with the man she knew so well and yet had only just discovered sitting six inches to her right?

"Jared, any news on that Silver Lake property?" Lloyd asked, passing the bowl of mashed sweet potatoes.

Jared spooned a healthy serving onto his plate and handed the bowl to Mila. Their knuckles brushed, and the silver serving spoon slipped from Mila's fingers and clat-tered to the ground.

"Shit." Mila clambered from the table to retrieve an-other spoon. "Sorry."

Caryl pointed a disapproving pout at her daughter. "Where's your head at, Mila?"

With a new serving spoon in hand, Mila returned to the table and nearly stumbled again. Jared's eyes burned into her, his lips curved into the tiniest hint of a smile. That slippery jerk knew exactly what he was doing.

"I'm just tired," Mila said. She slid back into her chair and spooned a heaping portion of potatoes onto her plate. If she couldn't quiet her nerves with wine, food would have to do.

"So," Lloyd said. "What about that property?"

Mila watched her father carefully. Why had he asked twice?

"Ah, no," Jared said. "It's a tough one. It's for such a specific buyer, and that buyer just hasn't materialized yet."

The brightness radiating from Jared's face dampened as he spoke. He stared down at his plate, trailing the tines of his fork through the mound of golden orange potatoes.

"Just wait until you're working somewhere like New York or Boston," Calvin said. "Silver Lake will look like peanuts compared to those multimillion-dollar homes."

The smile tugged at Jared's lips. "That does sound nice."

Mila's chest burned.

"You're not still thinking of moving to a big city, are you?" Caryl said. She'd stopped eating altogether, her fork poised midway to her mouth and topped with a cube of tender meat.

Jared cleared his throat. His eyes darted sharply around the table at the expectant faces. When they landed on Mila, she bit her lower lip to keep her expression neutral. New York. Boston. Hundreds of miles from here. Filled with smart, sophisticated women who took the world by the balls.

"I don't know," Jared said. "I mean, I'd like to. Someday."

The slow, methodical sound of Nicole chewing filled the room, and Mila fought to avoid her friend's pointed stare.

"What's wrong with Pine Ridge?" Caryl said. "You can't raise a family in New York or Boston. Living in a little apartment, paying ten dollars for a cup of coffee with no family around to help you out."

The color slowly drained from Jared's face, and his wide-eyed stare returned to his plate. He hadn't taken a single bite.

"I don't know," Jared said. "I'm not really there yet, you know?"

"Yet," Caryl said.

Mila begged the universe to swallow her up. The evening had taken a decidedly strange turn, and the frozen, petrified look on Jared's face told her he knew it, too.

"Well," Jared offered, "the goal in moving somewhere like that would be to make money. A lot of money. Then I'd have options."

"Money's nice," Caryl said. "But money won't keep you warm at night. Mila doesn't want to live in a big city, you know."

"Mom, leave him alone." The tone Mila meant to be firm came out whiny and small.

Caryl sent her the Bailey Look, and a sick sense of dread crept across Mila's chest.

They couldn't possibly know.

Could they?

"I'm only saying all the things his mother would say if she were here."

Jared snorted. He took a long drink of his wine and wiped his mouth with a napkin. He'd always had a very complicated relationship with his mother, and summoning her never relieved any tension.

"My mom wanted me to leave this town more than anybody," he said.

Mila sat up straighter. Mrs. Kirkland never made a secret of her aspirations for Jared or her opinion that he never worked to his full potential. Remembering the tense conversations between them made Mila's heart hurt.

"Your mother was a good woman," Caryl said. "I didn't know her well, but I know she made the best of a bad situation."

Jared snorted again.

"Hey, can we change the subject?" Mila said. Her stomach had turned in on itself, watching Jared squirm under

Caryl's intense scrutiny. He never wanted to talk about his mom, and coupled with his plans for the future, she feared he might simply up and walk out.

"Your mother's just curious where this all is going." Lloyd raised his fork and gestured to the space between Mila and Jared. "You know. Word travels fast around here."

Mila's tongue dried up as Jared's face turned a lighter shade of gray. The only sound in the room was Nicole's slow, purposeful intake of air.

"Yikes," Nicole whispered.

What are you referring to, Dad? Whatever could you mean?

The words echoed in Mila's brain, but nothing came out of her mouth. Instead, she summoned every shred of courage she possessed and lowered her shoulders in a warrior pose.

"It's none of your business," she hissed. "It's none of anyone's business."

Caryl tossed a hand in the air and rolled her eyes. "You're my daughter. It most certainly is my business."

"I'm sure Mila and Jared will tell us when they're ready," Nicole offered.

"You all act like I'm grilling her," Caryl said. "I'm just asking some simple questions. Is it supposed to be a secret? They weren't acting like it was a secret outside Utz's yesterday."

Mila shut her eyes, the one bite of food she'd swallowed threatening to resurface. Maybe they hadn't meant it to be a secret, but it certainly wasn't ready to be on full display at the Bailey family dinner table, where dreams came to die.

"What are you, spying on me?" Mila's voice barely choked out past tense lips.

Caryl rolled her eyes. "Spying? I was picking up my prescription, and I drove by and saw the two of you kissing in the parking lot. I'm not sure that qualifies me for the CIA."

"Oh God," Mila groaned. Caught kissing in the parking lot. Like a teenager.

"Hey, I'm all for it," Caryl said. "I just want to make sure you've both really thought this through. You're not eighteen anymore. Your decisions have consequences."

"Hey, Jorie McDonagh is pregnant again." Nicole's eyes widened as she shared the news, the rest of the table shifting uncomfortably in squeaky wooden chairs.

"Irish twins, huh?" Lloyd said.

The conversation shifted and allowed Caryl to pass judgment on a different Pine Ridge resident, but her earlier comments swirled in Mila's stomach like sediment in a pool. Everything she'd said was true, and yet speaking it out loud gave it strength, made it impossible to ignore.

While Nicole babbled on about Jorie and Matt and their two-under-two family scenario, Jared continued to push his food around his plate and remain eerily silent. Every few minutes he huffed a mild-mannered laugh and sipped his water. By the time plates were cleared and dessert served, Mila feared he'd never attend another Bailey family dinner.

"Hey, I should get going," Jared said.

His words rang across the table, drawing everyone's confused stare.

"Really?" Mila said. "We haven't eaten dessert yet."

He swallowed audibly and raked a hand through his hair. He had the same wide-eyed, glazed-in-fear stare he'd maintained since they'd sat down to dinner.

"I've got a ton of work to do before tomorrow morning," he said. "Plus, since you started recipe testing, I have to spend an extra hour in the gym every day. I'm starting to get a spare tire."

Just the thought of his smooth, tight abs made her throat dry up. Maybe after tonight she'd never get to see them again.

He moved around the room, hugging everyone warmly and saying goodbye in low, sweet tones. When he got

around to Mila, she glued her eyes to the sharp knife sliding in and out of the custard pie and attempted to ignore
him altogether.

"I'll call you tomorrow," he said.

She refused to turn, refused to hug him. She'd collapse
into tears, apologizing for her parents and begging him to
forget the last two hours of his life. She didn't want from
him what they claimed she did, didn't have those ridiculous
expectations. He could travel if he wanted. Work in New
York or Boston. He could live however he chose. No restrictions. Nothing holding him back.

Especially not her.

He stood there dumbly, waiting for something she couldn't
give.

"Okay," she said. She picked up two dessert plates, sent
him a tight-lipped smile, and turned away.

chapter **fifteen**

Gosh, I just don't know. I really don't care for this wallpaper."

Jared gritted his teeth. Everyone who'd ever seen an episode of anything on HGTV considered themselves experts on home renovation. Most of them just complained about wallpaper and carpet color and the lack of an open-concept floor plan.

"All surface stuff," Jared said. "Wallpaper comes down easily, and then you can pick the wall color you love. Turn it into a home. Your home."

Mrs. Abbott harrumphed again, and her husband shrugged his meaty shoulders. They meandered through the living room to the kitchen, staring up, while Jared stewed near the front door.

Typically he had all the patience in the world for commitment-phobic house hunters. He'd crack jokes, flirt with the wives, talk up the Loving Page bookshop's lively events and the delicious treats at McDonagh's Bakery. Today, uneasiness simmered in his gut, and he couldn't keep it from polluting his professional demeanor.

Dinner the previous night had been a total nightmare. The Baileys were incredible people, the closest he had to parents who understood him, but their traditional streak ran deep. They believed in family, financial stability, and keeping your head down. Big dreams need not apply.

He knew they wanted the best for their daughter, but he wasn't thinking long term right now. He simply wanted to enjoy Mila. He wanted them to have fun, explore sides of each other they'd never seen before, and take their time. He wasn't ready to open a joint checking account just yet. And every time he started to envision himself dating and marrying his best friend, he heard his mother's voice.

There's a whole lot more world out there, Jare. Don't let yourself get sucked in by the comforts of this town. You're headed for much bigger things.

The older he got, the more trouble he had seeing Pine Ridge as a death sentence. His mother had had her own unique experience growing up and living and dying in the small town, but why did that mean he had to replicate that life? Mila would never do to him what his parents had done to each other. She didn't have it in her.

Did she?

The Abbotts thanked him for his time and left him to close up the house. He took his time, flipping off light switches and locking windows. The faintest hint of a warm breeze blew through town, and he took full advantage of fresh air. Spring always meant an uptick in sales.

Could warm weather dredge up a buyer for Silver Lake? He punched the code into the lockbox on the front door and turned toward his car, hazy purple light settling over the treetops. He'd showed the property in summer when the sky turned cerulean blue, in autumn when burnt sienna and golden red and orange leaves painted the mountains in stunning broad strokes, and in winter when blankets of soft, powdery snow turned the house into a Christmas buff's wet dream.

A couple nibbles. No bites. Springtime—the muddiest, dreariest, most inconsistent season of them all—was his last hope.

The office sat quiet and abandoned when he arrived, all his colleagues having gone home for the night. He wasn't ready yet. His empty house fostered thoughts of the decisions that lay ahead of him, the expectations of everyone around him and one person—one overwhelming presence—who'd left him nearly two years ago. Work was work. All-consuming and unavoidable, no matter how hopeless his current docket seemed.

At nine o'clock, he toned down the desperation in his last email of the evening before hitting Send. Surely his contacts smelled the fear in him by now. He'd never been in a spot as tough as with Silver Lake. The proximity to failure didn't sit well in his gut.

He closed his laptop, locked up the office, and headed out into the night. As he cruised through the quiet, darkened streets of downtown Pine Ridge, he noticed the lights on at the Loving Page. He slowed his car to a crawl as he passed the big windows filled with Sydney's springtime display of paper flowers and brightly patterned book jacket blowups. Through the glass, just past the front tables, stood Mila and Sydney, chatting happily as they tossed paper plates and cups into a trash bag.

The book club. Had Mila made time for the book club tonight? She'd texted him earlier that she had a free night, but he'd had to take the Abbotts to see that property and a mountain of work to catch up on.

What an asshole. Mila had a free night, and he'd acted like he didn't have time for her.

He pulled his car into an empty space in front of the store and walked in, the bell jingling merrily over his head and announcing his arrival.

Mila looked up, her lips parted in restrained expecta-tion. Her sly eyes blinked a few times, and she bit down on the swell of her full lower lip. What had *ever* made him want to avoid her?

"We're closed, Kirkland," Sydney said with a smile. "You'll have to wait until the morning to peruse the erotic romance section."

She teased, but Jared had skimmed a few of those books. He'd had to stop himself after only a few paragraphs to prevent showing everyone in the store how much he'd en-joyed them.

"We were just heading out," Mila said. "Did you need something?"

He could see her defenses raised as if they'd been made of literal armor. Who could blame her? He'd run like a scared puppy from the Bailey family dinner, playing the role of typ-ical dude scared of being asked about his intentions.

"Hey," Syd said, reading the room. "I actually have to run. Mila, do you mind locking up for me?"

"Not at all," Mila said. "But you don't have to—"

"Eh." Sydney held her hand up. "Just talk to each other. But please don't have sex in here, okay?"

With a wink, Sydney grabbed her coat and slipped out into the night.

Mila toyed with the edges of the trash bag, avoiding his gaze as the air between them thickened.

"Sorry I bailed last night," he said. "Your parents freaked me out."

"You don't say?" When her eyes finally landed on him, they cut. Deep. He really was afraid of the tough stuff.

"I just wasn't ready to have that conversation," he said. "Especially not with your parents and Nicole and Calvin all waiting for me to pull a ring out of my pocket."

She shook her head, worked her lips as if summoning the courage to open the conversation. "Well, my parents are not me. That's not how I feel. I'm not waiting for a ring or counting on you telling me you want to live in Pine Ridge for the rest of your life."

The weight that had been sitting on his shoulders since yesterday suddenly lightened. "You're not?"

"Give me some credit," she said. "We're just having fun."

Huh. A sharp, tiny pang in his chest. Something like . . . disappointment? But what could he possibly be disappointed by? He wanted that. To explore her, to have fun with her, to enjoy her without the pressure of what came next.

Because they both knew marriage was not coming next.

"Okay," he said. "Well, great. Then we're on the same page."

"And fuck everybody else, right? Who cares what they think?"

Who *was* that girl? All the blood in his body rushed south. "Sure."

She released a long breath and reached for an open bottle of prosecco on the coffee table beside her.

"You want a drink?" she asked. "Otherwise I'll have to toss this."

"Um, yeah." He didn't need a drink. He needed to hear more about this theory of hers, the idea that they could just have fun. It sounded more like something she'd read in a book than something she'd come up with on her own.

She set down the trash bag and retrieved two empty champagne flutes from a tray on the coffee table. The soft gray sweater she wore slipped over one shoulder as she poured, and with that slip of skin, something seized his chest. She was comfortable and new, domestic and wild, his home and his heart all wrapped up in one. He didn't know what to do with such an overpowering feeling.

He'd grown up with two parents, but the older he got, the more he saw the reality of their fractured marriage. His father drank too much, and his mother disappeared under the weight of a life and a burden she'd never asked for. She'd spent her whole life dreaming of leaving Pine Ridge and, instead, had ended up being swallowed up by it.

As a result of her own regrets, she'd never once given Jared a pass. He'd never understood why everything Sam did was lauded and praised, and everything Jared did fell short. Sam had tried explaining—more than once—that their mother only wanted him to get the hell out of the town that had ruined her. Jared only felt the weight of her disappointment.

And what would she think of him now?

Mila handed him a cold, fizzing glass of prosecco, and she clinked hers against it before tucking an arm across her chest. The glowing table lamps lit her cheeks and made her nose stud sparkle like the North Star.

He cleared his throat. "I don't want us to just sleep together."

A surprised laugh skittered past her lips, and she pressed a hand to her forehead. "Okay?"

"Seriously, Lee, this isn't funny. I'm trying to talk to you."

She peered at him from under her hand and lowered herself onto the arm of the couch.

"You don't want us to just sleep together," she said. "You also want us to . . ."

"I want us to be us," he said, frustration heavy in his chest. "I want to be like we used to be."

She took a sip of her prosecco and ran a thumb under her full lip before glaring at him. "So if I'm hearing you right, you want to be best friends who also have sex?"

"Yeah." He shrugged. "I mean, I just don't want to lose everything we've been to each other up until now, you know?"

She paused, the weight of her stare making him itch. "Think about what I just said. You want us to be best friends who have sex. Does that sound suspiciously like something else to you?"

Anyone who claimed women were not smarter than men had obviously never talked to a woman.

"Okay," he said. "I get it. So then maybe we're in a relationship. Maybe you're my girlfriend. Is that crazy?"

"Do you *ever* think long term? What happens if you move to New York? Or Boston? Or North Carolina? What happens if you take a big job with Indigo?"

"You come with me."

The words fell out of his mouth as if a force from beyond had summoned them. *You come with me?* He'd never imagined them moving away from Pine Ridge together. But why not?

Her head fell backward, her shock of dark brown curls tumbling down behind her. When she looked back at him, her lips parted. "Seriously?"

"Why not?"

She tucked her thumbnail between her teeth and avoided his eyes. Suddenly the new Mila disappeared, shrunken down into her shell like she always did when the conversation got tough.

"You don't get it." Her voice barely carried across the few feet between them.

"What don't I get? You're so happy to tell me I don't get it, but you're never willing to explain yourself."

"Oh, fuck off." Her glowing, light brown eyes turned to steel.

"Great. That's helpful."

"Just forget it." She shook her head and focused on the champagne flute gripped tightly in her hands.

Silence weaved its way between them, filling the errant spaces and roaring in his ears. They'd had arguments in the past, but nothing that couldn't be resolved with a couple of jokes and a drink or two.

Tonight, she wasn't budging.

"How did you see this going?" he said finally. "You wanted to forfeit the friendship for the sex?"

She rubbed her lips together, gaze glued to her hands. "I don't know. I guess I thought as long as I was only focusing on one piece of it, the rest might settle on its own."

His skin prickled. *Settle on its own.* Did she think *he* would settle on his own? That he'd suddenly come around to marriage and kids and the type of domestic life he'd watched decimate both his parents?

"You told me what your parents said wasn't how you feel," he said. "That you aren't waiting on a commitment. Was that a lie?"

Her eyes lifted, her face momentarily blank. "No. It wasn't a lie. I mean, not completely."

His stomach tightened. He'd been hoping she didn't agree with them, but he knew her too well. Could she try to buck tradition? Move to New York or Boston or Raleigh with him and live a half-domesticated, half-nomadic lifestyle? She'd said she wasn't waiting for a ring, but now that he thought back on it, she hadn't explicitly stated she didn't want those things at all. She simply said she didn't want them now.

Nothing seemed clear anymore.

"I'm twenty-five," she said. "I'm not convinced this is exactly how my life will be until I die. But I also know that I love it here. I want to stay in Pine Ridge. I want to get married and have kids someday."

He winced. He hadn't meant to, but it happened.

"I mean, I think," she said. "I think I want to get married and have kids."

"Jesus, Mila." He pinched the bridge of his nose. "Don't tell me what I want to hear."

"I'm not." Her jaw set. "I'm telling you what's going on in my head. If I never meet anybody worth settling down with, then I won't. Marriage isn't the end-all. Being happy is the end-all. Being with somebody I love is the end-all."

He wanted it to be true. Wanted it to be true more than

he'd ever wanted anything in his life. "You'll meet somebody who wants to marry you. How could you not?"

"There are no guarantees in life. You have no idea how
any of this will go."

He ran a hand over his hair and walked over to the big
front window of the shop. His head spun again, and he
looked out at the street, dark and desolate at this late hour.
He imagined being in New York City, watching hundreds
of people roam, just starting their evening. He saw crowded
bars and well-dressed women and something new around
every corner at every time of the day or night.

But he turned back to Mila, perched on the arm of the
couch, the lamplight bathing her face in the type of glow
movie studios needed experts to create. Mila soaked up and
reflected all the light in the room on her own.

New York City didn't have her. No city ever would. The
way he felt about her terrified him to his core. Like she
could change everything he thought he believed. Everything he'd been taught was gospel.

"I feel like you want to be let off the hook for this," she
said. "That you want me to tell you I can't do this, and we
should end it completely. Go back to being friends."

Is that what he wanted? To never be allowed to kiss her
again? To never have access to the soft scent at her neck or
the deep moans she released as he roamed her body?

Maybe it was what his rational brain told him he should
want. It was what eighteen-year-old Jared would've screamed
at him to do. If he sat down with a psychic, his old man
would appear from the great beyond and tell him, "Run!
She's letting you off the hook! Go back to being friends!"

"No," he said. "I don't want to go back to being just
friends."

Her face softened. "So maybe we let go of our expectations a little. Maybe we try and just see what this feels like.
No boundaries, no definition, no labels."

He raised the prosecco to his lips and took a drink. In

the moment's pause, she stood up and met him at the window, bringing a subtle wave of lavender scent with her. Not the new perfume this time. Just her skin, the flowery lotion she used, the spicy, herbal scent of her shampoo.

It wrecked him.

"I don't want to hurt you," he whispered, not trusting the strength of his voice.

She licked her lips. "Then don't."

chapter **sixteen**

Mila trailed her fingers over the oranges' puckered skin, the smooth flesh of Honeycrisp apples, and the prickly fuzz of the kiwis. Without the restrictions of the first round, her mind should've relished the freedom of round two. Instead, she was stuck. Stymied. Completely void of inspiration. The produce section at the local grocery store did little to spark ideas.

She popped a green grape into her mouth and grimaced as the sour juice burst against her tongue. Just like her recent recipe tests. Sour.

"Not good, huh?" The husky female voice caught her attention from behind.

Mila turned to face Chef Constance, nearly unrecognizable without her chef's whites. She wore a gray ski cap over her short auburn hair, and a brightly patterned fleece jacket covered the rest of her round frame.

She grinned at Mila without showing teeth and plucked a kiwi from the bin.

"Ridiculously sour," Mila said. "Serves me right for stealing a grape, right?"

"You small-town people," Constance said, still grinning. "Too honest for your own good."

"Don't get me started on big-city types," Mila teased back.

"Eh. I'm from Heyburn, Idaho."

Mila laughed. "So I can count you among the too-honest small-town simple folk, huh?"

Constance inspected a plastic container of blackberries, grimaced, and put it back. "You got me. Twenty years in New York, and I'm still chasing after people on the street who drop a dollar bill. It's in my blood."

Mila readjusted her heavy handcart. "There are worse things to be."

With a narrowed gaze, Constance inspected Mila's cart. "Hm. Working on your pies?"

"Yes, but not with this haul." Mila looked down at her cherry tomatoes, garlic, dried pasta, anchovies, and lemons. "That would be one disgusting pie."

"I'd have thought rosemary and Concord grapes would be nasty, too," Constance said, "but you knocked that one out of the park."

A wash of flattery rolled over Mila. "You think?"

"Absolutely. It was one of the most inventive, well-executed pies I've ever tasted. And it could've gone horribly wrong."

Mila's lips curved into a smile. "Well, I'll take that as a serious win, then."

Constance crossed her arms over her chest and studied Mila. Her skinny brows lowered over scrupulous eyes. "What do you do for a living, Mila?"

She'd remembered her name. And her pie. Mila felt like prom queen and class president rolled into one. Constance's tough demeanor reminded her of Nicole, but the woman's own confidence and poise lured Mila into contentment. Peace. The space to be herself without judgment.

"I've got a bunch of jobs," Mila said. *Waitress* didn't have the same type of ring as *head chef.*

"Food service?"

"Um, yeah. I mean, I work at the diner mostly. Waiting tables."

Constance nodded. "That's great experience if you ever wanted to work in a kitchen."

In the comfort of her own home, creating pastries on her countertops, baking them in her oven, Mila was untouchable. Thrust into the professional world of food was something entirely different. She couldn't even enter her hometown bake-off without a push from beyond the grave.

"Sure."

"Listen," Constance said, "we've got a couple apprenticeships at the hotel . . ."

"I know," Mila said. "You told me. But I've never been to culinary school, and to be perfectly honest, I don't really see it in my future. It's just so expensive. If I won the contest, then maybe, but even then. To spend all the prize money on one thing for myself when so many people I know could use a little help . . ."

Constance pressed her lips into a disapproving glare. "You don't need to spend fifty thousand dollars on culinary school. I don't want to get ahead of myself, but if you do pull off this Spring Bake-Off thing, it'll be the résumé gem you need to land that apprenticeship. Real-world experience plus a win like that? You'd be ahead of the pack. Even without the formal training."

Mila's throat tightened. "Really?"

"Definitely." Constance inspected a Granny Smith apple and placed it in her cart. "Indigo supports apprentices at all levels of experience, especially in the culinary division. You'd be a fool not to apply."

With a single nod of her head, Constance grabbed a kiwi and moved past Mila to the meat counter. Possibility churned in Mila's chest. Maybe Constance represented an entire industry of people who looked at food service as a badge of honor, a stepping-stone to greatness, instead of a job some settled for.

If her parents had taught her one life lesson, however, it was that life didn't owe anybody anything. Good fortune did not beget good fortune, and nothing in life was certain. The lesson had been ingrained in her since birth.

Mila brought her groceries to the register and began unpacking her cart, her brain popping back and forth between Constance's tantalizing optimism and the crushing weight of her family's reality.

"You're not using your Georgie account for this, right?" Annette Bethel asked, screwing up her wrinkled lips as she began swiping packages across the scanner.

"No," Mila said. "I'll pay out of pocket for this."

"Whew. This would be one gross pie."

Mila licked her lips, replaying Chef Constance's words in the produce section. She'd be a fool not to apply. And she'd already come this far, entering the bake-off and then moving on to the final round. Maybe she wouldn't be the next Food Network star, but maybe she had more in her than she'd previously thought possible.

"How much is left in that fund?" Mila asked.

Annette pulled a clipboard from beneath the register and peered down through her bifocals. "Looks like twenty-seven fifty-four."

"Twenty-seven fifty-four?" The words snapped out of her mouth like a rubber band.

Annette glared.

"Sorry," Mila said. "I just, um . . . I didn't realize I'd spent so much money."

"It goes quick, doesn't it?"

As Mila hauled her canvas grocery totes over her shoulder, emotions swirled around her head. She'd depleted her funds at the hardware store, and now her account at the grocery store was nearly empty as well.

Twenty-seven fifty-four. The number sobered her, a stark reminder of her dwindling inheritance from Aunt Georgie. If she didn't come out the other side, she'd have wasted every penny of the money that could've gone to help her family with nothing to show for it but a big public humiliation.

And a ruined friendship.

As she drove back to her apartment, her car hugging the curves of the road she could drive with her eyes closed, she thought back on the past week. She'd had complicated feelings for Jared since they were kids, amplified by that day at the lake when he'd started treating her differently. Those long gazes, the blush that crept into his cheeks when she said something particularly dirty. It all meant something. All her suspicions, validated.

But what now? In one fell swoop, they'd changed the course of their friendship, and now everything looked different. She wanted things she hadn't previously let herself dream of, yearned for moments with him she never thought she'd be privileged enough to have.

Their talk on Monday had done little to squelch the burgeoning fears in her psyche. She knew what he wanted, and it wasn't a family with her in Pine Ridge. She tried to tell herself she could be cool, treat this casually, and take one day at a time. But she cared too much. The dull ache in her chest that bloomed as he kissed her was unavoidable. She'd never shake it now.

She arrived home, and her phone buzzed with texts as it connected to Wi-Fi. She set her grocery bags on the countertop and checked her messages, the first from Jared.

Need me to pick up anything on my way over?

She grinned. He'd sent the text twenty minutes ago and was probably already nearing her place. She fired back quickly that she didn't need a thing, and then added Well . . . with the eggplant emoji and sent it before she could talk herself out of it. Introducing sex jokes back into their repertoire gave the butterflies in her chest new reason to flap their wings.

Before she set her phone down to start dinner, she noticed another message.

Hey Mila. Give me a call when you have a minute.

"No, thank you." She deleted Vin's message and tossed her phone onto the couch. Whatever that asshole had to say could wait.

Her front buzzer rang just as she scraped the finely chopped anchovies into the pan, the satisfying sizzle bringing a smile to her face. Jared always jumped at the chance to try one of her creations, never shying away from an unorthodox ingredient. Anchovy pasta might be just weird enough to make him fall in love.

She buzzed him in, and moments later opened the door to catch him jogging up the stairs. In one hand, he clutched a bottle of wine, and in the other, a stunning bouquet of jewel-toned flowers. Blue hydrangea nestled next to brilliant purple anemones and ruby-red poppies.

Warmth rose to her cheeks as he approached, a little-boy grin tugging at his lips.

"Hi." He held out the bouquet and then quickly closed the space between them to plant a kiss on her temple. "Take two. This time, with feeling."

She took the bouquet with trembling fingers and breathed him in, the cold clinging to his leather jacket like a ghost. She lifted her face and kissed him. Quiet and slow.

Damn him. What had he gone and done now?

"I take it you like these?" he said.

She licked her lips, gazing down at the flowers and then back up at him. Take two blew take one out of the water. "Are these all *for love*?"

He shook his head in disbelief while a grin took over his mouth. "I was trying to tell you something, you crazy woman. You just didn't translate it very well."

"How embarrassing for me. All these years I've known you, and I still don't speak bumbling idiot."

His jaw dropped in faux indignation, and he squeezed her around the waist, gently pushing her inside. She closed the door behind him, and he collapsed into the couch with an exaggerated inhale.

"Wow," he said. "What smells so good? You told me this was a quick, easy dinner. I expected Easy Mac and Doritos."

"Have the words 'Easy Mac' ever left my mouth?" she said. "It's spaghetti with garlic and anchovies, and a little arugula salad with grapefruit and fennel. I made extra salad to give to my parents tomorrow. I have to take my mom to her physical in Utica, and I'm sure the doctor will have some words about her cholesterol."

With a wooden spoon, she stirred the anchovies in the pan, releasing another wave of pungent garlic-scented air into the room.

"Garlic and anchovies," he said. "I guess if we're both eating it, neither of us will be repulsed by the other one's breath later on?"

She shook her head and poured lemon juice into the pan, scraping up the brown bits and slowly turning the sizzling concoction into a simple sauce. After a few shakes of chili flakes, she turned off the heat.

"Call me crazy, but I'd take garlic breath over fake minty gum breath any day. Something about that taste reminds me of bad make-outs in high school."

When he didn't respond, she turned over her shoulder to find him peering at her phone.

"Nosy much?" she said.

He sat straight up, a startled expression on his face. "Sorry. I, uh . . . Vin's texting you."

She cocked her head, flattery simmering in her chest. "Why does he get under your skin like this? Of all the guys to be worried about . . ."

"I'm not worried." He crossed his arms and leaned back, spreading his legs in some forced display of machismo. "That guy's got nothing on me."

"Oh my God, you are so cute." She tore her gaze away to stir the pasta into the sauce. With her heart in her throat, she realized that this very moment was exactly what she'd been trying to avoid. Cooking dinner, flirting, joking, and all the while knowing they'd be naked and tasting each other in a matter of hours. It was everything she wanted, and everything she couldn't have.

"So what does he want?" Jared said.

She turned again, this time with a cocked eyebrow. "I don't know, I haven't read the messages yet."

He gnawed at his lip and shifted in place, tension setting into his jaw. She could have easily cleared it up, told him she'd already read one of the messages and Vin had simply asked her to call him. But an evil little voice deep down in her soul told her to let him squirm.

"You know," he said, "I know we said no labels and all that. But I wouldn't sleep with somebody else behind your back."

His words stung like a slap in the face.

"How dare you. I wouldn't, either, you asshole."

His eyes widened, his lips parted in surprise. "No, no, that's not what I meant. I meant . . . This seemed like a good time to just get it out there. In case you were wondering."

"Oh, good." Sarcasm dripped from her words. "Thank you very much for clearing that up."

She gave the frying pan a good shake and dumped the spaghetti into a large bowl, coating the top of the dish with crunchy homemade bread crumbs. With teeth clenched, she carried the bowl to the coffee table, where she'd already set out pasta bowls, forks, and napkins.

She sat down next to him, leaving a discernible space.

"Hey," he said quietly. He wrapped an arm around her shoulders and pulled her into his warm cocoon of biceps and soft wool and spicy cologne. "I'm sorry."

She refused to meet his gaze. Tears threatened her sinuses, but she'd be dead before she let a single one appear. If he pulled her any closer or forced her to look at him, she'd crumble.

"Trust me, okay?" she said.

He used his other arm to complete the hug, burying his face in her neck. "I do."

The phone next to her buzzed again, and she groaned as he pulled away. "God, what could he possibly want?"

She opened her messaging app to find three new messages from Vin.

Do you have a minute now?

Sorry to keep bugging you, but it's kind of urgent.

It's about your pie from round one. Please call me as soon as you can.

"What's wrong?" Jared asked.

Mila's brow twisted in confusion. She muttered to Jared that she had to make the call now and dialed Vin's number.

"Hey," he said after the first ring.

Mila stood to look out the window, knowing full well the conversation was fair game for Jared's ears but still wanting to keep some semblance of privacy. She feared the worst.

"Hi," she said. "So you've sufficiently freaked me out. What's going on?"

"As part of the contest, I have to go through and submit each contestant's recipe to the legal team at Indigo and prove that each contestant falls within the requirements set forth by the hotel. After double-checking the recipe and the ingredients, we found that less than half your ingredients were sourced from New York State, rendering your recipe ineligible."

The blood pulsed in Mila's ears, nearly drowning out Vin's words.

"Wait . . . what? That's absolutely false. I can provide receipts showing you where I got them."

"It's not the store you bought the items at, Mila. It's where the ingredients came from."

Her tongue felt too big for her mouth. "No, I know that. I just meant I can show you the brands, the sources. I know I was close to fifty."

"Based on quantities and yield, you came in at forty-eight percent." His clipped voice made her blood pressure rise. "The legal team consulted with a culinary staff. It's just facts, Mila."

Her head spun, and she placed a hand on the frosty window to steady herself. As her grape supply had dwindled, she knew the recipe had come close to the 50 percent mark, but she assumed the number was just a suggestion. It was March in the Northeast, how could they expect people to source butter, flour, sugar, and fruit locally this time of year?

"What now?" she choked out.

"That's it. You're disqualified."

All the breath in her lungs vacated in one slow, steady stream, taking the feeling in her limbs along with it. "You're joking."

"I'm really sorry. I wish things were different, but you're dealing with a huge company here. They have to protect themselves against anyone coming at them later and claiming one contestant was favored over others. You signed the paperwork when you entered, and so did everyone else. We have to follow the rules."

Vin's voice held no hint of warmth, no indication that he was now or had ever been truly sorry. She couldn't help but wonder if this would be happening if she'd continued to date him.

"I can't believe there's nothing I can do," Mila said. "We're one week away from the bake-off. I've worked so hard. I . . . I've been testing like crazy for this next round. I've spent so much money."

She hated the tone pouring out of her, the feeble, whining words. She hated to beg.

"I know," he said. Clipped. Cold. "And I really am sorry. But again, it's a legal issue. You made it to the final round with a dish that didn't actually meet the requirements. To make it fair, we'd have to go back and start the entire competition over again. We just can't. You understand."

"Sure." She huffed out an angry breath. *Sure.* Why shouldn't she understand? It was only everything she'd worked for crumbling at her feet. Karma showing its nasty face. Of course she'd been eliminated. She'd wanted it too hard. Believed in herself too much.

"All right, well," he said. "Again, sorry. Good luck with everything."

She slowly lowered the phone to her side, staring out over the dark parking lot outside her window, trusting that Vin had nothing important left to say.

A few airy moments of silence passed until Jared said, "What happened?"

"I'm out." The words fell off her tongue, seemingly coming from someone else's throat. She couldn't quite believe them. "I'm disqualified. My pie had less than half the ingredients sourced from New York State, and now Indigo's legal team says I can't continue in the competition."

She swallowed, moving through the living room as if pushing through whipped cream, then lowered her body down onto the couch next to him.

"You've got to be kidding." His words sizzled like water in a hot pan. "No. No fucking way. That's insane."

"Yeah." She sniffed back her disbelief and stared at the coffee table where their dinner sat, cold and forgotten. "It's insane."

"That can't be the last word on it. Give me the phone, I'm gonna call him."

"J." She looked at him, his face twisted up in anger. "Just don't. Can you do me a huge favor?"

"Anything." He leaned toward her, his angular face telling her he'd leap tall buildings for her. Stare down the barrel of a gun. Pummel Vin into oblivion.

"Drop it."

His eyes widened. "Drop it?"

She licked her lips, her entire being vibrating with nerves and anxiety and fear. "I need to think about this, and I need to process it on my own. Your anger will get in the way of that. I need you to eat this pasta that probably tastes like old feet by now, I need you to put on a funny movie, and I need you to hold me while I sleep. Can you do that?"

His mouth opened, an indignant cough passed his lips, and a deep blush rose in his smooth cheeks. "Honestly, Mila, I don't know. I'm so pissed off."

"I know. I am, too." She swallowed down threatening tears. "Pissed off and sad and embarrassed. Just let me process this on my own. Okay?"

With another huff, he fell back on the couch. He rubbed his hands across his face and stared at her, his mouth still hanging open. "Am I allowed to ask if there's *any* option for changing their minds?"

"Vin said that's it. There's nothing else they can do."

He leaned over his knees, dragging his hands down his face, back up again, and shoving them through his hair to leave the tresses in disarray. She couldn't help herself from thinking about how handsome he looked, indignant and sexy and properly angry on her behalf.

He shook his head. "Are you okay?"

Was she? Would she ever come back from this? Her skin

prickled, her head swam. She was not okay. "I will be. I just really need this from you, okay? I need you to be calm for me. At least for tonight."

She knew the advice sat heavy on his tongue. He couldn't help himself. But he remained silent, and she'd never been more grateful.

As she flipped the television on and found a mindless nineties sitcom, a warm hand crept across her lower back. He squeezed lightly, summoning tears she thought she'd already willed away. His fingers pressed into her skin and brushed the ridges of her spine.

She swallowed the lump in her throat and forced her gaze to his sweet face as he tucked into his spaghetti. She'd never loved him more.

chapter **seventeen**

Mila pulled the car into the strip mall parking lot, navigated her way into a space, and cut the engine.

"Ooh, that bakery," Caryl said. Her eyes lit up, and she clapped her well-manicured hands together at her chest. For reasons unknown, her mother always wanted to look her best for doctor's appointments.

"No bakeries," Mila said. "You heard the doctor. You have to cut down on sugar. I feel like your drug dealer at this point."

"Oh, please," Caryl said. "A slice of pie here and there isn't going to kill me."

Mila tamped down anything else she might want to say about her mother's diet and opened the driver's side door. The spring air held a touch of warmth for the second consecutive day, and briefly, like a prisoner forgetting they were on death row, she realized they had a good shot at an outdoor Spring Bake-Off.

The smooth, cold metal door handle brought her back to reality, and Mila allowed her mother inside the discount store ahead of her.

"What's that look for?" Caryl asked.

"Huh? No look. I was just thinking."

They wandered slowly past discounted Easter baskets and last year's chocolates to the women's clothing section, where packed rows of off-brand blouses and pants promised treasures within.

"This is sharp," Caryl said, snagging a fuchsia silk blouse. She checked the price tag. "Thirty dollars? For *this*?"

"It's pretty," Mila offered. "You should get it."

"Not worth it." Caryl shoved the blouse back into the sea of clothes and stepped slowly to the right, eyes fixed on the options in front of her.

Mila and her mother didn't often shop together, but she needed an excuse to stay out of Pine Ridge. She didn't want to be around people she knew, people who, by now, had surely heard the news. *Disqualified.* The shame. The utter ridiculousness of thinking she had a shot at any of it. Everything she'd feared had come to fruition.

Should've kept my freaking head down.

"Hello? Earth to Mila?"

Mila blinked, catching her mother's curious eyes. Deep, penetrating, golden russet brown, the same color as Mila's. Eyes a person can't escape from.

"Sorry," Mila said. "What did you say?"

"I asked where you wanted to have lunch after this. I like that Italian place over on Culver."

Mila cleared her throat. Her appetite vanished the moment she'd hung up the phone with Vin. Jared had eaten nearly the entire bowl of anchovy spaghetti by himself. "Sure, that sounds good."

With a hand still resting on the clothing rack in front of her, Caryl turned. She lifted one heavily penciled eyebrow and lowered her chin. "Are you going to tell me what's going on? You look like you've got the weight of the world on your shoulders."

"It's nothing." The news burned Mila's skin from the inside out, like trying to conceal live sparklers inside her mouth.

"I don't buy it." Caryl stood firm. Unmoving. Mila knew how this would go if she fought back.

"I got a call last night." She swallowed, trying to force the frog from her throat. "I've been disqualified from the bake-off."

Caryl's eyebrows knit tighter. "What did you say?"

Mila gnawed on her thumbnail, chewed nearly to the quick, and pressed against the silk blouses to keep out of another shopper's way.

"There was a rule," Mila said. "The recipe had to be made from at least fifty percent locally sourced ingredients, and mine wasn't. That guy Vin called last night to tell me mine wasn't within the parameters, and I've been disqualified."

"Oh no." Caryl shook her head. "No. That's absurd. How far off were you?"

"Two percent."

Caryl's head jerked backward as if someone had snapped her with a wet towel. "Excuse me? Two percent? No. *Hell* no. What did you say to him?"

"I didn't say anything, really. What am I supposed to say?"

"Mila Bailey." Caryl's ruby-red lips tightened into a thin line. "*What* are you supposed to *say*? You're supposed to fight. You're supposed to go straight to the president of Indigo Hotels or whoever has authority over this little worm Vin and you're *supposed* to tell them that this is unacceptable."

Mila stared dumbly at her mother. The woman who had never encouraged her to fight for anything in her life. From getting cut from the eighth-grade basketball team to being wait-listed at her first-choice college, Caryl's motto had always been *If you'd kept your expectations low, you wouldn't have been disappointed.*

"Is that what you would do?" Mila said, accusation lacing her tone. "You'd fight?"

"No!" Caryl tossed her hands in the air. "But I'm not you. I'm not half as talented, and I've never had half the opportunities you have. You've worked too damn hard for too damn long to give this up now over a measly *two percent.* Two percent? That guy's got some nerve."

Vin did have some nerve. She wondered if he'd fought for her. If he'd tried to talk to the higher-ups at Indigo and ask them to reconsider. But then, it wasn't his responsibility to fight for her.

Caryl turned back to the blouses, snapping individual hangers as if they'd done her personal harm. After a moment, she stopped and turned back to Mila.

"In fact," Caryl said, "forget lunch. Forget shopping. We're going now."

Mila's throat tightened. "We're . . . what?"

"Come on. We're going to talk to this guy." She zipped up her coat and gave Mila a nod of encouragement.

"Mom, no. The rules are the rules. I didn't follow the rules, and now I'm out."

Caryl leaned forward, forcing Mila to shrink back. "Let me tell you something. Are you listening to me?"

Listening? Her words reverberated in Mila's bones. "Yes, ma'am."

"There are moments in life to sit back. There are moments to keep your head down, listen up, and do what you're told. Trust me. I know a lot about that. I've done a lot of it in my life out of fear."

A dark cloud passed over Caryl's face, her eyes momentarily unfocused. Her voice dropped as if someone might overhear.

"I don't even know what I was afraid of," she said. "What I do know is that I've spent a lot of years wishing I'd done a few things differently. I've taught you and your sisters to be good, kind people who follow the rules. But there are also moments in life, daughter, to fight back. There are people in this world who want to tear you down because they think they know what you deserve. And the minute you step too far, they want to put you back in your place."

Tears glistened in the corners of Caryl's eyes. Mila couldn't remember the last time she'd seen her tough-as-nails mother cry. It terrified her.

"You're very talented," Caryl said. "We all know it. If you let this Vin guy tell you what you do or don't deserve, you'll never forgive yourself. Don't let somebody else tell you what you're capable of."

From her toes to her hair, Mila trembled. The pure, unadulterated conviction in her mother's eyes, the steel in her voice, the pride in her jaw. They hadn't seen eye to eye on so many things over the years. This was something new. Maybe Caryl had her own regrets. Regrets she'd never shared with her daughter.

"Mom, I don't know."

"Don't let yourself be walked over." Caryl's voice rumbled like the first roll of thunder before a storm. "It's too easy to get used to."

Mila set her shoulders. She didn't want to be a doormat. Not today.

"There's a meeting for the finalists this afternoon at the community center," Mila said. "Vin will be there."

Caryl's lips spread into a grin. "Let's go."

As they pulled out of the parking lot, Mila flipped on the car radio, but nothing could distract her from the task at hand. What would she say? What were her demands? Every possible line ran through her head as she drove them back to Pine Ridge, but everything sounded foolish. Vin was smooth and intimidating, and he held all the cards.

As they approached the community center, Mila's heart beat in her throat. Her sweaty hands gripped the steering wheel, and she stared out across the parking lot as a few of the other finalists greeted one another warmly. She used to be one of them. And now she was on the outside. Looking in.

"I don't know if I can do this," Mila said. "It's bad enough that I'll have to announce in front of everyone that I've been disqualified, but what if he's a jerk about it? What if he makes me feel stupid on top of it all?"

Labored breaths escaped her lips as she watched Bob Santangelo, clad in crisp khakis and a navy-blue windbreaker, pick his way across the uneven parking lot toward the community center. She'd have to do this in front of Bob and the other contestants. Would they laugh at her? See her for the do-as-you're-told, small-town girl she'd been her entire life?

Something just beyond the squat gray building caught her eye. In a black wool pea coat, his face set in grim determination and walking at an impressive clip, was Jared.

"What is he doing here?" Mila muttered.

Caryl's lips twitched into a half smile. "Looks like he's ready to bust somebody's lip."

Mila burst out of the car and jogged toward him.

"Hey," he said, lips parted in surprise. "You're here."

"Yeah," she said. "My mom convinced me to come and talk to Vin. What are you doing here?"

Jared's beautiful mouth curved up on one side, and he peered over Mila's shoulder to her car, where Caryl still sat in the passenger seat. "Your mom convinced you?"

Mila's eyebrows jumped. "I know."

"That's incredible." He reached forward to brush a curl off her forehead. Her skin tingled with his touch. "Well, I definitely wasn't here to talk to Vin myself. Definitely was not going to scream at him until he let you back into the contest. So you don't have to worry about that."

She tilted her head. "You were not."

"I just said I wasn't." Secrets sparkled in his eyes.

"J, I don't need you to step in and take care of things for me, okay?"

"I know you don't," he said. "I just couldn't stand by and let you give up on this opportunity."

"Well," she said. "I'm here to fight for it myself."

"Hell yeah, you are." He kissed her, quickly and with purpose, as if infusing her with all the belief she didn't quite feel yet herself. "Go get 'em."

Mila turned and approached the community center on heavy limbs, her heart slamming against her chest. She'd never confronted anybody in her life, save for the time in middle school when Megan Ratcliffe had abruptly stopped sitting with Mila at lunch. Mila asked her why, and Megan responded, in front of the entire lunchroom, that she'd been "skeeved out" by Mila's tiny house, where her family lived on top of one another, and Mila and her two sisters had to share one room like a "freaking jail cell." Mila had been so painfully embarrassed, so utterly doused in shame, that she'd never sought out that feeling again. Better to just keep her head down. The Bailey family way.

But there was no keeping her head down now. If she wanted justice, she had to fight. No matter what the outcome might be.

She pushed into the community center and glanced around. Nine finalists milled about, chatting amiably and removing outerwear. At the front of the room, in a tiny cluster, stood Chef Constance and celebrity judge Denny Torres, with Vin close by scrolling through his phone.

What would they do when they saw her? Turn their judgmental stares on her, remind her that she shouldn't be here, that she didn't belong? That no matter what she did, no matter what path she took, she'd always be on the outside? The awkward teenager, heavy with shame, rose up inside her and told her to turn around, run away, save herself from the devastating weight of other people's opinions.

"Mila!" Her heart stutter-stepped as Kim, the spunky redhead from Buffalo with a penchant for sidecars, bounced toward her. She squeezed Mila in a hug and pulled back, a beaming smile shining from her round face. "Oh, honey, it's good to see you. Isn't this all just so exciting? Home stretch."

Indigo Hotels had offered discounted accommodations at local bed-and-breakfasts for out-of-town contestants, and most were treating the week like a vacation. The carefree smile on Kim's face made Mila's stomach turn. What she wouldn't give for an ounce of that unbridled joy.

"Mila?" Vin's voice cut through the room. "What are you doing here?"

The room fell silent as Vin approached, his once handsome face now twisted in anger.

"What do you mean, what's she doing here?" Kim snapped. "She's a finalist like the rest of us. Why shouldn't she be here?"

Vin's chin jutted out as if physically trying to keep the words from spilling out of his mouth. "Mila knows what I mean."

"I was hoping we could talk," Mila said. She'd meant her voice to sound as steely and sure as Caryl's had two hours earlier, but instead, she sounded like a child asking for an extra cookie after dinner. She tried again. "In fact, I think you owe me that."

Vin blinked, his mouth falling open. "Oh, do I?"

"What's going on?" Bob Santangelo chimed in.

Mila straightened, readying herself for yet another bully's input.

"Nothing," Mila said. "I just need to talk to Vin."

"There's nothing to talk about," Vin said. "You're disqualified. That's it. No discussion."

"Disqualified?" Kim's voice turned breathy. "Why? Her pie was incredible!"

Mila choked back the wave of emotion turning her legs wobbly. All eyes landed on her, and she watched them as if through beveled glass. Warped, with confused stares and demanding postures. They wanted answers.

She bit down on her lip, waiting for Vin to speak. Over his shoulder, past the sea of folding chairs in the community center and out the front window, stood Jared. When their eyes met, he raised a hand and smiled.

A surge of confidence rose up in her chest. She summoned all the positive energy she could, trapped and caged everything Jared had tried to convince her of over the past few weeks, and planted her feet firmly on the ground. She had to do this.

Now or never.

"According to the rules," Mila said, "each recipe had to have at least half the ingredients sourced from New York State. Mine came in at forty-eight percent, and the legal team at Indigo Hotels decided it wasn't fair to the rest of the contestants. That I should be disqualified."

She cleared her throat, letting the news settle over the room. "I don't want anyone to bend the rules for me, and I was going to just take the ruling and walk away. But this contest means so much to me. It means a lot to my family. I've worked so hard, and I couldn't let two percent keep me from trying. So I thought I'd come here and see if there was anything I could do. Anything at all."

"But that's absurd!" Kim said, staring hard at Vin. "Who cares if she was at forty-eight percent? That's close enough, isn't it?"

"No," Vin snapped. "I'm afraid it's not *close enough*. There are rules. We can't just bend them for one contestant when everyone else fell within the parameters. This isn't Little League. We're not handing out participation trophies."

"Sounds like it's a legal issue," Bob Santangelo chimed in. "We're talking about a big corporation here, people. They've gotta cover their asses. Legally. If they say she's out, she's out."

Bob's bloated face turned pink as Mila shot him a tight-lipped glare.

"Well," Arthur Allen said, "I, for one, don't care. So she's at forty-eight percent. Her pie was damned good, and I'll bet if you asked her, she'd remake that pie with one hundred percent New York–sourced ingredients and it would still be in the top ten."

"I'm with him," someone else chimed in.

"Me, too," Kim said. She crossed her arms across her chest defiantly.

"Vin." Chef Constance approached. "Who did this decision come from? Corporate? I certainly didn't hear anything about it."

Vin's jaw ticked back and forth, and he set his hands on his hips. "I discussed it with corporate, yes."

Denny Torres sauntered toward them, his imposing football player frame daring anyone not to notice him. He ran a hand over his floppy hair, ruffling the already unruly style. "Seems sort of strict," Denny said. "They really said she should be disqualified?"

Vin swallowed, staring up at his friend. He crossed his arms over his chest, eyes darting around the group. No words left his mouth.

"Listen," Kim said, "I don't give a tick if only forty-eight percent of her ingredients were sourced from New York State. If she'd been at ten percent, okay, maybe. If my vote counts for anything, I say let her stay in the competition. She's damn talented, and if I'm gonna win this thing, I want to beat the best."

Kim winked, and Mila blinked back tears.

"I'm with her," Arthur Allen said. "Do we get a vote?"

More voices rose up from the room, everyone but Bob

Santangelo agreeing that if they had anything to say about it, they wanted Mila back in the competition.

"It's not up to me, okay?" Vin barked. "I talked to corporate. This is the decision."

"I dunno, man," Denny said. "Maybe give it another shot? Seems really unfair to let it go this far and then kick her out now."

"Again," Vin said. "*I* am not kicking her out. The rules are the rules."

Mila breathed deep. She appreciated the support, but this was on her.

"I know that," she said. "I'm asking if there's any way for you to reach out to corporate one more time and see if there's anything I can do. Please, Vin."

"Hope Indigo doesn't get sued," Bob barked.

Vin sucked his teeth and gave Mila a once-over, as if the answer waited in her outfit. "Fine. I'll call them after the meeting. But I'm not making any promises."

The group, save Bob, erupted into applause, and Mila released a nervous laugh, relief flooding her veins. One last attempt. It wasn't a guarantee. But it was something.

"Mila!" Sydney shouted over the low blend of voices filling Sam's living room and skipped toward the door to clobber Mila in a hug.

"Happy birthday, Syd," Mila said. With one arm she hugged the birthday girl, and in the other she balanced a dulce de leche cake.

"How dare you." Sydney took the cake as her eyes glittered. "Did Jared tell you this was my favorite?"

"You think my dopey little brother remembered your favorite cake?" Sam approached, slinging an arm around Sydney's shoulder and kissing her cheek. "I commissioned this work of art."

Mila's cheeks heated from the compliment and from being in the presence of two people so obviously in love with each other. Standing within a three-foot radius of Sam and Sydney together felt like sitting too close to the fire.

"Well, you're both amazing," Sydney said. "Thank you."

"Where's Jared?" Sam asked. "He didn't come with you?"

Word had spread through town like wildfire, and now everywhere she went, people asked where Jared was. As if they couldn't physically be separated or the town itself would implode.

"He's coming from Inlet," Mila said. "He had a house to show."

"But he'll be here soon?" Sam's brows met in the middle, and for the first time since she'd walked in, Mila noticed his demeanor. Fidgeting, nervous, blushing. Sam Kirkland didn't get nervous, and if he did, he certainly never showed his hand.

"What's your deal?" Sydney asked, her eyes still trained on the cake. "It's only seven o'clock. He'll be here."

Sam cleared his throat and shoved his hands into his pants pockets. "Just wanted him to get here already."

Sydney rolled her eyes. "You're really terrible at keeping secrets, you know that?"

The front door opened behind Mila, and she didn't have to turn to know it was him. The fresh spring breeze carried his scent in, nearly knocking her forward. He'd worn the same cologne since high school, but it smelled different now. Darker. More intoxicating.

"Hi," he said, his lips curling into a smile as he gazed at her. He brushed her hand by way of greeting, and she clamped down on her lower lip to keep from grinning like an idiot. His display of support at the community center earlier had meant the world to her, and she planned to show him as much at her apartment after the party.

The bake-off decision still swirled in her stomach,

threatening to derail her evening at any moment. But she kept her phone close, checked every few minutes for a missed call from Vin, and hoped for the best. Hope was all she had.

Mila poured herself a glass of wine and settled into a corner of Sam's couch to chat with Nicole, Calvin, and Denny Torres, who seemed to slip right into the Pine Ridge social scene like a fish to water.

They fell into easy conversation about the town's recent changes. Sydney's shop had been doing particularly well lately after *Good Morning America* featured the Loving Page. Between Indigo Hotels and the success of the bookstore, Pine Ridge thrived.

"I hope your man can fight the pull of Pine Ridge," Denny said, gesturing to Mila with a red plastic cup filled with beer. "We're trying to get him to come work with Indigo."

"I thought Vin vetoed that," Mila said. Even his name on her tongue tasted foul.

"Eh," Denny said, "Vin's got a chip on his shoulder. He worked his way up the company, and I think he feels protective. He's not a bad guy. He's just a little prickly. And he'd be lucky to have Jared on board."

Mila swallowed down the uneasy fizzing in her chest. She thought that plan had been nixed. One small victory on the path to keeping Jared in Pine Ridge. She wanted only good things for him, but if those good things kept him living five minutes away from her, all the better.

Mila's phone buzzed in her back pocket, and she sat bolt upright on the couch, her sauvignon blanc sloshing over the rim of her glass and onto Nicole's jeans.

"Smooth move, Lee Lee." Nicole sent her the evil eye, but Mila barely saw it. The name on her phone had her heart beating in her throat.

Vin.

She opened the text.

Gimme a call when you can.

Mila pushed past the clusters of party guests, apologizing as she went, until she reached the kitchen. She snagged Sam's cordless phone from the wall and slipped down the hallway into the guest bedroom, closing the door behind her.

"Hello?"

"Vin, it's Mila. I just got your text."

He cleared his throat. "Yeah, so I talked to corporate again. They said if all nine finalists agreed they wanted you in the competition, you'd be allowed back in."

Her teeth chattered, the chill in the dark bedroom seeping past her T-shirt and coating her skin in goose bumps. Bob Santangelo's sneering face floated through her mind. She had no idea why he disliked her so much, but if her success came down to his approval, she had a better shot of qualifying for the US Olympic rowing team.

"Okay?"

"I called each contestant. Bob Santangelo was on the fence, but ultimately he agreed. And so did everyone else."

"Oh God." Relief rushed out of her in one massive exhale, and she doubled over, letting the bed catch her as she dropped. "Thank you. Thank you *so* much. You didn't have to go out on a limb for me, but you did. I really appreciate it."

"Listen," he said. "I wasn't trying to be a dick. And I wasn't trying to punish you or anything."

She pinched the bridge of her nose and remembered his disgusted face at the hotel when she started to tell him she didn't want to go out again. No, definitely not trying to punish her.

"I didn't think that," she said.

"I just wanted to run the contest the right way. It's the first time I've been entrusted with something like this, you know? I'm the one who found Chef Constance, I'm the one who recruited Denny. The locally sourced ingredients were my idea. This whole thing is on my shoulders."

The bedroom door creaked open, and she turned. Backlit by the glow of the living room, Jared took one step inside. His green eyes widened.

"I understand," Mila said to Vin. "Truly I do."

"All right." He sniffed. "Good luck in the rest of the competition. And if you have any questions about the rules or anything . . ."

"I'll call you," she said. "Promise."

She punched the power button on the phone and looked up, her lips tightening in an attempt to control all the emotion churning inside her.

"You're back in?" Jared said. He whispered, the words skipping across her skin and landing deep inside her chest.

"I'm back in."

"Yes!" His eyes creased up, lost in the widest smile Mila had ever seen on him, and she leaped into his arms. With one hand firmly against her neck and the other clutching her back, he spun her around, all the adrenaline of the day seeping out of her like a sieve.

"God, I'm so relieved," she said. "I'm so freaking relieved."

He relaxed his grip, just enough to meet her gaze, and caught her mouth with his. She sunk into his body, letting him hold her up. Letting him support her. He'd held her hand throughout the competition, urged her forward when all she wanted was to turn back. Without him, where would she be?

His arms tightened, molding to her as if their bodies had once been cut from a single stone and were just now fitting back together. A greedy moan traveled from her throat into his, and he responded with fervor, her lips stinging from the intensity of the kiss.

"Hey." He broke away, his mouth slightly swollen and his eyes lowered and hazy. "We can't have sex in my brother's guest room at his girlfriend's birthday party. As much as I want to."

She trailed her tongue across her lower lip, still tasting him there. "You sure?"

A half-drunk smile crossed his mouth. "I mean . . . no."

With knowing fingers, she scraped her nails across his scalp, and he huffed out a breath as his eyelids closed. Just as she placed the tiniest flutter of a kiss on the hollow of his throat, three loud knocks broke through the moment.

"If you're banging in there, I'll punch you in the throat, J."

Jared laughed as his brother's voice effectively killed the mood, and he squeezed Mila's butt and raised his eyebrows. "Guess he's not cool with it."

"Maybe we don't have to stay too much longer," she said. Clouds filled her head, the release of the day's tension and the warm scent of his skin combining to turn her brain to mush. *Heaven on earth.*

"Once they sing 'Happy Birthday,' we're out."

With linked hands, they emerged from the bedroom and rejoined the party. Mila's heart lightened as if a lead balloon had been released from her chest. The good news fizzled out of her, and her friends crowded around, each of their faces reflecting the relief in her words. Nicole pummeled her in a hug, and Sydney squeezed the hand Jared wasn't already clutching.

She'd never felt so loved, so overwhelmingly in the right place at the right time. She wanted to bottle this feeling and wear it like perfume on the days she didn't quite feel herself.

"I knew Vin would do the right thing," Denny said. He puffed up his wide chest and grinned down at Mila with a lopsided smile. "Told you he's not all bad."

"Still wins Douchebag of the Year in my book," Jared said.

Denny gave Jared a gentle shove and laughed, tossing back the last of his beer. "Hey, dude, this town's all right. I thought this was gonna be the most boring three weeks of my life, but I'm having a pretty good time."

"Glad we could bust up your small-town stereotypes,"

Mila said with a smile. She watched Jared's face, hoping some of Denny's poeticism about Pine Ridge rubbed off on her not-yet-boyfriend. As content as she was with what they were doing now, she wanted more.

She couldn't help herself. The tiny flicker of a dream that Aunt Georgie breathed life into had turned into an inferno. Everything seemed possible now. And if she could overcome odds and make it to the final round of a contest she'd always been too intimidated to enter, why couldn't she have the man of her dreams and a family in her hometown to boot?

Mila poured herself another glass of wine, content to stay at the party as long as she wanted. There would be no hurrying home tonight, no escaping to her apartment for a night of good sleep before an early shift at the diner. Jared and her friends filled Sam's house, and she wanted nothing more than to remain a part of it.

"Holy shit!" Sam's buddy Greg's voice bellowed through the house. His large frame half filled the view out the sliding glass door, but everyone crowded around, eager to claim a bit of the space.

Mila wandered over as the words "engaged" and "proposal" wove through the group like steam. She peered through the sliding glass doors and down the darkened hill to where Sam and Sydney stood next to the water, their silhouettes illuminated by the moonlit lake.

"He's proposing!" one of the women squealed.

There was no bended knee, no grandiose gesture with lifted arms and fireworks and a massive diamond visible from the house. Syd and Sam stood without a slip of space between them, Sydney's chin bowed and Sam's hands trailing through her hair.

Huddled around the window, the group let out a collective gasp as he reached into his back pocket, pulled something tiny out, and clutched her hand at her chest. Another moment passed, and she was off her feet, Sam's arms wrapped tightly around her.

"*Ho-ly shit*," Jared whispered.

"Did you know he was doing this?" Mila asked. She couldn't believe her tears, couldn't believe something so sweet and removed from her own life could tug at her heart this way. But it was Sam and Syd. Two people so perfect together you had to wonder what kind of pod they came from.

Mila tore her eyes away from the window, ready to share the joy radiating from her skin with the man she hoped to someday share a similar future with.

Jared's face pinched. Cold and shadowed in gray. He sucked his bottom lip between his teeth, eyes fixed on the scene outside.

His lips tensed and tightened, a tiny muscle flexing and releasing at the sharp angle of his jaw.

Something was wrong. Very wrong.

chapter **eighteen**

The scene played out in front of him like a bad rom-com. The happy couple. Clinging to each other as if their very existence depended on physical connection.

Jared knew about Sam's plan to propose, but seeing it play out with his own eyes turned his stomach in ways he wasn't prepared for. And Mila's eyes bore into him, tears sparkling on her lashes, as if to say, *Am I next?*

"What's wrong with you?" she said. "Don't tell me you're not happy about this. You love Sydney."

He clenched his teeth. What could he say? *Please don't ask this of me.*

"I . . . I'm fine." It was all he could muster. "I'm just surprised."

He couldn't look at her. She'd see right through him. With his stomach twisting, he turned away from the window and went into the kitchen. He dug through the fridge in search of a fresh beer. The rush of cold revived him, gave him a moment to himself. He knew he'd have to face Mila eventually.

The sliding glass doors opened, and a raucous cheer rose up from Sam and Syd's best friends and family. Jared watched from a safe distance as the group swallowed them up, squealing and bubbling over with excitement.

Jared gulped his beer, his stomach still in knots. What in the actual fuck was wrong with him? Every move Sydney made, every word she said, only proved how much she loved his brother. She and Sam had been through hell and back, both separately and together, and as a couple, they just made sense.

Something in his gut, though, clanged like warning bells. *You're next.* Every bad sitcom he'd ever seen played on a loop inside his mind, the nagging wives, the exhausted husbands, the screaming kids. He saw his parents, actively avoiding each other within the walls of their little house and speaking to Jared and Sam but rarely to each other.

Syd and Sam deserved each other. But the unbridled joy surrounding their engagement made Jared feel like a fraud.

"You're being an asshole." Mila's voice cut through his anxiety.

He crossed one arm across his chest and refused her pointed gaze. "I'm just giving them some space."

"No, you're not. I know exactly what you're doing."

"Don't analyze me." His words lashed out, sharper than he'd meant them. But he didn't want to answer to anyone. Not now. And not to the one person who was supposed to understand him and everything he'd seen, everything he'd been through.

"Fine, Jared. You want to be a pouty little boy and take the focus away from your brother right now? Go ahead. But I'd be a terrible friend if I didn't tell you how selfish you're being."

She spun away, leaving him shakier than ever in a cloud of her new, sultry perfume. Despite his frayed nerves, his mind traveled back to their night at the hotel and a different part of him awoke. The softness of her skin, the way she shattered at his touch. He'd loved her as a friend his whole life, and now he needed her with something deeper, something more primal. He couldn't shake it, despite his gut reaction to the idea of forever.

Jared hovered near the kitchen table, unable to avoid his brother any longer. Sydney busted free of the crowd ahead of Sam and shrieked at Jared, launching herself at him and nearly propelling him into the table.

"Jesus," he said, wrapping an arm around her as she rocked back and forth. "You almost killed me, woman."

She pulled back, her face glowing and shiny with joy. "You're gonna be my brother, Jared! Does that terrify you?"

He laughed, a tiny fissure forming in his concrete heart. "Of course. You always make me feel so dumb when we watch football together."

Her face settled into forced seriousness. "I'll smarten you up yet, kid."

She squeezed his neck one more time before turning away and slipping back into Sam's arms. Jared watched cautiously as she nuzzled his brother's neck.

They're so happy. He shook the thought away. They were one in a million.

As Sydney trailed away, returning to the buzzing group behind her, Sam walked slowly toward his brother. One eyebrow raised in question.

"Congrats," Jared said, his voice as tight as his chest. "Smooth, too. Private, then public."

Sam shrugged. "I knew she'd want it that way."

How would Mila want it? He forced the thought away, chasing it from his brain with another swig of beer. Mila's engagement wouldn't involve Jared. Some other guy, some reliable, boring dude would ask her to marry him. He'd give her babies and a big house and a family of in-laws to spend holidays with. They'd all gather around the Bailey family dinner table, a picture-perfect postcard of something unsustainable.

"Best man?" Sam asked.

Jared groaned, even the thought of strip clubs and tuxes unable to get his juices flowing. "Fine."

Sam shook his head. "You really can't get it up for my engagement? You can't even fake it? The idea of marriage is so repulsive to you that you can't be happy when it happens to someone else?"

Shame sluiced through Jared. His issues with marriage were his alone, and he shuddered at the idea that he'd diminished Sam's night in any way. He didn't know why his heart hammered in his chest as if he'd just stared down a black bear. But Mila lingered across the room, her eyes finding him every other minute, and he knew what he was setting himself up for. Disappointment. Hers and his.

"That's not it," Jared said. "I'm . . ."

What could he say? *I'm a selfish prick, and I should get out of this town as soon as possible. Not so it doesn't ruin me, but so that I don't ruin it.*

"I'm sorry," Jared said. "I'm really freaking happy for you guys. You're getting everything you wanted, dude. It's all working out for you. That's it."

Sam hesitated, weighing his little brother with a thoughtful stare. He ran a hand across his beard. "I don't believe you."

"Just because I'd rather be dead than married doesn't mean I can't be happy for you."

A wry smile tugged at Sam's lips. "Hate to tell you, Jare, but I think you're inching closer to it than you even realize. You accidentally fell into the most perfect relationship you could find."

Jared's throat dried up. "We're just having fun."

Sam laughed. "Sure."

"Seriously," Jared said. "She's the one who said it first."

Sam turned, already on his way back to Sydney. "Just call me when you need help figuring out what kind of proposal you think Mila might want, all right?"

Jared stood alone in the kitchen until his beer bottle ran dry.

The room tilted and swayed in front of him, but it wasn't the alcohol. He'd had only a couple of drinks, but he'd had them quickly.

"I got him from here." Mila's voice cut through his soupy brain. "Thanks, Greg."

Jared collapsed into his couch, the squishy fabric enveloping him like the hug Mila had refused him all night long. He couldn't blame her. No one at the party seemed especially happy to talk to him.

The front door closed behind Greg, leaving Jared and Mila submerged in a stony silence. She stood in front of the couch with one hand on her hip, the other lifted to her face. The thumb wedged between her straight, white teeth, and her eyebrows told an entire story of her disappointment in him.

"Did you have fun tonight?" he asked. "I didn't need Greg to escort me home, by the way. I'm perfectly fine to drive myself home from my brother's house. I've done it a billion times."

Mila lowered her gaze, a subtle shake of her head sending her curls dancing around her face. She pushed the hair away with a labored motion, as if even that movement proved inconvenient.

"Listen," she said. "I'm gonna go. I just wanted to make sure you were okay."

"No," he said. "Don't go. Why? Why are you going?"

"Because you're hammered." Her lips flattened. That wasn't the reason. He could see it in her face.

"I'm not *hammered*. I had three drinks."

"I'm not arguing with you right now. It doesn't matter how many drinks you had. You've been annoying as shit all night long, and I'm not dealing with pissed-off Jared who is also intoxicated. Okay?"

He swallowed past his gummy tongue and pushed himself to the edge of the couch. He looked up at her. She hadn't turned on the lights, but the moon shone so bright tonight it might as well have been a spotlight. Her dark, glossy curls glowed, and her eyes bore into him like glowing orbs threatening to tell the future.

He owed her something. He raked a hand through his hair and cleared his throat. *Sober up. Sober up. Sober up.*

"Just . . . don't go," he said. "Please?"

The crease between her brows softened slightly, and her chest rose and fell on a contemplative breath. Her breasts pressed against her thin, striped cotton T-shirt, and he scolded himself for ruining the opportunity to sleep with her tonight. He'd been dreaming about it all day. And now this.

"You're an asshole."

"*I'm* an asshole?" Her sharp words stung his cheeks.

"No," he groaned. "I was talking to myself."

"I'll agree with that." She paused for another moment before lowering herself to the couch. She left a sizable distance between them.

"Can we just go to sleep? It's been a weird night, and I don't want to talk about it anymore."

She bit her lip and turned her gaze on him. Slowly. Thoughtfully. It made him itch.

"What?" he asked.

"I don't get it."

He cleared his throat and flopped back onto the couch. Fine. So they were gonna have this conversation now.

"You don't have to get it," he said. "You just have to respect how I feel."

A shaky breath left her lips. "Maybe that's the problem. Maybe I don't respect how you feel. You have this toxic view of marriage, as if anybody who participates is a total asshole."

He gritted his teeth. She understood him better than he thought. What she didn't know was that for close to twenty years he'd rolled his eyes at marriage, committed to sticking with his hatred of the entire institution.

Until that kiss.

The moment she'd let him lay his lips on her, his vision changed, like when the eye doctor clicked to a new lens. Forget the paperwork, forget the legally binding contract. Mila belonged to him, body and heart and soul. It didn't look like marriage, didn't feel like the shackles he'd always thought of it as. She was the rock. The one constant he never had to worry about. He found himself wondering every day what a life with her would look like.

And that scared the shit out of him more than anything.

"I told you I don't want to talk about this," he said. His words settled into the quiet, dark living room, and she snorted.

"Shocking. When shit gets tough, Jared Kirkland wants to crack a joke or run the other way."

"I don't have time for this." He pushed on his knees until he stood, and walked past her toward his bedroom. By the time he reached his bed, he expected her to be halfway to her car.

Instead, a strong hand gripped his shoulder and spun him around. Her jaw set, her nostrils flared, her eyes blazed like fire beneath furious brows. He'd never really seen her truly angry.

Damn, it was hot.

"No," she said. "We're talking about this now. I don't care if you never want to marry me, Jared. I don't care if this is the last night we ever spend together. If you don't explain to me what's going on inside your head, I'll fucking burst. I can't take the tiptoeing, the egg shells, the wondering. You had a saint of a mother. She did *everything* for you and Sam. The only parent with a full-time job who also managed to make it to every soccer game, every parent teacher night, every church Christmas pageant. She was your biggest cheerleader, and all you could do in return was roll your eyes at her and act out like a toddler who didn't get his way. After all this time, I still can't imagine how a woman that dedicated could make you think having a wife is a death sentence."

"You don't know shit." The words crackled against his teeth. "My dad never wanted to get married, did you know that? But he did it for her. Then after they got married and had a kid, he turned into a raging alcoholic. They ruined each other's lives. So then after the guy dies, she puts all her energy into punishing her youngest son, making him feel like he could never do enough. Why was I held to some ridiculous standard that none of the other men in my family were held to?"

Mila blinked as if trying to swallow the idea. "She wanted the best for you."

"I'm tired of that line." His voice simmered. "Look at how happy Sam is. She treated him like a golden child and me like the kid she hoped would move out at sixteen."

Mila licked her lips, the anger fading slowly from her features. She took a step toward him. "Did you ever ask her about it? Really talk to her? I'm sure she had her reasons, J."

"We argued about it all the time." His chest burned. It was half true. She'd call him on his bullshit—a skipped class, a D on an exam, one too many jokes cracked during soccer practice—and he'd lash out. Rinse. Repeat. Every year of his life until she died. And even as she lay dying in hospice, she asked relentlessly about his commissions, if he was applying to jobs outside North Country, if he'd read that article in the *Times* about the booming real estate scene in Minneapolis. When Sam showed up at the hospital, she asked only how he was doing.

Mila tilted her head, deepening her stare until Jared couldn't stand it anymore. He turned away from her and fixed his attention to his dresser, where a handful of loose bills and business cards required immediate sorting.

"Your mom's life didn't go the way she planned," she offered. "I knew her, J. She was quiet, kept to herself, but she had a heart of gold. She left me a twenty-dollar tip at the diner no matter if she ordered a cup of coffee or a full meal."

"Well, great." His fingers paused over the faded edges of a paper card touting insurance services from some jerk in Albany. "Happy to hear she treated you like the second kid she never had. You and Sam. Both privileged to sides of my mother I never got to see."

"Maybe you pushed her away," Mila said.

He twisted his lips in a bitter smile and turned his face until he could see her clearly. "I'm the kid, Mila. She's the parent. She's not supposed to let me push her away."

Mila swallowed, her delicate throat contracting. The tiny jewel in her nose sparkled as a thin shaft of moonlight fell on her face.

"She's not supposed to let you push her away."

He shivered, his skin puckering with goose bumps. The words hung between them and mutated until they both saw the twisted form clearly. All this time. He'd been waiting for his mother to make an effort, to prove that she loved her son more than she'd loved her husband. And in turn, he'd been waiting for Mila to prove something, too.

"How hard are people supposed to fight for you, Jared?"

His lips parted. "I don't know what you mean."

"I love you, do you know that?" Her chin trembled, the corners of her eyes creasing up. "And I've worked really hard for you. I've pushed past a lot of my own shit to try to meet you in the middle. I've tried to understand where you're coming from and be flexible with you because you have such hard-and-fast rules about marriage. I've been supportive of anything you wanted to do in your career, including moving away."

Shame hung on his shoulders like a weighted vest.

"I've had to confront my own shit," she said. "I've had to examine *my*self and try to figure out why I'm so scared of certain things. Why I'm afraid to try. Why I'm afraid to draw attention to myself. But I'm changing, Jared. I'm becoming a better version of myself. And all this time, you're staying the same. Refusing to move forward. Refusing to examine your own bullshit."

He waited for her to continue, waited for her to swing back around to the love part. She loved him. If she loved him, maybe she'd be patient with him. Maybe she'd hang around until he figured all this out.

"I've never had to think about it before," he said lamely. "I've always been on my own."

"You have not. You've always had Sam, and you've always pushed him away, too."

He settled his shoulders, straightened his spine. She didn't know what it was like. To be part of a family but always be on the outside. First Sam and his mother had each other, then Sam had Sydney. Jared had always been the second kid. The afterthought.

"I'm scared," she said. Her voice cracked and, with it, his heart. He'd do anything not to hurt her.

"What are you scared of?" He took a timid step toward her, giving her his full attention.

She pressed her lips together, and her eyebrows met in the middle. "I'm scared you're gonna hurt me. This thing we're doing is a huge gamble. I'm trying so hard to hang back and see where it goes, but I'm in, J. You could really hurt me if you wanted to. And that's terrifying."

His confidence slipped, like an ice floe breaking apart, each piece slowly shifting away from the whole. He could hurt her. Maybe he already had.

"Then maybe we should quit while we're ahead."

Her hands hung limply at her sides as she stared at him, the same tortured look pinching her face. "Are you serious?"

No. I love you. And I can't even imagine myself with anyone else. "You're right. You're gonna get hurt. And I can't let myself be the one to hurt you."

He had to look away. He tore his eyes from her, stared hard at the stack of business cards and dollar bills on his dresser top. A paper clip occupied his trembling fingers while his mind raced with thoughts of her. His best friend. His lover. The woman who'd claimed every space in his life and in his heart and who now stood before him, begging him to spare her.

He wouldn't turn into either of his parents. And he wouldn't take her down with him.

"You're really ready to let this go?" she whispered.

A foot to his left sat his bed. For a brief, blissful moment he imagined taking her hand and falling into that bed and pretending like no one else in the world existed but them.

His heart skipped, and his stomach roiled. That wasn't real life. Real life was hard and messy and painful, and he'd be better off alone.

"No," he said. "I'm not ready. But I think we both know where it's headed. I don't want to do that to you. It's not fair."

"You're a coward."

He nodded slowly. "I know."

A slow tear rolled down each of her cheeks, and she wiped at them furiously, as if she'd been betrayed by her own body. "All right. Fine. Then I guess this is it. You're free now."

With one last smoldering glare, she sucked her lower lip into her mouth, turned over her shoulder, and walked out.

chapter **nineteen**

The morning of the Spring Festival opening day, Mila awoke in a veritable puddle of her own sweat, her T-shirt clinging to her chest and her shorts bunched around her hips. The dream had been so real. Denny Torres had joined her family for Sunday dinner, and when she passed the bowl of sweet potatoes, he grimaced and told her he didn't eat meat. No matter how she tried to explain to him there wasn't any meat in the dish, he refused.

The more she relived the dream, the more foolish it sounded. But the simple act of a judge refusing food sent her into a spiral.

She crawled out of bed, shoved her feet into Sherpa-lined slippers, and shuffled into the kitchen. Coffee. She needed coffee. Only coffee could center her wobbly brain.

Coffee and Jared.

With fingers still trembling from her panic dream, she retrieved the coffee grounds from the cabinet and filled her French press. The French press she bought on their road trip to Vermont last summer during one of his breaks from Chloe. They'd spent the day hopping around breweries, hiking, and screaming the lyrics to their favorite eighties songs while they drove through a torrential downpour back home.

She twisted the oven knob to ignite the burner under her teakettle and stared hard at the flickering blue flame. God, she missed him. It had been only four days since Sam and Syd's engagement, but each day stretched on longer than the last.

She'd suspended all her beliefs for him. Paused the security force field around her heart to let him in. And he'd done exactly what she'd feared he'd do.

Maybe he'd already moved on. Maybe he'd called Chloe the second Mila had left his house to see if his ex would give him another shot. Maybe they were in his bed right now and he was saying all the same things to Chloe that he'd said to Mila during their night in the hotel.

She chewed on her thumbnail, her teeth finding barely any nail left to bite. Her mother would see her hands and raise that damned eyebrow, and Mila would feel even worse about what a disappointment this whole thing had been.

What a disappointment *she'd* been.

Her phone buzzed as the teakettle began to whistle. She filled the French press carafe with steaming water before opening her phone and checking the message.

She knew it wouldn't be him. And yet, she hoped.

You up? I'm nearby. I've got muffins.

Mila snorted a bitter laugh and told Nicole she was up.

Less than five minutes later, Nicole appeared at the door wearing her Adirondack Mountain Rescue jacket and carrying a paper McDonagh's Bakery bag. Worry etched her face.

"Breakup sweets, at your service."

Mila rolled her eyes and poured the coffee into two mugs. "It's not a breakup. We gave the romantic thing a shot, and it didn't work out. No big deal."

Nicole settled onto a kitchen stool and placed two giant blueberry muffins on the counter. The domed tops glittered with crunchy sugar crystals, and despite Mila's salivary glands jumping to attention, her stomach recoiled.

"I already ate," Mila said.

"You did not," Nicole countered. "Don't try to tell me you had food before coffee. I know you too well."

Mila tore a tiny chunk from one of the muffins and popped it into her mouth. Chewing and swallowing proved almost as difficult as forcing Jared from her mind.

"You know," Mila said, "you don't have to keep coming over here to check on me. I'm fine. I know the whole town thinks I'm going to crumble into some inconsolable lump of sadness, but I promise you, I'll be all right."

Nicole pursed her lips and tugged at her earlobe, the surest way to let Mila know a lie was forthcoming. Nicole always told the truth.

"I really only came over to bring you breakfast," she said. "I knew you took a few days off to test and make your bake-off pie, and I wanted you to have sustenance."

"You're very sweet," Mila said.

"Oooh," Nicole cooed, fixing her eyes on the counter next to the stove. "Apples. Did you reach out to Uncle Paul? Is that what the pie is? Apple?"

Mila had refused to share her idea with anybody, going so far as to visit Uncle Paul's apple farm herself and telling him the only way she'd promote the farm was if he promised to keep her pie plan a secret. She didn't want her neighbors' questioning eyes, their pitying stares. *Well, she's heartbroken over him, of course she made his favorite pie for the contest.*

Eventually she'd have to admit to herself that she'd chosen this particular pie because it linked her to Jared in a supremely intimate way: food. But she'd also taken that caramel apple pie recipe and turned it on its head.

Instead of peeling and slicing the apples, she set cored apple halves face down in the deep-dish pie plate, poured butter and brown sugar over them, and developed an airy custard filling to fill the space around the fruit. A thin layer of flaky sourdough crust covered the custard, and when the whole thing came out of the oven, crackling and bubbly sweet with caramel goodness, she sprinkled a barely there crumble of crispy bacon bits.

"I'm not telling you," Mila said. "You'll see it Saturday."

Nicole pursed her lips and raised an eyebrow, yanking up the sleeves of her hunter-green jacket to reveal the tiny rose tattoo she'd secretly obtained when she turned eighteen. Mila had gone with her and chickened out before she could finish writing her name on the paperwork.

"Whatever it is," Nicole said, "I know you're gonna kill it."

Mila bit down on her lip. She'd typically refute Nicole's optimism. Today, she felt it, too.

"Oh, also," Nicole continued, "Calvin has this friend I want to set you up with. He lives in Boonville, so a little bit of a trek, but he's a really nice guy. They grew up together. He has a good job, and Calvin's heard him say he's looking to settle down."

"Well, *golly*," Mila droned, donning her best Southern belle accent. "A big ole *man* willing to make me his li'l ole *wife*? Get me to the church on *time*!"

The forced smile melted from her face with her most dramatic eye roll to date, and she sipped her coffee, the caffeine not hitting her bloodstream quick enough for the potential-suitor conversation.

"You're such a brat." Nicole plucked a blueberry from

her muffin and tossed it at Mila, her friend deflecting the rogue berry into the sink. "I just want you to be happy. You've been holding out for Jared for so long, and I don't want you to waste any more time."

Mila bit her lower lip and dropped her gaze. *Holding out.* How pathetic. Waiting for someone to notice her, and then when she finally got her shot, the idiot didn't even see her worth.

Caryl's words echoed in Mila's head. *Don't let somebody else tell you what you're capable of.* A wave of determination rose up in her chest, flooding her senses. She knew who she was. She knew she was smart, talented, caring, and compassionate. She knew she'd be a great wife, a fantastic mother, a talented pastry chef. She deserved to be all those things. She deserved a chance to try.

"Well, you can rest easy," Mila said. She forced confidence into her voice and a smile to her lips. "I'm not wasting any more time. I'm gonna make this pie, I'm gonna win that contest, and I'm gonna get the apprenticeship with Chef Constance at Indigo."

The corner of Nicole's lips quirked. "Oh yeah?"

Mila tightened her jaw. "Yeah. I'm gonna kick the *shit* out of this contest. And Jared Kirkland will be sorry he didn't see how amazing I really am."

"Damn, Lee Lee!" Nicole leaped off the stool and thrust one fist into the air. "Hell yeah you are. Now take this fire and put it into that pie! I'll get out of your hair. And I'll see you tonight at the opening ceremonies. Six o'clock, yeah?"

"Six o'clock."

Nicole kissed Mila's cheek, gave her one last reassuring hug, and slipped out the front door. Mila turned back to her kitchen, tore the top off the muffin, and shoved it into her mouth. Crumbs rained down onto the counter in front of her, and through a full mouth, she said, "I'm gonna kill it."

* * *

'm glad you called me, man." Vin tapped on his phone, ignoring Hank the bartender who'd asked him twice if he wanted another.

"Hey." Jared's voice snapped with all the venom coursing through his veins since last week. He'd thought the toxicity would have faded over time, but instead it had intensified like some kind of nuclear waste lying in wait. "You want another drink or what?"

Vin looked up, his eyes wide behind the thick-rimmed glasses. Today he wore a flat-brimmed baseball cap with his tight hooded sweatshirt. If Jared hadn't been crawling out of his skin, more ready than ever to get the hell out of Pine Ridge, he'd never have called this dirtbag.

"Sorry, bro." Vin turned to the bartender. "Gimme another old-fashioned."

Jared swallowed down all the nasty things he wanted to say. But he needed this guy. Now more than ever. "So. You think I've got a shot?"

"Oh yeah," Vin said, tucking his phone into his pocket. "Just email me your résumé and I'll send it over to my buddy in HR as soon as I can find some Wi-Fi. Really, though, it's a formality. I'll have an interview on the books for you by end of day. It'll happen quickly. Everything at Indigo moves really quickly."

Good. Quickly. Exactly what he needed. He needed to stop looking over his shoulder every time he walked through town. He needed to avoid the judgmental glares of every local he passed on the street. He needed to get out of Pine Ridge, where every corner, mailbox, and pine tree reminded him of Mila, practically bashing him over the head with the realization that he'd never get over her if he couldn't get out of town.

"Hey, Hank," Vin called out. "Scratch the drink, yeah? I gotta run."

Hank turned around with the finished cocktail and a grimace. Jared waved him forward. "I'll drink it."

Hank turned his grizzle-framed lips down and eyed the full glass of bourbon in front of Jared. "You sure, Kirkland?"

"Give me the drink, Hank."

Hank snorted. "Good grief, boy. I hope you get laid soon. This isn't a good look on you. Mopey. Heartsick. It's plum embarrassing, if you ask me."

"Well, nobody asked you." Jared sipped his bourbon.

Vin shook his head and tossed a twenty-dollar bill on the bar. "Chin up, bro. Just wait till you get down to Raleigh. There's so many hot girls down there, you'll forget Mila ever existed."

The bourbon slid along his tongue, and his jaw tightened. He couldn't forget her. He didn't want to. He just wanted to get out of this place and pretend like he hadn't ruined the best thing he'd ever had.

Vin clapped a hand on Jared's shoulder before calling out to Sam and Denny as they entered the bar. Jared scoffed. Another thing he wouldn't miss about this place. Not a moment's peace anywhere.

Sam and Denny flanked him, both leaning on the bar with grim looks settled onto their faces. "You're going Saturday, right?" Sam asked.

"Nah." Jared swallowed another mouthful of bourbon, and the liquor-induced warmth spread across his chest. "She doesn't want me there."

"Are you planning to skip the opening celebration tonight, too?" Sam said.

He had never missed opening night at the Spring Festival. But what if Mila was there? "I dunno."

"You're a real prick, you know that?" Sam snatched Vin's abandoned drink from his brother and handed it to Denny. "Make yourself useful, big man, and drink this, will you?"

"With pleasure." Denny palmed the glass in his big hand and sipped with a curious look on his brow. "You're not really gonna skip the bake-off, are you? That's a real scumbag move, bro."

"Why would I go?" Jared snapped. "To watch her win? To stand back and *not* hug her during the happiest moment of her life?"

"To support her," Sam said. "To do the thing you should've done all week but were too much of a scared little boy to man up and do."

"Do me a favor and leave me alone." Jared's eyes trained on the worn bar in front of him, the wood nicked and marked with years of use and abuse. Broken glasses, spilled beers, crazy hunters with knives carving their initials when no one was looking.

"Hey, D?" Sam said. "Can you give us a minute?"

Denny held his free hand up and slunk away from the bar.

"Look at me," Sam snapped. Jared refused. What did his brother care, anyway? The guy had everything he could ever want. A beautiful fiancée, a business he owned and could be proud of, the comfort of knowing if he stayed in Pine Ridge, he'd have all the stability and community he could ever need.

"Fuck off, bro."

In one move, Sam reached out and snatched a swath of hair at the back of Jared's head and jerked his brother's neck back until Jared couldn't look anywhere else. Sam's eyes blazed with determination.

"Listen," Sam said. "About a year ago, you socked me in the face for being a total asshole and trying to ruin the best thing that had ever happened to me. Do you remember that?"

Jared grinned. Sam had accused Jared of trying to sleep with Sydney, and Jared had been so insulted and pissed off and angry at his pigheaded brother that he'd punched him square in the eye. Sam and Sydney reconciled shortly after.

"Yeah," Jared said. "You were being such a boner. Like I'd ever go after a girl you were so obviously obsessed with."

"Well," Sam said. "Do you want me to punch you in the face? Do you need a knock of sense to realize what you're doing?"

Jared yanked himself free of Sam's death grip and ran a hand over his hair. "If I go bald back there, I'm blaming you."

"Get your head out of your ass," Sam snapped.

"It's more than Mila. I've exhausted every opportunity in this tiny town. I want to make some money, man."

"What about Silver Lake?" Sam said. "I know you didn't close it yet. And I've heard on good authority that there's a ton of property to get your hands on around here. It's not about your career. It is *not* about more than Mila."

Jared exhaled, trying to keep his voice calm and clear. "She wants to get married, Sam. I can't give her what she wants. How could that ever work out?"

"You and the marriage thing," Sam grumbled. "One shoddy example growing up and you act like the entire institution is flawed."

"Why don't you talk to me when you're ready to discuss what *really* happened between Mom and Dad? Both miserable until they died too young. And then Mom spending the rest of her life alone, focusing way too much on her kids and what they'd end up doing with their own lives. If that appeals to you, great, but it's not gonna be me."

Sam's lips parted, his eyes wide with disbelief. "You never want to hear me when I talk about this."

"I hear you," Jared snapped.

"No. You never do. You think you were such a disenfranchised kid? Mom picked on you?"

"Yes!" He sat straight up and stared at his brother with wide eyes. "That is exactly what I think! It was the three of us, and yet it always felt like I was the sad-sack neighbor kid who got invited along to shit with Mrs. Kirkland and her perfect son, Sam."

A bitter laugh floated past Sam's lips and leaned back in the barstool, glancing around the bar as if someone might back him up.

"Ah, man. You're so warped."

"Seriously, Sam, if you're just gonna be a dick, then leave me alone."

"Listen to me." Sam ran a hand over his beard, his eyes blazing. "Mom was never worried about me. Ever. I was always gonna be fine. But you? You are *exactly* like Dad."

An icy chill crept along Jared's spine. Sam lifted his eyebrows as if letting it sink in.

"Loud, charismatic, pretending like life is gonna hand you a thousand opportunities no matter how many you squander." Sam leaned in closer. "You think she was gonna let you make the same mistakes she'd watched Dad make? That she'd just leave it up to fate?"

Jared choked back the realization as it threatened to knock him backward off the barstool. "Why'd she have to be so hard on me?"

"She did her best, J. Dad was a degenerate alcoholic. He gave Mom just enough of his paycheck to cover rent and food and clothes for us, and he drank away the rest of it. She had to pick him up from the bar more nights than you'd been alive by the time he died. She balanced raising two kids Dad never wanted in the first place on the pittance he gave her while trying to maintain her own sanity. You think she wanted to be cautious in her attempts at saving your ass?"

Jared forced a shaky inhale. "Why didn't she just leave?"

"Dude, you don't know *shit* about addiction or how it affects people's families. You think she had the money for a lawyer? For a divorce? And then what? She's alone with two kids and Dad's still Dad. He's still drinking. And to top it all off, then *he's* alone. You think a drinking problem gets better or worse when your family abandons you?"

The truth slipped into Jared's bloodstream like the bourbon in front of him. "What are you, an expert?"

"You know I've been going to therapy since the whole Liv situation," Sam said quietly. "I needed to confront all my own issues involved in wanting to help an addict."

Jared sipped his drink, but no amount of liquid could ease his sandpaper throat. His whole body flooded with confusion, as if someone had been pinching his nose and he could finally inhale again.

"Mom did whatever it took to make sure you got out of Pine Ridge," Sam said. "So that you didn't become either one of them."

Jared ran his tongue across his upper lip, tasting bourbon and regret. "Why wasn't she worried about you?"

"This might be news to you, but you and I are very different." Sam readjusted his baseball cap and leaned back on the barstool. "And I was older when Dad died. I think I knew a little bit more about him than you did. Enough to be scared out of the drinking."

"Why was she okay with you staying in this town?" Jared said. He needed all the answers, and he needed them now. "Sometimes you'd joke about leaving, but she saw you well into adulthood settling down in Pine Ridge. It seemed to make her so happy."

Sam shrugged. "I try not to think too hard about that. Maybe she thought you were smarter than me. More driven. But I'm okay with that. I'm happy here."

A quiet moment passed, and a voice that sounded a lot like Mila's sounded in Jared's head. *You could be happy here, too.*

"She'd be disappointed if I stayed here, huh?" Jared whispered. He couldn't fight the tears brimming his eyes.

"She'd be disappointed if you settled," Sam said. "To watch you give up on Mila or your job because it got hard."

Jared pinched the bridge of his nose, wishing he hadn't had that last bourbon.

"Listen," Sam said. "Mom's gone, and however you feel about her is something you have to figure out on your own. I'm gonna give you my therapist's number, and you can do what you want with it. But you have to start making your own decisions based on what's best for you. Don't walk away from things because you think you know what the outcome will be."

Jared shook his head. "I dunno, man. Maybe somebody like Mila just isn't in the cards for me. She's gonna be an amazing wife. What if I'm the shittiest husband?"

"You act like that's something you can't control."

Hank slid a glass of water in front of Jared and raised his eyebrows as a directive. Jared gulped the water. Boozing suddenly seemed foolish.

"Why were you sitting here with Vin?" Sam said. "You've forgiven him for trying to date Mila?"

Jared huffed. "Never. He, uh . . . he's hooking me up with a job opportunity in North Carolina. I'm heading down there Friday for an interview."

Sam's eyes narrowed. "Are you serious?"

"Yeah." Jared shrugged and turned away from his brother. Every concern he'd had about chasing after this job would beam out at him from Sam's all-knowing eyes, and he couldn't hide from the truth. He didn't want to look at him.

"Wow," Sam said. "North Carolina. That's a trek."

"Yeah, well. Shit's just not happening for me here, you know? I need to try someplace new."

"See," Sam said. "*This* is what would bother Mom. Letting all this slip through your fingers: Silver Lake. Mila. You've said yourself there's a lot of money to be made up here in North Country. Never thought you had it in you to cut and run from what could be the greatest things that have ever happened to you."

Jared wanted to snap back, argue with his brother, tell him he was totally off base. But he was tired. Tired of arguing, tired of pretending these things didn't matter to him.

The things he wanted most were the most difficult to obtain, but that didn't mean the reward wouldn't be worth the chase.

He exhaled, his posture caving with his resolve. "So," Jared said. "What do I do?"

"Easy," Sam said. A smile curled onto his lips. "You fight."

chapter **twenty**

Mila paused, taking it all in. Milky-blue twilight settled over Williams Farm, but the entire place glowed from within. Glittering white twinkle lights wrapped around posts flanking the entrance, and a massive wooden sign painted with **WELCOME TO THE PINE RIDGE SPRING FESTIVAL** in curly white letters welcomed guests to the festivities.

A sloping green hill led to a massive expanse of lawn and booths featuring Adirondack-themed pillows, hand-woven baskets, emerald-green wool blankets and cozy knit hats, and pungent, deep-fried treats at every turn. Kettle corn and home-brewed beer competed for air space with hot roast beef sandwiches and crunchy salt potatoes.

Mila breathed deep. People milled about, the air itself electric and alive with excitement for the first event of the warm-weather season. A gentle breeze ruffled the delicate silk of her knee-length skirt, and bunches of flowers filled baskets along the walkway leading patrons to the main event.

Tonight there would be a small fireworks display and a message from the mayor. The following weekdays featured performances from local musicians, raffles, and a kiddie parade, and on Saturday, the bake-off took center stage. Mila's fingertips tingled but she forced her hand to her side, willing her thumb out of her teeth.

No more nail-biting. No more bad habits. No more little-girl weaknesses. This week, she was a warrior, and pastry was her weapon of choice.

"Thank God for global warming." Nicole snuggled into Mila's side, clutching her denim-clad arm. "Of all the Spring Festivals I remember, I'd say four of them were warm enough for a light jacket."

"I hate to say it." A smile tugged at Mila's lips. "But yeah. It's just so much better outside. With the flowers . . ."

She breathed deep, hyacinth- and lilac-laced perfume filling her lungs. Tulips in shades of crimson, Creamsicle, and lavender stood at attention as she and Nicole walked slowly past the front entrance and into the festival.

Pine Ridge residents, young and old, hurried past them, each eager to visit their favorite vendors. Mila and Nicole always did a lap first before settling on their first purchase. As they neared the first stall, Sydney called out.

"Check it out!" Sydney scurried out of the booth and stood in front of them in a Wonder Woman pose, her chest popped out highlighting a royal blue T-shirt that read, in white, disco-themed font, Pine Ridge Is for Lovers.

"*Shut. Up.*" Nicole grabbed Sydney's arms and stared, wide-eyed and openmouthed. "Okay, well, forget doing a lap. You're my first purchase of the festival. Give me one of those right now."

Mila stood a few paces back, a smile stretching her lips as she watched her friends. She reached into her tiny purse in search of lip balm, and her fingers curled around a rigid slip of paper, folded once and tucked deep into the interior pocket.

She pulled the paper out and exhaled sharply. Photo-booth photos. From Spring Festival seven years ago. Jesus, she hadn't used this purse in a long time.

Four photos stacked on top of each other featured an embarrassingly young Mila and Jared, fresh-faced and happy and blissfully unaware of the doubts forming in each other's minds. In the first three photos, they stuck their tongues out, peered over outdated sunglasses, and bared all their teeth.

In the last photo, Mila pursed her lips. Jared stared. As if he'd forgotten he was being photographed. His face turned toward her, his spiky hair casting shadows on the wall behind him, and his lips parted slightly. If it had been anybody else, anybody but her and the guy who'd recently broken her heart, she'd call it love.

"Hey."

Her throat slammed shut as her gaze lifted to Jared's face. The man staring back at her left the little boy from the photo in the dust.

"Hey," she said.

He ran his teeth over his bottom lip, his strong, chiseled jaw working back and forth as he gazed at her. Tonight he wore oxfords with fitted jeans and a soft charcoal-gray sweater that set his deep green eyes ablaze in the ever-darkening evening. He stole her breath and threatened to keep it.

"What are you doing here?" The words slipped out before she could catch them.

His eyebrows jumped. "I haven't missed opening festivities at a Pine Ridge Spring Festival since I was born, and I'm pretty sure my mom came when she was pregnant with me. This seemed like an especially shitty year to stop coming."

His gaze fell on her warmly. So unlike the last time they spoke. She didn't want to believe he had different intentions tonight, but her heart nudged her forward.

"You nervous?" he asked. "About Saturday?"

She pursed her lips and forced a nonchalant shrug. *Not with a Jared-inspired pie in my arsenal.* "Nah."

The corner of his perfect lips twitched into a smile. "Nah? Well, look at you. Not intimidated anymore. Confidence looks good on you, Bailey."

The hair at the back of her neck prickled. "Don't insult me."

"I wasn't." The playful grin disappeared. "I'm happy for you. I've always thought you underestimated yourself. If you finally have the confidence you should've had the rest of your life, then I'm ecstatic."

So that was it. He was like a parent sending their kid off into the world. *As long as you're happy.* Anger bubbled up in her chest.

No. That wasn't how it was supposed to go.

"Happy you're happy, J." The sarcasm wasn't what she'd intended, but his lips parted in surprise and eased the disappointment.

His eyes darted around, and they both realized at once that they had an audience. Sydney and Nicole huddled silently together at the edge of the Loving Page's booth, Edith O'Hare blatantly stared while shoving kettle corn into her open mouth, and the entire McDonagh clan watched in rapt attention from farther up the hill.

Jared grabbed Mila's hand and tugged her away from the vendor booths and the prying eyes.

"Jared." She called out as he hurried past people and around the side of the massive barn where the Spring Festival would've been held had the weather turned. He slipped inside the building and thrust them both into a pool of darkness, festival noise muffled in their own little corner of the world.

"Say what you want to say to me." His warm breath whispered across her cheeks, and she instinctively lifted her face, every inch of her saying, *Closer closer closer.*

"You first."

The inky black of the barn settled over them, and as her eyes adjusted, the contours of his face appeared in the night. The full lips, the straight-bridged nose, the heavy eyebrows slightly marred by the old scar.

She couldn't help herself. She brushed a gentle thumb across his cheekbone, reveling in the sensation of skin on skin. His eyelids lowered slowly, his chin dipped in reverence.

"You could have me," she whispered. "If you just trusted yourself. You can do this. You can be everything I need you to be."

"I don't know where you get this faith in me," he said.

The weight of his hands on her hips deepened her need, and she softened into him.

"I know you," she said. "I know things about you that you don't know yourself. And I know because you've proven them over and over again. Your loyalty, your honesty, your grace. You make me feel so cared for, so seen. And you don't even have to try. It's not about flowers or saying the right thing. It's about showing up. You have always showed up for me. *Always.*"

He licked his lips, his tongue a breath away from her cheek. "You're wrong. You're the only one I've ever tried for."

She tilted her head. Her lips begged to brush against his. "Try again."

He swallowed, his throat constricting in the shadows.

"You want me," she said. "Don't you?"

A muffled grunt echoed in his throat, and he guided her hand to the front of his jeans, where the hardened length answered her question.

"Yes, I want you," he growled. "I want you right here."

"That's not what I meant."

"What else can I say to you?" His voice wrestled free of his throat, his body tightening under her hands as if he couldn't contain the energy coursing through him. "I want you in every way, Mila. It's not up for debate. I want you in my clothes, in my car, in my bed. I want you wrapped around me and inside me and dripping off me."

Her stomach caved. His intensity rolled over her in waves, stripping her bare and demanding her attention. They were the same people they'd always been to each other, and at the same time, different in every way.

She knew this wasn't reconciliation, a mending of what they'd fractured. But she didn't care. She'd never regret it. She'd never wish she could take back the irrefutable power they created when they were together. And so she forged ahead.

She covered his lips with hers. She plunged her tongue into his mouth, and he gripped her ass with both hands as she struggled for breath. Their teeth knocked together, but she didn't care. She needed him, grasping his neck and shoulders with desperate fingers.

They moved backward as one until the backs of her thighs bumped the top of a heavy wooden table. He hoisted her up and slipped between her knees, pressing against her pelvis.

"Do you want me, Mila?" The sound of her name, ragged and strangled and tripping off his tongue, caught her deep between her thighs.

"Yes." One syllable was all her muddled brain could choke out.

"Tell me," he said, working his hands beneath her skirt and raking nimble fingers along her tingling skin. "None of this kid shit. I want to hear you say it."

Her eyes closed, swirls of color spiraling behind the lowered lids. She sunk into the pressure of his hands on her hips, his fingers kneading her flesh and catching on the fabric of her lace thong.

"I want you." She swallowed, summoning her voice and all the words clawing at her heart. "Even if it's not forever."

His brow pinched, his eyes darkened. "Oh yeah?"

She steeled herself, refused the old Mila who warned her against getting hurt. *You can't handle this*, she said. But she could. She knew it now. It didn't mean she didn't love him. It meant she knew what she was capable of.

"Yeah."

He swallowed, doubt crossing his face for just a moment before he tugged her skirt up until it pooled on the table around her. On unsteady legs, he took a step backward and hurriedly unbuckled his belt, yanking his pants and boxer briefs down around his knees.

With one hand stroking the length of his cock, he reached out and dragged a thumb across her sex, the sensation only slightly dampened by the thin stretch of fabric holding her together.

Her chest heaved, her breaths came in sporadic bursts. She swiped a hand across her tongue and grabbed his cock, coaxing him toward her. No time for games, no time for lingering glances and drawn-out teasing motions.

In one motion, he fell forward, catching his weight on either side of her and drowning her in a wave of his delicious scent. She breathed in through her mouth, dragging her lips against his throat as her arms and legs slithered around his body.

She grabbed the hem of his sweater and pulled upward, dragging the garment past silky soft skin and over his head, ruffling his perfectly coiffed hair into something unruly and wild. The tresses matched the untamed look in his eyes.

"I want to see you," he rasped.

She ripped off her jacket, her T-shirt, and her bra, all while he hovered over her, eyes burning into her skin like a mountain lion that hadn't eaten in weeks.

The second the cold air kissed her skin, he lowered his

face and took one peaked nipple into his mouth. His teeth nipped gently as he massaged her breast, the pressure between her legs growing and pulsing with every rhythmic motion.

His erection pressed at her entrance, the cotton of her thong growing damp with anticipation as his mouth worked. She huffed and moaned, choked and panted. The climax threatened already.

"I need you," she said, raking her fingers through his soft tousled hair. She clutched him to her chest, his tongue lapping at her sensitive flesh.

Without removing his mouth from her breast, he tugged the thong aside and trailed the tip of his erection across her swollen lips. Her skin caught fire. How much more could she stand?

"Inside me," she gasped, the swirling colors behind her eyelids turning to sparks. "I need it, J, I need it. Now."

She fumbled around for the tiny purse abandoned behind her on the table and located the condom she'd tucked inside. She didn't need to wait for him to take charge of the encounter or give her the go-ahead. She had it covered.

With the condom snugly in place, she wrapped her fingers around him and coaxed him inside her. He thrust once, and a yelp escaped her lips. The sound bounced off the barn walls like an animal in a trap. Except she was the animal, and she wanted to be caught.

"You're unbelievable," he groaned. He clutched her body to him, burying his face in her neck as he guided his hips against her again and again.

She lost herself, swallowed up in his steely biceps, the soft curve of his neck, the warm, sweet scent of his skin. They merged and melted, blended together until she couldn't tell where she ended and he began.

His hands slid down to the table where she perched, using the heavy furniture as resistance while he rocked against her, coaxing the orgasm from the depths of her soul. With her fingers gripping his solid shoulders, her nails digging into his tight flesh, he pounded against her, and suddenly, she shattered.

She clung to him, the climax rolling out of her in waves. Her voice bounced off the barn walls, filling the space with a chorus of pure, unfiltered ecstasy. Her body shifted and pulsed, and he snaked one hand behind her neck to hold her as close as physically possible.

"Holy shit," she gasped. "Jared."

His body didn't stop. With slow but purposeful motions, he rolled his hips and met her gaze, the desire searing into her memory as if it were the last sight she'd ever see.

With a pinched brow and parted, swollen lips, he tightened his grip on her, and she squeezed her thighs around his waist in response. The simple movement seemed to be all he needed. His body seized up, and he pressed his open mouth against her neck, jerking and stuttering and crashing against her as a dazzling smile overtook her lips.

Every inch of her sparkled, glittering and bright, despite the darkness that hugged them from all sides. This was all she ever needed. Pies and apprenticeships and million-dollar homes be damned. Whatever awaited them in the future, nothing could spoil the pure bliss of having him just like this.

He stood up slowly and stepped backward, his eyelids lowered and his mouth open in dazed pleasure. As he pulled up his pants and secured his belt, his eyes never left her. She made no move to redress or climb off the table.

"If you don't cover yourself up soon," he said, "I'm gonna have no choice but to make you come again."

His voice, scratchy with lust, creeped under her skin and forced a fresh wave of electricity through her limbs. She widened her legs just a little bit farther.

His hands froze over his belt buckle, and his lips quirked into a grin. "Oh, so that's how it is, huh? More, Mila?"

She licked her lips, pressed her shoulders back. If it were

up to her, they'd never leave this barn. They'd create a life for themselves on this tabletop, giving each other brain-melting orgasm after brain-melting orgasm.

He sauntered toward her, his eyes floating between her breasts, heavy and peaked in the chilly night air, and her spread thighs. The scant bits of moonlight floating in through the open barn door hugged the firm planes of his chest and highlighted the ridges of his taut abs.

Desire pooled in her belly. No. She wasn't done yet.

"If I tried," he said, sinking against her, his breath hot on her neck, "could I make you come again? Right now?"

His warm fingers slid between her slick folds, toying with her already muddied brain.

"Fuck," he groaned. "You're so wet."

"Does that answer your question?"

She tilted her head back, soaking in every inch of his face as he buried two fingers deep inside her. A single cry escaped her lips as she tightened around him, instinctively drawing him even closer.

His thumb whispered across her clit, and her hips tilted, needing but not prepared for him all at the same time. As he worked his fingers back and forth, in and out, he lowered his mouth to hers and sucked her lower lip into his mouth.

"Tell me something," she whispered. "Anything."

A single exhale floated past her chin as he said, "You're the best person I've ever known. You make me believe things I never thought I could."

The timbre in his voice skated along her ear and down her spine, exploding her whole world into brilliant Technicolor. All her nerve endings sparked and fired at once, and before she could take another breath, her body gave in. She collapsed against his chest, her pussy tightening around him like never before.

As she breathed, one deep inhale after another, he traced a gentle hand from her neck to her jaw, resting his thumb and his gaze on her lips.

"I missed you," she said. She pressed her lips against his thumb and rested her face in his hand. He felt so good. Like coming home.

"I missed you so freaking much."

He slowly dragged his hand away from her and stepped back, giving her a moment to dress. After they'd both resurrected their semi-normal appearance, she took a step toward him. Her vision and rational mind clouded over with the events of the last twenty minutes.

"Listen." He rested his hands on her hips and lowered his brow. "I'm gonna say something, and you might not like it."

She straightened her spine. Whatever he had to say next, it wouldn't break her. Not now.

"What?"

He sniffed and widened his stance so that they stood eye to eye. His lips tightened. "I'm closer than I've ever been. I've done a lot of thinking and I've talked to Sam and . . . I want to be with you."

Shivers skittered across her skin. "Okay?"

He trailed his thumb across her hip bone. "I need to get there one hundred percent on my own. I need to know that I'm totally ready. Emotionally, mentally, financially, physically. Can you give me just a little bit of time?"

She wrinkled her brow. Time? He needed more time? She'd been prepared for one of two conversations to arise from what had just happened: moving on with each other or without.

How much grace could she sacrifice when she'd already given him so much? She heard Nicole's voice, her mother's voice. If Aunt Georgie were around to chime in, she'd have agreed.

You have such low expectations for the people in your life.

Jared's hopeful face shone like the lake in moonlight. If she gave in to him now, she'd keep the possibility of something more with him alive. A life together. A future. And all at once she'd be telling him he could treat her however he liked. Put her second. Make her wait.

No.

She was done with all that. Done with waiting. Done with putting herself on the back burner.

"Mila, I—"

"No." The word fell off her lips, confident and sure.

His forehead creased, and his thumb—previously making circles on her hip bone—froze mid-rotation. "No?"

"I've been on your schedule, Jared. I've waited for you. I've waited for *everyone*. I've spent a lot of time and energy making sure everybody else around me felt at ease. Need help around the house? No sweat, I'll sacrifice my friends and hobbies to make dinner and do the laundry before starting my homework. Dreams too big they might hurt the whole family if they don't work out? Cool, I can stay put at the diner and do the safe thing. Scared of marriage? Sure, I'll pretend like I'm totally fine without a commitment for the rest of my days."

His mouth tightened. "No, Lee, that's not—"

"No, *I'm* speaking." Every inch of her skin caught fire, alive with adrenaline and the remnants of desire. A lethal combination. "I'm done making other people feel comfortable at the expense of my own happiness. I want things, too. I want the apprenticeship with Indigo, I want to make pastries for a living, I want to stop working at the diner, and I want to get married and have babies with somebody who doesn't think that makes him a prisoner."

His hands fell away from her body in one defeated move, brushing against the legs of his jeans as he took a step back. "I have never asked you to forfeit your own happiness. I only tried to be honest."

"Being honest about being a coward doesn't make it forgivable."

She crossed her arms tightly over her chest and waited.

Now was his moment. He could argue. He could fight back. He could fight *for* her and everything they'd created up to now.

"I'm not on your timeline," he said. Even in the darkness she saw his cheeks flush red. Damn him for looking so beautiful even at the most inopportune time. "I'm trying my best, but I'm just not there yet."

She bit down on her lip, refusing to lift her thumb to her mouth. "I'm tired of waiting."

With her chin lifted, she turned over her shoulder. A tether—something like steel reinforced with the power of the gods—connected her heart to Jared's, and as she walked away from him, the line tightened. She'd never be able to truly say goodbye to him. He was in her, a part of her history like rings in a tree trunk. But her history didn't have to dictate her future.

chapter **twenty-one**

J ared ran a hand over his head, more a nervous tic than an actual effort at taming his already-smooth hair. He'd put extra effort that morning into making sure every single strand had its place and stayed there.

He hadn't worn a tie. A bold move in traditionally corporate settings. His suit hugged every curve, navy-blue summer-weight wool tailored to perfection, the crisp white shirt underneath recently starched. Wearing that suit, he could sell sawdust to a lumber mill.

And judging from the lilt in Mr. Romano's voice throughout the interview, he'd done something like it.

As Mr. Romano stood from behind the desk, buzzing his assistant to walk his interviewee out, Jared clenched his teeth. No suit in the world could erase the doubt floating around his mind. Nothing about this trip felt right. Not the twelve-hour drive down, not the swanky room at Indigo Hotels Raleigh they'd put him up in, not the hotel chain's sleek corporate offices, and not the perfectly pleasant guy who'd carried out the seamless interview.

"Thanks for coming all this way," Mr. Romano said. He shook Jared's hand in a tight grip and motioned to the door.

"My pleasure," Jared said.

"You'll hear from us soon. Jenny will walk you out."

Mr. Romano's assistant, Jenny, ushered Jared out of the office and chatted amiably about all that Raleigh had to offer: mild winters, beautiful summers, professional sports, and a thriving craft beer scene. By the time he shook Jenny's hand and found his car in the parking lot, he felt full to bursting with shiny nuggets about the City of Oaks. Jenny wasn't the only one effusive with praise for Raleigh; everyone from the hotel concierge to the barista at the Starbucks he'd stopped at that morning touted the city's myriad highlights.

The appeal slid off his shoulders like butter on Teflon. Raleigh didn't have Mila.

He'd originally taken the interview so that he wouldn't have a single regret, but after her speech in the barn, he'd kept it because he needed to know deep down in his heart that he wanted her above all else. He needed to be able to look her in the eye and honestly say, *I don't want anything as much as I want you.* She could argue with a lot of things, but she couldn't argue with the cold, hard truth.

If he was honest with himself, though, he'd also kept the interview because he had an old debt to pay. If his mother had ever been right about anything, it was to give himself the opportunity for more. He needed to know he hadn't stayed in Pine Ridge to continue old family patterns but because it was the best path for him.

He'd tried to explain that to Mila, but she'd refused. For all the difficulties she'd had to circumvent in her own life, he'd have thought she would have given him the space he requested.

When she said no, defiance flared up inside him. He took the interview for a lot of reasons. Maybe they weren't all the right ones.

As he pulled onto the highway, the voice mail icon popped up on his phone, and he hit the button to play it. Denny's surfer dude voice blared through his car's speakers as Jared's car hit sixty miles per hour.

"What's up," Denny said. "Gimme a call when you get this. I've got a question for you. Do you even check your voice mail? I never check mine. I'll call again later."

Jared chuckled. The guy had been a welcome addition to the Pine Ridge crew, especially considering Sam's impending nuptials. Next there would be kids, and he'd see his brother less than ever. He liked having Denny around to grab a beer or hit the gym with. Maybe Denny would hang out in town for a while after the contest ended. It'd be cool to have a new friend.

That is, if Jared stayed. He cleared his throat and tightened his grip on the steering wheel. Even his subconscious pushed him toward Pine Ridge.

Miles passed and hours fell away. Jared crept passed Virginia, DC, and Pennsylvania, and by the time he reached the New York border, he'd settled into something resembling calm. His phone rang somewhere around Binghamton, a caller with a 984 area code.

"Hello, this is Jared Kirkland."

"Jared." Mr. Romano's deep Southern drawl cut through the car as Jared navigated the dark, desolate thruway. "Hope I'm not catching you at a bad time."

"No, sir," Jared said. "Just about home, actually."

"Good. Jared, we'd like to offer you the position. I could play it coy like we're interviewing a bunch of other prospects, but 'coy' is not really in my vocabulary. I think you'd be great on the team, and we want you to start as soon as possible, so I'm calling you now and emailing the offer as we speak. I wouldn't normally hire someone at your level of experience, but you're very bright, and I just got a real good feeling from you. I like to trust my gut, and my gut's telling me you'd be a real asset to the team covering Bailey County."

A chill spread across Jared's skin, prickling the back of his neck as if a ghost had materialized in the passenger seat. "What was that?"

"Bailey County, Texas," Mr. Romano said. "It's the area we're looking at for our next development. You'd be based here in Raleigh but traveling frequently to West Texas."

Jared's mouth turned to dust. He'd never believed much in signs or omens, but this one was impossible to ignore. The name pierced his brain like a shot of adrenaline. Whatever calm he'd gained on the open road disappeared with her name.

He ran his tongue over his lower lip. It should've been the offer to end all offers. His dream scenario. Leaving Pine Ridge, making twice the money in a company rife with perks, and setting out on a path to success of his own making. Independent. Free.

But with one name, one single word, his decision became clear. New York, North Carolina, Texas. He'd never escape her.

He didn't want to.

"Thank you so much, sir," Jared said. "Once I'm off the road, I'll check my email and take a look at the offer, if that's okay with you."

"Of course. Take a good look at it and let me know if you have any questions."

Jared ended the call and turned his eyes back to the road. He checked his texts, just to see if anything had come through while he'd been on the phone.

Nothing.

He tried to tell himself Mila was probably prepping for the bake-off tomorrow. Maybe she was already in bed. Visions of her long legs danced in his mind. Her soft, freckled skin brushing against his as she dreamed, her lips parted in a world beyond her conscious mind.

He ached to be back there. To be with her. Where he always should've been in the first place.

You look gorgeous." Nicole wrapped loving arms around Mila's shoulders and squeezed. Caryl and Lloyd looked on, timid smiles on both their faces. The parental support she'd long sought, embracing her on all sides. A rare but divine moment in the Bailey family.

Indigo Hotels Adirondack Park's sweeping ballroom hummed with anticipation, eager contestants and their friends and families surrounded by the intoxicating aroma of freshly baked pastries, breads, and cakes. Weak but welcome sunshine filtered in through the soaring windows, which featured a glittering view of the lake beyond.

Mila's throat clogged as she imagined working here. Would she fit in? Indigo would be hard pressed to find another pastry apprentice who'd work harder than she would.

She'd gone to great lengths getting herself ready today. Curled lashes, raspberry lipstick, shimmering blush on the apples of her cheeks. The balmy spring weather afforded her an opportunity to wear a peach-flowered dress that skimmed her ankles and hugged her ribs with a dip at the cleavage.

Today might be her moment. Today might change everything. She had to be ready for anything.

For anyone.

Nicole pulled back, biting her lip to tamp down her smile.

"Quit hanging on her," Caryl scolded. "She's probably nervous enough as it is."

Nicole rolled her eyes but gave Mila a few inches of space. Truth was, Mila craved touch. Her bones begged for it. But it wasn't Nicole's hands she needed now.

Where was he? She knew he'd show up. She'd heard rumors he'd gone to North Carolina for an interview. The thought of him driving toward his future, thousands of miles away from her, turned her stomach inside out. But then she imagined his smile. Driving away from her but toward a successful existence outside Pine Ridge. Outside the town that had always held him back.

"There she is!" Sydney's voice carried over Mila's shoulder, and Mila turned in time for Sydney's tight embrace to knock her backward. "Good luck today, Mila. We're all pulling for you."

Mila grinned at her as she pulled away and Sam joined. Her friends. Her family. What more could she ask for?

A pang of loneliness hit her square in the ribs. *What else?* Just everything.

"He's on his way." Sam's eyes glittered, but he wouldn't go so far as a smile.

"He better be."

The group all turned surprised looks on Mila. She summoned every last shred of courage she possessed, dug deep down past her ribs, into the depths of scary places she hadn't dared to touch since that night in the hotel. Since Aunt Georgie gave her a shot. Since everything changed.

She wouldn't shrink down anymore. Jared owed her something. If she knew him as well as she thought she did, he'd deliver.

"Mila?" Vin interrupted her protective bubble, and her parents stepped aside to let him through. "They're ready to start."

The cavernous ballroom grew three sizes as she separated from her safe little world and followed Vin to the front, where the bake-off contestants waited on risers. She filled her lungs with cool, cinnamon-scented air, forced it out again, and put one foot in front of the other as Vin's broad shoulders led the way.

A strong, warm hand gripped her elbow. She turned sharply, her face open and expectant.

Jared.

The crowd around her slowed and stilled until it was nothing but an oil painting, background for the scene playing out between them. His eyes widened and blinked, his lips parted in a moment of hesitation. A soft, light blue button-down shirt hung open at his neck, exposing a stretch of lightly tanned skin at his clavicle that she had the sudden desire to run her tongue across.

"Just wanted to wish you good luck." His hand slid from her elbow to her hand, and with one reassuring squeeze, she was safe.

Her brain froze. She heard herself say, "It's a bacon pie."

His lips curled into a grin. "Bold."

She swallowed her fears and forced her spine straighter. "I'll see you after?"

"I'll be here."

She traced her thumb across his palm before reluctantly dropping his hand and hurrying to the front of the ballroom. Whatever had happened between them, wherever they stood now, he'd showed up for her. Just like he always had.

Mila climbed onto the risers and stood next to Sidecar Kim. The tiny redhead flashed Mila her widest smile, sending a flutter through Mila's stomach.

Mila steeled herself, scanning the eager face of each finalist. Whatever happened, it wouldn't break her. She wouldn't let it.

"Ladies and gentlemen!" Mayor Sweeney's voice boomed through the ballroom, a shrill moment of feedback silencing the crowd. "Whoopsie, sorry about that."

The hundreds of people crammed into the space looked forward, each shining face eager for the results and the announcement that would kick off an evening of celebration. Mila heard her own heart beating, her blood racing through her veins like it had somewhere to be.

As Vin joined the mayor onstage to welcome everyone

to the big event, Mila's gaze drifted to where Jared stood, next to the massive stone fireplace in the middle of the room, alone, hands casually slipped in the pockets of his slim-fitting black pants.

Her mouth dried up. His eyebrows lowered, but they didn't dim the fire in his eyes. He watched her intensely, the beam of his gaze lighting her up with otherworldly promise, as if everything ahead of them could be communicated through his stare.

"And now." Mayor Sweeney's voice cut through her fantasy. "Without further ado, our top three finalists for this year's Pine Ridge Spring Bake-Off!"

Mila clasped her hands behind her back to stop the trembling. She tried to tell herself it didn't matter, that everything she could possibly gain from this competition she'd already won. The money would be nice. But that apprenticeship. God, she wanted that apprenticeship. Going back to the diner to wipe down counters and pour coffee seemed like the ultimate insult after all this.

"In third place, Kim Plotzky from Buffalo, New York, with her cranberry pretzel bread!"

Polite applause tittered through the crowd, with a big boisterous redheaded group in the back of the room making up for the lack of rowdiness. Kim pressed her red-painted lips together, waved toward the group in the back, and accepted a purple prize ribbon from Mayor Sweeney.

Mila bit down on her lower lip, physically willing her hand away from her mouth. She'd never wanted to chew her thumbnail so badly.

She met Jared's gaze again. This time a smile played on his lips, and he winked. A tidal wave of emotion rolled through her, buckling her knees and testing her balance.

"In second place," Mayor Sweeney said. He checked his cards. "Mila Bailey from our own Pine Ridge, New York, with her caramel apple bacon pie!"

For one brief moment, everything stopped. Every sound

muffled, from the low murmurs of the crowd to the crackle and pop of the fireplace, as if someone had put a bag over her head.

She blinked once.

Twice.

Her eyelids closed and opened in slow motion, and she pressed her lips into a smile.

"Congratulations, Mila." Mayor Sweeney shook her hand, his mouth smiling but his eyes creased in disappointment. It would have been good for the town, too, if she'd won. And now . . .

She took the red ribbon and, in a haze of confusion, joined Kim.

Arthur Allen, grandpa of the group, took first place with his savory barbecue pork bread, and before Mila could center herself, the entire competition ended as abruptly as it began. Arthur Allen posed for photographs with the judges, the contestants returned to their respective groups, and Mila stood still among the chaos, wishing she could be anywhere but here.

Jared approached first, leading her to a vacant corner of the ballroom with his eyebrows raised in subtle concern.

"You okay?" he said.

She swallowed down her disappointment. How could she be honest with this person she needed more than anything, who knew her better than anyone, but who didn't want to commit? His strong hands held her arms, demanding her attention and tugging sadness from deep in her chest.

"Um, yeah," she said. "Disappointed. But I'll be okay."

"You want to run away? Get in my car and disappear for a while before you have to face everyone?"

A bitter laugh escaped her lips. "No. I have to talk to them sometime, right?"

He sniffed, his gaze settling on her mouth. "Second place, Lee. Maybe you didn't win the whole shebang, but you finally did it. You nailed a bacon pie. *Caramel apple* bacon pie. And that's a personal victory if I ever saw one."

A genuine smile finally found her. "Ever the optimist, huh?"

"Not always." Seriousness settled over his brow. "Listen, I know maybe this isn't the time, but . . ."

"Mila?"

Mila turned over her shoulder to find Chef Constance, looking as polished as she'd ever seen the woman, in a crisp white button-down shirt and a sharp tweed blazer. Chef Constance glanced from Jared to Mila and back again.

"Hello," she said. "Chef Constance Hathaway."

"Jared Kirkland," he said. "You guys made a huge mistake."

Mila's heart hiccupped in her chest. "Jared!"

His lips stretched into a winning smile. Chef Constance matched it.

"Let's just say not all the judges were on the same page." She dropped Jared's hand and turned her attention back to Mila. "Do you have a moment?"

Jared touched Mila's wrist, the simple brush of his skin on hers sending sparks up her arm. "I'll wait for you in the back."

I'll wait for you. She tamped down the hope blooming in her chest and watched him weave through the crowded ballroom toward her friends and family.

"I'm sorry the contest didn't go your way, Mila," Chef Constance said.

Mila shook her head, her curls dancing around her face. "Please don't be sorry. Arthur is so talented. And that pork bread was bizarre and delicious. He deserved to win."

"You're gonna have to work on that Pollyanna attitude if you're going to work in my kitchen."

Blood *whooshed* in Mila's ears. "What's that?"

Chef Constance raised one expertly arched eyebrow. "You're very talented, Mila. I think you'll get along very well with our pastry chef, Alonso, but you have to toughen up. Can you do that? Spend the next couple of weeks boxing or taking karate or something, so by the time May rolls around you can come to work with us as a pastry apprentice at Indigo Hotels Adirondack Park."

Mila's mouth fell open, her already wobbly composure threatening to break. "You're serious."

"Very serious," Chef Constance said. "The kitchen is no place for a demure attitude. But it is the place for badass bitches who make pies like caramel apple bacon with sourdough crust. I was hoping you'd turn out something as cool as that and prove to me you deserved the apprenticeship even if you didn't win the contest. I want you to teach your recipe to Alonso, and then I want to serve that on opening night at the hotel. Deal?"

Laughter exploded from Mila's mouth, and before she could stop it, a tear slid down her cheek. Emotions competed for space inside her gut like wrestlers in the ring. "Yes. Deal."

"All right, good." Chef Constance stuck her little hand out and Mila shook it, pumping once as a tiny nod to the badass Chef Constance knew she could be. "I've got your number and your email. I'll be in touch next week with details."

"Thank you," Mila said, swiping at her damp cheeks. "Seriously. Thank you so much."

Chef Constance nodded, turned, and walked away.

The space around her shifted and spun, her vision blurry as she moved through the ballroom and tried to focus on the drawn faces of her friends and family. By the time she joined them, they'd already started spouting their subdued congratulations on winning second place, mixed with hearty condolences for not coming out on top, but Mila had nearly forgotten what there was to be sorry for.

She let them surround her, hug her, apologize to her for the missed victory she so rightly deserved. As her parents patted her head and Nicole squeezed her hand, Jared stood a few paces back with a tiny grin on his curvy lips.

Once the official details and offer of her apprenticeship came through by phone or email, she'd tell them all. Until then, she wanted this secret. Only she didn't know if she'd be able to keep it from Jared. Something told her he already knew.

Lloyd announced they should all start enjoying the Indigo-sponsored event, but Mila hung back, letting the group file away and leave her alone with her best friend. The best friend she'd fallen in love with.

"Can I steal you for a minute?" he asked. "I want to show you something."

She bit down on her lower lip, the good news threatening to spill out. She wanted to tell him more than anything, but if she did, she also wanted to be able to sink into his arms and share her joy in a way that was possible only if nothing else stood between them. But not like this. Not how they were.

"Sure," she said.

Without asking, he gripped her hand and led her toward the exit. Neither spoke as they walked to the parking lot, climbed into his car, and took off driving east.

They drove silently, smoothly, around roads she knew as well as her own name. She could navigate them blindfolded, sure that no matter what else changed, she knew this place.

The sun hung high over the tree line, turning the sky a clear, brilliant shade of sapphire that nearly burned her eyes. Ahead, the mountaintops reminded her that winter still clung to the high peaks. She ran her hands over her bare shoulders.

"You cold?" He reached for the heat before she could answer. Warm air cascaded over her skin, and when she looked at him, she burned from the inside out.

"Jared . . ."

"Just wait," he said. "I want to show you this first. Before we talk about anything else. Is that okay?"

She licked her lips and watched as his jaw worked back and forth. Both hands gripped the steering wheel in a forced posture she'd never seen from him before. She couldn't afford to give him his space last week. Maybe she could try now.

"Sure."

Jared's car carried them over shallow hills and down unpaved roads until he finally made a left turn into a dense stretch of forest. The narrow dirt driveway turned to rocky gravel a quarter of a mile down and, after another minute, opened up to a wide circular drive.

Just beyond the driveway, looming in the late-afternoon sun, stood a massive home that hugged the curve of the lakefront, visible through giant glass windows. Each plane of the house showcased the incredible view beyond the lot. Mila's eyebrows raised in appreciation.

"Wow," she said. "This is pretty ridiculous. Where are we?"

"Come on." He cut the engine and climbed out of the car, jogging around to the passenger side before she could exit. He took her hand and drew her close as they approached the house.

After some fumbling with the lockbox, Jared opened the wide front door and ushered her inside. The interior of the home stole the breath from her lungs, and she gazed around in wonder at the empty living room. Twelve-foot-high windows, polished to perfection, featured the glassy lake outside and the emerald green forest beyond.

"Jesus," she breathed. "I knew there were spectacular homes around here, but I couldn't have even dreamed this one up."

Jared closed the space between them, took her hands in his, and lowered his chin. Fine lines appeared around his lips, the corners of his eyes creasing.

"This is Silver Lake," he said. "As of this morning, Denny Torres put an offer in on it."

"Jared." His name came on a breath, and her mouth fell open in elated surprise. She knew how much this meant to him. "Congratulations. Holy shit. You finally did it."

He licked his lips, the stony seriousness still etched into his smooth face. "Truth is, I would've come back and stayed in Pine Ridge even if I hadn't sold it. I went to North Carolina, and I interviewed for the job with Indigo. It didn't feel right."

So he *had* gone. Her chest constricted with the weight of the news. "If that's what you want . . ."

"It's not." He lifted a hand to her face, cupping her neck and gently trailing her jaw with his thumb. "For a long time, I didn't know what I wanted. I just wanted to be good at something. To be the best."

Mila nodded slowly. They'd come at their dreams from two very different angles. And somehow the path kept leading them back to each other.

"I was scared of staying here and failing. I wasn't selling this house, I wasn't moving forward in my career, and I kept falling short of being what you needed." He breathed deep, his gaze flickering momentarily to their hands, then lifting back to look at her. "You deserve everything, Mila. I can see how your life is gonna play out. You're gonna have the perfect guy with you. I just . . . didn't know if I could be that guy."

She gnawed on her lip. She wanted to argue and tell him she'd settle for whatever he could give her. But that wouldn't be fair to her. It wouldn't be fair to the potential she knew he had.

A grin tugged at his lips. "I think I sold myself short."

"Yeah," she said. "You did. Embarrassingly short."

A laugh sailed past his lips, and he lowered his face to hers, brushing the tip of her nose with his. "You know," he said, "you've got everybody fooled."

"Oh yeah?"

"Yeah. People think you're quiet and complacent. But nobody's ever challenged me like you. Nobody's ever pushed me to confront my bullshit like you."

Her heart surged. He couldn't know what a compliment that was. "You let me be myself," she said. "Until recently, I didn't know how to share that with other people."

"Well," he said. "Things have changed, huh?"

She nodded, their lips dangerously close to touching. "I'm not willing to back down from what I want anymore. And weirdly enough, that attitude seems to be working."

"I'm sorry I asked you to wait for me," he said. "I meant what I said. I couldn't look you in the eye and promise you things I wasn't sure I could deliver on."

She bit her lip. "I'm sorry I couldn't find the patience for you to explore that."

His mouth ghosted over hers. She exhaled, instinctively stretching to maintain the contact.

"But now?" he asked.

"You're back," she said. "And I . . ."

His thumb paused its gentle motion on her jaw, and his eyes darkened. "Yeah?"

"And I'm still in love with you."

She slid her hands around his waist, sinking into the firmness of his body.

"I am so in love with you." His eyelids sunk closed, and he leaned in, pressing his warm mouth to hers. She melted into the kiss as the adrenaline of the day peaked in her veins.

"I waited for you even though I didn't mean to." She grinned.

"I hoped maybe you would." His hand trailed down her neck, and he stepped backward, gripping her hands tightly once more. "I'm gonna be everything you need, Mila."

"You already are."

The room around her blurred in and out of focus as he let go of her hands, reached into his pocket, and dropped to one knee.

"Jared." His name fell off her lips in two wobbly sylla-bles. This couldn't be happening. A sob stuck in her throat and threatened to explode.

"Mila." He took her hand, his own trembling like the last leaf on a maple tree. "I love you. I have never known love like this in my entire life. You're the most selfless, kind, courageous, beautiful person I have ever known, and if you say yes to marrying me today, I'll work every day at being all those things for you."

Tears cascaded down her cheeks, falling heavily on the bodice of her dress. She wiped furiously. How dare they obstruct this precious view, the sight of his face, illumi-nated by sunlight and glowing with admiration?

"And if you say no," he said, grinning, "I'll wait. I'll wait forever if that's what it takes. I don't want to just be mar-ried. I want to be married to you."

In one move, she dropped to the floor, collapsing against him and burying her face in his chest. "Yes. Yes, J. Yes, I'll marry you."

He wrapped his arms around her, their bodies becoming one shaky entity, the nervous laughter spilling out of both of them. He pulled back slightly to take her left hand.

"So that was a . . ." He narrowed his gaze, the sparkling diamond ring poised over her hand.

"Yes, you dope."

He beamed at her, donning her finger with the gold band. The jewel glittered in the afternoon sunlight stream-ing in through the windows.

"You're sure?" she asked. Their eyes locked, her hands tightly clasped behind his neck while his gripped her waist, as if they each held on for dear life. "You're really sure about this?"

"More than sure," he said. "I've been sure about you the whole time. I just couldn't get the idea of you together with this messed-up vision of marriage I've always had."

He skimmed her cheek with a knuckle, brushing away the tears that continued to fall.

"So," she said, tightening her grip on him. "What changed?"

"Sam threatened to punch me in the face."

She laughed, nuzzling his ear. "Is that the only way you two know to figure your shit out?"

"Apparently." He kissed her, as if ten seconds was too long apart. "He cleared up a lot of stuff. About my parents. My mom. What happened to her and how she treated me and Sam because of it. Turns out you don't really know what anybody's relationship is like if you're not one of the people in it."

She trailed her hand down his chest, gazing warmly at the new piece of jewelry on her hand. The one that turned their friendship into something more. The one that symbolized forever.

"Imagine that," she said.

He breathed deep, kissing her again. His lips lingered on hers and pressed once more. "I'm not going anywhere, Lee. Ever again."

She waited for the doubt to creep in, the subtle pressure on her heart telling her something wasn't right. But as he looked at her, the confidence and assuredness etched into his face, she knew. He'd taken the long way. Maybe she had, too. But here they were. Together. For now. Forever.

ACKNOWLEDGMENTS

I will keep this short and sweet, because I am lucky enough to have a small, tight circle of people who helped me turn *Wild Love* into a book and have been there for me in full force on this one, too. I will probably have the same list of thanks on book one thousand.

To Eva Scalzo, who proved time and time again throughout this crazy process that she is much more than an agent: a brainstormer, a confidant, an editor, a translator, an interpreter, an advocate, and a friend. I am so grateful for all the hats you wear and how often you're willing to don them for your clients. I consider myself so lucky to be on #TeamEva.

To Brittany Kelley, Michelle McCraw, my RChat loves, the Berkletes, and everyone else who championed this series, I am beyond thankful. The writing community is supportive, but my writing community is a bunch of tough, smart, insanely supportive people whom I never stop appreciating for one day.

To Sarah Blumenstock, for literally guiding me through what it means to work with an editor and for being the best teacher a writer could ask for. Your kindness and patience and knowledge have made this series shine, and I think this book showcases that especially. Sorry my pun game is so weak. I'll get there. ☺

To Brittanie Black, Erica Ferguson, Natalie Sellars, and the rest of the team at Berkley Romance and PRH, who spend countless hours on marketing, copyediting, publicity, and all the rest of what turns a book into a product for the masses. I'm so grateful for your talents and for explaining it all to me in the simplest way possible! I'm crazy lucky to have such an amazing team behind my words.

To Mom and Dad, for still being my loudest fan group. It never stops feeling like the greatest gift to hear you say you're proud of me.

And to Josh. An apartment move, a dog, a new job, a pandemic, three books, and a baby to boot. I couldn't have gotten through half of what we've gotten through this past year without the best, most patient partner by my side. And I think we're just getting started. I love you.

Don't miss

bold love

Coming Spring 2022

from Berkley Jove!

The lake view wasn't nearly as impressive through the smudged little windows of the guesthouse, but Bee took it in all the same. A suburban kid, born and raised in Garden City, Long Island, she moved to Manhattan the day after she turned eighteen. The idea of nature didn't occupy much of her brain space. Abe and Johnny had suggested camping once, but she'd laughed them off. Why would anyone elect to sleep on the ground when they had a perfectly good bed at home?

As she peered out the cobweb-covered glass at the back of the converted shed, she breathed in the pine-scented air, and a peace settled over her. No car horns, no screaming people, no blare of sirens. Just chirping birds and the sweetly scented breeze blowing through the trees.

She slipped into her hooded sweatshirt and headed toward Denny's house, visions of the beefy football player dancing in her head.

Last night, as the sun went down over the lake and the

mountain air filled her head and the wine seeped into her veins, he began to look just a little too dreamy. *I want your taste.* He hadn't meant it that way, but her body certainly heard it that way.

She wanted to stay in that moonlit kitchen, gazing into his deep golden-brown eyes and wondering what his animated face might do if she kept talking, kept poking fun at him. But if she stayed, she'd start to fall. And she didn't have time for that.

She rapped on the imposing front door, and it swung open immediately. He grinned down at her. The morning light caught amber flecks in his damp, dark brown hair, and a wave of clean, cool soap scent wafted out at her. He must've just taken a shower.

A shower . . . rivulets of water cascading down those chiseled abs . . .

He cleared his throat. "Hey. Good morning."

Shit. She hadn't had time to suitably scratch her itch back in New York, and she'd pay for it now. She didn't imagine the findings on Tinder in Pine Ridge were particularly rich.

"Good morning," she said. "Ready?"

"Yep. Let me put some shoes on."

In his brief absence, she pulled her hormones together. He wasn't even her type. Robbie, her last significant relationship, was a heavily tattooed hipster always dragging Bee into his personal and financial issues. A performance artist, Bee had initially been attracted to him because of his creative ambitions and insatiable thirst for life. After Bee stuck by him during rehab for opioid addiction, newly clean Robbie decided it wasn't the right time for a relationship and disappeared from Bee's life.

Someday, Robbie had said in a voice mail he'd left while Bee was at work. *Someday my future partner will thank God I had a woman like you in my life.*

It hadn't made the breakup any easier to swallow.

"You look cute," Denny said, yanking the front door closed behind him.

Bee ran a hand over the word FUN on the front of her gray sweatshirt. She'd had no idea what to pack for early fall in the mountains but figured sweatshirts and jeans would get her through the next few months. Had she gone out of her way to make sure her hair was freshly highlighted and each outfit had some element of her personality in it in case he noticed?

Maybe.

"Thanks." She brushed away the compliment. "How far away is this place?"

"About a fifteen-minute drive." He walked over to his big black SUV and clicked the locks with a tiny remote. "I figured we'd grab breakfast first. That cool?"

She breathed deep, the crisp morning air filling her lungs. She'd declined his dinner offer last night because she didn't need any excuses to spend non–work related time with him. If she could keep her distance and restrict their interactions to decor-focused ones only, she had a shot at avoiding his glittering eyes and lopsided smile. If they started sharing their life stories over wine, she'd be toast.

But a girl had to eat.

"Sure," she said. "But we should make it quick. I want to really dive in today."

His brow furrowed. They climbed into the car, and as he started the engine, he shook his head. "Am I a gross eater or something?" he asked.

"What? No. I mean, I don't think so."

"This is the second meal you've tried to get out of with me." A grin tugged at his lips.

"That's not true." She cleared her throat and gazed out the window as they ambled over the rocky driveway. "I just want to get cracking, you know? I'm really excited about this project."

The smile on his face remained, as if he didn't believe her. *Whatever.* It was her story and she'd stick to it, even if it killed her.

They arrived a few minutes later at the Black Bear Diner. She'd driven by last night after Sydney picked her up from the train station. The heavy bacon scent floating in the parking lot air made her stomach groan with hunger. She'd inhaled her sandwich last night, but it wasn't enough to tide her over until morning.

Mila Bailey raised a hand to Denny and told him to sit wherever he liked. As Bee followed him through the bustling little diner, curious eyes trailed her. She stuck close to Denny, as if his towering figure could protect her from judgment.

She slid opposite him into the booth he selected, and picked up a menu to shield most of her from the room. "Are people here friendly?" she asked.

"They're the best," Denny said. A tiny smile curled onto his lips. "A handful of prickly assholes, but you know. Every town's got 'em."

Bee's eyes darted around the restaurant. People seemed to have returned to their coffee and conversation, but her heart still hammered in her chest. Put her in an arena full of city folks dressed up in drag and high on molly, and she could handle herself no problem. But a small town full of conservative people who would judge her based on her tattoos and the rainbow-flag pin on her purse? She clutched her menu like a life raft.

"Everything okay?" he asked. His gaze narrowed in concern.

"Fine." She shrugged. "I'm just . . . cautious. Around new people. I don't exactly fit in around here."

The tiny smile returned to his face. She wanted to touch that face, trail her fingers over his smooth brown cheek. He had the closest shave she'd ever seen.

"What's different about you?" he said. "Your tats? I can barely see them. Except for these."

He ran a gentle finger along the base of her thumb where the word *go* was written in curvy black script. With the same cool, deft finger, he traced the index finger of her other hand where the word *be* was written in the same script.

Goose bumps rose up on her neck as his gaze deepened. She swallowed her discomfort, but the feeling of exposure remained. She may as well have been naked, the way his dark eyes narrowed in on hers and stripped away her armor.

"What do they mean?" he asked. His finger still connected with hers, and the contact left her brain as thick as tomato soup.

She licked her lips, digging for an answer.

"Hey guys!" Mila barreled into their little bubble, and Bee looked up, startled. "Coffee?"

"Please." Bee held up her chipped white mug like a disciple waiting for the blood of Christ.

"Bee, it's so cool you're helping Denny decorate his house," Mila said as she poured hot, dark coffee into Bee's waiting mug. "Only took him a year to give in and admit he needs more than a mattress."

"I'm still not convinced," Denny said. He stretched to his full, impressively wide arm span and leaned back in the booth. "But Bee's got great taste, so I'm letting her try."

"Can't wait to see it." Mila placed her free hand on her hip. "Bee, if you need a break from this guy, let me know. I'm not sure if Sydney told you, but I work part-time as an assistant pastry chef at Indigo Hotels Adirondack Park, and we have a killer bar. I'd be happy to entertain you sometime."

Bee bit back a smile. Maybe people around here really were kinder than she'd given them credit for. She'd always thought small town equaled small-minded, but the warm, welcoming vibe at the Black Bear Diner and from Mila Bailey felt anything but.

"That's really sweet of you," Bee said. "I'm totally taking you up on that."

After Mila took their food order, she scribbled her phone

number on Bee's napkin and then disappeared. Denny's eyes returned to Bee's, all warm and probing.

"So," he said. "What do they mean? The tattoos."

Damn it. She thought maybe he'd forgotten. "They're reminders."

"Be?" he asked. "You need a reminder to . . . be?"

"In a way." She grinned. "As in, don't hold back. Whoever you are, do that. Go forward. Be."

He nodded slowly. "I like that."

"Also, I got them when I was eighteen as a little bit of a 'screw you' to my parents." Her mother had physically gagged, as if instead of a tattoo, Bee had shown her a dead mouse. Bee went out the next day and got another one.

Denny nodded again. "I like that, too."

"What does yours mean?"

He ran a big, strong hand over his shoulder, a nostalgic grin settling on his mouth. "*Honu.* The turtle. It symbolizes a long and prosperous life in Hawaiian culture."

"Ah, you're Hawaiian."

"Mostly Filipino Hawaiian, but my mom can trace her lineage on one side all the way back to native Hawaiian royalty."

She nodded, waiting for more. He scratched his nose, breathed deep, gazed out the window. When he looked back at her, something in his eyes shifted. Whatever vulnerability he'd approached in explaining his heritage disappeared in one flick of his gaze.

"So these are reminders," he said, touching her fingers again and melting her insides in one go. "What are the rest?"

"The rest?"

"The rest of your tattoos. I saw the roses in New York."

She suppressed a laugh. Most men who asked about her ink loved it because it turned her soft, feminine form into something bangable. It made her more dangerous, more complicated. In all the years she'd had them, not one sexual partner had ever bothered to study them. Or her.

"They've all got different meanings," she said. "Different stages in my life, different things that are important to me. And then there are the reminders."

Mila returned with steaming plates of eggs, pancakes, and bacon, and Bee's mouth watered. The restaurant patrons might have been different, but a diner was the same in Manhattan, in Pine Ridge, and everywhere in between. Bacon smelled the same wherever it sizzled.

The conversation stalled as they tucked into their breakfasts, and after a few bites, Bee looked up to find Denny's plate nearly empty. He shoveled huge forkfuls of eggs and potatoes into his mouth, and only after a few moments of her staring did he look up.

"What?" he asked, mouth full of breakfast food.

"Sorry." She bit her lip to tamp down the shock. "You just . . . Wow, you eat fast."

His cheeks filled with color, and he wiped his mouth and set his fork down. "Yeah. I always have. I come from a huge family, most of them athletes growing up, and if you wanted a full plate, you had to eat before somebody else came along to take it from you."

She nodded slowly. Her own family meals growing up were mostly silent. Her grouchy, overworked father—when he could be bothered to attend dinner at all—was usually too exhausted from a day on Wall Street to put effort into family conversation. Her mother picked at her sparse plate in an endless effort at achieving her goal weight, and Isaac texted his way through meals. Sometimes Bee brought a book.

"You know you're an adult now, right?" Bee teased. "You can order ten more plates if you're still hungry. And aside from me snagging a potato, no one's taking your food from you."

He crossed his arms over his chest, his sparkly eyes lighting on her once again. "No way in hell am I giving you a potato."

"Who said anything about giving?" In one quick movement, she speared a crispy potato with her fork and popped it into her mouth.

His grin curled further, revealing the edges of his straight, white teeth. "Well, that's it. You forfeit these."

He grabbed the nearly full plate of pancakes in front of her and set it down on his side of the table. "That's the rule. You take from me, I take from you."

"Unless you want a fork in your arm, I suggest you give that back."

They stared goofily at each other, their smiles belying their threats. He locked eyes with her as he dug into her stack of pancakes, cutting off a huge triangle and shoving it into his mouth.

If you kissed him now, he'd taste like butter and syrup. She exhaled, admonishing herself. She couldn't keep the lusty thoughts at bay.

This boy might ruin you.

After breakfast they drove a few miles north to Donnerville, where Adirondack Home Furnishings promised a wealth of mountain-themed decor. The sprawling store looked more like Bass Pro Shop than the quaint little place she'd anticipated, but when they entered, Denny's face lit up like a kid on Christmas morning.

"Holy shit." He bounded over to an eight-foot taxidermied black bear positioned next to the entrance in a frozen but ominous pose and ran his long fingers through the fur. "We gotta get this."

"Hi there!" A tiny salesman approached, a perma-grin pressed onto his round face. The top of his head gleamed like a cue ball, and he ran a hand over it before extending his reach to Denny. "Welcome to Adirondack Home Furnishings. I see you've got great taste."

"We definitely want this," Denny said.

"No," Bee said, stepping in between the men. "I mean, possibly. For now, we're going to keep looking."

Denny shot her a confused glare. "We can look for other stuff, but I know I want this."

She gritted her teeth. The last thing she needed was for the salesman to think they were impulse buyers with a lot of money. Worst case scenario, he recognized the wealthy football player standing in front of him.

"We just walked in," she said. "Let's see what else is available, all right?"

"Whoa-ho-ho," the salesman laughed. "I see who wears the pants in this marriage."

"You see who wears the *what now*?" she snapped.

"All right, just chill out." Denny put his big paws on her shoulders and steered her away from the entrance. "Thanks, man. We'll let you know if we need anything."

Bee's face flushed with anger as Denny led her into a secluded aisle featuring racks of scented candles.

"Take it easy, yeah?" he said. "I've got money. And that was cool as hell."

"We're here for inspiration," she reminded him. "I can get all this stuff at swap meets, garage sales, wholesalers. This place is tourist central, and everything is marked up like crazy. Plus, anybody who tosses out a misogynist line like 'Who wears the pants' does not deserve a dollar of our business."

"Was it that?" he said, grinning. "Or did it piss you off that he thought we were married?"

Her stomach fluttered as she looked up into his amused face. The guy must've been a terrible poker player.

"I don't know what you think you know about me, but I'm not some badass, anticommitment city chick. Marriage doesn't scare me. And some random dude in Hicksville, USA, assuming I'm your wife scares me even less."

Or maybe it made me super turned on.

"Hicksville?" His grin morphed from amused to disappointed. "Don't discount the people here. They might not know the difference between types of caviar, but they'll help you out when you need it. You of all people should know how valuable that can be."

He moved down the aisle, and she stood in her embarrassment. Of course she knew how valuable generosity could be. She'd essentially dedicated her whole life to taking care of other people, no matter if they thanked her or not.

The truth was, she was a fish out of water in North Country. Her defenses rose sky-high the minute Sydney's pickup truck pulled off the highway and onto the single lane road leading into Pine Ridge. What if instead of being embraced by the town, she was shunned? Mocked and held at arm's length because she came from someplace else? She'd been treated as an outcast in her family by everyone but her brother throughout her entire adolescence, and she'd sooner cut off her own arm than be made to feel that way again.

She'd settled into a comfortable existence in Manhattan, surrounded and supported by a community she'd never experienced or expected. Now that she found herself submerged in so-called normalcy, she'd never felt so exposed.

With her heart in her stomach, she wandered the store and found Denny in the bedroom furniture department. He stood stone-faced next to a four-poster bed made out of logs and covered with a buffalo plaid duvet.

"This is . . . something." She touched the smooth lacquered wood and tried to find a redeeming quality. "Fits the theme."

"I like it," he said. "Is it cheesy?"

She studied his face before proceeding. He seemed strangely affected by the bed, and she didn't want to insult him. "Maybe? But that's fine. Today I just want you to tell me what you're drawn to, and then I'll come up with some renderings and swatches and mood boards to show you. We don't have to make any decisions today."

He ran a hand up one of the four posters, and she admired the tendons popping out of his thumb and wrist and trailing up into his forearm. Her brain made the short leap to imagining him on the football field. She'd never lusted after athletes, but the strength in one of this man's appendages distracted her in an alarming way.

"Maybe something like this in the guest room," he said. His eyes remained trained on the bed, the blank stare frozen on his face.

"You could also tell me if you're looking for something specific, with your parents in mind."

Finally, his eyes flickered away from the bed and over to her. "Yeah? Is that weird? They'll probably be the ones to stay in the guest room most often."

"Not weird at all. It's your house. I want to turn it into something you'll love. Every room of it."

He stared at her for another moment before licking his lips and letting his hand fall from the bed frame. "My parents have really high standards."

Over the years, Bee had honed her ability to pick up on the tiny threads people tossed out in conversation. Threads they wanted you to tug on.

"Oh yeah?"

"Yeah." He looked back at the bed. "I mean, disgustingly high. My younger siblings are all really successful. I've got a brother who's a doctor, a sister who owns a tech startup she's in talks about selling to Google, and another brother premed. I'm the delinquent child."

Her heart seized up. "You are not."

He tossed her another glance, his lip quirked in a half sneer. "You don't have to say that. I am definitely the black sheep of my family. I basically gave up a career in professional sports. I gave up a lot of money."

She waited patiently for him to continue, giving him the space to open up in his own time.

"It just never seemed that important," he said. "I worked really hard at football, but I also happened to be good at it. I loved hanging with my teammates and running plays and practice. But the struggle never really seemed worth the pay-off, you know? The money was nice, I guess. When you're in the NFL for long enough, though, you see the really ugly side, and after a while I didn't know what I was working so hard for anymore. What I was putting up with all of it for."

She nodded slowly. His story was textbook. A kid who'd had to earn every inch of his parents' affection and spent his whole life working at the one thing he thought they loved about him. No matter what he did next in life, it would always be subpar.

"You never had fun playing?" she asked.

"Eh. Sometimes. They make you do charity work in the city you play for, and I always liked doing that. Working with little kids or serving people in shelters." His sharp cheekbones shifted, the tiniest hint of a dimple appearing in his cheek. "But that's such a small part of it. I hated the pressure. The way they could make you feel like cattle. I hated seeing guys get cut or traded. As I got older, I couldn't figure out the reason for putting myself through all that."

He ran a hand through his silky dark hair and then pasted on an easy smile. "Sorry. You didn't realize I hired you to be my therapist, too, huh?"

"I've been told I'm easy to talk to," she said. "So I don't mind."

His face softened, his eyes zeroing in on hers. "You are. Easy to talk to, I mean."

A fluttering between her legs made her clear her throat and take a step backward. A dangerous thought wiggled its way into her brain. What if they slept together—no strings attached? People did it all the time. They'd never end up together in a serious way, but what harm could come from helping each other out every once in a while?

The vibe between them flowed like ocean waves: power-ful and undeniable. He must have felt it, too. She pressed her lips together, watching him, studying his angular face, and wondering if he'd considered the same scenario.

He flashed his teeth at her, breaking the reverie. "Wanna take a look at the couches and stuff?"

She nodded, not trusting her voice. They wandered slowly through lanes of plaid couches, patchwork leather armchairs, and deerskin lamps. Everything screamed "mountain kitsch," while Bee wanted "mountain chic." His place would look so much better filled with minimal pieces with rustic appeal.

She pulled out her phone to tap a note to herself while he sidled up next to her.

"Let's go out for dinner tonight," he said. "You haven't seen the town yet, and on Wednesday nights Taylor's has trivia. It sounds lame, but it's really fun. Everybody goes. Mila, Jared, Sam, Sydney. A bunch of their other friends."

Dinner. She breathed deep, imagining that handsome, chiseled face lit by candlelight. Then she imagined a room full of people who all knew each other, friends who had already achieved a natural ebb and flow in their relationships. Without Johnny and Abe to lean on, she'd be on the outside. Again.

She gnawed her lip. "Well . . ."

Disappointment lined his eyes. She'd already caused that sad puppy face three times in the twenty-four hours she'd been in Pine Ridge. Maybe the evening wouldn't be so bad with Denny accompanying her.

"Okay," she said. *But no candles.* "But someplace casual."

"Really?" His whole face lit up and something small and quiet eased, down deep in her soul.

"Really." She sucked on her cheeks to contain her smile. "I mean, you don't even have Wi-Fi in the guesthouse. What else am I gonna do, read a book?"

"Oh shit." He smacked a palm to his head and tugged at his wild hair. "There's no Wi-Fi in the guesthouse. I didn't even think of that. Whenever you need it, come to the house. There's a key on that set I gave you, and I'll write the alarm code down for you. You're totally welcome. Any time."

"Thank you."

"All right." He crossed his arms over his chest, settling into a satisfied stance. "Dinner tonight. And then trivia after. It's not club hopping in Manhattan, but it's gonna be fun. I promise."

She grinned. With Denny by her side, it might be even better.

Ready to find
your next great read?

Let us help.

Visit prh.com/nextread

Penguin
Random
House